TURMOIL

A Nick Hunter Adventure

TURMOIL

A Nick Hunter Adventure

Paul Henke

— To Kenneth,

Best wishes!

Paul Henke

Methuen

First published in Great Britain in 2011

Copyright © Paul Henke 2010

Methuen
8 Artillery Row
London
SW1P 1RZ

1 3 5 7 9 10 8 6 4 2

The right of Paul Henke to be identified as the author of this work has
been asserted by him in accordance with sections 77 and 78 of the
Copyright, Designs and Patents Act, 1988.

www.methuen.co.uk

ISBN 978-0-413-77704-1

A CIP catalogue record for this book is available from the British
Library

Set in Palatino by SX Composing DTP, Rayleigh, Essex
Printed and bound in Great Britain by
CPI Bookmarque, Croydon

Acknowledgements

As always, when writing a story, there are people to whom I am indebted.

The first is my wife, Dorothy. She is, without doubt, my greatest fan and harshest critic!

Then there's my agent, John Beaton, who has helped and steered me throughout the long, challenging process of a manuscript becoming a book.

Chris Kane is my PR agent who has the uncanny knack of getting my name into local newspapers and arranging interesting radio interviews.

Then there's John Wyper, who cast an eye over the finished manuscript, finding those last corrections, so vital if the story is to flow and entertain.

And finally thanks to Peter Tummons, managing director of Methuen, my new publishers, with whom I look forward to working for many years to come.

Prologue

He drove along the dusty road, his eyes hidden behind a pair of sunglasses. He knew this would be the last time he made the journey. A feeling of contentment rose up within him, masking the trepidation and hesitation he had felt for nearly a month. Finally, however, the amount of money on offer had proved too great a temptation and he had agreed to do it.

The warning signs became more threatening as he drove. He was familiar with them. He had read them on many occasions, intrigued at first, bored by them later. In the distance, he could see Tilla Jogian, the highest peak in the Eastern Salt Range. When he had first travelled through the Punjab, the very thought of his destination had kept him on the edge of his seat. Not anymore. His last opportunity for promotion to Colonel had been the previous year. All his dreams for the future were flushed down the toilet because of one man – his previous commanding officer who was now a minister in the new government. His lack of advancement was due solely to poor family contacts and this fact rankled deep within him, as he saw less capable officers being promoted ahead of him. To add insult to injury, three weeks earlier he had been informed, using military jargon, that he was SNLR –

Services No Longer Required. He had been told that he would be leaving in one month's time, with three months' salary plus a small pension which was totally inadequate for his needs. He had tried to discuss the possibility of another posting, but to no avail. The political appetite was for cutbacks in every section of the armed forces.

As the thoughts tumbled through his head, hatred overwhelmed him. He took several deep breaths, steeling himself for what lay ahead. At last, he could see the outer fence, topped by razor-sharp wire. The facility – where the country's nuclear arsenal had been developed and was now stored – was one of the most heavily guarded in Pakistan. He was aware that electronic trip-wires showed if anyone approached the establishment's boundary. A minefield had been carefully laid with enough powerful hardware to blow the tracks off a tank. There were no warning signs to indicate the danger to any unauthorised visitor to the place. Cameras sat along the top of the fence and recorded every inch of it. The place earned its top secret reputation.

The sentry box at the gate came into sight, the red-and-white-striped pole across the road a token obstacle. Just beyond it was the solid metal pointed barrier, sticking half a metre out of the concreted entrance. A guard stood in the middle of the road and held up his hand. The driver stopped. He and the guard knew each other – they had been stationed at the same facility for the best part of two years – but he knew he would still have to show his identity card. The guard's face was stony, no welcoming smile as the card was handed over. Then and only then did the guard relax.

'I thought you were on leave, sir.'

'I am, but you know how it is,' the Major responded

indicating the two bags on the seat behind him. 'I need to test some equipment in the cavern.' He shrugged and shook his head. 'If you ask me, it's a waste of time but you know the Colonel. Orders are orders.'

The guard nodded sympathetically. He saluted, raised the pole and said something over his shoulder to his colleague inside the sentry box. There was a whirr of machinery and the barrier sank down to fit snugly into the recess, allowing access to the next gate. The Major drove slowly towards the control room which housed the guards who monitored the establishment's surveillance system. At the side of the building was a room containing a squad of armed men, ready to be deployed at the first sign of trouble. He stopped and showed his pass to the soldier at the window. They also knew each other.

'What brings you here, sir? I thought you weren't due back for another week.'

'That's right,' the Major nodded, 'but I need to check on some equipment in the cavern.' Feigning exasperation he added, 'You know what it's like.' Gesturing to his bags, he added, 'I need these monitors to do the job. It shouldn't take too long.'

The guard nodded, saluted and gave instructions for the barrier to be lowered.

The Major returned the salute and waited for a few seconds until the second barrier vanished. He drove slowly towards the sheer cliff in front of him. Turning the engine off, he climbed out of the car. His mouth was as dry as the land was arid.

The facility, one of the most heavily guarded in Pakistan, was where the country's nuclear arsenal had been developed and was now stored. Ahead lay large double doors embedded into the solid rock of the mountain.

Railway tracks ran along the ground from a buffer before vanishing under the doors 200 metres away. If the rockets were to be fired, the tracks could hold as many as a dozen carriages, each carrying a single rocket. To the right was a side entrance for personnel.

He looked around. There were a few cars in the car park but he knew the owners would be on the second floor. Their job was to monitor the bombs, ensuring there were no radiation leaks. To date, there had been no problems and none were expected. Nobody went down into the depths of the cavern unless it was absolutely necessary. In the three years he had been stationed there, he had been in the arsenal less than a dozen times and on each occasion it was to show visiting dignitaries around the complex.

He opened the back door and grabbed both bags and then slammed it shut with his knee. At the side entrance he dropped one of the bags, looked up at the camera, waved, swiped his ID card, entered the code to unlock the door and waited for the loud click. He dragged the door open, picked up the bag and stepped into an empty corridor that inclined gently downwards towards the lift in the distance. The corridor was stark, painted a light green with strip lighting every few metres. He pulled the door shut and lifted the entry-phone receiver.

'Aamir, I'm going down into the cavern. I am checking something for the Colonel.'

'Do you want any help?', Aamir asked.

'No. It's fine thanks. I can manage.'

'Okay.'

The Major walked down the corridor. At the double doors to the lift he entered the necessary code numbers using his thumb. The doors opened immediately. He stepped inside and pressed the button to go down. When

4

the lift doors opened at the bottom of the shaft he was greeted by a solitary guard who was on duty for eight hours at a time with no respite. There was a room to one side which contained the makings of tea or coffee, a small fridge for something to eat – although the food was usually inedible – and a basin with running water. Another door led to a toilet. Like all the guards, the man was bored with nothing to do. He stood up and smiled. Even if it was only for a few minutes, the distraction was welcome.

'I have come to check on some equipment,' the Major explained to the guard, raising the bags in his hands. 'I have to run the data through these.' He opened the bags to reveal two black boxes.

The guard had no idea what he was talking about and couldn't have cared less but nodded in acknowledgement. He knew the Major had unrestricted access.

Using a special key and numbered code, the Major opened the heavily reinforced steel door and stepped inside. Everything at the facility was heavily reinforced. This fact amused him, in view of what he was about to do.

Along one wall was a single row of nuclear rockets, each sitting on a flat-bed carriage. Their range was far enough and their power great enough to wipe India off the face of the earth. Stalemate was more comfortable to live with than nuclear annihilation. The facility and what it contained was well known to people in the proper circles – such as the military high commands of India and the West – and without such knowledge the place was no deterrent. However, except for a handful of engineers, senior officers and the Pakistani High Command, nobody knew that the facility also housed a number of so-called dirty bombs. Although plutonium-based, they did not

5

create a nuclear explosion. Instead, when detonated, high density radioactive material would be scattered over a wide area. In a city or town, the explosion would probably kill a few hundred people in the vicinity. The immediate fallout would cause the deaths of considerably more in a short period of time. And the long-term effects? The truth was nobody knew. The widespread devastation caused by the radioactivity would be crippling to any country, especially if the detonation was in the financial sector of a capital city like London, Paris, Rome or Berlin. He savoured the thought.

Ahead of him was a steel door. He swiped his pass card through the reader, waited for the light to turn green and entered a five digit code. There was an audible click. He spun the central wheel and pulled the door open. The lights came on automatically. The bombs were stowed in a rack to his right. He counted them. Ten in all. He took a handkerchief out of his pocket and wiped the sweat off his face and nervously licked his lips. This was the last opportunity for him to change his mind. Once he took the next step there would be no turning back. An overwhelming feeling of fear washed through him momentarily but this was soon replaced by simmering anger when he remembered what had happened to him. It took only seconds to lift down two of the devices and replace them with the identical boxes he had brought with him. The boxes were smooth aluminium, painted black and lined with lead. The aluminium made the bombs slightly lighter, the colour made them more difficult to find. The lead ensured no radiation leaked out and set off any possible detectors.

He carefully placed a bomb into each bag. He shook his head at his inexplicable caution. There was no chance of an explosion unless the detonators had been set. He left the room and locked the door. He now needed to kill time, to show that he'd had a reason for being at the facility. He paced back and forth. The nuclear rockets towered above him, an intimidating reminder of the power wielded by the Pakistani government. His thoughts reinforced his hatred and determination to continue down the path he was on.

Ten minutes had now elapsed. He unlocked the door. Tugging it open, he stepped into the corridor. Although it was unnecessary, he opened both bags and showed the guard. The man nodded briefly as he looked inside. There was a simple reason for showing the guard what was in the bags. When the Major failed to report for duty there was bound to be an investigation and the unauthorised visit would quickly be discovered. An internal investigation would follow but the guard would be able to confirm that he had seen the Major enter and leave with the same contents in the bags. It was possible that would cause a delay in the bombs being examined. It would give him that much more time to vanish.

'See you next week,' he said as he walked over to the lift. If the guard had noticed the sweat on his brow he had made no comment. He wouldn't dare.

At the main door he lifted the phone. 'I'm all done Aamir. I'll see you next week.'

'Yes sir. Enjoy the rest of your leave.'

Once outside, he walked quickly back to his car and placed the bags carefully on the back seat. But his thoughts were filled with doubt. What if the bombs were not as stable as he thought? What if the guards knew what he was up to and were waiting for him to make his move? What if . . .? He forced himself to concentrate on what he

7

was doing. He started the car and headed for the main gate. This was his most fearful moment and it took willpower not to have the shakes. If he was stopped and the bombs were found, he would be lucky just to face a firing squad. His punishment was likely to be far more extreme before death finally released him. Everything looked normal however and he was waved through without a hitch. He need not have been alarmed.

He felt elated as he gradually increased his speed, heading for a rendezvous 200 kilometres away. He couldn't care less what happened to the devices after that. With ten million dollars he could go anywhere, do anything. Revenge was sweet after all.

1

If Nick Hunter hadn't been idly gazing into the dregs of his coffee, he would have noticed the men sooner and been able to act more rapidly. The outcome would probably have been vastly different. As it was, he had been brooding over his girlfriend, Ruth, or to be more precise, his former girlfriend.

Hunter had never had any difficulty attracting women. At just over six feet in height, he was extremely fit, with short black hair and blue eyes. He had been enjoying himself with the opposite sex since he was sixteen but now, as far as Ruth was concerned, it was time to move on. She had left the UK and returned home to Israel after an accident shattered her knee. She had been in danger of losing the leg above the knee but brilliant work by the surgeons on board HMS *Ark Royal* had not only saved her leg but rebuilt her knee. Further treatment by skilled surgeons in Israel ensured that she could walk without artificial aids, albeit with a limp. Hunter had pursued her and tried to plead his case but his words had fallen on deaf ears. Ruth's experiences had killed stone dead whatever love she had felt for him. He struggled to accept her decision, but eventually he did. With a heavy heart he had left Israel and, taking some leave, arrived at

Larnaka on Cyprus for a few days, to think about his future.

As a Lieutenant Commander, bomb and mine disposal officer and diving specialist in the Royal Navy, Hunter was aware that the rapidly-shrinking fleet meant that promotion above Commander, a rank he could reasonably expect to achieve, was now fairly remote. Unusually however, he had a realistic alternative: a job in the family firm. He knew that the worldwide shipping business owned by the Griffiths family, one of a dozen divisions established by his great-grandfather, Sir David Griffiths, had room for him. The shares controlled by the family trust were sufficient to ensure he was given a directorship. But he knew it wasn't the answer. There was work to be done at TIFAT – The International Force Against Terrorism – where he was one of the organisation's most senior officers.

TIFAT was based at Rosyth in Scotland. Manned by special services personnel from across the world – the elite of the elite – it had become the most desired posting in the world for special services operatives from America, Europe, Russia and elsewhere. Whenever effective, but unobtrusive, muscle was required TIFAT was deployed.

Impatiently, Hunter shook off his gloomy mood and looked up. It was a beautiful, sunny day on the island. The temperature was in the low eighties. A gentle breeze was blowing off the sea and he had planned to go windsurfing later that afternoon. Placing some money alongside his empty cup Hunter was about to leave when he paused. Instinctively he felt there was something wrong but couldn't put his finger on it. He settled back in his chair and casually looked around. He was sat at a table which looked out towards the street and numerous other cafés

10

and restaurants. Tables and chairs lined the pavements on both sides and at that time of the day, the whole street was in shade and most of the cafés were full of people enjoying the gentle pace of island life. They were busy chatting and smoking as they sipped either a coffee or an early aperitif.

After a few moments Nick Hunter's attention was drawn to three customers, each sat at different tables. The men appeared to be taking an interest in a young woman sitting alone at a table next to the road. She was fiddling with a spoon in her saucer, nervously touching the shoulder-length, light brown hair that covered her right ear and hid half her face. Hunter watched as she held a phone to her ear and then, without speaking, placed it in her handbag with evident irritation. There was something familiar about the way she held herself, but for the life of him, he couldn't think what it was. He wondered about approaching her to see if she cared for a drink, but quickly dismissed the idea. Maybe the men watching her considered her attractive as well. However, a niggling doubt remained. And then – using his finely honed instincts and TIFAT training – he realised. They were the *only* men taking an interest. Despite being seated at separate tables, they had briefly exchanged looks with each other, and it was these slight movements which had initially caught his attention.

There was no doubt they were from the Middle East, possibly even Pakistan, but they were of different ages. One of them looked around and glanced briefly at him. As he did so Hunter noticed a scar on his face which ran down the length of his left cheek. There was an uneasy tension about the man that didn't fit with where he was and what he was doing. The three of them then exchanged imperceptible nods. Hunter's antennae were now on full alert and alarm bells were jangling loudly in his head. Something was going down.

Hunter took a moment to survey the road and saw a big Mercedes which had been stopped by a traffic policeman while he shepherded a gaggle of schoolchildren across the road. The three men looked at the car and stood up. Hunter didn't know what was going to happen, but whatever it was, he didn't like what he was seeing. He quickly jumped to his feet.

'Fiona? Fiona! Hello! I thought it was you!' he said in a loud voice, as he hurriedly weaved through the café.

The Mercedes sped along the road, swerved in beside the woman and screeched to a halt. Hunter reached the woman just as the back door of the car was thrown open. As she looked up, startled, the three men simultaneously surrounded them. Hunter's presence confused them for a moment or two, giving him enough time to spot the gun pointing at the woman from the back seat of the car. He responded quickly, but then he'd had a few more seconds to prepare himself. The man standing on Hunter's right was nearest the car. He smashed the man across the throat with his open palm, grabbed his shirt and flung him towards the open car door. The man collided with the gunman and the gun went off with a gentle *phut*. The bullet pierced the man's lung, exited and expended its energy on the pavement. Grabbing a heavy glass ashtray from the table the young woman did not waste any time as she hit the man with the scar across his temple. Blood poured from his face and he collapsed into a table where an older couple were sitting. They began to scream.

The youngest of the three men reacted slowly. All he

could think about was that everything had gone wrong. Hunter lashed out with his left foot, caught the man in the stomach and, as he bent over, used both hands in a blow to the back of the man's neck. All Hunter's frustrations of the past few days were in that blow and the man collapsed unconscious.

The man in the car was trying to disentangle the gun from underneath his colleague when Nick said to the young woman, 'Come on. Let's get out of here before reinforcements arrive.' A whistle blew in the background, loud and shrill. Reaching for his gun the traffic policeman began to walk over to see what all the fuss was about. 'Or worse still, before the police get involved.'

'Good idea,' the woman said in a southern English accent.

Hunter suddenly looked at her more closely. He was sure he'd seen her somewhere before. She was very attractive, about 5ft 7ins tall, slim and fit-looking. As her hair flicked back he caught sight of the earpiece. Such gadgets were not uncommon these days but Hunter knew it was a short range radio. They tried not to draw attention to themselves as they walked swiftly along the street. Behind them they left the policeman trying to control the unruly crowd that was now gathering near the car. They had covered a lot of ground and were about to turn a corner when the Mercedes jerked and accelerated with another screech of tyres on the hot and dusty road. As Hunter looked back he could see it was driving towards them. The rear window was open and the gunman was leaning out pointing an automatic at them. In the open, they didn't stand a chance.

'Quick. In here.' Hunter grabbed the young woman's hand and dragged her into a shop selling leather goods.

The startled owner looked up from the counter. Hunter thrust a 100 euro note at him. 'Where's the back door?'

The nod towards the door at the rear told Hunter all he needed to know and he hurried through the shop, pulling the woman with him.

'Let me go, will you?' she shouted as she snatched her arm away. 'Who the devil are you?' She frowned at him and her eyes narrowed as she looked at Nick. 'I know you, don't I?'

Hunter grinned. 'Yes. We've met before. I'm with TIFAT.'

'You're Nick Hunter.'

'And you're . . .' he paused, searching his memory, '. . . Samantha Freemantle.' He suddenly looked towards the shop window as the Mercedes skidded to a halt outside. 'Are we going to stand around exchanging pleasantries or are we going to get out of here?'

'Let's go.' Samantha hurried ahead. Nick followed. She was speaking into her left wrist. 'Charlie One, this is Delta, over.' She shook her head in frustration. 'Damnation. Nothing. What the hell's happened to them?'

They found themselves in an enclosed yard bordered by a high wall topped with broken glass. There was no gate. In the middle of the yard was a gnarled fig tree under which was a wooden table and four chairs. To the left were three outhouses, each securely padlocked, while to the right was a ladder lying beside a wall. Next to the shop door stood a large galvanised bin. Loud and harsh voices in guttural English wafted through the open door.

'Sod it!' Hunter exclaimed realising they were trapped. 'Quick, over there behind the tree!' Hunter darted across the yard and turned the table over. Samantha was right beside him.

14

'What are we going to do?' Samantha asked. If she was frightened, it wasn't evident in her voice.

By way of an answer, Hunter ran back towards the shop and ducked down behind the bin. As he did so he noticed a fist-sized rock lying beside the wall and picked it up. Samantha paused by the tree. Suddenly two men, both carrying guns fitted with silencers, emerged. They only had eyes for Samantha as she stepped behind the tree. One of the men said something and the other, with his gun on automatic, blasted away at the table. The impact of the bullets slammed it to one side. He stopped firing and said something to his partner who then stepped to his right and shifted his aim to the tree yelling 'Come out! Now!' His companion slowly moved to his left. A few more steps would bring Samantha into their field of vision. It was time to move. Hunter stood up and stepped out from beside the bin directly behind the gunmen. Something – a slight movement in the air – warned the man on the right and he began to turn around. He was too late.

2

Rehman Khan was as satisfied as a man could be who had just received a death sentence. Until he had absconded a few months earlier he had been a Captain in the Pakistan Inter Service Intelligence Agency. His family connections would normally have ensured that he reached the very top in the Pakistani Army. As it was, one factor had held him back. He was an Islamic fundamentalist to his fingertips. This was known to his superiors. As such, they didn't trust him. Pakistan was determined to come into the twenty-first century and there was no room for fundamentalism. This was the reason Khan had been with the ISIA and out of the mainstream of army life. His bitterness at the way he had been treated had turned to hatred, which in turn had made him even more determined to achieve his objective. What little time he had left would be put to use in the service of Allah, the one true God.

The headaches had begun at about the same time that Khan had made his decision. They had gradually become more frequent and painful and, finally, when normal painkillers were no longer effective, he had consulted a private doctor who had no idea who he was. Unsure of his diagnosis, but suspecting what was wrong, Khan was then referred to a specialist who ran additional tests and confirmed the first doctor's suspicions. Khan had an inoperable brain tumour.

When he was told, fear clutched at Khan's stomach, almost making him gag. 'Are you sure?' he had whispered.

'Yes, quite sure.' The doctor nodded sadly.

Khan nodded and accepted his fate. His God, he knew, would look after him. Then he asked 'How long?'

'It is hard to say.' The doctor had looked at Khan with respect, recognising his strength of character.

'Give me an educated guess' Khan pressed him for an answer.

'Six months.'

Khan had nodded. It was time enough. 'Can you give me something for the pain?'

The doctor paused for a moment. 'Yes. However, I should warn you that towards the end the pain will be so bad you will need hospitalisation.'

'Thank you, doctor. Somehow I don't think that will be necessary. You will, I trust, keep my visit secret?'

If the doctor had been offended he did not show it. 'Naturally. You have my assurance that I honour the doctor/patient code of ethics.'

'Thank you.'

'Take this along to the pharmacy at the end of the corridor,' the doctor said handing him a prescription. 'These tablets are highly effective.'

'Thank you again. Is that all?'

'Yes. Please pay my secretary on the way out.'

It had been as good a dismissal as Khan had ever heard, and he stood up to leave. His determination to achieve his objective strengthened as he left the office. Nothing would stand in his way now, nothing.

Khan made his way to the airport in Lahore. His false papers would see him out of the country just as they had protected him since he had left his post all those months ago. The work of Allah was never done. It was a thought that sustained him whenever he was feeling low. He smiled without mirth. He remembered the ease with which he had tricked that fool of an engineer. Ten million dollars! Instead of which, a bullet in the head had been his reward.

*   *   *   *   *

The rock smashed into the side of the man's face shattering his jaw and cheekbone. He fell with barely a grunt. His companion spun round, a mixture of fear and hatred etched on his face. Hunter continued with the swing. It was why he had hit the first man in the face with a downward blow. Due to the amount of force Hunter had used, the man's head was swept out of the way and didn't impede the blow. The rock struck the second man's wrist. The gun clattered to the ground, dropped by nerveless fingers as the ulna and radius broke at the joint. The man didn't even have time to scream as Hunter rammed the palm of his left hand into the man's nose. The man moved his head a fraction and, his nose broken, collapsed unconscious.

Hunter looked across as Samantha approached.

'Thanks for your help,' Nick said dryly.

'I could see you had everything under control,' she responded briskly. 'Besides, I didn't want to use my gun unless I had to. No silencer. Shall we get out of here?'

'Sounds like a good idea to me. Front door or back?'

'There's no gate.'

'We can use the ladder.' Hunter retrieved both guns from the unconscious men, flicked the safeties on and tucked them into his belt. They were damned uncomfortable. 'They might come in handy.'

Samantha was about to say something when she heard more raised voices in the shop. 'It looks as though we don't have any choice. I'll cover the door if you get the ladder.'

After placing the ladder against the wall, Nick grabbed an old rug that was lying on one of the chairs and scrambled up the rungs. He flung the rug over the glass embedded in the top of the wall, threw his legs over and dropped into the alleyway. Samantha was right behind him. Placing her gun out of sight under her jacket, she coolly took his arm as they strolled out of the alley. Hunter stepped around Samantha and walked next to the road. Behind them he could see the Mercedes parked outside the leather goods shop, both its nearside doors wide open. The few pedestrians passing did not bother to bend down to look in, but skirted around the doors with exclamations of irritation. If they had bothered, they would have seen the wounded man, blood seeping from his side, lying in agony and gasping for breath.

Nick and Samantha walked swiftly on and soon turned a corner.

'Mind telling me what's going on?' Nick asked.

'I can't. You're not cleared.' She spoke into her wrist again. 'Charlie One, this is Delta, over.' She repeated her broadcast several times. 'Something's wrong.'

'So it seems. I'm cleared for most things, however, so why don't you fill me in?' Hunter said as he looked down into her brown eyes. Worry and fear were etched on her face.

'I'm sorry. I can't.' She shook her head and sighed. 'Look, thanks for your help back there but I must get going.'

They were just about to turn another corner when Hunter grabbed Samantha's arm and thrust her back.

'What the . . .' Samantha cried out.

'Look, there, on the other side of the street. Two scruffy men. They are looking for someone or something. Moving right to left. They'll be looking for us.'

Samantha carefully looked diagonally across the street. She spotted the two men about fifty metres away, coming closer, looking back and forth, both with their right hands firmly in their coat pockets.

'I think you could be right.' She stood there for a moment thinking.

'Stay here. I'm going over to that alleyway ahead of them,' he said, gesturing with a nod of his head.

'Why? Let's just get the hell out of here.'

'That's not an option,' Nick said. 'They'll be in a position to see us in the next minute or so. There are not many people on that side, but enough over here so that if they do see us and start shooting, innocent people could get killed. Besides, I don't fancy a bullet in the back. They don't know me. After all, I was only on the scene for seconds but they'll have had you under surveillance for days.'

'Right. I'll stay here and cover you.' Samantha reached under her jacket and placed her right hand around the butt of her automatic.

Hunter tucked his head down slightly, averted his gaze from his quarry and hurried across the road towards an alleyway a little further up the street. He stood in deep shadow cast by the tall buildings either side of him and kept his back to the wall nearest the men. Across the street he watched Samantha, still unseen at the corner of the building. The two men had now walked further up the street and one of them looked down the alley as they passed. He didn't appear to notice Nick for a second as his eyes adjusted to the contrast from sunlight to shadow The other man was looking at the far side of the street and suddenly exclaimed as he put a hand on his companion's arm, speaking rapidly in Arabic. The man closest to Nick was barely half a pace away from him. Both men were now looking directly at Samantha who had deliberately left the protective shadows. As they prepared to fire Hunter stepped forward, raised his left arm and struck the first man a devastating blow to the jaw. The man fell backwards into the alley, caught his head on the corner of the wall and fell to the ground motionless. The second man began to turn towards Nick who clamped his right hand around the barrel of the gun and twisted it round to point at the man's stomach.

'Say hullo to your God.' Hunter said venomously as he twisted the man around to face the alleyway and fired the weapon with a sudden jerk. Gunshot echoed around the buildings as the bullet smashed through the man's stomach and spine and into the wall at the far end of the alley. Hunter dragged the body backwards into the alleyway and dumped it next to his companion. Nick quickly looked up and down the street and then, grabbing the collars of each body, dragged them a few metres up the alley and hid them behind an industrial-sized rubbish bin. He checked their pockets and removed everything he found. He stuffed paperwork, passports, money, credit cards into his jacket pocket. He also took the first man's gun. He was, he thought cynically, collecting an arsenal.

Nick glanced across the street but Samantha had vanished. He smiled. It was only to be expected. He started to walk back to his hotel and the people of the town went about their business, blissfully unaware of the events of the past few minutes.

On his way back to the five-star Palm Beach Hotel, Nick bought a screwdriver kit with various attachments. Once back in his room, he called TIFAT HQ in Rosyth, Scotland.

'It's Hunter. Is the General on board?' TIFAT HQ was a shore establishment, and had originally been a Royal Naval base and as such was referred to as though it were a ship.

'Yes, sir. Shall I try and find him?'

'Yes please. Thank you.'

There was a pause of only a few seconds. 'Nick, my boy, where are you?' the General boomed in his ear. For a small, dapper man, General Malcolm Macnair had a deep and resounding voice.

'Cyprus, sir. Something's come up and I need to run it by you.'

'Go ahead.'

'We've had some trouble here. Remember Samantha Freemantle from MI6? She applied to join us in some sort of liaison capacity. I met her briefly in the wardroom one evening when she was at *Cochrane*.'

'I'm led to believe she's getting the job. Since she already helps MI6 to liaise with MI5 she seemed ideal. Such co-operation could help reduce the number of cock-ups we experience. But she's been delayed for a few more weeks. Some operation or other, I think. What about her?' Macnair asked.

'Well, she's here on Cyprus.' Hunter briefed Macnair about what had happened explaining, 'I've got the papers

22

I lifted from the two men. Both have French and Algerian passports. Apart from money and credit cards, I've also found driving licences issued in both Saudi Arabia and Britain.'

'Forgeries?' General Macnair asked.

'Damned good ones, but I'm no expert. I've compared the British licences with my own and they appear identical. But I'm not sure . . .,' Hunter hesitated.

'What about the credit cards? Which country were they issued in?'

'Pakistan.' Hunter explained.

'Sounds like the United Nations. Right, tomorrow morning go to the base at Akrotiri. I'll arrange for a courier to collect what you've got. In the meantime, I'll make a few enquiries and get back to you.'

3

Using the screwdriver kit Hunter dismantled the guns into tiny pieces. Once he had finished, he wandered around the town, ditching the fragments in rubbish bins or dropping them down drains. He took his time and was conscious that he might still be a target. As always in such situations, imagination ran riot. Innocent men standing on a street corner, or looking up from a table where they were enjoying a drink, were a potential threat and he treated them as such. He knew it was the right thing to do. The day you didn't was the day you died, one instructor had told them, a few years earlier, so don't feel like an idiot. It was a lesson Hunter had never forgotten. Halfway through his task, he sat down at a table outside a small bistro and ordered a coffee. It was only now, as he sat sipping the curiously bland concoction, that the aftermath of the violence, death and destruction hit him. It always happened. The quiet moment, the inactivity, brought it all back. No matter how much the enemy deserved to die, even if the killings were in self-defence, it still left a bitter taste in the mouth.

To relax after an operation, Nick and his other TIFAT colleagues frequently drank too much or engaged in strenuous activity, such as running or a tough workout in the gymnasium. For some, it was the latter followed by the former. Whatever they did, it helped them to remain sane. It was often said that what they were needed to do to keep the world safe should be in books and films only, for entertainment, not in real life. A small world and a short life. Wasn't it time that humans learned to get on with each other? Hunter shook his head, mentally dispelling his gloom. Nothing of his thoughts showed on his face or in his body language. For all his introspection, he knew that someone had to do it. How could he expect others to act if he wasn't prepared to play his part?

Nick left most of the coffee and continued his apparently aimless wandering and finally rid himself of all the gun fragments. The last thing he needed was to be picked up by the police in possession of an unauthorised weapon. Back at his hotel, he made himself a whisky and soda from the guest bar and took a shower. While he dressed, he watched the early evening news on the television. Not surprisingly, it was mainly taken up with the shootings and resulting chaos. An identikit drawing of a man wanted for questioning by the police was shown. If it was meant to be of him, there was no resemblance at all. But then, with so much happening, who had been paying that much attention? When the programme ended Nick went down to the restaurant. The steak he'd had the night before had been tough, so he opted instead for a lamb kebab, baked potato and side salad. The meal, washed down with a couple of glasses of the local red wine, was excellent. Once back in his room, he considered finding a bar or a nightclub, although it was still early for most people to be out sampling the nightlife of Cyprus. His mobile rang. It was just on 9.00pm local time, 7.00pm in Scotland.

'Hello Nick. It's Josh. General Macnair asked me to pass on some information.' Joshua Clements was an American Delta Force Captain and had been attached to TIFAT from the very start. Slim, average height with brown hair, he could give an Olympic marathon runner competition. The joke with the teams was that he could get lost in a crowd of two.

'Fire away,' Nick said.

'Be at the Cypriot base by 08.00 tomorrow. You will be met at the main gate by Sergeant Reynolds of the Royal Scots Dragoon Guards. The Royal Scots have the weight out there right now. Give him what you've got. He lives in Edinburgh and will bring the stuff here,' Josh explained.

'Right,' Nick said. 'Anything else?'

'Macnair is raising holy hell about something. Right now he's on a video conference call with MI5, MI6 and the Joint Chiefs of Staff. God only knows what's going down.'

'Thanks, Josh. No doubt I'll hear something in the morning.'

'When will you be back, Nick?' Josh asked.

'Sunday,' Nick explained. The call ended and Hunter sat back pensively. What had riled Macnair so much, he wondered? He learned sooner than he expected when his phone rang thirty minutes later.

'Lieutenant Commander Hunter,' Macnair said in what Nick thought of as the General's official voice.

'Sir?' Hunter stiffened.

'Your leave is cancelled.'

'Understood sir.' Hunter knew better than to protest, asking instead 'Am I being recalled?'

'No.' Macnair sighed and said in a more reasonable tone, 'You've a job to do there. Samantha Freemantle and her team have disappeared. MI6 are, I was going to say

26

concerned, but panicked is a better description.'

'What's happened?' Nick asked.

'We have no idea. Get yourself to the base where the Duty Officer will take you into their communications centre. It's all arranged. Hopefully, I'll have a clearer picture by the time you get there. I'm sending Josh Clements, Jan Badonovitch and Doug Tanner to Cyprus.' He gave an uncharacteristic sigh. 'It doesn't look good Nick.'

'I'm on my way.' He knew better than to ask questions. He'd get answers once he got to Akrotiri but he couldn't help wondering what was up, especially in view of the men who were being sent to join him. Clements, Badonovitch and Tanner were amongst the toughest and most able men TIFAT had to offer and, when you considered the calibre of the remainder, that was saying a hell of a lot. TIFAT was stretched to breaking-point – with operations in Iraq, Iran, Afghanistan, Pakistan, Nigeria and the Sudan – and Hunter knew the three men had just returned from an operation in Afghanistan where they had taken out two warlords who had been fighting over a heroin crop and making life misery for the local population as a result.

Nick drove along the coast road in his hired BMW convertible and pulled up in front of the main gate at the British base. The Akrotiri peninsula, the southern tip of Cyprus, was occupied by a sovereign British base, manned by a British army regiment on a two-year rotational basis, and included an RAF squadron of fighters and visiting bombers. As he showed his ID card, it quickly became evident that he was expected. Nick was escorted to the communications centre by a member of the guard detail. Once there, he was shown into a private, sound-proofed room, hardly bigger than a broom cupboard, holding a table and four hard-backed chairs. He dialled Rosyth and was connected to General Macnair, who was now ensconced in the TIFAT operations room.

'What's happened, sir?' Nick began.

'A team of four operatives, including Freemantle, have vanished. We're working on it now, along with GCHQ.'

'Any transponders?'

'Just one so far. Lousy reception but GCHQ says the signal appears to be coming from somewhere in or around the old harbour at Limassol. We're trying to refine it further. From the satellite pictures it should be enough to work on. ECHELON is locked into the area even as we speak.'

ECHELON was the codename for the greatest surveillance and spy system ever created. Controlled by the American National Security Agency, it captured and analysed phone calls, faxes, e-mails and telex messages. It operated in conjunction with Britain's Government Communications Headquarters, the Canadian Communications Security Establishment, the Australian Defence Security Directorate, and the New Zealand General Communications Security Bureau. The ECHELON system was relatively simple in design. Intercept stations consisting of satellites, land-based intercept stations and intelligence-gathering ships sailing the seven seas, hoovered up everything in the ether. Codewords, passwords and trigger words downloaded the information for further examination. Computers sifted and sorted the data collected and, when necessary, triggered a message to an analyst. A thousand such intercepts were checked every hour, twenty-four hours a day. The elaborate process had been continually refined and, as a result of the 9/11 attacks, was now highly successful in tracking down known terrorists. But more importantly, ECHELON had proven to be the West's most potent weapon in the war declared by Osama bin Laden and his followers. The one drawback the system had, was that the vast amount of information it collected could result in some important event slipping through the net. The biggest problem, which was acknowledged by the West, was that the system had to be lucky one hundred percent of the time; the terrorists only once in a blue moon.

'What can you tell me about the operation, sir?' Nick asked.

'Freemantle was chosen because of her job as liaison with MI5 and MI6. MI5 had uncovered an Islamic plot in Britain while MI6 was involved because of the overseas aspect to it all. The details are on their way to me,' Macnair explained.

'They didn't need us?' Hunter asked.

'It wasn't considered necessary. They were on a fact-finding mission. If they had found anything they could use, they were going to pass it to us,' Macnair continued.

'Do we know what happened?' Nick was puzzled.

'Not precisely. Three of the team were on stakeout. Samantha was off-duty. You know the drill. It helps keep them fresh. She was about to go back to work and had been trying to contact the others when you turned up on the scene. The rest you know.'

'And you are sure there's only the one transponder?'

'Positive.'

'You know what that means sir, as well as I do.'

Macnair replied, heavily, 'Yes. Dead with the bodies in deep water.'

'That's the usual reason we don't get the signals.'

'I'm afraid you're right. It was my immediate thought when I learned about this.'

'Can you authorise me to collect a weapon here? I'll go down and take a look at the harbour.'

'I've already spoken to the CO and it's all arranged. It's recce only. Wait until Clements and the others get there.'

'What about the local authorities?'

'I'll speak to them if necessary. In the meantime, keep a low profile. As you know only too well, our mandate is unlike any other in the world. Though it may not be for much longer.'

'What do you mean, sir?'

Macnair paused before replying. 'It's not for now Nick but while you've been gallivanting around the Mediterranean a few problems have raised their ugly heads politically. Let us just say that we do not enjoy the same support with this sanctimonious s-o-b of a Prime Minister as we did the last one. At least his predecessor was far more pragmatic. However, that's my battle, not yours. In the meantime, I have the authority, so you take a quiet look while I make the necessary calls.'

'Yes, sir, but one thing. We're not controlled by the British Parliament. Ours is a worldwide mandate.' Hunter couldn't keep the puzzlement out of his voice.

'Precisely. It makes for interesting times.'

Shortly after that, Hunter left the room deep in thought. Outside he met Captain Trevellyan of the Royal Dragoons, the duty officer, along with the Sergeant Major in charge of the armoury. After an exchange of pleasantries Hunter handed an envelope to Trevellyan.

'This is for Sergeant Reynolds. I understand he's travelling to Edinburgh tomorrow,' Hunter said.

'That's right. On compassionate. His wife gave birth

yesterday. He should have been there for the event but something cropped up,' Trevellyan explained.

'It always does,' said Hunter wearily.

'I'll take you to the armoury. There are one or two interesting pieces we've picked up over the years which may be of use. Off books, so to speak.

'Have you guys enjoyed it out here?' Hunter asked as they walked to the armoury.

'Yes, normally we would, but to be honest we're hardly ever here long enough to enjoy the place.'

'Iraq?'

'You got it in one. It's not fair on the wives. They come over expecting a jolly and we're away most of the time. I've put in my papers. I'll be out in four months and counting in spite of the fact I've been offered Major with effect from next year, and an almost cast-iron certainty for my Colonelcy,' Trevellyan replied.

'So why go?'

'I don't trust the government.'

'No one in the services does. What about you, Sergeant Major?'

'Another fifteen months and I'm out with my full pension.' He spoke heavily. 'They offered me a further five years but I declined. When I go, I'll have given thirty years, man and boy, to my Queen and country. That's more than enough. I can't wait to get the hell out now.'

'Why?' Hunter had a perplexed look on his face. In the past, a man in the Sergeant Major's position would have given his eye-teeth for another five years.

'I don't feel it's my country anymore. Me and the missus are moving here. We've already bought a nice wee bungalow and I've put my name down for the local yacht club.' He chuckled. 'All I need to do now is improve my sailing!' The Sergeant Major stopped in front of an imposing metal door and lifted a heavy key to a lock that had been installed in the early part of the nineteenth century. It was merely for show. After twisting the key he placed his palm on a sensor and unlocked the door.

Hunter left the armoury with an Austrian Glock 18 strapped to his left side. It was the operatives' preferred weapon when close-quarter work was called for. Over his shoulder was a khaki, lightweight jacket, in the pockets of which were spare ammunition and a silencer. When quizzed about where the gun had come from Captain Trevellyan shook his head in mock sorrow.

'From a well-armed and well-financed Pakistani who thought he could control the borders between Pakistan and Afghanistan. He learned the hard way that he couldn't,' Trevellyan explained.

'So how did it end up here?'

'Funny that,' the Sergeant Major had replied. 'But these illegals have an occasional use.'

Hunter nodded thoughtfully and smiled.

4

It was a few minutes before 3.00am and Hunter darted surreptitiously around buildings looking at fishing boats and private vessels berthed in the old harbour. Behind him stood the towering walls of Limassol Castle, where King Richard the Lionheart had married Princess Berengaria of Navarre in 1191. The night was deathly still, the sky cloudless. The sun wasn't due to rise for another hour. His black shirt and dark blue jeans helped him blend into the background. Nobody was about – even the nightclubs were quiet – and none of the boats had lights on. The harbour was jam-packed with craft, berthed three or four deep along the inner wall. He stopped frequently, using his senses to assess the night. He was aware of the slightest of sounds – the creaking of hulls, a distant car taking late night revellers home, voices far away – but he could not see or hear anything of interest. It was his sense of smell that came to his aid.

The stench of the old fishing boats and rotted fish was unmistakable. However, a slight breeze came in off the water and brought with it a very faint smell of cigarette smoke that Nick almost missed. He tilted his head back and took another sniff. Yes, to his right. Nick turned his head and looked. At the end of the outer wall, sticking out at least fifteen or sixteen metres either side, was a coastal steamer of a sort frequently found in that part of the Mediterranean. She was, without doubt, badly berthed. As Hunter pondered why, the answer became obvious. There was actually nowhere else for the ship to come alongside. At least not that he could see. That being the case, it would have meant anchoring offshore, outside the harbour and moving back and forth by boat. This was something to be avoided whenever possible, especially if the ship was intending to pick up a passenger or two without being observed.

The harbour wall was littered with old, discarded and, in some cases, in-use fishing baskets for catching crabs and lobsters. A few nets were also scattered across the stones. Keeping low, Hunter made his way towards the end of the pier. As he inched closer, he could make out a crane on the starboard side, nearest to the wall. She was a tramp steamer, though her engines had been replaced with more modern diesels. Usually carrying only four men in the crew, they picked up and landed freight in harbours too small for larger, deeper draught vessels. He guessed it was for that reason the coaster had been allowed alongside. He could make out the name: *L'Escargot*.

He stopped about fifty metres from the end of the wall, behind one of the stacks of lobster pots. Slowly, almost on his knees, he moved forward. A small red glow suddenly brightened as someone standing on the stern of the ship inhaled deeply on a cigarette. Good. It meant that the man wasn't concentrating on his job – he was busy, his hands and mind on his cigarette and his night vision was slightly impaired – and that was often all that was needed. Hunter was now less than ten metres away and lying flat on the stones behind a discarded fishing net. As the man took another deep drag Hunter thought he recognised him as one of the men from the café. Suddenly, the tramp steamer's engines started, belching smoke and noise in equal measure. Once warmed through the *L'Escargot* would be leaving. After a few minutes someone stepped out onto the port bridge wing and shouted something in Arabic to the man standing down aft. He jumped ashore, untied the stern rope and threw it onto the deck, then dashed along the wall and did the same with the bow rope before leaping back onto the ship. Slowly the *L'Escargot* began to turn to starboard, away from the wall. It was an unusual time to depart – especially with no lights showing – and if proof of intent was needed, Hunter figured he'd seen enough. Without hesitation, he darted to the end of the wall and calmly stepped across the opening gap and onto the rubbing strake which ran from bow to stern around the fattest part of the hull, protecting her from damage when striking walls and jetties. He guessed she was about 800 tonnes deadweight and twenty years old. As she left the wall, Hunter could feel the slightest swell under his feet as she moved placidly through the calm Mediterranean sea.

Hunter withdrew his Glock, now fitted with a silencer, from under his shirt and passed close to the aft starboard derrick where he paused, crouching behind a wooden cargo hatch coaming. As he knelt there, a man appeared, flicked a cigarette over the side and immediately lit another. The scar on his left cheek was briefly illuminated in the light and Hunter now knew without a doubt that this was one of the men from the café. Suddenly the man turned to look at something behind him. Hunter didn't hesitate. With his thumb tucked into his palm, he hit the man with a larynx-crunching blow to the throat. There was no sound as the man collapsed. Hunter pressed his hand around the man's neck, blocking his carotid artery and killing him instantly. He dragged the body over to the lifeboat and hid it from view under the tarpaulin covering.

The ship had reached the harbour entrance and was picking up speed. As a result, her engines were creating a great deal more background noise, drowning out any sound that Hunter made. At that moment the port and starboard lights came on, as well as the two masthead steaming lights and the stern overtaking light. Moving forward cautiously, Hunter found a door into the super-structure and opened it quietly. The only lights were knee-high night lamps but he could see he was in the main passageway that ran the full length of the ship. He quickly reached another door. He listened intently, but could hear nothing over the noise of the engines. He twisted the handle, paused and then pushed it open slowly. Night lamps on either side of the bulkhead illuminated the galley. He closed the door and moved on. The first door to port opened onto an unoccupied single cabin. The next door along on the starboard side revealed a mess deck for eating. He checked all the cabins and found they were empty as well. At the end of the passageway a door faced him and alongside was a set of stairs which he guessed led to the bridge. That meant he was facing the door to the captain's cabin. Carefully, Hunter started to ascend but when he heard what sounded like a slapping noise coming from below he stopped. There was no mistaking the scream that followed, nor the angry, muffled tirade of a female voice. It sounded like the captain's cabin was in use. Immediately, he heard a laugh above his head and a voice said something in Arabic. The reply was in English.

'I have told you many times, you must speak English. It

is important for when we get to Britain. Do you understand?'

'Yes,' was the sullen reply.

'Say it again, this time in English.'

'I said, I hope Hasan leaves something for us to enjoy.'

'Don't worry my friend, he will. He knows what is good for him. That infidel woman will provide fun for us all.' There was a satisfied laugh.

Hunter took another step up and stopped, his eyes level with the deck. The bridge was laid out before him and behind him was a bulkhead. Two men – one at the wheel, the other leaning on an open windowsill – were standing in front of him.

'Close the window. It is getting cold,' said the man at the wheel.

As the window was pushed up Hunter took another two steps and fired twice. The first shot hit the man near the window in the back of the head and exited through his right eye before smashing the window to smithereens. The second shot hit the man at the base of his spine, breaking it in two and exiting through his stomach. The wheel slipped from his nerveless hands and began to turn slowly to port as Hunter stepped onto the bridge. Hunter grabbed it and put the ship on a heading of due east and jammed the foot of a stool between the spokes. The wheel spun a few degrees to starboard before it stopped moving. Left like that the ship would turn in a massive circle some twenty miles in diameter over a period of about three hours. That would do. He went below and paused outside the door. From what he had heard, he guessed there was only one other person in the forward cabin that needed his attention. Hearing another slap followed by a scream he took hold of the doorknob, twisted it fully, paused and then pushed the door open and stepped over the low coaming.

The cabin was relatively spacious, stretching the width of the superstructure. A small desk was to port with a chair behind it and to starboard was a recessed bunk. A man was seated on an upright chair with his back to Hunter. Slightly to one side Nick could see the naked form of Samantha Freemantle tied to a similar chair. Her eyes widened in surprise as she caught sight of Hunter. She was beginning to yell, 'Nick, behind you,' when Hunter saw the man out of the corner of his eye. He also saw the knife in the man's hand.

*　*　*　*　*

Zim Albatha stopped in a side street in the city of Bursa, famous for having been the first capital of the Ottoman Empire. Now it was a modern, sprawling, prosperous place humming with vitality and personality. The city centre was bustling with shoppers as they walked from shop to shop or went purposefully into one of the numerous banks. Albatha strode along the street past Ulu Cami – the Grand Mosque – and into the main square. Minutes later, he entered a restaurant. It was only half full and lunch was still at least an hour away. The place was dimly lit. The tables all had four chairs around them and each was covered by a black and white chequered cloth. Albatha was a big man, 6ft 6ins tall and weighing 220 pounds. He seemed to fill the doorway. He was a modest man with one vanity – a luxurious handlebar moustache. Albatha was a Captain in the Turkish State Security Organisation with a special roving commission, reporting directly to the Director General, Varol Sandal.

Why they were meeting in such an out-of-the-way place he had no idea. Albatha spotted his boss immediately, sitting in a corner, nursing a soda water. Seeing him, Sandal waved a hand in his direction. Albatha slid into the chair opposite.

'Sorry about meeting you all the way out here Zim but I thought it wiser to see you out of the office.' The Director General was of average height and weight and was highly astute, having proved his courage over his years as an operative. He now ran the security force with a rod of iron. He was highly respected by his staff and a few even liked him. Albatha was one of them.

A waiter appeared. 'Coffee,' said Albatha, looking at the man, 'strong and black.' He turned his attention back to his boss. 'So why here?'

'I've been given some information that I need you to follow up, but I don't want it going through the usual channels.'

'Why not?'

Sandal screwed up his face, as though considering whether or not to answer. 'There are too many questions being asked about current operations.'

'Who by?'

'Syed Azam.'

'The Minister of State for Immigration?'

Sandal nodded. 'Also, a self-confessed Islamist. Not quite a fundamentalist but near enough.'

Albatha shrugged. 'That's more to do with getting elected than belief.'

Sandal smiled cynically. 'Maybe. I'm not so sure. I believe there's actually more to it than that.'

Albatha's coffee arrived. Nodding his thanks he spooned in some sugar and took a sip of the hot, sweet drink, before asking, 'Why? We've nothing special on at the moment.'

'I appreciate that. But there's something in the offing. Something big.'

'How do you know?'

Shaking his head in frustration, Sandal replied, 'I don't *know*. It's just that the rumours I'm getting suggest that there's something brewing.'

'Where are these rumours coming from?'

'The usual,' Sandal said. The usual meant his boss's contacts, built up over many years of patient hard work. They had proved invaluable in the past.

'And where does Syed Azam fit into all this?'

'His name has cropped up a few times. Also, he's been sniffing around the department, asking questions.'

Albatha frowned. 'I don't get it. He's never done that before.'

'Which is why I'm highly suspicious.'

'What do you want me to do Varol?'

'Drop everything. I could be wrong, but I want it checked out. Which is why we're meeting here. Until I know what's going down, I want it kept between the two of us.'

Albatha nodded in agreement.

* * * * *

The man had been leaning against the bulkhead, studying the naked form of Samantha, anticipating what he was going to do to her. Unfortunately for Nick, he had the reactions of a cat and immediately took a swing at him. The knife handle smacked into Hunter's forehead, knocking him backwards. Nick's head hit the corner of the door and – dazed – he crumbled to his knees. Nick had just enough presence of mind to sway with the kick unleashed by his assailant. Even so he lay groggily on the deck, dimly aware of someone shouting. The next thing Nick knew, he was sitting on a wooden backed chair, his arms tied so tightly to the armrests that his fingers were already tingling due to the lack of circulation. His feet were also tied to the chair legs in a similar fashion, and they were beginning to go numb as well. One man stood looking down at him. When he saw that Hunter was conscious he hit him on the side of the jaw with his clenched fist. While Hunter closed his eyes and tried to clear his head there was a loud yell from outside and the man who had attacked Hunter came rushing into the cabin, screaming in English. He had a strong Birmingham accent.

'They're dead! They're dead! He's killed them!'

The other man's face drained of blood. As the Englishman raised his knife to kill Hunter, his friend stopped him. He also spoke English, but with a strong Middle Eastern accent.

'Do not kill him, my friend. We must find out who he is and what he knows. Is he alone? Are there others with him and if so, where are they?' He looked at Hunter. 'You have killed my friends. You will have a very painful death.'

'You're right, Achmed.' He then looked down at Hunter and said, 'I'm going to enjoy killing you.'

Hunter, very wisely, said nothing. There was no point in antagonising either of them. Another fist in the face was best avoided if possible.

'We'd better go back on the bridge,' said the man with the Birmingham accent. 'Once we're clear we can deal with this swine.'

Both men left the cabin. Hunter looked at Samantha and managed a weak smile. 'Some rescue, huh?'

41

Samantha shook her head. 'I've known better. Any more bright ideas?'

By way of an answer, Hunter forced his toes down and tried to lift himself off the deck. He sat back down heavily.

'What are you trying to do?' she asked.

'Break the chair. If we're going to escape we need to do it now.' He started slowly to inch his way towards the bulkhead. It was exhausting work, and his hands and feet were gradually becoming numb. He paused to rest for a few seconds and then, rounding his shoulders as far as he could, he flung himself backwards smashing the back of the chair into the bulkhead. Gripping the armrests, he summoned all his strength into his arms and heaved upwards. The tendons on his neck were sticking out with the effort. The wood splintered with a loud crack. Nick leant forward and the chair dropped back onto the floor. He tried again and this time the back of the chair broke. Once his hands were free he hurriedly untied his legs and tried to regain some feeling in his feet.

'Get me free,' Samantha said.

'Hang on, I can't feel a thing in my fingers,' he said, rubbing his hands together. Suddenly he heard a change in the engine and the old ship began to slow down.

'Hurry, Nick, untie me.'

'No time. When the door opens start struggling like hell.'

Hunter hid the broken chair and pieces of rope in a corner, grabbed another chair from behind the desk, and sat down. It wasn't a moment too soon. The door opened and the man who had been addressed as Achmed entered. In his hand he carried a knife.

Samantha began to struggle, yelling and groaning. Achmed looked at her, still advancing towards Hunter and smiled. 'We will enjoy ourselves with you before we kill you. While you,' he looked at Hunter, now only an arm's length away, 'you will die very slowly and you will tell me all that I wish to know.'

The only word to describe Hunter's next move was 'eruption'. The man looked in total astonishment as Hunter's right leg smashed into his stomach, winding him. Hunter brought his left knee up in another focused move and brought his coupled hands down on the man's neck. It snapped like a dried twig.

Samantha had lapsed into silence.

'Scream,' Hunter told her.

'What?' She looked at him in bewilderment.

'Scream! Now!'

Samantha let loose a piercing scream. They heard a voice yelling. Hunter picked up the knife and stepped over to Samantha and cut her free.

'When I say so, give a really loud scream.'

'Why?' she whispered.

'He'll think everything is alright and won't be tempted to investigate. He's the man with the gun. I want him to come down but I don't want him to be armed. He may use it before I can deal with him. Yell something that will attract him but which won't arouse suspicion.'

'Like what?'

'How the hell . . . Like rape or something.'

Hunter stepped over the coaming, closed the door so that the man on the bridge wouldn't be able to see the body of his friend and went to the other side of the stairs to the bridge.

Suddenly a muffled scream rang out and Samantha called, 'No! No! Please don't rape me! No! Help me. Somebody please help me. Oh, my God. Help!'

The temptation proved too much. The man came down the steps with a smile on his face. Hunter saw that his gun was in its holster. As he reached the door, Hunter stepped up behind him and hit him across the temple with the handle of the knife. The blow knocked the man to his knees. A second blow rendered him unconscious. Hunter lifted the man up by his shoulders, dragged him into the cabin, dropped him onto the chair vacated by Samantha and tied him up. Samantha was busy getting dressed. Hunter averted his eyes.

'I'm going up top. The galley is just along there. Will you see if there's any juice in the fridge. Also, I expect there's a first aid kit in there. It's the most usual place to keep one. See if you can rustle up a few aspirin or something.'

On the bridge, a glance around the horizon showed very few ship or boat lights. The autopilot was engaged and was set on a heading of 100 degrees at about six knots.

After about ten minutes, Samantha joined him with a bowl of warm water, a cloth and some Codeine. 'Let me take a look.'

Carefully, she cleaned the blood off Nick's face. There was a graze, plus a small bump and a bruise. Hunter winced when she wiped it.

'What about your chin?'

Tentatively, he gave it a gentle nudge back and forth. 'It'll do. I've had a lot worse playing rugby.' He threw three Codeine down his neck and washed them down with half a litre of orange juice.

'That's better. Feel like talking?' Nick asked her.

Taking a deep breath, she replied, 'Yes, what do you want to know?'

'What happened? How did you end up here?'

Samantha shook her head. 'I've no idea. I left after I saw

you were okay. I hadn't gone very far when I felt something sharp in my bottom and the next thing I knew I was tied to that chair.' She paused and then added, 'Naked.' She shuddered, tears welling, her eyes blinking rapidly.

'Take it easy. We can talk later.'

'You needn't patronise me, Lieutenant Commander,' she spoke sharply but immediately regretted it saying, 'I'm sorry. I didn't mean that. It's just . . .' she paused.

'Don't give it a thought.'

'No. I want to tell you what happened. After they stripped me and tied me to the chair, they took great pleasure in telling me what they'd done to the others. They joked about it. They shot Harry Sparrow and Fred Nelson in their arms and legs and threw them overboard. Colin Frobisher . . .'

'Frobisher?' Hunter asked, interrupting her. 'He was one of the team here?'

'You knew him?'

'Yes. He and I exchanged information sometimes, informally. It worked better that way. We weren't exactly friends but we'd shared a few drinks.' Hunter's voice hardened. 'What did they do to him?'

She closed her eyes for a moment, composing her thoughts, and then said, 'They broke his wrists and ankles with a hammer. Then . . . then they tied weights to him and threw him overboard.'

'Alive?'

'And fully conscious as well.'

'Which one did it, do you know?'

'Yes. The man down below.'

'I'm going to have a chat with him. You stay here. Keep a lookout for other ships' lights. The Mediterranean can be a busy place, especially at this time of the year with so many pleasure craft about.'

'Even at this hour?'

'Yes. People use their autopilot to head to their next port of call and don't often keep a proper watch, usually because they've had too much to drink. Believe me, I've seen it often enough.'

'Nick,' her voice quivered, 'I want to thank you. If you hadn't come along . . .'

'Hey, it's fine.'

The man in the chair was still unconscious. Hunter went in search of a bucket, found one in the galley and filled it with water. He returned and threw it into the prisoner's face.

'You broke the wrists and ankles of a friend of mine and threw him alive into the sea,' Nick said in a measured tone. 'Is that true? Is that what you did?'

In return he received a mouthful of abuse. Turning the chair around, Hunter tilted it back and dragged it across the deck. Then, with some effort, he dragged it up the steps to the bridge. The man continued swearing at him.

'What are you doing?' Samantha asked.

'You'll see.' He leant down and this time yelled in the man's face. 'Why did you do it? If you were going to kill them why not get it over and done with quickly? *Say*, you piece of vermin.'

The man cleared his throat and was about to spit at Hunter. Before he could do so, Hunter took a half-step back and brought both open palms hard against the man's cheeks. The blows stung more than did any real damage. Hunter was exercising a great deal of self-control not to hurt the man and hurt him badly. Another mouthful of abuse followed. Hunter stepped further back and nodded at Samantha, who crossed the bridge and slapped the man as hard as she could. Whether it was the shock of the slap, or the fact it was done by a woman, the man fell silent.

'Now listen to me,' said Hunter, his anger under control, his voice level, almost conversational, 'if you don't tell me your name, I'll let Samantha here get to work on you. Is that what you want?'

'I won't say a word. Not to you. Never.'

'Samantha, go and search the cabins. See what you can find, passports, driving licences, anything.'

She left without a word. Hunter waited in silence. About fifteen minutes later, Samantha returned and handed a British passport to Hunter.

'You'll never guess who he is,' she said.

'Hasan Husain,' Hunter said before he opened the passport.

'How did you know?'

'I had a suspicion. Nothing more.' Nick looked at the passport and continued 'Hasan Husain. Top of our Most Wanted list. Connected to both the Lisbon and London bombings. Believed to have helped with the planning of the Glasgow fiasco.'

'I am a Jihadist. I fight for Allah and for . . .', Hasan Husain began to chant.

'You're nothing of the sort. You've killed innocent people for your own perverted ideas of Islam and the mockery you've made of it,' Hunter cut across harshly.

Husain said, 'I demand to see the British Ambassador. And a lawyer.'

Hunter couldn't help it. He laughed.

5

At the sound of Hunter's laughter, Husain fell silent.

'We have some questions for you,' said Hunter.

'I'm telling you nothing.' Husain replied defiantly.

Hunter gave an exaggerated sigh. 'Listen Husain, we can do this the easy way or the hard way. You're going to die. There will be no court of law. No defence lawyers. I've found you guilty of both terrorist crimes and murder. So what do I mean by the easy way or the hard way? It's the way you'll die. Either way, you will talk. Believe me.'

Husain's mouthful of abuse washed over Hunter's head.

Hunter looked at Samantha and asked, 'Do you know what's going on?'

'A little. We received a tip-off. We also picked up some information from wire taps. It was enough to set off alarm bells which brought us out here,' she explained.

'Four of you is rather heavy duty.'

'I know. We're pretty sure something big is going to happen, but we have no clue as to what.'

Hunter looked out pensively towards the horizon. Dawn was breaking and it promised to be a beautiful, sunny day. Astern, daylight revealed the Cyprus skyline. There were numerous lights twinkling across the sea, all showing that the vessels they belonged to would pass clear of them.

With the strengthening daylight, the age and dilapidated state of the *L'Escargot* was beginning to show however. Bloodstains and bloody footprints on the deck were also becoming visible. Hunter spent a few minutes filling the bucket with sea-water and throwing it over the deck, washing the blood into the scuppers around the bridge. It gave him time to think even though his head hurt like hell. He helped himself to some more Codeine and a carton of orange juice. Then he went out onto the port bridge wing and telephoned TIFAT HQ. It wasn't long before he was speaking to General Macnair, who didn't complain about being woken up in the middle of the night when he heard about Hasan Husain. Hunter brought Macnair up to speed.

'Is there any chance we can get Clements and the rest of the team helicoptered out to the boat?' Hunter asked. 'And I need some SSM. Thinking about it, it'll be easier and less messy than anything I can do.'

'Leave that to me. What will you do with the ship?'

'I'll abandon her somewhere.'

'I don't want Husain on trial,' Macnair warned Nick.

'Sir, I'll get back to you in fifteen. I'll take a fix, plan a track and give you my position for 14.00 hours. That should be time enough for the others to get here.'

He read from the *L'Escargot*'s basic 'satnav' system and transferred it to the chart lying on the table at the back of the bridge. It was a French Garmin Blue Chart, well worn with pencil marks and tracks, some rubbed out. He planned a track and sent a text to Rosyth with their predicted latitude and longitude for 14.00. He then examined the chart more closely. He could make out a fresh pencil line which he followed with a pair of dividers to its western edge. He pulled more charts from the

49

battered folio kept in the drawer under the table. The track continued west. Chart followed chart, all the way to Dieppe, all 3,200 nautical miles, as near as dammit. The *L'Escargot* was due to dock in three places: Pozzallo in Sicily, Gibraltar and Lisbon. Without stopping in between and assuming reasonable weather and a speed of ten knots, Hunter calculated that it would have taken them about thirteen days. Add on twelve-hour stopovers in each port to take on water, diesel and fresh food, and allowing for any delays, they would have made it easily in just over two weeks.

'Keep an eye on things here, please, Samantha. I'm going to take a look in the engine room. I won't be long.'

The engines were in good working order, properly maintained and, significantly, Hunter thought, fairly new-looking. There was plenty of diesel in the ready-use tanks; the back-up tanks were also full and oil levels were correct. It took a few more minutes to establish the fact that the holds were empty. He returned to the bridge and stood looking down at the chart.

'What are you doing?' Samantha asked.

'Checking on something.' He looked across at Husain who was staring at the deck, his head drooping forward. Hunter knew that by ignoring Husain, the fear would be growing in his mind. He wouldn't be able to stop it. It was a technique well known to the security services. It was part of the softening-up process before the interrogation started. Instead Nick picked up the ship's log and checked figures down the right hand page. Course, speed and distance travelled were shown in a list, although the timing apart of the ship's position was intermittent at best. *L'Escargot* steamed at a steady ten knots.

'Well I've been looking through the ID cards and other

papers' she explained. 'Husain also has a Pakistani passport, but it's in the name of Majid Sardar.' She looked at Husain and hesitated. 'Can't we put him down below so I don't have to look at his ugly face?'

'Sorry, no. Too much effort. Bringing him up here was hard enough.'

She looked at Husain who had started struggling against the ropes. What he thought he could do was beyond her. However, she did know that the fear in him would be ratcheting up, his actions virtually beyond his control.

Hunter looked at him for a few moments. 'Husain, I am a Royal Naval officer. I know more about ropes and knots than a boy scout. The more you struggle the tighter the ropes will become. They are known as one-way slip knots. Do you feel them getting tighter? You should because your circulation will start to be affected.'

Husain stopped struggling and looked, with hatred and growing fear, at Hunter.

'You see, you're feeling it already. Soon your fingers and toes will become numb and start to turn blue. If I don't slacken the knots gangrene will set in. Should you live long enough to develop it. However, one thing is sure, the extremities of your arms and legs will soon be hurting like hell.' Hunter was lying through his teeth about the knots but his words had the desired effect. Husain stopped struggling.

'Do you want to keep watch or get us something to eat? I could do with something.' Nick asked Samantha.

'I'll get some food.'

'The galley's halfway along the corridor on your left. I take my coffee strong, white and without sugar.'

'Okay.'

Hunter stood on the starboard bridge wing, enjoying

51

the promise of another warm and sunny day. He deliberately gave no thought to Husain and what he had done. Otherwise, in spite of his training and self-discipline, he would do some serious harm to the little bastard. Samantha soon returned, armed with fried egg sandwiches and a pot of coffee.

'I've never seen so much tomato ketchup outside of a supermarket.' She laughed as she held up a red plastic bottle. She closed her eyes and turned her face up to the sun. 'God, that feels heavenly. I never thought I would feel the sun again.' She looked at Nick. 'Thank you again.'

'No thanks necessary.'

'I owe you.'

'You owe me not a darn thing. Forget it. What's the food situation like?'

'Very good. Well stocked with tins of all sorts. The fridge is packed with frozen lamb, minced beef and fresh vegetables.'

'I thought it might be.'

'Why?'

'I'll tell you later.' They ate in companionable silence.

Samantha put down her empty cup and suddenly yawned. 'Hell, I'm shattered.'

'I'm not surprised after what you've been through. Can you find us something to sit on?'

Nodding, she went below and returned with a couple of folding chairs she had found in the mess room.

'Thanks. You sit out on the port wing, I'll take the starboard.'

She sat in the doorway, in view of Hunter. Moments after sitting down Samantha fell asleep, her head drooping forward awkwardly.

'Samantha . . . SAMANTHA!'

She awoke with a start. 'Sorry, I must have nodded off.'

'Why don't you go below and get some rest? I can manage.'

She shook her head. 'I'll be all right. I'll get some more coffee. That should perk me up.' She went below, made some fresh coffee and returned. She sat on her chair, drank half her coffee, placed it on the deck and settled back to enjoy the sunshine and was soon fast asleep once again. She looked extremely uncomfortable. Hunter quietly woke her up and persuaded her to go and get some sleep, pointing out there were cabins below that hadn't been used by the crew. Left alone on the bridge Hunter sipped his coffee while he examined more of the ship's papers. Some were in English, others were in Arabic. He began photographing them and transmitting them to TIFAT using his phone. He then checked the ship's position and adjusted the course and speed as they headed towards the rendezvous point. He called the General and told him what he'd discovered.

Thoughtfully, Macnair said, 'Dieppe, huh? That's very interesting.'

'There's something else, sir. I couldn't understand why they planned to call at Lisbon. After all, it isn't that far from Gibraltar.'

'Maybe they had a good reason to do so.'

'They did. They were going to fill the ship with wine. Port, to be more accurate.'

'How do you know?' Macnair asked.

'I found a manifest amongst the papers.'

'Wine to France?'

'No sir, England. Stopping at Dieppe to refuel.'

'That's a nice touch. It gave them a good reason to come to Britain.'

'Yes, sir. That's what I thought.'

'Dieppe is obviously for some sort of rendezvous.'

'Agreed, but there's no indication of what,' Nick said.

'Let me know if you find anything. If there's nothing else we can speak later.'

Hunter sat with a blank sheet of paper and a pencil. After a few moments of thought, he began writing. When he'd finished, he cast an eye down the list. He nodded to himself and stuffed the paper into his hip pocket. Shortly before 14.00 he checked their position again and was satisfied they were within half a mile of their rendezvous point. He could hear the unmistakable clatter of a helicopter. A glance at the anemometer showed a light breeze coming over the starboard bow. Hunter called the pilot using Channel 16, the emergency and initial contact channel, and ordered him to go to Channel 8.

'I'll hold this course and speed. Come in over the port quarter, wind is ten knots, green two zero. The road is green,' Hunter said, indicating to the pilot that he was in charge and it was safe to approach. Had he used the phrase "the road is red" they would have come in ready for a gunfight.

'Roger that. Sea is clear ahead. Coming in now,' replied the pilot.

The helicopter hovered over the stern. Moments later Josh Clements appeared in the doorway and was winched down to the deck. Jan Badonovitch and Doug Tanner followed in rapid succession. The helicopter veered away, back to Cyprus, and the three men headed to the bridge.

They may have belonged to a tough, elite force, but they never took avoidable risks. The team wore the latest Kevlar vests, their weapons were the finest to be found in the arms industry, and they rarely went into a situation without having a good idea of the odds. As General Macnair said often enough, they hadn't been so expensively trained to waste it all.

'Hi, boss,' Badonovitch greeted Hunter, casually standing in the port doorway.

'Hi, Jan,' Hunter replied, smiling. It had become a game with the pair of them. The tougher the situation, the more laid-back they were when meeting.

Jan Badonovitch was one of the toughest men at TIFAT. Squat and broad-shouldered, his strength was legendary. He spoke Russian, English and Polish, and got by in German. A sergeant in the Russian *Spetsnaz* – which, if translated literally, meant 'of special purpose' – he had been with TIFAT since its foundation. His posting had been for two years initially but that had been extended indefinitely after General Macnair successfully made a case that all TIFAT operatives should stay as long as they wished. That suited some, not others, depending upon each person's ambition for promotion. Within the non-commissioned ranks, few were lower than sergeant or its equivalent, depending on the service and country they came from. The major factor that made TIFAT so appealing was the respect the organisation was held in which was why there was a long waiting-list of volunteers. At headquarters there was a ranked hierarchy; in the field there was no such thing, except if orders had to be given, and these were usually minimal. Each man knew exactly what was expected of him and performed to the best of his ability. And that was outstanding, by anybody's measuring stick.

'What's up, Nick?' Josh Clements asked as they shook hands. 'What happened to you?'

'Just a slight altercation,' Nick said wryly.

'And the other guy?'

'Waiting for you on the bridge.'

'Hullo, boss,' Doug Tanner waved to Hunter. Tanner was a big man in every way. An American SEAL he was well over six feet tall and as black as the ace of spades. Tanner enjoyed pointing out that he never needed to use any 'can't-see-me' cream when on night ops. Most people looked up to him, even Nick. Those who didn't know him very well were unaware of the orphaned children's homes he supported, using the money he'd accumulated while with TIFAT. As well as financial help, he spent his leave in different parts of the world, helping to construct or renovate buildings to be used as orphanages. On the rare occasion he was asked, he claimed that, being single, he might as well spend his cash on something worthwhile. He never mentioned the fact that he had spent most of his childhood and youth in an orphanage – usually in trouble of one form or another – and it was the US Army that had saved him from prison, while the SEALs had given him pride and belief in himself.

Hunter brought the team up-to-date. He nodded towards their prisoner. 'Meet Hasan Husain.'

At the mention of the name the men's faces broke into huge smiles.

'After all this time, we've finally got the sod. There must be a God after all,' said Josh Clements. 'Any idea where he's been hiding?'

'From the look of the passport we found, I'd say mainly in Pakistan and Afghanistan. He's also spent some time in Saudi Arabia. Did you bring the SSM?'

'Yes,' said Clements. 'Luckily, the base had some after their last deployment in Afghanistan.'

'Incidentally, we've got an MI6 agent sleeping below. Samantha Freemantle.'

'The woman who's going to be our liaison between MI5 and MI6?' Clements asked.

'That's the one. Right, let's get started. The sooner we finish, the sooner we can get off this heap.'

SSM was a powerful cocktail of drugs. It was a mixture of Scopolamine – a constituent of henbane – the barbiturate Sodium Amytal, and Mescaline – a naturally occurring psychedelic alkaline – and had taken years to develop. It was proving highly successful but there was one unusual characteristic of the drug. It was at its most effective when used on somebody who was in pain. The SSM took away the pain and soothed the subject's nervous system. As a result, the brain was more willing to co-operate when questions were asked.

'Boss,' Jan Badonovitch said, 'you know how I hate to state the obvious,' he didn't seem to notice the exchange of looks and smirks between the other three, or chose not to, 'but what questions are we asking?'

'Here you are.' Hunter reached into his pocket and handed over the list he'd compiled. 'Anything else you can think of, jot it down.'

'Is there a timescale?' Clements asked.

'Not really. We'll play it by ear. Take him below. Jan, you and Doug deal with him. Josh, can you start searching the ship? Samantha had a cursory look, which is how we found the passports and ID cards. But there could be more. I'll stay up here. I've already found some papers which I've forwarded to Rosyth. I'll take another look and see if there are any more.'

'Right, boss,' replied Doug Tanner. Once he had cut Husain free, he hauled him up and threw him towards the stairs. Husain stumbled and yelled. Tanner was right behind him and shoved him down below. Husain landed with a thud and a mouthful of curses. The treatment was all part of the softening-up process.

Hunter stopped Badonovitch and said, 'There's one really important item Jan. How in hell did they know about MI6's involvement? We need to find out urgently.'

Badonovitch nodded.

'What next?' Josh asked.

'I need to take a look at the charts,' Nick said.

'Are we going anywhere in particular?' Josh asked Nick as he set off downstairs.

'Into deep water. We need to get rid of this thing.'

Hunter took the bridge apart in his search for information. At the back of the shelving that held the ship's charts he found a loose panel. He used a set of dividers to pull it off the bulkhead and reached inside. There, he found log books and registration documents. A quick flick through showed that they referred to the coaster, but showed three different names and ports of registration. Hunter took the documents and sat out on the starboard bridge wing examining the chart of the area. He made up his mind, altered course to port and settled back down in the sunshine. If they merely abandoned the coaster it was bound to be spotted and boarded. Far better to get rid of all the evidence. He liked the thought that whoever was pulling the strings of this operation would be left confused.

There were no screams from below, no raised voices. When Hunter went below to the galley there was nothing to be heard above the rumble of the engines. SSM was a highly effective drug. He knew that each question would be asked many times in different ways, to check if what was said was true. Tanner and Badonovitch were used to the procedure. There was, however, a major flaw with the drug. If the recipient believed what he had been told, it was impossible to use rational argument to contradict that belief.

Moments later Clements appeared with Samantha in tow.

'Found anything?'

'Not a thing. What about you?'

'Charts from here to Britain. Along with logs and registration documents for this ship, but with different names.'

'Interesting,' Josh said thoughtfully.

'That's what I thought. Let's hope Husain gives us some answers. You okay Samantha?'

Stifling a yawn she nodded. 'Once I get some more food inside me. I'll go and make us something to eat. Cheese sandwiches do? There's plenty in the fridge.'

'Already taken care of,' said Hunter. 'Sandwiches and a flask of pea soup are over there on the chart table.'

'Oh, how domesticated you are, Lieutenant Commander,' Samantha teased.

Nick laughed. 'Considering the size of the crew, the ship is well provisioned in the basics, including powdered milk, tins of fruit, tea, coffee, you name it.'

They had started to eat when Jan and Doug joined them.

'Any joy?' Nick asked.

'Some,' Jan replied, helping himself to a sandwich.

'What have you found out?' Josh asked.

'They've come from Pakistan and went in to Cyprus to refuel and take on water,' replied Badonovitch.

'That's confirmed by their charts and log,' said Nick.

'And that's what we'd been told' Samantha said. 'That was why we were on Cyprus. Waiting for somebody or something, like this ship.'

Hunter shook his head. 'Listen, Samantha we're not idiots. You must have had better intelligence than that to have justified your presence here. Your lot are not exactly renowned for investing money on the off-chance of a potential problem.'

Samantha shrugged. 'We'd been expecting something, though not necessarily this lot.'

Hunter didn't pursue it. 'Did you know they were on their way to Europe?'

'We knew that whoever we were looking for would be heading our way. How did you know that's where they were going?' Samantha asked.

'From the charts. They have the right charts to get them to Britain.' Hunter turned to Tanner. 'Did you find out why they were making the journey?'

'He doesn't know. They were told to go to France and wait for instructions. Someone would meet them at either Le Havre or Dieppe. Their job was to take whoever turned up to England and land them somewhere quiet. He had no idea what for.'

'How did they know about MI6's involvement?'

'Husain had no idea where the information came from. They'd been told that MI6 was here and that the *L'Escargot* was the target. They were then ordered to get rid of the team.'

'So why did they torture them before throwing them overboard?', Samantha asked.

Badonovitch shook his head in sorrow. 'They wanted to know what you knew.'

'I noticed in the log that they had put to sea for a few hours to test the steering gear. Was that when it happened?'

Tanner replied. 'Yes, boss. They had to return to port to refuel, because the fuel barge hadn't been available earlier. That's when they picked up Samantha.'

'They all have false passports and ID cards,' Nick explained to Doug. 'But more importantly, they have ship's documents with different names as well. Paint out the name on the ship's side, put different papers in the folder, change the log and hey presto. Customs and harbour officials come on board and give them a clean bill of health. It's one cleverly planned and implemented operation. Anything else?'

'We did get the name of one contact.'

'Who?' Hunter paused with his sandwich halfway to his mouth.

'A man by the name of Shaikh Nabhani.'

'Never heard of him. Anybody else?' asked Hunter.

'No,' Samantha said. 'But Nick, you know these people come and go all the time. The foot soldiers are considered expendable in the service of Allah. Look at suicide bombers. Only the masters stay alive.'

The others nodded. They'd seen it many times. But then it was true of any organisation that acted outside the law, not just Islamic fundamentalists.

'Do we know where we find this Shaikh Nabhani?' Hunter asked.

The answer was surprising.

'London,' said Badonovitch.

6

They got nothing more of any value from Hasan Husain. A second dose of SSM rendered the prisoner unconscious. They weighted his body and threw him overboard.

They were directly over the chasm and running parallel to it when they received word that a helicopter had lifted off from the base to collect them and was headed their way. Hunter quickly gathered up all the paperwork they had discovered and, after checking there were no ships or boats in the vicinity, the team opened the *L'Escargot*'s sea cocks. Darkness had fallen and though the moon would be at least three-quarters full, it had not yet risen to cast its influence on the Stygian night. The sea was lapping the gunwales when the distinctive noise of a helicopter was heard.

* * * * *

The following morning, after only a few hours sleep, Hunter was woken with the message that General Macnair was on a secure line in the communications centre. Groggily, Hunter climbed out of his pit, washed his face and slipped on a tee shirt, shorts and running shoes. Minutes later he picked up the telephone.

'Good morning sir.'

'Ah, Lieutenant Commander. At last,' General Macnair said. 'We've gleaned some useful information from the papers you found. Both MI5 and MI6 already had their suspicions of Shaikh Nabhani and he has been under observation here for some time, but only intermittently. There has never been enough to justify anything more. However, something has come up that interests us. There's a man by the name of Abu Talha, a Jordanian, who is currently living on Cyprus. His name appears to be linked with a series of bombings across the Middle East.'

'In what way, sir?'

'We think Abu Talha is the paymaster, or at least one of them,' Macnair explained. 'We're searching databases right now to check if the name Talha appears anywhere else and to see if we've got a photograph of the man. It seems he's a member of Jamiat Ihyaa Minhaaj al-Sunnah. You may know them as the Movement for the Revival of the Prophet's Way.

'Yes! Those lunatics!' Nick exclaimed when he heard Macnair mention JIMAS. 'They're worse than al-Qaeda.'

'Of that, there's no doubt. We're having an inter-service briefing on them in a few days here at Rosyth. You should be back in time for it.'

'What do you want me to do about Abu Talha, sir?'

'Try and get whatever information you can out of him. Then I suggest you send him to the Islamic equivalent of hell. What did you think I'd want you to do?' Macnair snapped. Lack of sleep was making the General unusually tetchy. It was the middle of the night back in Britain and he had been up almost twenty hours straight working.

'Just checking, sir.'

'Sorry, my boy. I didn't mean to bite your head off.'

Macnair paused briefly. 'From what you sent us, along with information we've collected from other sources, it looks as if something serious is going down.'

'Do we know what?'

'No. All we can tell is that there's a wave of expectation rippling across the Middle East. Fancy words I know, but they come from MI6.'

'When is this likely to happen?'

'We've a few hints but no more than that. There's no real indication of timescale, location or who's involved. By combining the stuff you sent us with what MI5 and MI6 know, we're sure something's up. But that's as far as it goes. We need to fill in the gaps. At the moment, we think it could be bombs in London, Manchester or Glasgow. Or even the downing of aircraft. You know the sort of thing. I'm hoping you'll get some additional information from this Abu Talha.'

'Where can I find him, sir?' Nick asked.

'We're still looking for him. I wanted to give you a heads-up. Isobel's lot are trawling various Cypriot computers right now. We know he's not listed as a property owner and he doesn't have a social security number – neither of which is surprising – so right now they're searching company records. It's more likely any property is owned through a front company. After all, Cyprus is renowned for ensuring anonymity. I'll be in contact as soon as we know anything. Incidentally, Ms. Freemantle must return to London. She's been given her orders by MI6. Get her to the airport. I've arranged a ticket. She's coming here to Rosyth.'

'Will do, sir.'

'We'll speak later.'

*

The sun hadn't yet risen but Hunter was wide awake and unlikely to get back to sleep. He jogged over to the excellent running track the Cypriot base possessed. Already warmed up, he began running – jogging for two minutes, sprinting for thirty seconds – and half an hour later, panting and perspiring heavily, he eased to a gentle jog. Nick regained his breath and then worked his way though a series of katas. These were set routines of fighting movements, using hands and feet, and incorporated a variety of different fighting styles from tae kwon do and kendo to pure karate. There were few people who could equal Hunter, or even come near him, and his only real competition was his best friend Matt Dunston, TIFAT's Church of England Chaplain. They often sparred together, each good-naturedly claiming he had beaten the other at the end of a bout. As he worked through the exercises Nick became reflective and he thought about how it had all begun.

*   *   *   *   *

Nick's father had been a journalist, hired to write the history of the Griffiths family. The first book about the family had taken six months to write and had been a bestseller. The day it had hit the Number One spot in the non-fiction lists had been the day his father had proposed to his mother. They had settled down in a small cottage on the estate so that Tim Hunter could have access to the Griffiths' papers so he could write the full story. A year later, Nick was born. A year after that, with the Griffiths' story finally written, his father's journalistic wanderlust had kicked in and he had told his wife that he wanted to go to South East Asia to report on the war there. The first fifteen years of Nick's life were spent overseas, mainly in the Far East. He and his sister, Louise, had attended various international schools and were occasionally taught by private tutors. Christmas was inevitably spent back in Britain with the family, and the first two months of each new year were spent skiing in Europe.

Another memory flashed to mind from when he was barely six years old and in Hong Kong. He had seen a sign in a window advertising martial arts and was so intrigued that his mother took him inside. From then on, he joined a martial arts club wherever he lived. Different countries meant different styles. It was a good way to learn discipline, focus, mental agility and develop lightning-fast reflexes. He had also developed a passion for sailing and so, interspersed with his martial arts training, he had taken up the pastime and joined sailing clubs wherever he went.

When Nick was fifteen he and his family returned to Britain. There he had encountered his first and only experience of bullying. They had settled down near Brighton and he had attended the local boys' grammar school. Louise was at the girls' school further down the road. It was their habit to meet and cycle home together. A number of girls had been teasing his sister, egged on by some older boys from his school. He intervened. The boys threatened him and two started hitting him on his shoulders. In under two minutes both boys were on the ground, one with a broken nose. The others had run away. The girls also ran away, threatening to get even with Louise. The fuss that followed was whipped up by the lies told about Hunter and Louise. They left their schools before they were expelled and were shipped off to a boarding school in Switzerland. Neither regretted the move.

From there to Dartmouth and the Royal Navy had seemed a natural step.

*   *   *   *   *

Following a shave and a shower, Hunter went along to the officers' mess for breakfast. Dressed in an open-necked, short-sleeved white shirt and light brown trousers, he was in contrast to the other officers who wore tropical style uniforms. The convention for having breakfast was the same in all of the officers' messes – newspapers were read while eating, even if they were a day or two old – and Hunter was reading yesterday's *Times* when the other three drifted in. Hunter explained what Macnair had told him. At the mention of JIMAS, Clements snorted in disgust whilst Tanner had a frozen look on his face. He'd come across them in the past.

'They're idiots,' said Badonovitch.

'Yes, but damned dangerous ones,' said Clements. 'I've studied them at length. The members of JIMAS are mainly Saudis – Wahhabis to be precise – and are easily recognised. The men cover their heads with a red and white chequered Saudi scarf. They wear trousers that reach just below the knees and have massive, bushy beards. They condemn all faiths including all Islamic sects that are not JIMAS, object to any form of music and attack Muslims who are clean-shaven. When they speak of the Qur'an or the Prophet Mohammed it is only about the events of the seventh century, ignoring fourteen hundred years of progress and scholarship in the religion. Their women wear clothes that reach the ground and keep their hands and faces covered.'

'I've been reading about them as well,' said Hunter. 'In

Britain the Wahhabis are responsible for more recruits going to Afghanistan and Iran for *jihad* training than any other sect of Islam. They're known to hate anything and everything Western, particularly values such as freedom, tolerance, equal rights for women, compromise and pluralism. They're also the main recruiters for al-Qaeda worldwide. The problem is, they are backed by the Saudi royal family and its money. When it comes to dealing with the sodding problem represented by JIMAS, thanks to the Saudi connection, we're between a rock and a hard place.'

Just then, Samantha appeared. 'I'm off. A taxi's outside. See you guys later.'

A chorus of farewells followed her retreating back.

After a leisurely breakfast, the team found a swimming pool and did a few lengths. Bored with inactivity, they drifted off to a well-equipped gymnasium and began working out. The four of them were hard at it when some army lads arrived. The squaddies challenged them to a game of four-a-side football which they accepted. When it came to fitness and speed the army didn't stand a chance. When it came to kicking the ball into the net the TIFAT team bordered on useless. After 20 minutes each way, with the score 15-all, a draw was declared. They parted in high spirits and with a good deal of cheery banter. The remainder of the day was spent dozing and reading. Finally, as the sun was setting and his thoughts were turning to a cold beer or two, Hunter was called to the communications centre.

'Nick? Hiram here.' Hiram B. Walsh was a Colonel with the American special forces organisation, Delta, the same as Josh Clements. Two failed marriages testified to his dedication to duty.

'Hullo, Hiram. Where's General Macnair?'

'Sleeping. He's been at it non-stop for nearly thirty hours.'

'What have you got for me?' Nick asked.

'There's good news and bad. Abu Talha doesn't appear to live on Cyprus, in spite of the other information we've received. However,' he drawled out the word, 'he does appear to own an ocean-going vessel of some description, probably a modern yacht.'

'Sounds expensive. Where did he get the money from?'

'Good question. Right now we've no idea,' Hiram explained.

'Saudi Arabia?'

'Possibly.'

'It's not the coaster we sank, is it?'

'No. We're sure it isn't. We're still trying to trace the ownership of the coaster on the off chance that it leads us somewhere. So far, we've trawled through three dummy companies, each owning only the one asset, the ship. The registered owners of the companies don't appear to exist, which isn't surprising. Isobel is going nuts. Cuthbert's working hard enough to blow a gasket.'

Isobel Sweeney was in charge of the TIFAT computer section. With her two senior aides, Gareth and Leo, they could hack into any computer system in the world. Getting back out again without being detected was the real skill, as Isobel often pointed out. TIFAT's computer system had been given the nickname Cuthbert. After a mess dinner one night, with too many glasses of vintage port under her belt, Isobel had confided in Hunter that she had named the computer after her genius half-brother who worked for a financial conglomerate in New York.

'If Cuthbert isn't getting far then we have some serious problems,' Nick said worriedly.

'I agree. However, Isobel assures me it's only a matter of time,' Hiram replied.

'How sure are we about the yacht and Abu Talha?'

'Pretty sure. We'll track him down.'

'Okay. If there's anything else I'll be on my mobile.' Hunter left the communications centre and strolled outside, enjoying the warm night and clear skies. Minutes later his own phone rang. He answered.

'Nick? Hiram here. Better go secure.'

'I'll be back in communications in five minutes.'

Minutes later, Hiram continued, 'We've received some help from GCHQ. At our request they've been hoovering up everything in the area. They got a lucky break. Abu Talha received a phone call from somebody in Britain. Talha is transferring two million euros from a number of banks in the Netherlands to three banks in London.'

'Do we know which ones?'

'Yes. Full surveillance is being arranged even as we speak. MI5 will deal with it, backed up by armed officers from Counter Terrorist Command. We've been asked if we'd like to send a liaison officer as part of the inter-service co-operation we're all enjoying these days.'

'Who do you have in mind?'

'Douglas Napier is going. He's about the only person we have available.' Napier was a Royal Marine lieutenant who had a reputation for tactlessness.

'Is that wise?' Nick asked.

Walsh chuckled. 'I've laid down the law. Told him to mind his manners and zip his mouth.'

'And what about at this end? Where is Abu Talha?'

'He's on a boat about half-a-mile offshore. I'll give you the exact co-ordinates. Satellite pictures show a super-yacht at anchor. They were taken about three hours ago but have only just come through the system. We've been working on it, and we're pretty sure it belongs to a member of the Saudi royal family. The yacht is called *The Flower of Allah*. We can't read the name but the photographs identify it. We are now targeting the yacht for updates every ten minutes.'

'Armed guards?' Nick asked.

'Yes, four, all patrolling the upper deck. From the look of them they all appear to be members of JIMAS. I'll send you the images we have. Wait a second, Nick. Something else is coming in.' There was a pause and Nick could hear a faint 'Thank you.' This was followed by another pause. 'Goddamn it all to hell!' Walsh let loose a mouthful of expletives.

'Hiram! What's up?'

'Nick, you've got to move fast. That son-of-a-bitch Talha has just given the green light for bombings in London, Manchester and Glasgow. Hell! From the look of this they're going to attack the base out there on Cyprus as well.'

'When?' asked Nick looking at his watch.

'Tonight. Or, I should say, the early hours. According to the intercepts it will be a co-ordinated attack at 05.00 hours.'

'Any idea of numbers? Types of weapons?'

'Nothing.'

'Is Mick Fellowes back yet?'

'Yes. He got back an hour ago. I'll call him in a minute and give him a heads-up. Nick, we're hoping that any information you find on the yacht will tell us about the attacks here in Britain. We need full details. Suicide or left luggage?' Left luggage was the code for a bomb hidden somewhere, be it in a vehicle, a building, a rubbish bin or even a left luggage locker in a railway station. Hiram continued saying 'Take as many prisoners as you can. There's an American Task Force about 300 miles away. I'll put them in the picture. They can lift and shift the lot on their journey to Guantanamo. We'll leave our American friends to carry out the necessary inter-rogations as they go. You never know, we might learn something useful.'

'Roger that.' Once the call had finished Nick hurried across the parade ground to the OC's office. Nick had met Colonel Fellowes a number of times and found him to be an astute Irishman with a wicked sense of humour. Medium height and weight, he had boxed for Sandhurst, which accounted for his broken nose. He was also one of the highest decorated officers in the British Armed Forces. A light was visible under the door. Hunter knocked and went in.

'He's just arrived,' Colonel Fellowes said as he greeted Hunter with a nod. The Colonel gestured to a chair and continued speaking to Hiram Walsh. Fellowes' eyes narrowed and he sat up straight. 'Bloody hell. Okay, we'll be ready. I'll call when it's over.' He replaced the handset and said, 'Nick, nice to see you again. Pity it's not under more pleasant circumstances.'

'Hullo, sir. I take it Hiram's just explained what the fuss is all about?'

'Yes. Bikini Red.'

The Bikini state was used by the Ministry of Defence to warn about different levels of terrorist activity. Bikini Red meant information had been received about a specific target. It also meant 'red alert' and signified that Britain was at war and there was the likelihood of a nuclear strike.

'I'll be with you in a moment. I'll let my second-in-command know what's happening. We'll be ready in less than twenty minutes.'

'Sir, we have our own operation.'

'So I understand. Is there anything I can do?' Fellowes asked.

'Do you have any oxygen re-breathers?'

'Sorry, no. There's no call for them. If the Special Boat Service come here they bring their own gear.'

'Damnation.' Looking out of the window, Hunter watched the fronds of a palm tree rustling in the wind. 'Any sports diving gear?'

'Plenty. It helps keep the lads occupied,' Fellowes explained.

Hunter nodded. 'Okay, not to worry. There's enough wind. We'll take the air sets.'

Fellowes understood what he meant. The bubbles would be dispersed as they hit the surface, intermingling with a slightly choppy sea. It would take a highly alert guard to notice anything.

'I'll get my lot together and get out of your hair as soon as possible. Where will I find the equipment?'

'Give me a few minutes and I'll get someone to show you where it's stowed.'

The door opened and the Regimental Sergeant Major walked in and saluted.

'At ease, Bill. This is Lieutenant Commander Hunter. He needs some kit. Get Smith to take him to the dive shack.'

'Very good, sir.' The RSM was ramrod straight, fit-looking and nearing retirement.

'How are we progressing?' Fellowes asked.

The RSM allowed himself a smile. 'Almost there, sir.

We'll have a chance to try out Standing Operating Procedures for real!'

'Excellent. I'll brief you fully in a few minutes when Major Montgomery gets here. Anything else, Nick?'

'One thing, sir. Can we have an inflatable and a helicopter?'

'Bill, sort it, will you?' Fellowes asked.

'Yes, sir.' 'Half an hour suit, sir?' Bill asked Nick.

Hunter smiled. 'Thanks. That's ideal.'

Hunter rejoined Badonovitch, Clements and Tanner outside the dive shack. While Hunter brought them up to speed, they established what gear they needed. Then the phone rang. Hunter was required back in the OC's office. On arrival, Colonel Fellowes handed Nick a bundle of photographs. A quick glance at them showed they were of *The Flower of Allah* and the surrounding area.

'These just came through,' Fellowes explained.

'Thanks, sir.'

7

The base was silent by 01.00 hours. Half a kilometre outside the perimeter of the fence, the men of the Royal Scots Dragoon Guards were bunkered down in their Standing Operating Procedures positions. The procedures laid down exactly what was to be done under the circumstances. Little thought was required. Each regiment that rotated to the base carried out the same defensive exercises. In this case, not only did forewarned mean forearmed, but the regiment was made up of seasoned troopers who had spent time in Iraq and Afghanistan. They knew precisely what to do. There were four obvious places for an attack. Those who were wearing night-vision goggles were deployed at each location. Each man was armed with a Heckler-Koch HKMP7A1 sub-machine gun. For the work required that night it was ideal. At 02.00 all positions checked in to the Command Post set up near the guardroom by the main gate. It was going to be a long and tense night.

*　　*　　*　　*　　*

Hunter and the team finished their preparations. It had been a hell of a mad rush. The photographs of *The Flower of*

Allah were examined carefully and their options discussed in detail. The yacht's specifications had been located online and forwarded to the team. She had capacity for a crew of six and could cater for ten guests in luxurious quarters. The owner's suite was up forward, directly under the bridge superstructure. They assumed that was where Abu Talha was to be found. After sorting out their gear and weapons, they changed into wetsuits. The only noise, a few minutes later, was the clatter of the Wessex HU5 helicopter as it rose into the air, a rigid raider with an 80hp outboard motor slung under its belly. They headed seawards and, once over the Mediterranean, turned to port and a course of north-east. The team settled down to the short flight and it was not long before the pilot announced that they were going down. It only took minutes to climb into the boat and unhook from the helicopter. They were five miles from where *The Flower of Allah* was anchored. Fresh information from Rosyth confirmed that there were still only four guards on the upper deck. Two were sitting on the bridge with one in the bows and one at the stern.

The raider's engine was muffled and could hardly be heard a dozen metres away, even at the speed they were travelling. Within twenty minutes they were in position. Half a mile from their target and about three cables off the beach, they lowered the anchor over the side. Hunter used binoculars combined with his night-vision goggles to study the yacht. It was a cumbersome arrangement but it meant he could clearly see the guard on the starboard bridge wing.

The water was less than ten metres deep. Badonovitch was diving with Hunter, Tanner with Clements. A buddy line was attached to each of their right arms, giving them a distance apart of three metres. Hunter and Tanner both carried a diver's board with a compass and depth gauge. Badonovitch and Clements towed short, neutrally buoyant sledges crammed with gear.

After aiming their compasses at *The Flower of Allah*'s anchor lights, the divers left surface, twisted over into a horizontal position and began swimming at a depth of two metres. The wind rippling the surface ensured that the bubbles from their breathing sets dispersed and could not be seen easily. The black water was lit up with the microscopic, fluorescent organisms that flourish in the Mediterranean, appearing like sparks as the men swam through them. The only sound was that of bubbles blown out through their mouthpieces. Twenty minutes into the swim, Hunter began to surface. Badonovitch swam gently down at the same time, preventing Hunter from hitting the surface too quickly. Nick was not surprised to find *The Flower of Allah* directly in front of him, less than half a cable away. Seconds later, he was back under the surface and they headed towards the stern of the hull. Clements and Tanner headed to the bows and the anchor cable.

At the stern, a ladder was built into the starboard side. Neither Hunter nor Badonovitch said a word as they discarded their diving sets, weight belts and fins, hanging the lot over the lowest rung of the ladder using their buddy line. Slowly and silently he stood on the ladder and eased himself out of the water. The breeze continued to help, whistling gently in what little rigging there was, masking the slight sound of water dripping from his wetsuit. While Hunter climbed the short ladder, Badonovitch trod water with his silenced automatic in his hand. Three rungs, and Hunter's head was level with the deck. He removed his silenced automatic from a waterproof pouch and, sliding off the safety, aimed at the guard's back less than three metres away. Each shot – one into the heart, the other into the spine – was barely louder than a gentle sneeze. Hunter stayed on the ladder, listening. Nothing. He climbed over the guard-rail and checked the body. Wrapping one of their weight belts around the waist of the dead man, they slid the body over the stern, where it floated for a few moments before the air escaped from its clothes and it sank. If anyone came on deck for any reason, a dead body would mean an immediate alarm, whereas a missing guard could be getting himself a coffee or relieving himself in the heads. Quickly, they hauled up the sledge. Inside were dry clothes, jungle boots, mobile telephones and explosives of various kinds. Stripping off their wetsuits they climbed into 'can't-see-me' suits, pulled on soft-soled jungle boots, strapped on their webbing and prepared their weapons. Silently Badonovitch moved along the port side. Hunter went along the starboard side.

It was just after 04.30.

*   *   *   *   *

'Eight men approaching from the west.'

'Roger that. We have another eight from the east.'

'This is Point Alpha. We also have eight men in single file. They are passing us now.' A few seconds passed. 'They are spreading out along the wire. They are hunkering down.' That was at the northern end of the base perimeter.

'Roger that. Same here at Point Charlie.'

There was a few seconds delay and then, 'Confirmed at Point Beta.'

'This is Romeo One. Wait for the order. We'll let them get busy. Then we open fire.'

Minutes later the radios crackled into life again. 'This is Point Alpha, I see two of the ragheads closing up to the wire. Looks like they've got wire cutters.'

'This is Romeo One. Close up. Open fire if you're spotted. Otherwise wait for the order.'

While two attackers in each of the three corners of the perimeter fence started work cutting the wires, the others moved closer. Their excitement was palpable; their focus, the base. Not for a moment did they expect anyone to be behind them – especially not heavily-armed soldiers – and the unexpected stream of bullets fired by the Guardsmen's sub-machine guns was like a scythe cutting down hay. The effect was devastating. Not all of the attackers died quickly and easily. Some lay in agony, bodies smashed, dying from loss of blood or damaged vital organs. Some exploded as the bullets tore into the waistcoats of explosives they had strapped to them. Not all the attackers wore the waistcoats – it was too dangerous. A bullet striking a waistcoat and causing an explosion could easily result in sympathetic detonations amongst all the attacking force. Hence only every fourth man had them. They would be the ones to surrender. They would walk up to the infidels – who would not shoot a man who was surrendering – and detonate the device. They would kill many British.

In less than two minutes there was no one left standing. Two of the waistcoats had detonated; this helped cut down the odds even more. It was over. Silence reigned supreme, as the loud chattering of the guns ended. Nobody from the regiment moved. They stopped and listened. Nothing. None of the enemy appeared to be moving, but it was better to be safe than sorry. A suicide bomber or two could still be alive. So the soldiers waited. And waited. Finally, after nearly fifteen minutes, one man at the northern end of the base began to moan. Armed with an Accuracy International L96A1 sniping rifle, the Regimental Sergeant Major kept low as he approached the sound. At fifty metres he stopped and examined the scene through binoculars. The moonlight enabled him to make out the terrorist holding his stomach, his legs curled up to his chin. He was calling on God to help him. The Regimental Sergeant Major pushed the safety catch on the left rear of the action forward, lined up the cross-hairs of the sight on the target's torso, and fired. The round passed through the man's chest. However, that was not what killed him. The bullet detonated the explosives strapped to him, blowing him to pieces, whilst the bullet expended its energy ploughing into the ground.

No one else moved or made a sound.

*   *   *   *   *

The steps up to the bridge wings were wide and shallow. Hunter and Badonovitch took them slowly. A faint buzzer sounded in the earpiece each man wore. It was the signal that Clements had climbed the anchor chain and was just below deck level, near the hawsehole. Hunter and Badonovitch took the last few steps, quickly and openly. Hunter's target heard him, and was just turning his head when Hunter opened fire. Both were torso shots which flung the man against the bulkhead, his gun dropping with a clatter. The noise caused the guard in the bows to look up and call out. This allowed Clements the luxury of two shots into the guard's back. Badonovitch also killed his man with double-tap chest shots. Just then there came a rumbling beneath their feet as the diesel engines started up. Moments later a man appeared on the bridge and was turning on electronic equipment – the radar, the communications console and the 'satnav' system when an internal phone rang. It was the engineer, reporting that everything in the engine room was running smoothly and that he was going back to bed.

It was 05.00 and *The Flower of Allah* was preparing to put to sea.

* * * * *

Rehman Khan's false documents brought him safely to Saudi Arabia. Two changes of airlines and passports helped him to cover his tracks. Although wanted by the Pakistani authorities for abandoning his post as a Captain in the Inter Service Intelligence Agency, he doubted the airports were being watched. And, having come so far and with his objective firmly in his sights, he had no intention of taking risks. He walked through passport control, nodded his thanks to a bored official, and crossed over to the domestic side of the airport. Outside, the sun shone and the forty-five degree heat brought an immediate sweat to Khan's brow. He had his instructions and he followed them. Minutes later he walked into the blessed coolness of the domestic terminal. He made his way to a coffee bar. Looking around, he saw two pilots wearing khaki uniform and dark reflective glasses at a table drinking coffee. The pilots watched Khan as he approached. He nodded his head twice.

One put his hand out and said, 'Passport.'

Khan showed it to him – his real one – and in return, he

received a nod that bordered on the condescending. The two men immediately stood, and discarding their drinks, walked towards the exit. Khan followed.

The helicopter was a Bell 214 ST Super Transport, painted in Prince Khaled Aziz bin Abdullah's colours. Inside, Khan strapped himself into a window seat while the pilots ran through their start-up procedures. Suddenly, like a bolt out of the blue, pain exploded in Khan's head and he fumbled for his pills, taking two. Closing his eyes, he leaned back against the seat and waited for his head to clear. As the helicopter rose into the air, his blinding headache gradually eased. The helicopter headed out to sea and towards the island of Qishrān, fabled stronghold of Prince Khaled Aziz bin Abdullah. Khan was anticipating the visit very much and was looking forward to making his report. A member of the mighty Saud family, the prince was able to indulge his guests' every wish, no matter how outlandish or perverted.

8

Doug Tanner climbed swiftly up the anchor chain and stepped onto the deck. He hauled his sledge up and carried it into the shadow cast by the vessel's superstructure. Tanner opened the sledge and he and Clements armed themselves with Heckler-Koch PDWs and knelt down quietly to wait. It wasn't long before a member of the crew appeared, calling out loudly to one of his mates that he was about to raise the anchor. Tanner emerged silently from the shadows and stepped up behind the man. He wrapped a massive arm around the man's neck, shoved his head hard forward and broke his neck with a loud snap. Tanner slowly lowered the body to the deck and stepped back into the shadows. Another member of the crew appeared on the bridge. He leaned over the guard-rail and angrily shouted something in Arabic. Badonovitch was closest to the man. He moved towards him stealthily and thrust a long, sharp knife between the man's ribs and into his heart.

Hunter joined Badonovitch on the bridge. 'What now, boss?'

'Let's get her underway and head out to sea.' Hunter went back onto the bridge wing. 'Josh,' he called in a loud whisper.

'Here, Nick.'

'Can you raise the anchor?'

'Hang on a second. Let me take a look.' A few moments later came the reply: 'Sure, no problem. It's an electric winch controlled by a simple on/off button. Why? What are you planning to do?'

'If we get underway,' Hunter explained, 'anyone else left on board should relax and go back to sleep and won't bother us. If we don't, someone may come looking to see what's wrong. We don't know how many guests there are nor how many of the crew are still alive.'

'Okay.' Clements moved the lever up, pressed the on/off switch and the anchor chain immediately began to rattle inboard, pulling the yacht through the water. As it broke from the seabed, Clements signalled to Hunter who moved the engine control into 'Slow Ahead'. The yacht got underway. It took only a couple of minutes for Hunter to figure out the automatic steering gear. A turn of a dial changed the yacht's heading to 090°. The radar was operating and a glance showed the sea ahead and on either side to be clear of shipping.

'Doug is ditching a couple of bodies over the side,' Clements said as he appeared on the bridge.

'Good. Give Jan a hand and do the same with those on the wings. I'll get rid of this one.' Nick looked at the headscarf on the dead man and asked himself how many more JIMAS members were on board.

The bridge was extremely well kitted-out with the very latest equipment. There was a captain's chair on the starboard side and a very comfortable owner's chair to port. The chart table was at the back of the bridge, a good five paces away. There was a curtain that could be drawn around the table for the navigator to work on his charts at

84

night without spoiling the vision of whoever was on watch. It was a highly professional set-up, which impressed Hunter. But then, as the yacht cost at least $150 million, it needed to be.

'Jan, you stay here. We'll scour between decks. We'll start in the engine room, just in case it's manned. From there we'll check out the lower deck where the crew live and eat. Then we'll take the main deck. Let's move out,' Nick said.

Access to the engine room was on the starboard side, through a doorway sealed with a watertight metal door, which led to a sound-proofed control room. Although the engine room was fully lit, there was nobody there. Hunter could see and recognise the alarm systems that fed the same information on the console in the control room to the console on the bridge. Minutes later, they had reached the lower deck, and stood in an uncarpeted passageway. No expense had been spared to make the quarters and public rooms for the guests luxurious, but down here was a different story. It wasn't, by any stretch of the imagination, a dump, but it left something to be desired.

Clements opened a door on the port side to reveal a small, scruffy cabin. A man was lying on his bunk, reading a pornographic book. The Qur'an was on his bedside locker alongside his JIMAS headscarf. It was the engineer and he was having trouble sleeping. Clements startled him and though he reacted quickly he had no chance. As he rolled off his bunk onto his knees Clements shot him twice. Nobody else was found on that deck. The remaining cabins were empty, as was the mess deck. That left the main deck where the guests were quartered. The opulence of the corridor was quite amazing. Deep pile carpet covered the deck and original paintings by world-famous artists were hanging on the bulkheads, which were made of highly polished yew. The three doors on either side were oak – thick, heavy and sound proof. After all, it wasn't polite to listen to what went on in the cabins when the doors were closed. With the owner's cabin, which extended to the width of the ship, there were seven cabins in all. The question was how many were occupied? The team had entered the corridor by the aft doorway off the deck with the swimming pool. Hunter took the first door on the port side. Clements took the door opposite. Tanner kept watch along the corridor. Hunter and Clements nodded to each other, turned the door handles and simultaneously pushed the doors inwards.

The cabins were identical in design. They both had a double bed situated aft of the door and against the outside bulkhead. In each was a sleeping figure. Clements put his right hand over the mouth of his target and used his finger and thumb to cut off the man's airflow. The man struggled for a few seconds and then fell unconscious. Moments later he had the man on his stomach, his wrists behind his back, secured with tie wraps and a gag over his mouth. Hunter had not been so lucky. The man in the cabin struggled, pushed Hunter's hand away from his face, and took a deep breath to yell. Hunter had no option. Using the knuckles of his right hand he hit the man in the throat. Thanks to his expertise, it wasn't a fatal blow. The man gurgled, his eyes popping as he gasped for breath. He was now powerless to retaliate and was quickly laid out on the floor, bound and gagged.

As Hunter and Clements moved further along the corridor, the door leading to the owner's suite opened and a man stepped out. He immediately saw the two men and let out a loud yell followed by a tirade in Arabic. The tirade became muffled as the man retreated into the room and, before Hunter or Clements could react, slammed the door shut.

The ear-splitting sound of an emergency siren shrieked throughout the vessel. Hunter and Clements flung open the doors of the next two cabins and stepped inside. In each was a single occupant. Hunter's target was still groggy from sleep, while Clements' target was out of his bed and getting dressed. A pistol lay on a bedside table, and as the man made a grab for it, Clements shot him twice.

Hunter pistol-whipped his man and bound and gagged him like the others.

The final door on the port side opened and a bearded face appeared. Because the doors were hinged on the forward side the man looked aft, straight at Tanner as he fired. The head vanished and both Tanner's shots missed. Abruptly, the noise of the siren stopped. A voice yelled something in Arabic. Another voice answered from the starboard cabin. The voices were muffled, barely discernible. Then there was silence.

'Internal phones,' said Hunter. He and Clements lay flat on the deck outside the third of the doors. 'Ready?'

'Let's go,' Clements whispered.

Reaching up, they turned the handles and simultaneously pushed open the doors. From inside submachine guns opened fire, shredding the doors.

*　*　*　*　*

Zim Albatha relaxed in the steam room of the Turkish baths. Throwing more water on the hot coals, he relished the increased temperature as the sweat oozed out of his pores. He admitted to himself that he didn't use the place often enough. The problem, he acknowledged, was lack of time. He was only there now to meet one of his contacts.

'Zim? Zim?' The pine door opened and a scrawny figure with a towel wrapped around his waist tentatively looked in.

'Hello Akar. Come on in and shut the door. Keep the heat in.'

'I can hardly see you. You always have it too hot!' Akar whined petulantly.

'Never mind. Come and sit down.' Albatha threw more water onto the heat. 'What do you have for me?'

'I have been all over Zim. I have asked everyone.'

'I hope you have been discreet?'

'On my word. I . . .' the man licked his lips, 'I have never known anything like it. Nobody is saying a word. Usually when there are rumours about, if someone knows something they like to brag about it.'

'That is true, my friend. Only this time . . .?' Albatha asked.

'Only nothing. Yet there is something. I know it. I can feel it.'

Albatha nodded. 'I know there is too. You are not the only one to tell me this. I have never known the like. Have you any idea where it is coming from?'

'No. At least, not really. I have heard . . .' he paused.

'What?'

'It could be from Atakoy by the airport.'

Albatha said nothing. He had already heard the same thing from a number of sources. Atakoy was an area well known for its Islamic fundamentalists. Many people there were implacably opposed to Turkey joining the European Union, no matter what benefits would be derived for the majority of the population, and they made no secret of their hatred of all things Western and non-Muslim.

'Here, take this.' Albatha slid a small brown envelope from under his thigh and passed it to the other man.

'Thank you.' Moments later the man was gone.

Albatha leant back and closed his eyes, deep in thought. So what to do next? There was only one thing he could think of. And it was illegal. He smiled. When did that ever bother him?

* * * * *

Their basic training meant that Hunter and Clements were both standing instinctively on opposite sides of the doorway, which was just as well since the bullets from the sub-machine guns ripped into the wood of the bulkheads. Neither of the two men was hurt.

Tanner pulled the pin from a grenade, counted to four and lobbed it into the port side cabin. The explosion was deafening and final. The reverberations had barely subsided when he did the same to the starboard cabin. Hunter and Clements cautiously put their heads around the door to find their targets almost shredded. A grenade exploding in such a confined space caused unbelievable damage. That left one cabin to go. They approached the door slowly and cautiously.

'Boss, the forward porthole cover is open. The man's shoved a desk and chair across the door and is using his phone,' Badonovitch called out.

'Thanks, Jan. A shaped charge here Doug.' Hunter used his finger to outline a circle three feet in circumference on the bulkhead next to the door. 'Pity about the Hockney,' he added, referring to the painting hanging to the right of where he wanted the plastic explosive placed. Tanner and Clements pushed the charge securely against the bulkhead and placed detonators – their firing mechanisms activated – on either side of the circle. The three men stepped to one side. Fifteen seconds later a loud explosion ripped through the yacht, blowing a circular hole in the bulkhead and sending wood panel fragments flying, missing the occupant by inches. The man was standing on the opposite side of the cabin, a phone held in one hand, a gun in the other. He was short, stocky, had a huge bushy beard and wore trousers that stopped just below the knees. On his head was the red and white chequered JIMAS scarf. Snarling with rage he pointed his weapon and opened fire. Shots smashed into the thick, wood-lined bulkhead and others, more by luck than judgement, flew through the blown hole and smashed into the wood lining of the passageway. Two rounds hit a knot in the wood at the edge of the hole and ricocheted upwards, ripping through the sleeve of Hunter's left arm, and tearing a hole in Doug Tanner's right trouser leg, narrowly missing him. At that moment Clements opened fire. His aim was deliberate and cool. His first shot hit the man they believed to be Abu Talha in the right shoulder, disarming him and sending him staggering to one side. His second shot hit Talha in the left hand, smashing a hole through his palm and shattering the phone he was holding. Clements contemplated a third shot but decided against it. Their combined muscle pushed the door open, shoving the desk and chair to one side. Hunter and Clements entered. The terrorist was still on his feet, snarling with hatred and anger. Whatever was thought or said about the men of JIMAS, they were not cowards, especially in the face of death. They were, after all, doing God's work and should they die whilst on *jihad* their reward would be to spend eternity in paradise.

In spite of his injuries, Abu Talha stepped forward and kicked at Clements with all the fury and hate he had in him. Clements swayed backwards, snatched Talha's foot and lifted it upwards, continuing the momentum. The man flew backwards, hit his head with a sickening blow on the bulkhead behind him and was rendered unconscious.

'You okay?' Hunter asked Tanner.

'Fine, boss. Straight through the cloth. You?'

Hunter pulled up his sleeve and looked at his arm. Blood trickled down his arm to his elbow. Hunter walked over to a well-stocked bar in a corner of the cabin and found a linen napkin, doused it in vodka and wiped his arm. It stung like hell. He handed a second napkin to Tanner who wrapped it around the wound.

'See that safe? Blow it,' Hunter ordered Jan as he entered the cabin.

The safe yielded papers – which were scanned and transmitted to TIFAT – as well as a stack of cash.

'I'll check on the prisoners.' said Clements. 'Get them ready for shifting.' Hunter submitted a request for an American helicopter to remove the prisoners.

Clements was back in minutes, yelling as he ran. 'They're all dead.'

'*Dead*?' Hunter couldn't keep the surprise out of his voice.

'From the look of them, I'd say poison.'

'Damnation!' Hunter hit his fist into the palm of his hand.

'Hell!' Tanner moved first. He stepped over to the inert body of Talha, wrenched his mouth open and stuffed a rag inside.

'Is he still breathing?', Clements asked.

'Yeah. He's OK.'

'What do you think? Some sort of capsule in their back teeth?' Hunter asked.

'Probably,' replied Clements. 'We'd better check Abu Talha. If the others had them then he's probably got one too. I'll get some pliers.' He went down the stairs and headed to the engine room. Talha was still unconscious when he returned. Clements handed the pliers to Tanner, and, gripping the man's jaw, held it wide open and shone a torch into the mouth. 'The upper back teeth on his left side are missing. On the right there are only two molars left. One up, one down.'

'Just pull one,' said Hunter. 'If he's got a capsule he won't be able to crush the sodding thing. And gently does it, Doug. Try not to crush the tooth in case it's the one with the poison.'

Tanner placed the end of the tapered pliers around the tooth and moved it back and forth. It took a few seconds before it loosened. He then lifted the tooth straight up and held it closely. 'This is the one, boss. Look.' He squeezed the tooth slowly between the pliers and the enamel split open. A small capsule fell to the deck and he lifted it up to show the others. 'I'll throw it overboard.'

At that point, Abu Talha moaned and began to come round.

'I'll tell General Macnair,' said Hunter. 'He won't be happy about this, but at least we've found Abu Talha.'

The General being merely unhappy proved to be an understatement. However, having vented his spleen – which was directed at events rather than the team – he said, 'Nick, there's a disquieting fact coming from all this.'

'Yes, sir, I know. This isn't their style,' said Hunter. 'We know they'll happily die for the cause but not take their own lives. At least, I've never known it.'

'Neither have I.'

'Which means they've done this to avoid being interrogated. More proof, if it's needed, about the size and significance of their operation.'

Macnair grunted. 'Agreed.' He paused. 'Right, change of plan. I want you to have first crack at Abu Talha. We might just learn something useful that bit sooner. I'll update the Americans and ask for the helicopter to be with you in, what, four hours?'

'That should be fine, sir,' Nick agreed.

'Then let's say 10.00. They can continue working on him on the way to Guantanamo. We'll speak soon.'

Abu Talha groaned and pushed himself up slowly. Leaning on his elbow he spat the bloodstained rag onto the deck. He began cursing and yelling in Arabic. Hunter understood some of what Talha was saying, particularly the profanities.

'Doug, gag him and get him below.'

Tanner grabbed the prisoner by the hair, forced his head back, stuffed another cloth into his mouth and secured his hands behind his back using tie wraps. He dragged him on his back across the deck, down the stairs and into the state room. All the while, Talha glared his hatred at his enemy. Tanner dumped him onto a straight-backed chair with armrests and cut the tie wraps. As he did so, Talha threw himself at Tanner who had been expecting such a move; indeed, had wanted it. In response, almost casually, he slapped Talha across the side of the head, knocking him to the deck. Tanner then put him back in the chair and tied his wrists very tightly to the armrests. In a corner of the cabin was a basin. Tanner took a glass of cold water and threw it over Talha. The third glass brought the man groaning back to consciousness. They injected Abu Talha with SSM and Clements and Tanner began questioning him.

Hunter dragged the bodies of the dead men on deck, weighted them and – with no ships or other vessels in sight – threw them over the side. Next, he pulled up any carpets with blood on them and did the same thing. Intermittently checking the horizon for contacts, he began sluicing away the blood in the cabins. Even after he'd finished, it still looked as though a battle had taken place. However, there didn't appear to be anything more he could do and they were running out of time. He abandoned the cleaning and returned to the bridge.

He'd only been there a few minutes when Clements yelled up to him, 'Nick, you'd better come and listen to this.'

Hunter looked down the steps and called, 'What's up?'

'Come and listen' Clements insisted.

Hunter had decided to leave the speakers on and it was at that moment that Macnair came over loud and clear. As soon as he started talking they could tell he was in an agitated state. 'We've a long way to go before we finish translating the papers you sent us but it appears some sort of nuclear device is on its way here,' he started to explain.

'*What?*' Hunter couldn't disguise the shock in his voice.

Clements stepped onto the bridge. 'Sir, I was just about to get Nick to listen to what Talha has to say. He more or less said the same thing.'

'Where did it come from? Do we know?' Hunter asked.

'The bomb, if that's what it is, is of Pakistani origin and was passed to al-Qaeda. They in turn gave it to JIMAS, as part of their holy war against the West, and they were entrusted with detonating the bomb in Britain. This is our biggest nightmare coming true.'

'So what now?' Hunter asked, breaking the stunned silence. Thinking such an event was possible was one thing; knowing that it was going to happen was something entirely different.

'The problems,' said Macnair, 'are finding the bomb, stopping the men who are transporting it and, most important of all at this stage, preventing the news leaking to the public. The chaos, panic and pandemonium that would ensue are unimaginable.'

'Where do we start looking?' Hunter asked.

'There's a mention of it in the paperwork you found. We should know the answer fairly soon.'

'In the meantime should we follow the planned track they've laid down?'

'Where were they heading?' asked Macnair.

'Egypt. Through the Suez Canal to be precise.'

'Keep going. The fact of the matter is, right now, there's nowhere else for you to go.'

'It'll be virtually impossible to keep this under wraps and you know it. Somebody will tell a relative to get the hell out of London. They'll tell somebody else. Before you know it, there'll be a stampede, a mass exodus. People are going to be hurt or even killed no matter what we do.'

'I pray you're wrong. We need to move fast. That's why if at all possible, we must not involve anyone else. You'll have to be the ones dealing with it.'

'Have you told the Prime Minister?' Hunter asked.

'Not yet, but I have no choice,' was the heavy reply.

TIFAT's mandate was a key part of any operation. It allowed them to operate with far more flexibility than the usual security and law enforcement services found in any country. However, when a particular country's security was at risk, it was only right that its powers-that-be were informed of events. General Macnair interpreted his orders loosely. Usually, he made the information available as late as possible, sometimes after the operation was over, which, wasn't unreasonable in his opinion, given the number of leaks from national governments especially when such leaks put the lives of his men at risk. Government leaders didn't agree, but then, he couldn't please all of them, all of the time. Not that he tried.

'Sir, you know as well as I do that this Prime Minister is one of the most gutless men ever to hold that position. My guess is he's about to leave London for a break, due to a heavy cold or some other such rubbish.'

'It wouldn't surprise me. However, there's nothing I can do about it. If anything leaks out and it's referred to me, I'll deny it. In the meantime, I should be able to get a Hercules C130 to you in plenty of time, though we're still working on it. Refuelling points and pilot hours are proving a bugbear. However, that's my problem, not yours. Incidentally, we'll pay the transit fee for the canal.'

'Right sir. Any idea yet as to who's coming?' Hunter asked.

'Don Masters, definitely. You might need an engineer and he's the best we've got. I'll see who else we can spare.'

'All right, sir. But we need everything. We'll transmit a list as soon as we can.'

'Right. I'll call you if something turns up. Wait a moment.' There was a pause while General Macnair spoke to someone at his end. 'We've just learned that the device isn't a nuclear bomb. It's a dirty bomb.'

'Where the hell did you get that information from?'

'From the material you sent to us. I suppose it's a step down from a nuclear bomb but even so, wherever it detonates, the city and country will be contaminated for God knows how many years to come.' The General's voice was heavy with anguish but he quickly returned to normal 'What's the condition of the yacht?'

Hunter answered. 'Mechanically, excellent. Cosmetically, however, it's a bit of a shambles.'

'Can't be helped. Paperwork is being sent even as we speak, proving that you're renting her for a three months' cruise.'

'If we do have to go through the Suez, what about the damage?' Hunter asked. 'How do we explain that?'

'Any damage in public places?' Macnair was referring to the bridge, the upper deck and other parts of the boat that visitors, such as customs and excise officers, could be expected to see.

'It's all between decks but if they want to search the vessel . . .'

'You can cross that bridge when you come to it. If it's suggested that they want to look around, use bribery and corruption. It usually works where you're going.'

Clements asked, 'What about the Saudis? What if someone screams blue murder that the yacht's theirs?'

'I don't think that'll happen, simply because of the timescale we're under.'

'Sir, I take it we're pretty positive? The papers we sent you confirmed it?'

'As sure as we can be. Even if there's only a twenty percent chance that this information is correct we daren't risk it. And based on the evidence I'd say it's a damned sight higher than that.'

'The helicopter's just arrived, sir,' Nick explained to Macnair.

'Okay. Get rid of that scum and we'll talk later.'

After Abu Talha was lifted off, Badonovitch and Tanner went below to get their heads down. In view of what they now knew, sleep was very hard to come by.

Four hours later, the yacht was steaming at thirty knots, on a heading of 190°. Hunter was sitting in the captain's chair, his feet on the console in front of him. Clements sat in the owner's chair, also with his feet up.

'Nick, this is the toughest yet,' he said.

Hunter looked across the bridge. 'That, old friend, is the understatement of the year.'

9

It was in a sombre mood that they approached the coast of Egypt at a few minutes short of 23.00 hours. Hunter had spent the journey looking up various publications, from *Sailing Directions* to the *List of Lights*. The charts used on the yacht were French, not British, and not as detailed.

General Macnair came on the loudspeaker. 'Can you hear me?'

'Yes, sir,' Hunter replied.

'We've discovered there is some sort of rendezvous taking place in the Arabian Sea. We only have the co-ordinates.'

'We think we have them as well, sir. Let me just read what's here on the chart.' He gave Macnair the latitude and longitude of a cross marked on the chart of the Arabian Sea.

'That's it. Good. We have some corroboration. We need to find the name of the ship and take it from there.'

'Sir, I presume you want us to deal with this, rather than the Americans, because we need to find the device?'

'Correct. If they blow the ship to smithereens, which they can do in a nanosecond, we won't know if the bloody thing is there. If they storm the ship, the terrorists will have time to ditch the dirty bomb over the side and we still won't know for sure if they had it. As you said, knowledge about the device will get out and the whole world will be in a frenzy. So we must get our hands on the thing come hell or high water.'

'Agreed sir, I'd better go. There's a boat coming.'

'What gets me,' said Clements, watching the approaching boat, 'is that we didn't declare war on Islam or Muslims. They declared war on us. And now we're in it up to our necks.'

'The problem,' Hunter said, in philosophical mood, 'is that we have no one to declare war on. If a dirty bomb goes off in London, who do we attack? What use is Polaris? Do we wipe Pakistan off the face of the earth? Or Saudi Arabia? We now know the connection between JIMAS and al-Qaeda, but a group of terrorists isn't a whole country.' He sipped at his coffee while he gradually slowed the yacht down to five knots. 'We can't strike at a whole population, most of whom would be as aghast as we are at the prospect of what we're facing.'

He went out onto the port bridge wing. 'Ready, Jan?'

'Ready, boss.'

A boat approached, turned in the yacht's wake and came alongside the jump ladder that Badonovitch had dangled over the side. A man in uniform stepped onto the lower rungs and climbed up the side of the yacht. He was quickly followed by a second man in a similar uniform but with a distinctively different cap badge. Badonovitch led the men on to the bridge. Handshakes were briefly exchanged and papers and passports shown to the man from immigration. The second man, the pilot for entering the port, stood shoulder to shoulder with Hunter and indicated where he wanted them to go. At that time of night theirs was the only vessel moving, although the waters of Port Said were jammed with ships of all shapes and sizes.

'Nice boat,' said the immigration officer, in a heavy accent, practising his English. It was, after all, the international language of the sea and air.

'Yes, she is,' Hunter replied with a smile.

'Yours?' asked the immigration officer.

'No. We've chartered her. My friends and I are circumnavigating the world. It has long been an ambition of ours,' Hunter explained. 'You know how it is.'

The two Egyptians exchanged looks that clearly said that they were in the presence of madmen. 'Your papers are in order. I thank you.'

'Don't you want to see over the boat?'

'That will not be necessary because you are not stopping in Egypt.'

'We will anchor in a few minutes, Captain. Please be ready for the first convoy at zero five hundred hours,' said the pilot.

'The first convoy?' Hunter queried.

'Yes. There are two southbound convoys each day and one northbound. You will be the end ship. The tail-end Charlie, I think you say. You will anchor in the Great Bitter Lake near Station Seven.'

'How long will it take to transit?'

'It depends on many things, but anything from twelve to sixteen hours. I cannot be more accurate than that.' The pilot frowned and then added, 'From the number of ships in the first convoy, I would estimate it will be closer to twelve hours than sixteen. Many factors affect the time it takes to travel the canal, not just the number of ships in each convoy. You will be going at about eight knots. We will anchor here.' He pointed to port and Hunter spun the wheel and reduced speed even further.

'Tell Jan to stand by,' Hunter told Clements.

Clements repeated the order and Badonovitch, standing in the bows next to the quick-release shackle holding the anchor in place, waved acknowledgement.

'Here will do,' said the pilot.

Hunter put the engines into reverse and said, 'Let go.'

'Let go, Jan!' Clements called out.

There was a metallic clunk as Badonovitch used a hammer to hit the shackle, followed by the noise of the cable running out.

'I bid you goodnight, Captain,' said the immigration officer. The pilot nodded and led the way down the port steps. They clambered over the side and down the jump ladder to the boat that was still alongside the yacht. The pilot waved briefly as the boat pulled away and picked up speed towards the bright lights of Port Said.

'I'm surprised they didn't want their palms crossed with silver, if not gold,' said Clements.

'The new Egypt,' said Hunter cynically. 'A large whisky and soda would go down rather well right now.'

Clements gave a chuckle. 'Hypocrisy rules the waves. I found a rather fine malt amongst the bottles in a hidden bar in the state room. I'll just be a moment.'

A few minutes later he reappeared with a tray bearing four glasses, ice, soda and a bottle of Glenfiddich. He also brought a bottle of vodka for Jan.

They poured the drinks, large ones, and drank to a successful operation. Then they tossed coins for the order they would keep watch. Hunter had the second stint on what would be a long night.

Hunter appeared on the bridge fifteen minutes early.

'Can't sleep?' Clements greeted him.

'Too much on my mind.'

'Me too. If we fail and this bomb goes off, where will they attack next? Will they stop with one bomb? Or will they keep going? Keep trying to impose their will on the West with threats?'

'God knows. Is there only one device? Or do they have more? At the moment the Pakistanis have admitted there's only one, but you know what they're like to deal with.'

'Yeah. Shake hands and count your fingers afterwards.'

Hunter shrugged in frustration. 'All that and more has been running through my mind.' He paused. 'You know what the biggest motivating emotion is?'

'Sure. It's fear of failure.'

'Fear of failure. The consequences of failure this time are unimaginable. But suppose we don't stop them? What then?'

In the glow of the heavily lit anchorage Josh shrugged. 'We'll do our best. It's all we can do. Hey, come on Nick. This isn't like you. You're one of the most optimistic s.o.b's I know.'

Hunter's snort and smile weren't reflected in his eyes. 'Not this time, Josh. Anyway, you get below. Anything to hand over?'

'Not a thing. Two boats went past, one to that tanker over there and one to that cruise ship. Apart from that, all quiet. Goodnight, Nick. I'll see you in a few hours.'

Hunter went below, made himself a cup of coffee and

returned to the bridge. He began pulling the requisite charts from their folios and drawing lines on them and planning their route. He looked up details about the canal, checked landmarks for references and marked distances to go to the end of the Suez Canal. It was essential information but it also helped to pass the time. He woke Badonovitch and went below for an hour's rest. He tossed and turned the whole time.

By 05.00 they had raised the anchor and were making ready to move. The port was full of ships. Each one had been allocated a number and position in the convoy. A 150,000 tonne oil tanker was leading the way. Fully laden, this was the largest ship allowed through the canal. Anything bigger usually went via the Cape of Good Hope. At 05.10 they dropped anchor again. It was obvious that it would be at least an hour before they were called upon to move. They settled down to a breakfast of scrambled eggs, toast and coffee. There was no bacon. The hypocrisy the JIMAS members had shown by having alcohol on board did not extend to bacon. They sat in the sunshine as the sun rose above the horizon, coffees in hand, feet propped up on handrails. It was, they all knew, a welcome moment of peace before the very rough storm that lay ahead. They had, over the years, learned to accept such moments with good grace and gratitude. They stayed where they were for a further hour. Finally, they were called on the radio, and they got underway – without doubt, the tail-end Charlie of dozens of ships. They would be anchoring again about two-thirds of the way along the canal, in the Great Bitter Lake. As they entered the canal, the sound of a train whistle came loudly across the water. To starboard they saw a long, heavily-laden goods train overtaking the convoy. The tracks ran the length of the canal, all the way down the western side. Hunter engaged the autopilot. He stood by the controls, watching it perform. After a few minutes he was satisfied. Course alterations were marked on the chart. The convoy's speed was showing at 7.8 knots. He wrote the actual times to alter course in a navigator's notebook. Because the Mediterranean and the Red Sea were at the same sea-level there were no locks to delay them. The reason for the slow speed was because of the wash created by the larger ships. Only a few decades earlier, before speed restrictions had been imposed, the wash of larger ships would hit the shore and flood settlements, injuring people and animals. At the same time, the canal walls had also been damaged. Thanks to the slower speed this was no longer the case. Looking out of the yacht's windows, port and starboard, the team saw many migrant people transiting the area. Where they were going and why was a complete mystery.

The sun was blazing hot, but the air conditioning maintained the temperature inside the yacht at a comfortable twenty-two degrees centigrade. The massive cranes in the busy port rapidly gave way to bleak desert on the eastern side and small towns and villages to the west. The land to the west was cultivated, cotton being an important crop in the region. There was an air of timelessness, an historic grandeur found only in a very few regions in the world. The building of the canal was truly one of the greatest achievements of the nineteenth and twentieth centuries.

'Nick, I'll take over if you'd like to get some rest,' Doug Tanner said as he appeared on the bridge at 11.00.

'Thanks. I need to call the General first.' Hunter put his finger on the chart. 'We're here, ten miles from Bahr el Tumsah. You can see the lake. That town in the distance is

105

Isma'iliya. When we get to Station Three we'll have done just over fifty miles.' Hunter then explained how to set and disengage the autopilot and showed him the dial to alter course. 'Just follow that cargo vessel ahead.' Two cables ahead of them was the black and white hull of a dilapidated ship. Its registration and flag showed it to be Libyan, a flag of convenience almost as popular as Panama.

'Okay. I've got her. How's the arm?'

'Fine. It's beginning to itch.' Hunter rubbed the top of his arm. He had found a first aid kit in a cupboard on the bridge and had replaced the napkin with a plaster. The bleeding had long stopped and a scab had begun to form.

Behind the bridge was a small but well-equipped communications room. Hunter established contact with TIFAT HQ at HMS *Cochrane*.

'Hullo, sir,' he said to Macnair. 'I thought you'd like to know we're about a third of the way through the canal.'

'So I see. We have you on satellite. Any problems? How's the arm?'

'Fine. Josh has been all over the boat. We're well-stocked for food and drink. The yacht's diesel tanks are full and we've discovered an automatic fresh-water-making machine in the engine room. All in all, we're looking good. Did you find out anything else?'

'There appears to be another asset somewhere.' The frustration of the situation was clear in Macnair's tone.

'Another ship of some sort?'

'Perhaps. We're not sure. What if asset is merely code for another device?'

'God alone knows.'

'One good thing, proof of ownership is so difficult to establish you shouldn't have any trouble with Customs and Excise.' Macnair paused and then said 'Lieutenant

Commander, you don't need me to tell you what we're facing. When Benazir Bhutto was assassinated, Pakistan was on a knife-edge. The current President, Shahid Tahir, is holding the country together, but for how long? The nightmare that the Taliban or al-Qaeda get their hands on a nuclear device or a dirty bomb appears all too real.'

'If it *is* true, do we know where they got it from? Is it Pakistan?'

'We can't be sure, but it looks like it. There is another possibility, however.'

'Iran?' Hunter ventured thoughtfully.

'Correct. We're pretty certain they don't have a nuclear bomb yet, but a dirty bomb is something entirely different. And they're mad enough to do something like this.'

'That's for sure. Even if they did supply it, that isn't the problem.'

'No. It's stopping the thing.'

'Have you told the Americans yet?'

'Yes. We need all their resources to look and listen. GCHQ has also been given a heads-up, although I've only told Ivor Paterson and Sarah Fleeting the reason why.' Paterson was the boss at GCHQ. Sarah was his deputy. She often worked closely with TIFAT and was well liked by General Macnair and Hunter. The government listening post in Cheltenham was a vital cog in the war against worldwide terrorism. Like ECHELON, it hoovered up as much information as it could, put it all through a vast computer system and used trigger words to analyse what was being transmitted, be it the spoken or the written word. In view of what was happening, co-operation between the Americans and the British was at an all-time high. Unfortunately, the same could not be said for other members of either NATO or the United Nations. When it came to gathering and keeping information, both organisations leaked like sieves.

'How long can you keep a lid on things, sir?'

'Not long, that's for sure. Days rather than weeks. But we'll keep denying everything until we're blue in the face. Not that it'll do much good.' Both men were aware that their conversation echoed their discussions from the previous day. Then it had been merely the Prime Minister in the know. Inevitably, the information was spreading and it would continue to do so until all hell broke loose with the media or, heaven forbid, the device was detonated. Cynically, Hunter wondered for a moment which would be worse. Mentally, he shook himself. There was no question which it would be. He realised that such stupid thoughts came from lack of sleep. Their goodbyes were brief.

Hunter went below to the owner's cabin, fell onto the bed and was almost instantly asleep. He missed the transit of the lake of Bahr el Tumsah and the stretch of the canal leading to the Great Bitter Lake. He was woken by the sound of the anchor chain rattling through the hawsehole when the yacht heaved to at the northern end of the lake, opposite Station Five. Not for him the luxury of slowly coming to and enjoying the gradual awareness of his surroundings. Instead, Hunter was instantly awake, full consciousness flooding his mind and memory. Climbing off the bed, he looked through a porthole. The arid desert bank was half a cable away. The gentle throb of the engines beneath his feet died and, apart from the hum of the air-conditioning, complete peace embraced the yacht.

'Everything all right?' he called up the stairs.

'Fine, boss.' Badonovitch appeared at the top of the stairs. 'We've been told it'll take about fifty minutes for the northbound convoy to pass then we'll get going again.'

'Thanks, Jan.' In the en-suite and luxuriously fitted bathroom, Hunter shaved and showered. In the dining room, he found Tanner and Clements eating fried steak and onions, with french fries and a side salad.

'Looks good.'

'Yours is in the oven, Nick,' Josh said. 'We've got some good news.'

While Hunter collected his food Clements continued, 'General Macnair called. He said not to bother waking you. They've got the co-ordinates for the rendezvous. The ship is an old coaster which is registered through dummy companies to Abu Talha. You know, he was either a very cautious operator or paranoid.'

'The former I expect,' said Hunter. 'Also, an operation like this, out of necessity, will be kept as tight as possible. One source of money – Saudi. One source of fighters – JIMAS. Overall control – probably Pakistan.'

Clements nodded. 'That's more or less what we figured.'

'Did you run it past the General?'

Clements nodded. 'He concurs. He's satisfied the Chinese have nothing to do with it. Also, Dr. A. Q. Khar has raised his ugly head.'

Hunter nodded in understanding. Khar was known as the father of Pakistan's nuclear weapons. Although the West had been aware of Khar's work, it had done nothing to stop him. Unfortunately, it was a known fact that Khar had passed his atomic secrets to North Korea, Libya, and Iran. Khar had been instrumental in the proliferation of nuclear weapons.

'What's he been up to this time?'

'They're still working on it back at Rosyth but it looks like he's the creator of a plutonium-enriched bomb.'

'Makes sense. If anyone can do it, he can,' Hunter said heavily.

'How in hell has he got away with it?' Tanner asked in disbelief. 'Why haven't we stopped him before now?'

'Mustaraff is protecting him,' replied Hunter. Seeing Tanner's puzzled frown, he added, 'do you know about the disputed border of Kashmir, between India and Pakistan?'

Tanner nodded. 'Sure. They've been squabbling over that piece of real-estate for decades.'

'Exactly. Well, India got nuclear weapons. They were threatening to use them on Pakistan if the territory of Kashmir wasn't handed back to India. Pakistan resisted, protested vigorously to the UN, and effectively created holy hell about the dangers of a nuclear war. Or at least, the prospect of nuclear fallout in the region. It was all a smoke screen. The Pakistanis were working furiously to create their own nuclear weapons. They did it and tested their first nuclear bomb in 1998. Then they threatened India. The result, a classic Mexican-style stand-off. The hero, Dr. Khar.' Hunter took a deep breath. 'What a sodding mess. Now it looks as though Dr. Khar has supplied a dirty bomb to the fanatics.'

'Perhaps not,' said Clements, thoughtfully. 'Maybe someone stole it.'

Hunter shrugged. 'That's possible, I suppose. It's academic now. Stopping them is the priority. Where's the rendezvous?'

'Arabian Sea, a hundred miles south of Karachi,' Clements replied.

Hunter frowned. 'That'll be somewhere near the Tropic of Cancer if I remember rightly.'

'Spot on. The ship is called the *Union of Sark* and is

registered in Panama. Currently, she's a few miles offshore of Karachi. The Lloyds' details have been transmitted to us. She's twenty-five years old, fifty thousand tonnes of general cargo, with a crew of fifteen. In a nutshell, a tramp steamer. She was originally registered in the Channel Islands. Which would account for the name.' Clements took a mouthful of coffee.

'Are we tracking her?'

'Yeah. ECHELON and GCHQ are monitoring all her transmissions and messages. So far, there's been nothing out of the ordinary. But you can never tell.'

As sophisticated and clever as the West had become in battling terrorism and terrorist states, so had the enemy. It was a vicious circle, spiralling out of control.

10

The Flower of Allah finally exited the Suez Canal a few minutes after 18.00, just as the sun was setting. The one hundred and one miles of canal had passed without incident and should have been an experience to savour. Unfortunately, for the four men on board, this was far from the case. They had spent the day discussing tactics and options. Messages and updates had passed back and forth between TIFAT HQ in Rosyth and the yacht. A Hercules C130, with a team of heavily armed and well-equipped men on board, would be despatched in time to make the rendezvous. Hunter was highly gratified to see who was in the team. They were the best TIFAT had to offer – meaning the best in the world.

Now that they were free of the canal, Hunter eased the yacht out to starboard and slowly increased her speed, catching up with the cargo vessel they had been following through the canal in minutes. They had the Gulf of Suez to traverse – followed by the Red Sea – in all, some one thousand five hundred miles to the Gulf of Aden and their rendezvous with the Hercules C130. According to the information TIFAT had now gathered, *The Flower of Allah* was due to meet the *Union of Sark* in five days. In the meantime, the *Union of Sark* would sail along the coast of

Pakistan in a south-south-easterly direction, steering clear of the country's territorial waters.

Information was the most valuable resource that existed on the planet. Finding it was one thing. Understanding what it meant, quite another. Luckily, due to the events of the past 48 hours, the West had been given a heads-up on what could still prove to be the most shocking event in history. One piece of news did come from the BBC and was relayed by the General. It had been announced that the Prime Minister's family had left London for a break. It was rumoured the Prime Minister would follow soon. The men on the yacht agreed that this was no surprise.

They gradually settled into a routine. Tanner was no mean hand when it came to cooking – the food and drink supplies on board were superior to what they usually enjoyed – and he volunteered to keep them fed and watered. He also helped with watch-keeping duties. Eight hours on, eight hours off. According to the 'satnav' fixes, the yacht was making a good 29.8 knots. At that speed, in the busy waters of the Red Sea, two men were needed at any one time, especially during the night. Within 27 hours they were off Port Sudan. The night was peaceful, the moon and stars bright. Hunter was standing on the bridge, a cup of coffee in his hand. Badonovitch had just fixed *The Flower of Allah*'s position and her engines were running smoothly. They still had enough diesel in the tanks for their needs, although dropping fast at that sustained speed.

Which was why the broadcast on Channel 16 was all the more galling.

'Motor vessel ten miles from Port Sudan and travelling at thirty knots. Heave to immediately. This is the Sudanese

113

coastguard. You are to comply now.' The message was repeated in French and Arabic.

'What do we do, Nick?', Badonovitch asked.

'Nothing,' Hunter replied. 'There's damn-all they can do about it. I doubt there's a coastguard cutter in the world that'll catch us. We'll keep going. There's plenty of shipping around to stop them doing anything stupid like opening fire. And after all, they don't have a clue who we are. As far as they're concerned we could be stuffed full of VIPs. Harming us could cause the sort of international incident that the Sudanese definitely don't want.'

The message was repeated, only this time it was more ominous. '*Flower of Allah* heave to immediately. Stop or risk being sunk.'

Hunter and Badonovitch exchanged frowns.

'How in hell did they get our name?'

Badonovitch shrugged. As he did, there was a loud explosion near the starboard beam.

'Famous last words,' said Hunter, knocking off the autopilot and taking the wheel. He eased the throttles forward the last few notches and the yacht picked up another seven knots. Now she was flat out. Even so, apart from the sound of the wind in the small amount of rigging attached to the superstructure, she made very little noise, testimony to the sound-proofing around the engine room.

Clements and Tanner had been eating but the change in the tempo of the engines brought them hurrying to the bridge.

'What's up, Nick?' Clements asked.

'Sudanese gunboat ordering us to stop. What's more, he called us by name.'

'That makes no sense,' said Clements. 'Why on earth would they want to stop us? Unless . . .' He trailed off.

114

'Precisely. Unless they've been told to stop us,' Hunter said as he eased the wheel a few degrees to port. One problem they faced travelling at that speed was that too much wheel risked the yacht heeling so far over she could be in danger of capsizing.

Before Clements could say any more, Hunter asked, 'Can you see the gunboat?'

Badonovitch had the binoculars up to his eyes and was looking aft. 'Yes, boss. They're right astern and following fast. I can see their bow wave.' The moon was halfway up the sky, casting what they now considered to be an eerie light, as opposed to the beauty of earlier.

'Incoming,' said Badonovitch quickly when he saw the muzzle flash of the gun trained on them.

* * * * *

During the past 24 hours, General Macnair had spoken to three different professors at the universities of Edinburgh, Oxford and Hull. All three were specialists in worldwide terrorism. They each knew of Macnair and were only too willing to discuss the issues he raised. Explaining that he was collecting material for an exercise he asked what would happen in the event of a dirty bomb exploding in London. They agreed on a number of facts. Britain would be bombed back at least one hundred years in terms of its economy and probably even more than that. From being one of the ten biggest economies in the world Britain would be more like a developing nation, a Third World country, on a par with Ethiopia, or, if they were lucky, Nigeria. Anarchy would be the order of the day. How would people feed themselves? How would companies operate? With the stock market wiped out which companies would actually exist? And so it went on as each conversation mirrored the last and added a slightly different perspective scaring Macnair to the core of his being. Once he had finished speaking to the third man, he sat back in his chair pensively. He faced one major problem. The politically correct preferred to call them issues, but Macnair was not, and never would be, politically correct. The major headache that needed to be faced was the Islamic influence in Britain and on British politics. A recent survey showed that 40 per cent of Britain's Muslims supported al-Qaeda and wanted Sharia law introduced to Britain. They also supported the idea of their children being educated in *madrassas* rather than mainstream schools. Many Muslim children, especially those born to Pakistani parents, already attended Islamic *madrassas*, in the evenings and at weekends. MI5 had infiltrated many of them. In more than a few, the children were being educated to hate the West and everything it stood for. They were taught by rote and were brainwashed into believing that the only laws that counted were the laws spoken by Mohammed. When MI5 reported what was happening to the government, they were told to monitor the situation but do nothing. Macnair stood up and crossed his office to the coffee machine. The coffee was stewed but he poured himself a mug anyway. When the law did interfere, human rights raised its ugly head and all hell broke loose in the Courts. Interference with their religion and way of life, screamed the *mullahs*. It had taken years to prosecute one cleric and get him thrown out of the country. His family was now supported by the state and lived on benefits. Yet they weren't even British. Macnair was tired and in need of sleep yet he knew he had to do everything in his power to resolve the situation. And if it meant breaking the law, then so be it.

He pressed the intercom. 'Hiram, can you spare me a minute?'

'Right away, General.'

Moments later Hiram Walsh, his second-in-command, entered. He settled into the chair opposite his boss. 'What's up, sir?'

'Hiram, we need more information. Hunter and the teams will do their best,' he paused, 'but we must be ready for any eventuality.'

'What have you got in mind?'

'You've seen the intelligence we've gathered to date. Reading between the lines there could easily be at least one other dirty bomb.'

'I'd say there's no doubt about it.' Walsh stood, walked over to the coffee machine, smelt it, pulled a face and poured the contents of the pot down the drain. Beginning to make fresh coffee, Walsh dropped all formality. 'Malcolm, we are in deep doodah. Real deep. I don't know how else to put it. You've seen the stuff we've decoded. Hell, we've identified at least sixty active members of al-Qaeda here in Britain. *Active*, mind you. And that's just us. I bet MI5 and MI6 can easily raise that number tenfold.'

'More like a hundred.'

'Probably,' Walsh agreed. 'And what are we going to do about it? Nothing. Not a damned thing. Why? Because if we try any rough stuff we'll have human rights lawyers crawling all over us.'

Walsh paced the office rapidly as he spoke, running his hand through his hair. Macnair listened without interrupting. At times like this Walsh had a habit of saying something, hitting the right note, and deciding on a course of action that often fitted in with his own thoughts. But Macnair liked to leave the American Colonel alone, to come to his own conclusions.

'We have said this a thousand times. It has been in every briefing, in every report we've commissioned or seen by other agencies. We have to be lucky all the time, the terrorists only once. We're fighting with both arms and legs tied behind us and a ball and chain wrapped around our waists for good measure.'

'The law is the law,' Macnair said without emphasis.

Walsh walked over to the fresh coffee, raised the pot in a gesture to Macnair, who shook his head. Walsh poured himself a mug and sat down opposite the General. 'We can't *not* take action. It's unthinkable.'

'When did you come to this decision?'

Walsh sighed. 'About four o'clock this morning while lying awake in my pit.'

'I agree. What do you have in mind?'

'Are you kidding? Plenty. From taking out as many of the bastards as we can to nuking Pakistan. Mind you, *that* thought was okay at zero crack sparrow fart, but not in the cold light of day.'

Macnair nodded. 'I had thought about a direct threat to the Pakistan government.'

'Along the lines of what?'

'Along the lines of: if a plutonium-based device explodes in Britain, we *know* you're responsible – or people in your government are – and we will wipe Pakistan off the face of the earth.'

'Only the government can make a threat like that. We don't have the nukes,' Walsh stated the obvious. 'If we were under threat back in the good old US of A and we told the Pakistanis we'd wipe them off the face of the earth, we might be believed. But here?' He let the words hang in the air. He didn't need to spell it out.

'So, you know as well as I do it'll never happen,' Macnair said. 'Besides which, you can't wipe out an entire population because of the actions of a few madmen. The truth is the vast majority of Pakistanis are decent people who just want to make a living and bring up their families. They pay lip-service to their religion, much like we do with Christianity, and get on with their lives. It's only the fanatics who are to blame. Fundamentalists. And let's be honest, Christian fundamentalists and Jewish fundamentalists are just as bad as Muslims. They are all brainwashed to an amazing, self-deluding degree.'

Walsh nodded, gingerly sipping his hot coffee. 'Yeah, I couldn't agree with you more.'

'It's time to put JIMAS under pressure, considerable pressure, along with the supporters of al-Qaeda. I take it the situation with the Hercules C130 is still the same?'

Walsh nodded. 'Affirmative. There's nothing further we can do for them, except cover their backs if we need to. At the moment, it all looks quiet out there. Nick and the boys are enjoying a pleasant cruise in the sunshine, but it won't last for long.'

Macnair nodded. 'I'm having a web conference in two hours. I'd like you to be there.'

'Who with?'

'Clive Owens. Bring Samantha Freemantle along as well. Liaison between us will be of vital importance.'

*   *   *   *   *

Hunter spun the wheel sharply to port. They were ten degrees off track when the falling shot hit the sea, sending a geyser of water cascading over the starboard deck. 'How far until we are out of their territorial waters?'

Tanner checked the chart and their position. 'Eight miles.'

The Flower of Allah passed half-a-mile under the stern of a large tanker travelling south at a sedate fifteen knots. He eased the yacht to starboard and paralleled the tanker's course, now hidden from the gunboat.

Clements stepped alongside Hunter. 'They had to know we were coming. It's the only explanation. Nobody is mad enough to fire on a yacht – or any boat come to that – without some cast-iron reason. So much for our hidden ownership and being incognito. I'll signal TIFAT.'

'Do that. We've no weapons so all we can do is run. We'll be past the tanker in a few seconds. Keep your eyes peeled for that bastard behind us and any other vessel that might be tasked to stop us. How are we doing, Doug?'

'We've opened up another two miles.' Tanner said checking the radar. 'The Sudanese are now just over five miles astern. All the ships on screen are heading either north or south. From the look of things, nothing's changed course to try an intercept. Distance to Sudan's territorial boundary is six point three miles.'

'Hot pursuit?' Clements suggested.

'That's what I would guess,' said Hunter.

Hot pursuit was the term used when international boundaries were ignored and the military forces of one country went racing into the territory, whether land or sea, of another. The excuse being the criminals or enemy they were chasing would escape otherwise. It was frowned upon, argued about at the United Nations, was the subject of many international enquiries and was frequently investigated by the World Court on Human Rights. Even so, hot pursuit occurred all too frequently.

'Incoming,' Badonovitch shouted again, watching the muzzle flash from the gunboat.

In his last two manoeuvres, Hunter had turned to port to head closer to Saudi waters, but this time he altered course to starboard. The shot fell a cable to port – very close to where they would have been if he'd followed his previous actions. Another ship was eight cables to starboard and fine on the starboard bow. They headed directly towards her and passed less than half a cable under her stern. Hunter altered course to port by a few degrees, ran close alongside the ship, a coaster this time, and shot out ahead. A few more degrees to port and they were hidden from the Sudanese navy vessel. Another irate order came over Channel 16. It was made clear in no uncertain terms that they had better stop and surrender.

'Josh, talk to them,' Hunter ordered.

'Sudanese gunboat, this is *The Lucky Strike*,' Clements said in the broadest American southern drawl that he could muster.

'*The Lucky Strike*?' Hunter looked over his shoulder.

'It was the first name I could think of. Go to Channel 12.' Clements didn't bother waiting for an acknowledgement but flipped the dial to 12. 'Sudanese gunboat, what you all shooting at us for? I'm reporting you to my government as soon as I can get a signal off.'

'Stop now. Stop, I say, or we will blow you out of the water.'

'If'n you do, then I reckon you'll have on your hands what we all call an international incident and I guess old Uncle Sam will be sending in gunboats of his own.'

'You are international terrorists and are under arrest,' came the reply.

'This here is *The Lucky Strike* and we are on a peaceful cruise around the world. I suggest you check the Lloyds Register. You'll find us there.'

'We will check after we have arrested you. This is the Captain. I demand you stop now!'

'Well, Captain, I can't rightly say as that we trust you and your navy that much so I don't think we will. However, I am sending a protest now to my government. No doubt they in turn will be on at yours. And in view of all the aid in good old American dollars we send you every year, I figure heads could roll over this. Yours, savvy?'

The radio was awash with garbled messages from frantic captains demanding to know what was happening and who was firing at whom and why. Messages from ships were filling the ether as they sent desperate messages to their head offices. Had war broken out in the region, with nobody aware of this fact?

'Any word from Rosyth?' Hunter asked. The team could expect any transmissions to have been monitored and hence the question.

'Coming in now.' He ripped the message off the teleprinter. 'Evade as best you can. Am protesting via the American State Office and the American Embassy in Sudan using Flash. Standby. Good luck. Out.'

Flash was the highest priority signal that could be sent and was only used in cases of dire emergency. Knowing General Macnair as they did, they figured the message would be sent straight to the American Secretary of State. Even so, it would take time. More time than they had.

'Range?' Hunter called out.

'Six miles and opening,' Tanner replied.

'Sudanese gunboat,' Clements broadcast, 'I have now sent a message to my government in protest. Also to my Embassy in Khartoum. I wouldn't want to be in your shoes. I reckon a Court Martial is waiting for you. Maybe even a firing squad.'

'A firing squad?' Hunter asked with raised eyebrows.

Clements shrugged. 'God knows. Can't hurt to put the fear of Christ into the bastard. If he's acting on his own and not on orders from his government it might make him stop and think. You know as well as I do that the Sudanese support Muslim terrorists every which way they can.'

Hunter nodded. It was true. And yet Western governments – hoping to influence the Sudanese – gave them huge amounts of aid which was then squandered by the elite, the military and the mullahs. It was a no-win situation that beggared belief. Or, as General Macnair once put it, pontificating over a large whisky in the wardroom, proof positive that the lunatics were running the asylum.

'Distance apart is opening a lot quicker,' Tanner reported. 'There they go. They're turning back towards Sudan.'

Hunter eased back on the throttles. The extra few knots had resulted in fuel being sucked up at an unsustainable rate.

'Coffee?' Tanner suddenly asked.

The other three men grinned and then laughed. It was all that was needed to break the tension that had been palpable on the bridge.

'Coffee is an excellent idea.' Hunter blew out his cheeks and then said, 'That was too damn close for comfort.' He put the yacht back on autopilot. 'Keep a watch for any

123

vessel not travelling the sea lanes and anyone crossing.'

The Red Sea was split into sea lanes, just like a motorway. Travelling north, the ships stayed to the west; travelling south they were to the east. Once in a lane, apart from over-taking, the ships had to remain in that lane. Crossing from one side to the other was only permitted at right angles to the lanes. The ships were obliged to obey The Rule of The Road. These rules governed everything a vessel did at sea, from the lights it showed and the sound signals it made, to how the vessel was driven. It was analogous to driving a car, only far more complex.

Hunter stood at the console, binoculars around his neck, scanning the other ships and watching their lights and their movements relative to themselves. Badonovitch was at the radar, Clements was in the communications shack reporting to Rosyth. All he got back was an acknowledgement.

'When all is said and done,' said Clements, 'I don't suppose there's a hell of a lot the Old Man can say.'

Hunter replied, 'Not to us, maybe, but I suspect he's burning the wires trying to find out what the hell's happened. None of us believes in coincidence. So it probably means we've been blown. If so, to what extent? I mean, who else on the terrorists' side knows we're on board this boat? And have they informed the terrorists on the *Union of Sark*? And if they have, how did they manage it without us intercepting the message?'

When Tanner reappeared ten minutes later, with coffee and cheese sandwiches, everything looked clear. They were now in that stretch of disputed water known as no-man's-land, between Saudi Arabia and Sudan.

Just before 09.00 their time, General Macnair made contact.

'How are you doing?'

'Fine, sir, thank you.'

'Good. I didn't tell you before because we couldn't be sure how effective it would be, but since noon yesterday we have been intercepting and filtering all messages sent to and from the *Union of Sark*. Most of the transmissions didn't arrive. We made sure of that.'

'Won't that cause a load of suspicion, sir?'

'We don't think so. Normal shipping traffic we allowed. It was everything else we stopped. Some of it had to do with you.'

'Where did the signals originate from, sir?' Clements enquired.

'We're not sure yet. The signals about you were short and sharp and difficult to trace but we're listening out for more. It doesn't seem as though the sender was expecting a reply. One thing we are absolutely certain of however. Somewhere there's a traitor at work.'

11

There were no more attacks, no more threats over the radio and no further calls to heave to for boarding. However, in view of the distance they had already travelled and what lay ahead, they decided it would be a good idea to fill the yacht's diesel tanks. Aden – at the western end of the Gulf – was the best port of call. Hunter contacted Rosyth and asked them to make the necessary arrangements so that their arrival would not be a surprise. Payment was not a problem. The safe in the stateroom made sure of that. Once the arrangements were made, and with more than enough fuel to get them to Aden, they increased speed again. Better to have time in hand than to be playing catch-up.

* * * * *

Clive Owens was the newly appointed head of MI5. The government hadn't liked it when he was given the job, preferring a candidate of their own choosing. Someone who would do as he was told. However, they'd had no choice. If anyone else had been appointed, it would have been recognised for what it was – government interference. Owens was the product of Eton and Sandhurst. Having spent eight years with the Household Calvary he resigned his commission in 1981 and joined MI5 as a trainee. His rise to the top position was due to two factors. The first was his undoubted ability. The second, and of equal importance, was the fact that he was extremely well-connected. Those connections had been instrumental in forcing the government to accept his nomination. Whatever career he had chosen, he would have risen to the top. As it was, he had done so in the service of his country. He was yet to receive his knighthood which was usual for one in such a position. Over a late night drink with trusted colleagues, Owens would laugh at the thought that it was the government's way of getting their own back.

Two hours later, Malcolm Macnair, Hiram Walsh and Samantha Freemantle were sitting opposite a large computer screen on the wall of the communications room at Rosyth. Each had a webcam aimed at them, showing them live on the screen. A few moments later, Clive Owens, using a password supplied by Macnair, appeared in the top left-hand corner. He was thin-faced, with sharp blue eyes, and black hair going grey at the sides.

'Thanks for joining us Clive.' Macnair frowned at the screen. He'd thought about what he was going to say, only now his opening remarks, to his mind, sounded fatuous. 'I'd like to take this opportunity to have a frank and open discussion. But first, let me introduce my second-in-command, Colonel Hiram Walsh from the American Delta Force. Samantha Freemantle you know.'

'Pleased to meet you,' said Walsh.

'Good afternoon sir,' said Samantha.

'Good afternoon. Nice to be with you. Where do you wish to begin?' Owens kept his face noncommittal. He'd listen at least.

'You know only too well what we're facing. Unless these fanatics are stopped, the consequences don't bear thinking about.'

'Agreed, but my hands are tied,' Clive explained. 'Malcolm, I've read the reports of some of your past operations. They're very impressive. If it hadn't been for you, the deaths of those men taken prisoner on the west coast of Scotland would have been catastrophic. Then there was the Israeli mess. Their policy of land-grab is wrong. We all know it. But Dayan would have carved out a huge sector of the Middle East if he'd been allowed to get away with it. Then there are the Russian crime cartels we're facing. Thanks to so-called human rights we're fighting organised crime with our hands tied as well as our eyes blindfolded. Or we were. At least TIFAT made a dent in the sodding syndicates. The last major caper about the white backlash was truly inspirational. The outcome would have been horrendous. I don't need to tell you all this but I am. What I'm about to say will, no doubt, be a nasty surprise.'

Macnair felt the worm of concern nibbling at the edge of his stomach. He was pretty sure what was coming.

'Yesterday, I was called to a meeting of Secretaries of State.' Owens hesitated then continued. 'After the usual briefings on worldwide events, the Prime Minister announced he was coming to the real reason for the meeting. Whether to continue supporting TIFAT or not.'

Macnair hardly blinked. Walsh said nothing. It came as no surprise to either of them. They'd known which way the wind was blowing. General Macnair pressed the transmit button on the computer. 'Go on,' he said.

Owens shrugged. 'Let me start by saying that I do not agree with them one iota. The operations I recapped a few moments ago are the ones I used in argument to ensure that TIFAT not only survives but is expanded, if possible. However, all I got was rule of law, human rights. Can't go round shooting people not found guilty by our Courts. And so on and so forth. You don't seem surprised.'

'I'm not. How were matters left?'

Owens shook his head ruefully. 'About what you'd expect, a review. A judicial enquiry with Parliamentary oversight. I am sworn to protect this country from her enemies. I think it's rich beyond belief that our enemies are so many vipers in our bosom.'

'What do you propose?'

'I suggest we meet with William Summers at MI6. He and I both have information we would like to discuss with you.'

'What about?' Macnair asked.

'What we're facing. You don't know the half of it.' Owens could barely control the anger in his voice.

'What on earth do you mean?'

In reply, he received a shake of the head. 'Later. Let me speak to William first and we'll make some arrangements. He and I have already discussed the possibility of meeting you.'

'Where do you suggest we meet?' Macnair enquired.

'Not here. You might be seen and recognised and word could get back to our political masters. Why don't we come to Scotland? To *Cochrane*?'

'In that case, if you can get yourselves to RAF Brize Norton I'll arrange transport from there. It'll be quicker than anything else.' Then he added, 'and anonymous.'

'I think we can be at the Station by,' Owens glanced at his watch, 'say two o'clock tomorrow afternoon. With the weekend tomorrow we won't be missed.'

12

Clive Owens was a tall, distinguished-looking man. Sir William Summers, on the other hand, was short, round, with a cherubic smile that hid an astute brain and a cynical mindset. They were sitting alone in Macnair's office. The General offered and poured coffees. It was Owens who started the discussion.

'William and I have significantly increased the frequency of our meetings and exchange of information for some weeks now. No more arguments about need-to-know and territorial turf. There's been far too much of that in the past. Our *joint* remit,' he emphasised the word and Summers nodded, 'is the national security of this country. Until now we have been left to do our jobs to the best of our abilities. Our successes have, as you know, been extensive if not spectacular. You must have seen some of the reports.'

Macnair nodded. 'I have. I believe that you do excellent work. It's slow, painstaking and soul-destroying. But there's no alternative.'

Summers spoke. 'Well, it's all changing. The level of government interference is hampering us in a number of different ways.'

'Such as?'

'Continuous briefings of Ministers and Secretaries of State. Comment on operations and suggestions that are tanta-mount to orders. The oversight committees are beyond a joke. Every one of them has a lawyer of some description on them. We have proof of al-Qaeda operating in numerous places across Britain. Names, faces, dates of events. Yet we can do nothing about it and do you know why?'

Macnair shrugged. 'I can guess. Illegally obtained. Wire taps without a Court order. Ditto for mail and e-mail intercepts.'

'That isn't the half of it,' said Summers. He was like his counterpart from MI5 – a complete cynic when it came to dealing with the government. He had joined the Foreign Office after graduating with a reasonable degree from Hull University. From there, more by accident than design, he had ended up working for MI6 while in an embassy job in China. Since then he hadn't looked back. He had been in post now for almost eighteen months. He had another eighteen to go to retire – if he survived in the job that long. He had received his knighthood at the Queen's last birthday honours. It was a title he rarely used, except, he joked, when booking a table in a popular restaurant. 'I have been called in and ordered to explain an upcoming operation, which I have duly done, only to discover that it's been cancelled two days later. No explanation. None of the criteria of what's best for Britain. If I had my way, I'd arrest the whole lot of them as traitors.'

'Without evidence to be used in Court?' Macnair asked dryly, raising his eyebrows.

The other two chuckled. Macnair's comment helped to break the tension a little.

'What's to be done?' Macnair continued. 'I suspect you came to see me with some sort of idea, a plan?'

Summers replied. 'At this point in time, there's nothing we can do about the politicians. After all, constitutionally, we don't have a leg to stand on. Either we toe the line or we get sacked. TIFAT could be slung out of Britain at any time. At the very least, the announcement of its closure could be made. They would have to give you time to relocate. If other nations decided to support and use you, then not even this government could object. Unless, of course, you were based in another European country. Then they could make all sorts of objections, especially in view of the Lisbon Treaty.'

'Damned traitors,' said Macnair. 'They'd promised us a referendum.'

'Be that as it may,' said Owens, 'there's nothing to be done about it now.'

The other two nodded. All three were pragmatists. It was a cliché, but they worked with the cards they were dealt. Complaining did no good. Lateral thinking and underhand working did.

Owens continued. 'If that were to happen, there would be no British involvement, which would be a disaster. All British personnel serving with TIFAT would be sent back to their units.'

'Worse than that,' Summers added, 'we wouldn't know what was happening. We'd be out of the loop. The consequences of that would be horrendous. We would become more and more isolated. Not on the face of it – between governments – but where it really matters. Between us and the rest of the intelligence community.'

Macnair nodded. He had already arrived at the same conclusion. Gloomy introspection clouded their faces. The General said, 'then there's the problem of you not having any input.' The reality of the intelligence world – acknowledged by agencies around the globe – was that Britain still had one of the most effective and extensive networks of agents in existence. It was a legacy of the Empire. Britain was also one of the most favoured destinations for those who lived in former British Empire countries. It made for a powerful bargaining tool when information was needed.

'We appear to be singing from the same hymn sheet then,' said Macnair. 'So?'

'How should I put this,' said Summers thoughtfully. 'The prospect of a plutonium-based device going off has helped to focus the politicians' minds. Even so,' he said, nodding at Owens, 'they expect us to deal with it. We'll do our best, obviously, but the all-important mandate . . .'

'Makes it impossible,' interrupted Macnair.

'Precisely,' said Owens. '"Halt or I fire!" yelled three times isn't exactly effective when trying to stop a bomb. William and I are agreed. They won't have time to do anything about TIFAT until after the crisis at the earliest, whichever way it pans out. All being well, we'll make a huge fuss about the role you play. I know,' he held up his hand, pre-empting Macnair, 'you like to keep things as quiet as possible. We respect that. We'll deal with our political masters in private. But if that doesn't work we'll go public.'

Macnair nodded slowly. 'That makes sense.' He stood up. 'It's past 18.00 hours, gentlemen. Can I offer you a glass of sherry or a whisky? I have a rather fine malt from Islay.'

They opted for the sherry and while he poured the drinks Macnair said, 'You didn't come all this way to tell me that. There must be something else you have in mind.

Something of far greater significance.' He poured himself the malt.

'Malcolm, we have information which we believe you should know. Information that we were both told to keep from you.'

Macnair handed out the glasses. 'By whom?' He took a sip of his malt, sure of the answer he would receive.

'The Home Secretary,' said Owens.

'That stupid . . .'

'Bitch?' suggested Summers.

'I was going to say cow, but you get the idea. She is one of the most incompetent and gutless Home Secretaries we've had in years. What in hell is her problem?'

The rhetorical question was answered by Owens. 'She sees good in everybody. They might be mistaken, uneducated, brainwashed or plain stupid, but as far as she is concerned, people are decent and good.'

The three men, having seen more than their share of evil in their time, shook their heads in sorrow tinged with anger. The safety of the realm was being placed at risk because of a bunch of lily-livered incompetents.

'We have brought with us a great deal of information,' Owens continued. 'Much of it pertains to people in this country but there is also plenty about foreign nationals, especially in Pakistan. All the information was gathered illegally. Take that as read. However, it does not diminish the value of what we've got. And believe us when we say, it's dynamite. Plutonium-based dynamite.'

The evening progressed and the men shared the intelligence that their respective organisations had collected. It was not only considerable, it was frightening beyond imagination. While they worked, food was delivered from the wardroom, but for the most part remained uneaten on their plates. The evening wore on until finally, just before midnight, they came to a halt.

'It's unbelievable,' said Macnair for the umpteenth time.

'That's what we kept telling each other,' said Owens, 'which is why we wanted to see you.'

'And the Cabinet has seen all this?'

'Most of it. We presented the information at a COBRA meeting three days ago.'

'What happened?'

The two Military Intelligence men exchanged looks and shrugs. It was Owens who answered. 'You can guess. Nothing. All that was said was there was a consensus that any action had to be within the letter of the law. That there was nothing we could do with what we've got.'

Macnair had known for some months that things at Cabinet level were getting worse, thanks to the Prime Minister and his lapdogs, but that it had gone so far and so fast came as a shock even to him.

'Let me ask you something.' The General sat back in his chair. 'Do they believe the threat we're facing?'

'Ah, you've put your finger on it. Half of them do, the other half don't.'

'Who are the half that do?'

'The ones that don't count,' was the cynical reply from Summers.

'That figures. What do you want me to do?' With that question the meeting took on a different atmosphere. Until that moment it had all been doom and gloom. Now, it was time for action, possibly.

'The oversight committees that effectively control us, that oversee our every move, do not affect you,' said Owens. 'It's part of your mandate. It's the main reason this government wants you closed down and thrown out of the

UK. At least they can then wash their hands in public and yell it has nothing to do with them if a TIFAT operation goes wrong.'

'It hasn't yet,' said Macnair defensively.

'We know that,' said Summers. 'Indeed, it's the reverse. But now I have seen our so-called leaders in action, I can see where they are coming from. I don't agree with them in any way. Quite the opposite. I am dead set against what they'll try to do. It's as though they are frightened of,' he shrugged, 'well, truth to tell, I don't know what. World opinion? The history books? If we fail to stop a dirty bomb exploding in Britain, *that* will be the time to be frightened of the history books.'

'We are going around in circles,' said the General. 'What is it you propose?'

Owens's smile was predatory. 'We have the information. You have the ability to act.'

Macnair nodded. 'That's true. However, this afternoon I was given a caveat.'

'A caveat?' Owens asked, frowning. 'What sort of caveat? From whom?'

'The Home Secretary. That's why I knew which way the wind was blowing. She told me in no uncertain terms what she wanted to do. She wants the European Union to close us down. She insisted that any action taken on British soil was subject to human rights and oversight by her department.'

'My God, I don't believe it,' Summers spoke in a loud whisper.

'Oh, do believe it,' said Macnair. He walked across his office and picked up the whisky bottle. He waved it in the direction of the two men. Both nodded. This news called for a drink stiffer than a sherry. He sat back in his chair. He smiled, though there was little merriment on his face. 'What she doesn't seem to understand or acknowledge is that she can't impose her will on TIFAT, as much as she would like to. She can't change our mandate. Such an event by politicians was foreseen. We'd lose a great deal of our ability to act. Sure, collectively they can. That's obvious. But not unilaterally.'

'That's what we understand.' Owens took a large sip of the smoky-flavoured malt.

'As you know, we're currently getting into position to take out a ship we believe is carrying a plutonium-based device.'

'Do our lords and masters know?' Summers asked, taking an appreciative sip from his glass.

Macnair nodded slowly. 'I made a great tactical error. I told the Prime Minister. I thought it was a courtesy. After all, we believe Britain is the target and so I thought I had no choice. I asked him to keep the information to himself. However, there is no doubt that it's leaking out. Radio, e-mail, telephone intercepts prove that. ECHELON and GCHQ are working on it for us.'

'Can you trust them?' Owens asked.

'Implicitly. It's thanks to them my team is still closing on the target. Without them, I don't know where we'd be.'

'We learned something interesting from the ISIA,' Summers said. The Inter Service Intelligence Agency of Pakistan was ostensibly there to do the bidding of its government, although it was a known hotbed of Muslim fundamentalists, Taliban and al-Qaeda supporters. 'A man named Rehman Khan appeared on our radar a few months back. He's the grandson of General Khan who, you may remember, took control of Pakistan in a military coup before being killed by a bomb on an aircraft in 1988.'

Macnair nodded at the recollection.

'Rehman Khan's a fundamentalist to his fingertips. Not only does he support al-Qaeda but he's also a supporter of JIMAS. He's been supplying them with arms and explosives for years. Khan has now vanished off the face of the earth. We're looking for him, right now.'

'Anything to do with what's happening?' Macnair asked.

'We believe so. Khan was working closely with Dr A. Q. Khar on something.'

'The nuclear missile man?'

'Correct,' said Summers. 'That's also Khan's area of expertise. We think that unknown to the Pakistani government they have been trying to develop suitcase-sized bombs. So far they've manufactured the dirty bombs.'

'Are we sure their government isn't involved?'

'Pretty sure, yes. What would be the purpose? The whole point of having nuclear weapons is as a deterrent, not to use the sodding things,' Summers replied.

'So who do we think is bringing it? Khan?' The General took a gulp of his malt.

'We believe so,' replied Owens.

'Do we know where Khan is now?'

'We're as sure as we can be that he's in the badlands of the Pakistan and Afghanistan border,' Summers said. 'A nasty place to operate.'

'But somewhere to start,' said a thoughtful Macnair.

'Exactly,' replied Owens. 'The big question is, what do we do about it?'

'Presumably, that's why you're here?'

Summers reached into his inside jacket pocket and retrieved a USB flash drive. 'On here is some of the most damning information you'll ever see. We can show movement of money and men around the world, as well as arms and explosives coming into this country. The ringleaders are easily identifiable, but so are many of their minions. Those Pakistanis who are not actively involved are tacitly prepared to go along with some of JIMAS' plans.'

Macnair shook his head. 'I just don't get it. Why?' The last word was almost plaintive.

'Mainly because they don't know the full extent of what JIMAS is planning,' answered Owens. 'If they did, they would be as shocked and angry as we are.' Then he spoilt it by adding, 'Maybe.'

'We've given it a great deal of thought,'Summers said. 'We double-checked TIFAT's mandate, just to be sure. We can arrest, detain and take to Court many of the people listed and have the cases chucked out, as so often happens.'

'Inadmissible evidence and a reluctance to show how we acquired that evidence,' Macnair suggested.

'Correct. But in reality it has all changed now. We must be seen to be acting within the law, whilst you can operate using the TIFAT mandate. Malcolm, we're drifting into the most dangerous period of our history. For a decade, our greatest fear has been the terrorists getting their hands on a nuclear device. Well, the nightmare is coming true even if it's a dirty bomb and not a nuke. We have to stop them. Come hell or high water. If that bomb explodes anywhere in Europe, then – apart from those killed in the blast and its immediate aftermath, and in the long term by the radiation – there'll be rioting, looting and many, many Muslims will be murdered.'

'You've come here with some sort of plan, I guess.'

Owens nodded. 'First, we plan to arrest many of those

on that USB flash drive. We've decided to come clean in the Courts. Explain how we got the information. Let the solicitors and barristers howl about illegal acquisition of evidence. We'll let the public decide whether we acted in the best interests of the country or not. This is all about preventing a major catastrophe.'

'So what do you want me to do?' Macnair asked.

'We need your help. You can raid bank accounts, create huge problems for individuals and get away with it. We can't. It's impossible. By disrupting their lives we may get some of them to panic. Make mistakes. Make a run for it, which might lead us somewhere. There are also a number we don't want arrested. Just dealt with.'

'I see. And if any do a runner, I take it you want us to follow through?'

'We don't have the resources in manpower or equipment,' replied Owens, 'whilst you do.'

Macnair frowned and nodded. 'Yes, but we're stretched mighty thin.'

It was Owens who put into words what they had all been thinking. 'I don't care how many known al-Qaeda or JIMAS sympathisers are hurt. A thousand of them are of less value to me than one loyal British person, irrespective of gender, colour, religion or ethnic origin. So we need to act. And soon.'

'There's yet another consideration,' Summers said. 'If a bomb goes off and Pakistan is blamed what will happen? Worldwide boycotting of everything Pakistani? Nobody in or out of the country? No trade? Rioting and death on a huge scale? The country will descend into anarchy. What then? If the fundamentalists have their way and get control then Pakistan will be thrown back into the Middle Ages. That prospect is too terrible to contemplate because of their access to nuclear weapons. Then the big one.'

'Wiping Israel off the face of the earth.'

'The Islamic dream,' said Owens.

Macnair nodded. He'd known where this was leading all along. 'Israel will retaliate with her own nukes.'

'Nuclear war,' said Summers, awe in his voice. 'Nuclear Armageddon. That's what we foresee.'

The night wore on as the three discussed their options and what could be done. In the early hours, when they finally said goodnight, the course of action had been decided. There was no doubt. The men responsible for the security of the United Kingdom were in revolt. Turmoil was in the offing.

13

They refuelled at a small jetty near to the entrance of the port. Customs and Excise had called and left again. Hoses had been hooked into access points and pumps started. Cans of petrol had been topped up. The petrol was used by the yacht's runabout, a six-seater luxury speedboat.

'This'll take about an hour,' Hunter said looking at the gauges. 'Jan, why not grab a taxi and go into town? There's a hypermarket called LuLu. Get some fresh fruit and veg.'

'Right, boss. I'll get my passport.' Minutes later Badonovitch was on his way, his pocket stuffed with some of the cash they'd liberated from the safe.

Clements and Tanner were down in the engine room. They checked the oil levels and gauge readings were compared to those on the bridge. The ready use tanks for fuel were dipped. It wasn't unknown for air bubbles to give the wrong readouts.

'Where does this go?' Clements asked pointing to a pipe vanished between the deck and a watertight bulkhead. Sighing, he added, 'We'd better check it out.'

'There's a hand-sized access hole.' Tanner put his fingers in. 'And a catch.' He pulled it upwards and a section of the deck and bulkhead folded open. Inside they found an incredible hoard of weapons. Apart from automatic rifles and handguns, they also found a FIM-92A Stinger Weapons' System.

'We'd better close this up until we're at sea,' said Clements. 'We don't want some port official wandering in and seeing this lot. I know it isn't likely, but better safe than sorry.'

They closed the covers and went back up to the bridge.

'Why am I not surprised?' Hunter said when he was told what they'd found. 'Presumably, for use somewhere in Europe.' A taxi approached the berth. 'Here's Jan. Let's get ready to go. I'll pay the fuel bill.'

Hunter went ashore and along the pier to the small hut at the end. There, he handed over more of the terrorists' cash and added a tip for good measure. The thanks heaped on him were effusive. He found there was a certain satisfaction in giving away the money. Departing the port was quick and easy. There were no other vessels and they were soon back at sea. Once clear of the land, Clements returned to the arms hoard. He reappeared on the bridge hefting the Stinger.

Hunter asked, 'Is there a serial number?'

Clements grinned. 'Great minds. I've already looked. It's been removed with acid. However, I'm fairly positive we supplied a load of Stingers to the Pakistanis at the end of the nineties. The great thing about this weapon is that it needs no maintenance. Aim, lock on, fire and forget. It's idiot proof. That's why it's so popular in Third World countries.'

'That,' added Hunter, 'along with the fact it's usually free, a present from the United States.'

'Britain's just as bad,' Clements replied.

Hunter nodded. 'Amen to that. I won't even try to deny it. So are the French, Chinese and a host of other countries.

The enemy of my enemy is my friend. As if!' His voice was filled with derision. 'Any way of finding out who supplied it?'

'Possibly,' said Josh. 'Ultrasonic sound aimed at where the serial number was will show up clearly on a screen. I've seen it done.'

'I'd better call this in and let them know what we've found,' Hunter said.

A watch-keeping rota was agreed, and soon the team was sitting in the sun eating the fruit Badonovitch had bought. The melon was particularly tasty. For the next twenty-four hours they enjoyed what could only be described as a luxury cruise. The weather was ideal – warm, sunny and with a light breeze from the east. After they left Aden the team had spent what was left of the forenoon examining and firing the weapons they had discovered. They also checked out the P4 plastic explosive and timing mechanisms.

'This stuff is state-of-the-art, and no mistake.' Doug Tanner's comment summed it all up.

Rosyth kept Nick informed about the *Union of Sark*. In the late afternoon the ship had turned on to the fourth side of a box track. The waste of fuel and steaming time alone were enough to prove that a rendezvous was going to take place. Was it to receive goods, such as the arms and explosives found on board? Or was it to off-load something?

In the evening, as the sun was setting, Hiram Walsh contacted them. 'Nick, just to let you know that we have had independent confirmation that the Pakistanis do have dirty bombs.'

'How?'

'Somebody high in the Pakistani government told MI6.

We don't know who. MI6 said they needed to keep some secrets. After all, the person who told us will be in real danger if his identity leaks out.'

'We've been monitoring the news. It doesn't appear as if anything's leaked yet.'

'It hasn't. We're doing everything in our power to keep a tight lid on things.'

'Any confirmation that it's on the *Union of Sark*?' Nick asked.

'Nope. We can but hope.'

'Okay. I'll speak to you later.'

*   *   *   *   *

Macnair walked across to his window and gazed towards the majestic Forth Road Bridge and beyond. He was thinking about what MI6 had just told him. How much worse could it get? His tired mind wandered into the politics of the situation. Aware for some time of what was going on, he had not been able to see what he could do about it. If the British Parliament decided they didn't want TIFAT in Britain any longer then it would be closed down. End of story. Relocation wouldn't be a problem: international access to world events would be. Speed of response was important, which was why Scotland was ideal. No. If they were thrown out of Britain they'd be thrown out of Europe. The only place left to go would be America. Democrats or Republicans, at least their politicians were pragmatists. He shook his head, trying to clear his brain. He would cross that particular bridge when, or more to the point, if, he was driven to it. In the meantime, Macnair would do whatever it took to stop the planned atrocity, and damn the consequences and damn the politicians with their politically correct claptrap. The potential destruction of London by a dirty bomb was too much to gamble. Far too much. The terrorists had to be stopped at all costs.

He thought fleetingly of Christine Woolford, Member of the European Parliament, with whom he had an arrangement. An old-fashioned word for an old-fashioned couple was the way Macnair liked to think about it. There was no doubt in his mind that one day he and Christine would get married. In the meantime, they were both highly motivated pursuing their respective careers. Macnair smiled, this time with a little mirth in his demeanour. After this caper, maybe it wouldn't be an issue. He could become a house-husband. At the thought, he couldn't help a chuckle escaping his lips.

He left his office, walked out of the building and crossed the square. Using a keycard he opened a high-security door and entered. He passed through a foyer and approached another door which required a four-digit code to unlock it. Inside was one of the largest and most comprehensive computer set-ups to be found anywhere in any armed service in the world. It also had one of the most powerful communications systems in existence which was as good as that found on any American aircraft carrier. A dozen people worked there. Not enough, the senior officers at TIFAT all agreed.

Isobel Sweeney was in charge. She sat at her desk, on a dais half-a-metre high, eyeing her domain. Slim-built, 5ft 6ins tall, with fair hair, she was attractive rather than pretty. When she smiled, her face lit up with an inner radiance that had captivated more than one man's heart. However, Isobel described herself as a confirmed spinster, in love with her computers. She had many male friends, and had been intimate with a number of them, but her relationships never led anywhere. She was, she once told Macnair, adept at building brick walls, lousy when it came to bridges. That was when she had just broken up with her latest boyfriend.

'Good morning, Malcolm.'

'Morning Isobel. Any coffee brewing?' He took the seat opposite her. He knew she was addicted to caffeine and had excellent coffee on the go at all times. Isobel poured two mugs. 'Did you get anything?'

Isobel looked over her shoulder and nodded. 'Yes. So far we have confirmed eight participants from the list we were given.' She handed Macnair his coffee. 'Actually, let me correct that. It's eight families. Extended members are also involved. Of that, there's absolutely no doubt.'

'That's what Owens thought. Nice coffee.'

'Thanks.' She opened a buff file on her desk and glanced at it. 'We have been able to tap all the names we received from MI5. Leo and Gareth have been at it all night.'

'Good work. I'm afraid there's some bad news however. One of our informers in the Pakistani government contacted William Summers. He confirmed the bomb. Plutonium core,' Macnair explained.

'No surprise there.'

Macnair nodded. 'He thinks there are two devices. MI6 is trying to confirm this.'

Isobel had spent too long in front of her computers and too many hours out of the sun to have acquired any sort of tan. Nonetheless, her face still drained further of colour. 'Dear God. *Two* devices!' She could not keep the horror out of her voice. 'Are you sure?'

'Sure, no. Think so, yes. Which is why we have to move and move fast. So what have you got?'

Isobel glanced down at her notes and then discarded them. 'We've spent the night tracking the bank accounts of all eight families and their members. Over thirty million pounds have been transferred in the last three weeks. Between them they own properties around London valued at some ten million pounds and additional properties in Leicester, Bradford, Oldham and three in Glasgow.' Isobel pursed her lips and then added, 'Every one of them has been heavily mortgaged in the last month.'

'Where's the money?'

'It's been transferred out of the country.'

'Why not sell the properties?' Macnair asked, reasonably.

'Quicker to remortgage than to sell.'

The General nodded. That made sense. 'Do we know where the money is?'

'Yes, we do.' Isobel took a sheet of paper from the pile in front of her and handed it over. 'These are the account names and numbers and where they are. The balances are as of eight o'clock this morning.'

'Are these all the accounts? No deposit accounts left in building societies? No children's savings accounts anywhere?'

'Not that we can trace. You have in your hands a total of one hundred and ninety-eight accounts worldwide. You can see the countries they are in, and which banks. Most are with the Bank of Pakistan, but some are with the Bank of America and the Al Rajhi Banking and Investment Corporation in Saudi Arabia.'

'What about credit cards? Any other investments?' Macnair asked.

Isobel shook her head. 'We're still working on it. However, they appear to have divested themselves of all of their investments, from Pakistan Steel to the HSBC

148

Bank. We are still sifting through what information we have, but I would say they have liquidated everything they own.'

'Total amount?'

'It appears to be in the order of at least fifty million pounds.'

'That's a hell of a lot of money.'

'We checked their tax returns as well.'

'And?'

'And they paid less tax than someone on the minimum wage.'

'Why am I not surprised? Are we ready to go?'

Isobel nodded. 'Just say the word and we press the buttons.' Isobel's computer monitor pinged. She looked across the room at Leo who nodded to her. 'We have now tracked down all credit card details by using the information from their bank accounts.'

'Excellent. Take the lot.'

'With pleasure.' She stood up and called out. 'Listen people. Take the lot.'

A cheer went up as hands began to fly over keyboards.

14

As Farid Kasim bowed before the Imam with the rest of the congregation, he kept his face free of emotion. The elation he felt was under control. Strict control. One day, his fellow worshippers would know the truth. Then, he would be honoured in households across the world. Or at least in Islamic households. In the meantime, he must keep his peace. In three days he would leave this foul, accursed land for good. The thought gave him a great deal of comfort.

Noon prayers over, he got to his feet. He left the mosque with his brother, Borat, and two cousins. At forty-four years of age he was deemed the head of his extended family. Pakistani by birth he had lived in Britain since the age of three months. His parents became naturalised British subjects on Farid's seventh birthday. It had been a day of great rejoicing in the Kasim household. His father, Farid Kasim Senior, owned one general store and managed three others. He did not believe in paying his fair share of taxes, having decided that the Queen had enough without any extra from him. Instead, Kasim Senior took cash to Pakistan where he invested in property and built a significant portfolio. He was killed when the light aircraft he was travelling in crashed in the

Punjab. Farid Kasim was just seventeen years old. At the time of his death, Kasim Senior was by anyone's standards, a wealthy man.

The son did not inherit the father's business acumen, but he did inherit his aversion to paying tax. It was a tradition he kept up all his life. Embracing fundamentalist Islam was as natural as breathing to Farid Kasim. To his way of thinking, women were evidently inferior to men. Wasn't this proven by Allah once a month when women bled? So it showed in the Qur'an, along with many other examples of man's superiority. The fact that Kasim had never read the Qur'an, nor made any attempt to understand what was written there, was immaterial. So spoke the mullahs! He followed as closely as he could what he was taught. Hence he had four wives. One he had married in Britain, the other three he had married under the auspices of Islam, in remote areas of Pakistan's hinterland. The three women he had brought back to England and installed in a house near to his number one wife's house. It was an arrangement all four woman professed to be in agreement with, since it was the will of Allah.

Thanks to the good life he had enjoyed, Kasim was running to fat. His round face was hidden beneath a bushy beard, his lack of stature hidden by cleverly designed shoes that added to his height.

Stepping out of the mosque he said to Borat, 'I'll get some money from the machine.' He left his brother and two cousins standing together.

Kasim took his credit card from his pocket and inserted it in the hole-in-the-wall, entered his PIN and pressed the button to withdraw cash. He elected for £500. At that moment he had the shock of his life. Instead of giving him the money, the machine proclaimed it was a stolen card

151

and shut down. Kasim stood staring at the closed shutter with his mouth agape.

'What, by the holy name of the Prophet, peace be upon him, is happening?' His brow was dark with rage. 'What is the meaning of this?'

'Maybe you did not pay your bill,' said one of his cousins, who immediately regretted saying anything when Kasim turned his wrath on him.

'Fool! Of course I paid my bill. Besides, the limit of credit on that card is twenty thousand pounds! I have never been over one thousand pounds. We will see about this.'

The machine was embedded in a wall of Barclays Bank. 'Wait here,' he said to the other three, and stalked in and marched to the front of the queue.

'I demand to see the manager,' he said in a loud voice to the teller, who was serving an elderly lady. 'Here, you! I demand to see the manager.'

'If you don't mind, sir, there is a queue. If you wait, I will check and see if the manager is available.'

The calm, reasonable tone used by the teller only infuriated Kasim more. 'I demand to see him right now.'

'Wait your turn,' said the elderly lady standing in front of the window. 'Get back in line.'

In Kasim's world women did as they were told. On top of his card being taken it was too much for a man like him. 'How dare you speak to me, you old . . .old . . .' He was spluttering with rage.

'Less of the old, young man,' said the elegant lady, with a gleam of anger in her eyes. 'Now get back in line.'

Instead of doing as he was told, Kasim turned to the teller yet again. 'You there, get the manager immediately.' He then made a serious error. He barged into the woman with his shoulder, causing her to stagger sideways to stay on her feet. This was the last straw. At eighty-two years of age, Hazel Edmunds had a commanding presence. Highly intelligent, very active in her community, she had the spirit and drive of a person half her age. When she had left her house that morning the clouds had threatened rain and so she had taken her umbrella with her. Not for her a dainty, woman's bit of rubbish as she liked to say, but a proper man's black umbrella. She didn't hesitate. She raised it to shoulder height and smacked Kasim across the back of his legs, hard. Kasim yelled out in pain and shock. She raised the umbrella again and swung hard, this time connecting with Kasim's left shin.

'Stop it, you old cow,' Kasim screamed. He stepped towards Hazel and as the umbrella came down again he snatched it from her hands. In his blind anger and hatred, Kasim raised the umbrella to strike her across the face. At that moment, a man in the queue stepped forward, grabbed Kasim's arm and bent it back, forcing him to drop the umbrella.

'Listen, you don't strike a woman. Not in this country. Now get the hell out of here.' He twisted Kasim around, placed his foot on his backside and pushed hard, sending the Pakistani stumbling across the room.

The other members making up the long queue had finally woken up to what was happening and cheered. To cries of, 'Get out!' and 'Don't you dare hit a woman!' Kasim slunk out of the door, hatred in his heart.

'Oh, my,' said Hazel, 'I feel quite faint.'

'Well done, love,' said the man who had helped her. 'If I wasn't happily married I'd ask you out.'

Hazel smiled coquettishly, the sparkle in her eyes reinforcing her youthful look.

Farid Kasim went storming along the road, barging into

people, ignoring pleas to watch where he was going. The others followed him. He crashed through the front door of the house he lived in with his legitimate wife and stalked into the living room. Luckily for her, she was over at the other house, enjoying the company of the three women she considered her sisters.

Kasim paced back and forth, venting his anger. 'Bastards! I'll show them!'

'Farid, control yourself,' said his brother, in a placating voice. 'We will show them. Soon. All of them. When the bomb goes off . . .'

'Shut up! Have I not told you before to watch what you say? This house could easily be bugged.'

Keeping his own anger under control, his brother nodded wearily. He was fed up with hearing the same rubbish. If the place was bugged, they would have been arrested long ago. What he had no way of knowing was that microphones had been installed within the previous twenty-four hours. No Court order had been obtained. There was not going to be a trial of any description. The gloves were off. The stakes were too high.

Kasim's phone rang. He grabbed it. In a petulant voice he said, 'Who is this? What do you want?'

'Mr. Kasim? Mr. Farid Kasim?' The voice was oily, as only a banker's can be.

'Yes! What is it?'

'This is the HSBC. I regret to inform you that you are well over your overdraft limit on your account.'

'What? That's impossible!'

'No, I am afraid it is the case. I have personally double-checked the figures after the computer flagged you as, hem,' the voice paused with a gentle cough, 'a problem account.'

'What? What did you say? Who do you think you're

talking to?' Kasim spluttered with rage. 'I shall have your job for this. I shall . . .'

He got no further as this time the oily voice turned to steel. Again, as only a banker's can. 'Mr. Kasim, I do not make mistakes. The figures have been checked and double-checked. I insist that you regularise the situation immediately. Good day, Mr. Kasim.'

Hearing the dialling tone, Kasim stood there with a dazed look on his face.

'Who was that?' asked his brother.

'That was the bank,' Kasim said in a strangled whisper. 'The bank. They say I am overdrawn. That I owe them money.'

'You do. That was part of the plan.'

'Yes, but not like this!' He turned on his brother. 'We must ensure we are squeaky clean before we leave. That way there can be no comebacks. No trail. No matter what happens, no matter what damage we cause, the British will hunt for us. Make no mistake about it. They are not a forgiving race. I want to live out my life without looking over my shoulder all the time. I do not want to spend my days in a cave like bin Laden.'

'Isn't it a bit late for that Farid? You cannot have the glory without the suffering.' His brother spoke in a portentous manner.

'I can! I will! Now leave me to . . .' He got no further. The phone rang again. He snatched it. 'Yes?'

He listened for a few moments and then interrupted the woman's voice. 'There is a mistake, I tell you. I will deal with it shortly.'

'Mr. Kasim, I have to inform you that your account has been suspended. Please do your utmost to correct the situation. To regularise your position.'

That word again! Was it part of bank-speak these people were taught? He slammed the receiver down. Fear enfolded his heart in its icy grip. Again the phone rang and he looked at it with trepidation. It rang and rang. Finally, he picked it up and said tentatively, 'Hullo?' His voice was hardly more than a whisper.

'Mr. Kasim? Mr. Farid Kasim?'

'Yes. Yes. Who is this?'

'This is Emirates Airlines. I am sorry to inform you that the payment using your American Express card for your tickets has been cancelled.'

'Cancelled? What do you mean?'

'The original authorisation has been cancelled. I know it is very unusual but it has happened in your case. I am very sorry.' What he was apologising for was impossible to tell. 'Do you have an alternative method? A different card perhaps?'

'No! Yes! Wait!' Panic was clouding his brain, making it difficult for him to think coherently. 'Yes, I . . . I have a Visa card. Hold on a moment.' He dug in his jacket pocket, withdrew his wallet, took out his card and said, 'Here. Use this number.'

'Thank you Mr Kasim. Please wait while the card goes through.' A few seconds later and the voice came back, 'I am sorry, sir. But that card has been rejected as well.'

'It . . . It's impossible, I tell you.'

'Be that as it may, sir, I have no alternative but to cancel your tickets.'

'You cannot! You must not!' But there was no one there. As he put down the receiver, shock tinged with bewilderment was overshadowed by fear.

The phone rang yet again. He stood frozen, looking at it. His brother picked it up.

'Yes?'

'Is that Mr. Kasim?' The enquiring voice didn't specify which one and so he replied, 'Yes. Can I help?'

'This is the Halifax Bank. We seem to have found a most unusual anomaly. Most unusual.' The voice was urbane, educated, male. 'You appear to have a mortgage against your property that is double the property value. How on earth this has come about I can't tell.'

'What do you mean?' Borat Kasim asked, more perplexed than anything.

'I don't know how to explain it. When I arrived this morning and logged on to my computer, a message came up telling me that the value of your property was half the mortgage and to check it immediately. I have pulled the file and it appears to be the situation. I was wondering if you would like to come to my office so we can sort the matter out? I am sure there is some simple explanation, though for the life of me I cannot see it.'

'Can I come next week?' He was stalling for time. He hoped to be in Pakistan before the end of the week along with his brother.

'I am sorry, Mr. Kasim, perhaps I didn't make myself clear. Unless you come in and explain matters to my satisfaction then I shall have no option but to call in the police. With a good lawyer, you will no doubt get bail and be released within hours. Naturally, we shall insist that your passport be confiscated.' Then, the voice added, for good measure, 'both of them.'

Now it was Borat Kasim's turn to panic. He smashed the receiver back into its cradle and stood looking down at it as though he expected it to rise up and bite him at any moment. The other three had no idea what had been said but they recognised the horror on Borat's face. Suddenly heavy knocking on the door reverberated throughout the house.

'Don't answer it,' said Farid Kasim, fear gripping him. When in control, he was calmness itself. When anything didn't go his way, panic was always just below the surface. The knocking became heavier.

'Mr. Kasim! Mr. Kasim! Open up. I have a writ which I must serve. Open up, I say. We know you're in there! Don't make me come back with the police.'

'What shall we do?' Borat Kasim whispered.

'Don't answer it!' said one of the cousins. 'They will go away. Then we can leave. We must get away.'

'And go where?' the other cousin asked.

'We can get our money. We can travel. We can take the car and go to Dover. Get on a ferry. Go to France.'

Farid Kasim's attention was drawn to something happening outside. He moved to the window. 'What . . . What is going on?' A vehicle pick-up truck was lifting his Volvo onto its back. 'What is the meaning of this?'

'My car is being taken also,' said one of the cousins, horror in his voice.

There was more knocking on the door. 'We'll be back, *Mr.* Kasim.' The ironic emphasis on the 'mister' was not missed by the men in the house.

Farid Kasim sank onto a sofa, leaned forward and put his face in his hands. His younger brother, himself on the verge of panic, watched Farid with contempt etched on his face. The man he had looked up to all his life, his hero, was falling apart.

'I am leaving,' said his cousin.

'So am I,' said the other one. 'I must get to the bank. Get some money. Get my passport.'

They hurried to the front door. One looked over his

shoulder and said, 'I will phone you when I know what is happening.'

The two men rushed out.

'What does it all mean?' Borat asked in a bleak whisper.

'I do not know.' Kasim paused for a moment and then said 'We must get away. And quickly. Ring for a taxi.'

Borat picked up the receiver and held it to his ear. He was greeted with silence. He juggled the buttons on the top of the phone before smashing the receiver down in frustration. 'It has been disconnected.'

'Then use your mobile, moron,' his older brother snarled at him.

Reaching into his pocket he looked at the small screen. 'It says unobtainable.' There was defeat in his voice.

'Rubbish!' Farid Kasim took out his own mobile and looked at the screen. It showed the same message. 'I . . . I don't understand. What is happening?'

The brothers looked at each other in complete horror. At that moment the house phone rang. The noise startled them both. How could it be? It rang and rang. Finally, Farid Kasim reached out a tentative hand and lifted the receiver.

Nervously he said, 'Hu . . . Hullo?'

'Ah, Mr. Kasim, I trust you are well.' The voice was bonhomie itself with an American twang to it.

'Who . . . Who is this?'

'I, Mr. Kasim, am your worst nightmare,' said Hiram B. Walsh. 'Outside your front door is a Transit van with its side doors open. Please walk out to the van and get inside.'

'Why . . . Why should I?'

'Because I said so. And it isn't "I", it is "we". We want your brother as well.'

'Why should we? Are we under arrest? If we are, where

are the police? I demand to see a policeman. A warrant.' The last two words were said in a shriek, as hysteria took hold.

'Did you think for one second that you would detonate a plutonium-based bomb on British soil with impunity? We have been on to you from the very start. All of your co-conspirators are under arrest. Even as we speak, men are being rounded up in Pakistan. Those that are lucky will be shot. Others are being held for interrogation. Now come out with your hands clear so that we can see them and get into the vehicle.'

In a panic, he slammed the receiver back down. He said to his brother, in a strangled voice, 'They know! They know about the bomb.'

'It is not possible. You said it would be easy. That they would never know. What have you done, you fool? What about Fisal? Does he know? Has he been arrested?'

Farid Kasim was not a brave man. He was a bully and a coward. The events of the past few hours had left him numb, unable to think clearly. In a daze, he walked towards the front door, opened it and stumbled out, his brother at his heels.

When they climbed into the van they were thrown onto the floor, their arms twisted painfully behind their backs, and handcuffed. The door was slammed shut.

'Welcome,' said Colonel Hiram Walsh, 'to hell.'

15

Isobel, Gareth and Leo spent what should have been an enjoyable twenty-four hours destroying the financial credibility of eight different extended families. The pleasure was missing because of the dire consequences of failure. What they were doing was a challenge that required all their acumen and imagination. One idea led to another; one line of attack to a second and a third. It was evident that the people they were targeting were up to their collective necks in Islamic fundamentalism.

'How on earth,' asked Leo, taking off his glasses and rubbing his weary eyes, 'did these people get away with it for so long?'

Gareth looked up from his monitor. Where Leo was short and fat, and forever on a diet, Gareth was tall and skinny, even weedy-looking. They were the best of friends with one thing in common. Both men had superb brains when it came to computers. Although neither was ambitious, they had half-a-dozen patents in the computer industry that earned each of them more in a month than their salaries paid in a year. Isobel managed their money for them, fussing over them like a mother hen. It was she who made their investments and handled their tax returns. To show their appreciation, the two men showered her with gifts.

She was still on cloud nine after being given the keys to a new Mercedes sports car she happened to admire in a magazine recently. Naturally, she had scolded them both for being so extravagant but secretly, she was as pleased as punch. She alone knew how much her two boys were worth, but they didn't. They were obsessed with their computers. Invading other systems either for information or to disrupt the enemy was what they loved doing.

'I've issued repossession orders on all their properties. That's an amazing fifty-seven across the country,' said Leo.

'Any joy with the Bank of Pakistan?' Isobel asked Gareth.

Gareth chuckled and rubbed his hands. 'Oh boy, yes. As of two minutes ago. Transfers are taking place even as we speak. Where there are overdraft facilities I'm going to the maximum. Hullo,' he suddenly sat bolt upright in his chair and stared at the screen for a few moments. 'Well, well, well. It seems the Bank of Pakistan does not have quite the same level of control that Western banks have. All the accounts are going over their overdraft limits.' A few more seconds passed. 'And by some considerable amount, I can tell you.'

'Good. Only don't go too far,' Isobel warned him.

'Why not?' Gareth asked.

'We don't want the bank investigating, looking for the money.'

Leo snorted with derision. 'Fat chance. They'll never find the money Isobel. They won't be able to begin to trace it and they certainly won't find us at the end of the food chain. Gareth and I have been working on this programme for months. We've just been waiting for a chance to use it.'

'Did you create it with anything in mind? Knowing you two I'd be surprised if you didn't.'

'We were going to suggest attacking Mugabe's billions and redirecting the money back to ordinary Zimbabweans.'

Isobel smiled. 'I like that idea. And I am sure the General will also. Once this is over we might suggest it. That should be a very satisfying project. In the meantime, let's continue to make life uncomfortable for these people.'

*   *   *   *   *

President Shahid Tahir of Pakistan was pacing across his office. 'What do you mean, one of our submarines is missing?'

'Just that, sir,' replied Admiral Tariq Kamal Hassan, Chief of Naval Staff for the Pakistani Navy.

'Do you mean it has had an accident? Been in a collision? Blown up? *What*?'

'We don't know, sir. We lost contact three days ago.'

'Three days ago?' The President stopped pacing and looked at the other man. 'Why wasn't I told earlier?'

'Sir, we have procedures in place. The submarine sends twenty-four hourly situation reports which include their position, course and speed. We don't worry if we miss one. We are perturbed if we miss a second and we hit the panic button if we don't receive a third. That signal was due three hours ago.'

'I see. So what do we do?' Tahir asked.

'I have instigated a full air-sea rescue, in accordance with Standing Orders.'

'Sit down, Tariq. There's something else, isn't there?'

The Admiral nodded. 'Yes, Shahid, there is.' Both men went back a long way and once the formalities were over, they relaxed into being the friends they were.

'What is it?'

'I had my aide, Captain Iftikhar Mirza pull the files of the crew. There are thirty-six ratings and five officers. The sub is the PNS/M *Khalid*, S137. It's an Agosta 90B. A French diesel attack-boat. Very reliable. We wanted to be ready in case we needed to inform the next-of-kin. What he found was highly disturbing.'

'Oh? In what way?' Tahir asked.

'As you know, our armed forces are riddled with fundamentalists. We keep an eye on them and do our best to keep them apart. In our case on different ships. Going through the files, Captain Mirza noticed a number of them had been identified as being amongst the more extremist elements we have serving. So he dug further. We have the same method of crew change as the British Royal Navy. We no longer change the whole crew at one time but employ trickle drafting, which means the crew changes over a period of time. For the last six months, every member of the previous crew has been replaced with a fundamentalist. A known radical.'

'What about the Captain?'

'A Commander Mohammad Anwer.'

'I know the name from somewhere.'

'He's the son of Sayyid Anwer, the industrialist.'

'*That* Anwer. He's worth about half a billion dollars, or so they say.'

'So I understand. Which is why we could not prevent his son getting command. This is in spite of the fact that we know him to be fundamentalist in the extreme.'

'Too much influence?' the President asked wearily.

'Far too much.'

'So how many of the crew are in the same category?'

'All of them.'

'What can they do?' A note of hysteria was creeping

into Tahir's voice as the enormity of the problem became clearer. 'Attack someone? Attack some shipping? What?'

Admiral Hassan shrugged. 'We have no way of telling. All I can say is that I don't like the way things are one little bit. What they could lead to.'

'How could this have been allowed to happen?'

'The officer responsible for the drafting of these men has disappeared.'

It was a simple and logical explanation.

'We may be reading the signals all wrong. It could be something simple, like loss of communications or an accident.'

'You don't believe that, do you?' President Tahir asked.

The Admiral shook his head. 'Not for one moment.'

*   *   *   *   *

'I demand to see my solicitor,' said Farid Kasim.

He was sitting in a room three metres square by three metres high. There were no windows and only one door. The walls were painted green. Tucked away in a corner of the base, with highly effective sound-proofing, it made an ideal interrogation complex. This was the first time it had ever been used. Sitting opposite him was Hiram Walsh of Delta and Clive Owens from MI5.

'Did you not hear me?' Kasim asked as he leaned forward, doing his best to generate anger instead of the fear he really felt, his mouth turned down in an ugly sneer. 'If you do not get me my solicitor it will be the worse for you.'

At times like this it was important to keep the person under interrogation completely off-balance. Owens and Walsh had both spent the last few minutes perusing a file that Isobel had e-mailed to them. Walsh looked up at Kasim, who was now leaning even further across the table, and nodded. Casually he backhanded Kasim across the face, knocking him into a corner of the room.

'What! What!' Tears formed in the Pakistani's eyes.

'You have ten seconds to get back onto your chair,' said Walsh, evenly. He knew the effect he was having.

This was unlike anything Kasim had ever experienced in his life. When he was in the van he had envisaged being arrested and then charged and later, brought before the courts. He would hear evidence brought against him at a trial conducted before his peers, or at least the British equivalent of his peers. Prison was one thing. This was something entirely different.

From somewhere Kasim found the courage to say, 'You cannot do this. I demand my rights. My human rights!'

He got no further as Walsh stood up and stepped around the table. He leaned down, grabbed hold of Kasim by his lapels and lifted him effortlessly to his feet. As he smacked Kasim against the nearest wall with a resounding crash, he kneed him between the legs, hard. Kasim went a deep purple colour and would have collapsed if Walsh hadn't been holding him up.

'Now listen to me. We know about the dirty bomb. We know about your part in it. We know all about the different families who have been helping you. So let me make one thing absolutely clear. There will be no solicitor. No trial. No way out. You will die in this room.' While he was speaking, Walsh shoved Kasim back into the chair and began using leather straps to tie Kasim's arms to the armrests.

'What are you doing!' Kasim screamed.

Owens continued in a friendly, conversational voice.

166

'We are going to inject you with a truth drug. You will tell us all you know. You will be insane by the end of the process, but we will learn all that we need to. We will do the same to your brother and your cousins. Incidentally, we've been looking for one of them, Shaikh Nabhani, for some time. We know he was the contact between the crew of the coaster *L'Escargot* which had been en route to France, Dieppe to be precise. I'm going to enjoy watching him answer questions.' Drip-feeding information to someone under interrogation was another good softening-up process. How much did they know?

There was no response as Kasim looked at Owens with horror and fear chasing themselves across his face. 'You can't do this,' he whispered.

'We can and we will,' said Walsh.

At that moment Kasim lost control of his bladder and soiled his trousers.

'Clive, switch on the intercom.'

Owens pressed a button on the black box on the table. Suddenly the air was rent apart with an agonising scream and a voice begging someone to stop. Kasim recognised his brother. Walsh nodded at Owens who cut off the sound of sobbing.

'That was your brother, in case you didn't recognise him,' Walsh said. Then he lied. 'He was having one of his testicles cut off with a blunt knife. A Swiss army knife, if you're interested. The same will be happening to your two cousins. Each one of them is going to die a truly horrible death.'

'What . . . What about me?' Kasim croaked.

'Me, me, me. That's all you can think about.' Walsh spoke in a false, jovial voice. The revulsion he was feeling about what they were doing didn't show as he dropped

167

Kasim back into his chair and returned to his own side of the table. Nobody had used a knife on any of the prisoners. The mere threat was sufficient to cause the screams. Especially when a knife-blade was flicked against a naked scrotum.

A thought suddenly occurred to Kasim. 'If you have a truth drug, why are you doing this?'

'That's a very good question,' Walsh replied, as though he was taking part in a civilised discussion. 'The fact is, SSM works better when the recipient – which is you, in this case – is in pain. We even know why that is. You see, if you are in pain – excruciating pain – the drug numbs it. The brain likes that. It responds. It knows that to stop the pain you need to answer our questions. Naturally, the drug itself is also at work. It's a sort of combined effort, you might say. Very often we'll shoot somebody in the elbow or knee. But here,' he shrugged and looked around the room, 'too much blood really. Too much mess.'

Owens leaned forward, 'Where is the dirty bomb coming into Britain?'

Kasim mustered his last shred of courage. 'I do not know what you are talking about.'

'Then I shall explain. We know all about the *Union of Sark*.' He looked at his watch. 'In less than six hours, it will be attacked. If we find the device on board, all well and good. If we don't . . .' he left the statement hanging. 'Believe me when I tell you that we will track down every member of your family. By the time we are finished with them, they will curse your name. If you think for one moment we are going to let you get away with killing thousands of people, then think again. We know the devastation that will be caused if this dirty bomb explodes anywhere in Britain or Europe. The pollution alone will be horrendous. I am not sitting here pretending anything else. We will have our revenge. You are Pakistani. We will wipe Pakistan off the face of the earth. Before we do, we will tell the world why. You see, when there is nothing left, you leave us no choice. Your name and the name of all your co-conspirators will be vilified through the ages.'

'You cannot . . .' Kasim's voice was hoarse.

Walsh leaned forward and hit the desk hard with the palm of his hand. Kasim flinched. 'Don't tell me what I can and cannot do!' he thundered. 'No one knows you are here! No one! Do you understand me? We can do with you as we like.' He nodded to Clive who pressed the button on the black box.

A voice laden with anguish was heard to say, 'I tell you, I do not know. Only Farid knows. You must ask him. Please. Please!' The voice broke down into strangled sobs.

'So only you know. You will tell us,' said Clive Owens, leaning forward in his chair while Walsh leaned back and crossed his legs. Owens slapped Kasim hard across the side of his face. Kasim's head whipped to one side, though he retained his seat. The shock was intense and tears welled up, rolling down his cheeks.

'You pathetic coward,' sneered Owens. 'Look at you, crying like a baby.' He pointed over his shoulder. 'See that camera?'

For the first time, Kasim noticed the small camera in the top left-hand corner of the room, pointing at his face. 'The world will see you blubbering. Like my colleague here said, we will vilify your name and that of your family to the ends of the earth.'

From somewhere, Kasim found the strength to say, 'Human rights activists . . .'

He got no further as Walsh smacked him across the side

of the face to shut him up. 'That's what we think of human rights activists. And if you think they will raise their sanctimonious, pious heads after a dirty bomb has exploded you can think again. There's a line and you people have crossed it. I have seen the *Sijjin* and your name is on it for what you intend doing.'

The *Sijjin* was a scroll on which was written the names of those who would be going to hell.

The two men watched as Kasim collapsed in on himself. It was an incredible sight. Not only did he appear to shrink down within his body, but the very essence of the man appeared to disintegrate. He began blubbing, his shoulders shaking.

Walsh and Owens exchanged looks. Walsh shrugged and said, 'Let's see if he'll answer any questions.'

'What is your name?'

'Farid Kasim,' was the whispered and hesitant reply.

'Where do you live? What do you do for a living?'

The questions were answered without prompting.

Owens said quietly to Walsh, 'I've heard of this, although I have never seen it before now. It's a complete mental collapse. Didn't the CIA write a paper on it?'

'Actually,' said Walsh, frowning, 'it was the KGB. The CIA got access to the papers when some defector or other crossed over back in the seventies. The Agency did some more work on it, but what exactly, I don't recall.'

Owens snapped his fingers. 'That's right. Am I right in saying there's no return? That he'll enter a vegetative state that can last for the rest of his life?'

'I don't know.' The Colonel looked uneasy. 'Will his mind deteriorate to such a level that he's no use to us? That he won't remember anything?'

Owens shook his head. 'I can't remember. Get to the

important questions. Skip all this background crap.'

Half an hour later, Owens and Walsh were appalled but satisfied by what they had learned. Kasim had taken a turn for the worse. Up until that point he had been lucid, although his answers had become more rambling. Now, as if the switch had been twisted further, he spoke gibberish. It didn't take them long to realise that it wasn't an act. Kasim had gone over the edge into madness. Whether his insanity was permanent or temporary there was no way of knowing or telling. However, they did see an advantage. All four of the prisoners were placed in a cell together. The other three watched and listened to Farid in total horror and fear. It took only minutes for them to demand to speak to someone, anyone. To tell them every last thing that they knew, rather than risk insanity.

16

Macnair couldn't keep the anger out of his voice. 'The bastards. The utter bastards.'

'It may not be true,' said William Summers. The Director General of MI6 spoke more in hope than expectation.

Macnair's look summed up the feelings of the four men. Walsh poured whiskies while they each helped themselves to ice and soda water.

'What do we do now?' Walsh asked.

'I've spoken to Nick. We've confirmed the presence of the dirty bomb on the *Union of Sark*. I've emphasised there's to be no mercy. We now know there is definitely a second device and that it's being brought overland. We have no details yet. We don't know where it is or who is carrying it. However,' Macnair took a mouthful of whisky, getting his anger under control, 'we are now sure it's coming. We also know – and okay, okay, it's a statement of the obvious – that *someone* knows the details. We need to find that someone. We do whatever it takes. Agreed?' He looked enquiringly at the other three men. They each nodded unhesitatingly.

'Good. William, can you bring in anybody to help? Senior people who won't hesitate to do whatever it takes. We'll second them to TIFAT, working under my rules.'

Summers smiled. 'Certainly. I should think they'll be delighted.'

'And you, Clive?'

'Same here,' Owens said.

'So we'll work to the letter of TIFAT's mandate and brief.'

'The letter?' Summers queried.

'Our interpretation of it. We will act without permission and definitely without oversight. We will lift as many people as we see fit if we think they are involved with the terrorists. If we make a mistake, then so be it. Tough. It will be an honest one.'

Macnair stood up and walked over to the sideboard to refresh his glass. 'I'll arrange to get rid of the bodies. There are going to be a hell of a lot more and we don't want them cluttering the place up.' He looked out of the window at the bridges over the Forth. From there he had a clear view of both North and South Queensferry. The four prisoners had died from a painless poison added to their food. Compared to the men, women and children caught in the blast and aftermath of a dirty bomb, they were lucky. Very lucky.

* * * * *

Hunter stood on the bridge wing in the early evening and watched the Hercules C130J circle over the yacht. The rear ramp was open and pallets of equipment were sliding out as parachutes were blossoming overhead. After only a few short minutes he saw the TIFAT operatives tumbling through the air. They opened arms and legs and stabilised facedown. It was known as the frog position. They each opened their parachutes at the last second. It meant that they were in the air for the minimum length of time, and therefore were targets for the shortest period. And although there was nobody there to shoot at them, it was good practice. Clements took the speedboat out to pick up the men and their equipment. The men climbed into the boat while the gear was towed, supported by automatic inflation units. Badonovitch and Tanner helped to haul everyone and everything onto the yacht. It didn't take long. The Hercules circled overhead, did a wing-wag and was soon heading back to Oman for refuelling.

'Everything all right?' Hunter greeted David Hughes.

'Yes, sir. Everyone's just sorting out their pits,' replied the SAS Sergeant. The little Welshman was one of the toughest men Hunter had ever known. He had been due to return to his regiment in Hereford the previous month but had requested an extension to his tour with TIFAT. Macnair had ensured that he got it.

At that moment Peter Weir arrived. Weir was TIFAT's sniper, able to put ten shots out of ten into the centre of a target five centimetres in diameter at one thousand metres. Most people couldn't even see the target at that range. When asked, Weir just said it was instinct. What he didn't say was that his hands were rock steady and that he didn't drink alcohol, to ensure they stayed that way.

'Some boat, boss,' Weir said as he greeted Hunter. 'It must remind you of the family yacht.'

Hunter grinned, knowing the banter was well-intentioned. They all knew about his connection to the Griffiths family, though he never paraded his personal wealth in front of the team. He ensured he lived – more or less – within his military salary. Even his car – his pride and joy – was an old MGB convertible, though sadly on its last legs.

'It's a bit cramped, when all's said and done, but it'll do for you lot. We're having a briefing in the main saloon in an hour. There's a hell of a lot to cover. Hopefully, we'll link up with the General.'

'What a lousy journey. We've been travelling non-stop for nearly thirty-six hours,' David Hughes said. 'It's been one delay after another. We've been told what's going down but we don't have any details. Any more about the bloody bomb?'

'It's been confirmed that there's one on the ship we're after. It's not a nuke in the normal sense. It's plastic explosive with a plutonium core.'

'A dirty bomb,' Weir said softly, 'the bastards.'

Hunter added, 'we also know that a second bomb is on its way but we've no idea where it is, who has it and when it's due.' He changed the subject abruptly. 'Food's ready in the galley.'

'Great. I'll tell the lads. The crabfats aren't exactly known for their cuisine.' Weir spoke disparagingly about the RAF who had flown them out from Britain.

Less than an hour later, with the yacht on cruise control, the team congregated in the main saloon. General Macnair had just joined the meeting using a live video link.

'We've been misinformed,' he began, 'we're sure the bomb isn't on the ship yet.'

The room erupted in pandemonium, everyone speaking at the same time. Questions followed comments followed curses. When order was restored, Hunter asked, 'Sir, you said yet.'

'Their own people believed it had been delivered. We think it would have been there if they had stuck to their timetable. But, as we know all too well, the simplest things can foul up an operation and that's what's happened in this case. MI6 have confirmed some information that had come our way.' He didn't explain that MI5 and MI6 personnel were now at Rosyth and a lot more information was being confirmed or discarded. 'We are now sure the device will be delivered to the ship tomorrow at dawn.'

'Sir, how can we be sure?' Clements asked.

'A series of signal intercepts that originated with the ship. At first, they didn't make any sense. It was Isobel who spotted the significance. Or suggested it. It's a submarine. It looks like it's going to rendezvous with the *Union of Sark* to hand over the device just before dawn.'

'I take it,' said Hunter, 'that it's a Pakistani submarine?'

'Correct.'

'How is that possible?' Hunter frowned.

'The Pakistani navy has an air-sea rescue operation in full swing. They've lost Pakistan Naval Submarine *Khalid*.'

'Interesting.'

'It gets more so,' said Macnair. 'We have just learned that the CO is one Commander Mohammad Anwer.'

'How did we find that out?', Nick asked.

'His father is a very rich and influential man by the name of Sayyid Anwer. He's raising holy hell for the submarine to be found.'

'Not surprising, but so what?'

'Isobel fed Commander Anwer's details through Cuthbert and came up with some interesting information. In spite of his father doing everything in his power to keep his son away from the Muslim fundamentalists, he appears to have failed. The only reason he is still in the navy is because of his father's contacts. Isobel suspects his father wanted him to stay there to reduce the influence of the radicals on him but she has since come to a different conclusion. She has no proof, mind you, but she thinks the son stayed so that one day he would be able to use his position in a military manner.'

'Do you think that likely?'

'Who can tell. We know these people think and plan long-term, so yes, it's more than possible.'

'Based on what's happening, it does make sense.'

'There's more. We asked our contact in the Pakistani High Command if he knew anything about the rescue operation and he told us an interesting fact. It seems the whole crew are Islamic fundamentalists to their fingertips.'

'Is he sure?'

'As sure as he can be. It's got their government in an uproar.'

'In what way, sir?'

'Potential military action on behalf of the Jihadists. It could cause enormous problems. Right now they're debating if it's a rescue operation or a find and sink attack.'

'What about the second bomb? Any word?', Hunter continued.

'Nothing as yet.'

'What do you want us to do tomorrow?', Hunter asked.

'The *Union of Sark* is still ploughing a square furrow. We've looked at various options and come up with one we believe will work.' General Macnair spent the next few minutes outlining the operation. His audience remained silent, rapt in their attention. It was audacious as well as clever. And though there was some risk, it was manageable. Probably.

Once the video conference was over, the men dispersed. Most of them went to their bunks to snatch some sleep, while a few went to check on their equipment.

Sitting on the bridge, mulling things over, Hunter briefly thought about writing a just-in-case letter to Ruth, but then decided against it. Yet again, he told himself that life had moved on for both of them. Which was the same conclusion he had come to on Cyprus when this whole blessed thing had kicked off. His last will and testament was in order and there was nothing to write to his parents about. They understood the concept of duty. Hunter stood up and stretched. This was ludicrous. Compared to other operations he had been on, this one was hardly that dangerous. The planning was meticulous, the information pretty exact but there was, without doubt, still plenty of room for error. There always was. It was nothing new. So why the gloomy thoughts? Lack of sleep, he decided. Raising binoculars to his eyes he swept the sea around him. Although they were transiting a very busy stretch of water, there was not another vessel in sight. From this height above sea level he could see about seven miles to the horizon where the shipping lanes were to be found and where the ships were ploughing through the calm waters. A glance at the radar showed two vessels at twelve miles, passing down the port side. If it wasn't for the task ahead then this would be an ideal cruise Hunter thought. His grin was mirthless. Apart from the fact there were no women on board.

An hour later TIFAT informed them that their target's course and speed had altered. The *Union of Sark* was now heading for a rendezvous point which Hunter plotted on a chart. Adjustments were made to the yacht's course and speed to intercept. More signals were received by the *Union of Sark*. Precise instructions were given and acknowledged.

'Nick, the Pakistani government have issued a find and

sink order for the submarine. It's pretty drastic, but apparently they see no other way of stopping them,' General Macnair explained during their next conversation.

'I'm not surprised. If they are intending to create chaos a submarine is a damned good weapon to have.'

Egg sandwiches and coffee were served all round. They ate in gloomy silence.

'I suppose,' said Lieutenant Douglas Napier, Royal Marines, Special Boats Service and day one at TIFAT, 'it's only to be expected. Having a dirty bomb around isn't exactly conducive to a relaxed atmosphere.'

The others nodded. If the operation went as planned, they'd end up with the bomb. A daunting prospect to say the least.

Hunter tried to change the mood. 'Everyone happy about what we're going to do?'

'Sure, boss,' said Badonovitch. 'Although I've never taken out a submarine before.' He looked pensive. 'It'll be an interesting operation.'

17

They were dressed in wetsuits, which were more comfortable than drysuits and gave more freedom of movement. The nylon line had been prepared and a small apple-float placed halfway along it. Their weapons and the oxygen rebreather sets had been checked and double-checked. They were ready to go.

Four teams of two, three for the ship and one for the submarine – at least initially.

Hunter, teamed with Badonovitch, stood looking at the radar screen.

'There she is, less than five miles away and exactly on track. Fishing lights on?'

'Affirmative,' said Clements. By displaying fishing lights they hoped to confuse the enemy into thinking they were a trawler. It would account for their slow speed.

'Is the submersible ready?'

'Yes, boss. Whenever we are,' said Badonovitch.

'Okay, let's get into the water then the yacht can move out of the way. We don't want to make the ship alter course.' He glanced at his watch. 'Fifty minutes to sunrise. Just about perfect.'

The other teams were Josh Clements and Peter Weir, Doug Tanner and Don Masters, and finally, Sam Macready and Captain Simon Henri. Macready was another day one man from the same outfit as Napier. He specialised in using plastic explosives, small surface craft and diving. Henri was French and had come from the French Legion. He was new to the team and was still making an impression. So far, from all Hunter had seen, the impression had been highly favourable. He was, without doubt, one of their most experienced parachutists. The men slid into the water, buddied up and checked each other's diving sets for leaks. All clear, they were handed down various pieces of equipment. Their weapons were either at their waists, strapped to their legs, or across their backs.

Hunter and Badonovitch took the ten metres of one inch, extra flexible steel wire rope (EFSWR) and inflated the three buoys, one at each end and one in the middle. The wire hung heavily in the water, just below the surface. The last item passed down to them was the chariot. Hunter and Badonovitch climbed onto the two seats, Hunter in front at the controls. The teams strung out behind holding onto a nylon rope. Communications were checked and the yacht moved away under the command of Douglas Napier ably assisted by David Hughes, the Welsh SAS Sergeant.

'Dolphin One, this is Marina, the coaster is still on a steady course, speed four knots. Over,' Hughes transmitted. Each team had a call-sign of Dolphin One through to Dolphin Four.

'This is Dolphin One. Roger that. Still no sighting. Out,' Hunter replied. 'Okay, here we go. Follow me and try and stay in line.'

Hunter engaged the electric motor of the chariot and it moved sedately through the calm sea, a metre below the surface, towards the path of the *Union of Sark*. Hunter and Badonovitch had their heads just above the water. One man from each of the Dolphin teams had his arm through a loop in the rope. The other member of the team carried the electro-magnets. Without the chariot it would have been impossible for the team to reach their target. The weight of the equipment alone would have been debilitating. As it was, the swim was tough going and very few operatives could have carried it out successfully.

'Dolphin One, distance to go, two point five miles,' Hunter heard in his earpiece. Replying he said 'Roger that. I have the forward mast light visible. Also the starboard light. Am moving forward a few yards. Out.' Hunter took the chariot forward ten yards and then another ten as he adjusted their position. Then he said, 'Both red and green visible.'

'Roger that. I would say there is less than half-a-mile to go.'

By now *The Flower of Allah* had moved five miles away and was on a slightly divergent course to the *Union of Sark* which had not altered course.

There were no further transmissions. The stem of the hull was looming over the divers as they left surface and sank six feet down. The noise of the ship's engines was loud but steady as she approached. Both men in each team were connected by a rope, each team having different lengths. Now one man was to port of the *Union of Sark*'s bows, the other to starboard. Then the ship was on them, ploughing between them, snagging the rope with her bows. They felt the nylon rope tighten and then drag them through the water like fish on a line. Using their shoulders they hit the sides of the ship with scarcely a bump. The diving gear was ditched and those carrying the electro-magnets began immediately to climb the hull. The magnets were controlled by buttons in each hand and were strapped to their hands and knees. The secret of using them was co-ordination and practice. They started with both hands and both knees stuck firmly on the side of the ship. By pressing the left-hand button, the current was cut and they each moved their left hands and knees up six inches. Then the same on the right. Then left again and so on. They each went up the three metres of deck in under fifteen seconds. Knotted ropes were dropped over the side for the other divers to climb. Meanwhile, Hunter and Badonovitch sat where they were, on the chariot, just below the surface, listening to the reports coming in.

'Deck is clear,' said Josh Clements. 'Okay, looks like we're on.' In the background they could just hear the faint sound of the engine control bell. 'Yep, slowing down now. Exactly on schedule.'

They had achieved the most important part of their mission: to access the ship without alerting the crew. Now all they needed was for the submarine to join them.

Excited voices speaking in a foreign language could be heard in the background and Clements whispered, 'I can see the submarine. She's just appeared.' He looked at his watch. 'Exactly on time. Yep, it's an Agosta all right. It means five officers and thirty-six crew. No pennant number though.'

The *Khalid* came slowly closer to the ship. At about one hundred yards, or half a cable, a loudspeaker burst into life. In English.

'*Union of Sark*, we will send the inflatable across with the merchandise. Please lower your ladder.'

There was a great deal of fussing, but eventually, the port access ladder was lowered successfully. Clements could see an inflatable boat entering the water from the submarine. Dawn was now less than fifteen minutes away, enabling him to see the package being carefully handed down. Hunter engaged the drive for the chariot and headed to the submarine, three metres below the surface. Transit time was four minutes. The *Khalid* was maintaining headway of about one knot to stop her rolling. At the stern of the submarine, he and Badonovitch left the chariot and swam away with the EFSWR in tow. Hunter had a thin nylon rope attached from his waist to the chariot. Methodically, they wrapped the wire around the starboard fin, jammed it in the rudder and then took it to the port fin where they carefully threaded it against the pin and sprocket. They looped it back through and jammed it tightly around the starboard fin again.

Hunter pulled in the rope attached to the chariot hand over hand. The two divers climbed onto it and headed along the starboard side of the submarine. They stopped when they arrived at the engine water coolant intakes. It took only a minute to set and prime a shaped lump of plastic explosive. The *Khalid* would not be diving anywhere. Or if it did manage to submerge, it wouldn't be down for long.

'Inflatable on its way,' came over Hunter's earpiece.

'Roger that. We're leaving. What's happening?'

'Lots of laughter, waving and cheering.'

'Then they are in for one hell of a surprise. We're at your stern right now.'

'Roger that. It's clear.'

Hunter surfaced and Sam Macready threw him a line and made it fast to a stanchion at his end. Hunter tied the rope to the chariot. They passed up their diving gear and then climbed on board the ship. From the submarine's klaxon came the harsh diving signal as the crew prepared to leave the surface. At the same time, the coaster's engines grew louder as their speed increased. The *Union of Sark* was paralleling the submarine and in the strengthening light Hunter watched as the submarine, its conning tower almost under the surface, suddenly came back up.

'Okay. Time to get to work everyone,' Nick said. 'You know what to do.'

He and Badonovitch headed for the bridge. Dolphin Two went to the engine control room, Dolphin Three headed for the crew's mess and Dolphin Four started on the cabins. They didn't go smashing in, making a fuss and a great deal of noise. They killed quietly and efficiently. The crew may have been Jihadists but were clearly not fighters. They died in uncomprehending shock. Badonovitch went up the port side of the bridge, Hunter to starboard. Standing on the bridge wing, with his back to Hunter, watching the submarine, was a man wearing a black jacket and a flat black cap. The man looked to his left and said something to someone in the bridge. He must have caught a glimpse of Hunter out of the corner of his eye for he looked around, the wide smile freezing on his face. Hunter guessed that the man was the captain. Two silenced rounds into his chest killed him instantly.

A voice was heard yelling, 'Captain! Captain! What is . . .'

The man's mouth dropped wide open as he looked into the barrel of the pistol Hunter was pointing at him.

'No . . . No . . . Please . . . No . . .' he said as he backed away. 'What do you want?'

'That.' Hunter pointed to the container at the back of the bridge that held the plutonium bomb. It really did look like a suitcase.

'What . . . What do you mean?' This time the words came out in a hoarse whisper.

Badonovitch was on the other side of the bridge. A third man was at the wheel in the centre of the bridge. He was looking over his shoulder at Hunter. There was a gun in a holster hanging beside the binnacle and the helmsman snatched it up.

Badonovitch's first shot was in the back, through the spine, knocking the man to the deck. The gun fell from his motionless fingers as Badonovitch stepped up and put a second round into his skull.

'All clear, boss.'

'Thanks, Jan.'

'Where's the second bomb?', Hunter enquired in a reasonable tone of voice.

'What second bomb?' The man licked his lips. Of fear he felt plenty, but he would not disgrace himself. He would not cower before them. Not before Allah and these infidels.

'Wrong answer,' said Hunter, lining up his pistol on the man's forehead and pulling the trigger. Reports began coming in from the remainder of the team. The ship was theirs. No crew member still lived.

Don Masters appeared on the bridge. 'Is that it?', he asked, nodding towards the case.

Hunter nodded in return. Masters flicked two catches and opened the lid. He was confronted by a black panel with lights and switches. An instructions leaflet was resting on the panel. Picking it up, he glanced through it. It was written in English, which wasn't surprising, there being so many different languages and dialects across Pakistan. It was obviously needed, as the person setting the bomb to explode would have no idea what to do.

Hunter looked forward. The submarine was still on the

186

surface, about a mile away and getting nearer. Clements appeared, found a pair of binoculars and focused them on the submarine.

'I can see a boat in the water and some men on the casing down aft.'

Just then the radio on the bridge crackled into life. '*Union of Sark* this is submarine, over.' They ignored it and the subsequent repeats.

Hunter walked over to the captain and took his cap. In his black wetsuit and with the cap on his head, he would be mistaken for the captain long enough to suit their needs. Out on the bridge wing he waved to the men on the submarine. Somebody in the conning tower waved back. It was clear that the crew of the submarine were not expecting any trouble. They were busy trying to cut themselves free from the EFSWR.

'Stand by,' said Hunter. 'Shoot the men in the conning tower first.'

18

It had taken great patience but Zim Albatha had successfully placed bugs in both Syed Azam's office and the house where he lived with his wife together with the apartment where he kept his mistress. The transmissions were recorded on disc, and were voice activated. Without the new software that identified voices Albatha wouldn't have had the time to listen to 10 per cent of the recordings. As it was, he still had hours of boredom, even when the Minister was in his office and engaged on official business, although that wasn't all that often. Syed Azam appeared to hold a great number of meetings at other locations. It was tedious, mind-numbing work – the Minister of Immigration's wife and mistress seemed to spend hours watching television – which was not unusual for surveillance duty.

Finally, Albatha struck pay dirt.

'Are you sure the device will pass this way?' Azam asked.

'No. However, we must be ready for anything. Our plans have to be flexible if we are to succeed,' Rehman Khan cautioned.

Syed Azam chuckled. 'It will be a great day for Islam. Think of it, my friend! A dirty bomb . . .'

'Enough! Say no more.'

'Rehman, you worry too much. I am a Minister of State. No one would dare do anything to me. I would have their heads if they tried.'

Syed Azam was tall and thin to the point of emaciation. His prematurely grey hair and beard gave him an air of authority he worked hard at cultivating. His supercilious manner annoyed his fellow parliamentarians, while his vanity was echoed in his elegant clothes. A private income allowed him to do as he pleased. Or so he thought.

'That may be. But we cannot be too careful,' Rehman Khan warned him.

Azam sighed, as though he was speaking to a slow-witted child. 'As you say. But even so, with the devastation and panic we will create, Turkey will become a force in the world. A force for good. With our military might and our position we will wield great influence between the West and the Islamic countries. Perhaps I may even run for the Presidency one day.'

So Varol Sandal had been right Zim thought to himself. The rumours flying around the world about a plutonium-based bomb exploding in Europe were true. To date, all there had been in the news was innuendo and rumours. All had been repeatedly denied by Western governments but mainly to no avail. Zim picked up his mobile and rang his boss. Whatever decisions were to be made were well above his pay grade.

*   *   *   *   *

It was a turkey shoot. Peter Weir used a recently acquired Vapensmia NM149S, five-shot sniper rifle. Developed for the Norwegian army and police force, it was also available

189

commercially as a target or hunting rifle. It used a standard Mauser three-lug bolt, a 6 x 42 telescopic sight and came fitted with a sound suppresser. For such close work he used his elbows to take the weight of the rifle.

There were two men on the conning tower. One was looking across at the *Union of Sark*, concerned that the vessel was less than eighty metres from the submarine and closing on a convergent course. The other was watching the work party at the tail of the submarine and was Weir's first victim, killed instantly by a bullet that entered his forehead and blew out the back of his skull.

As the second man, the captain, looked around for their assailant, Weir shifted aim and fired. The shot entered the captain's left temple and exited through the right.

The men on the casing continued working, oblivious of the danger they were in. The sounds of the two shots were barely heard on the other side of the bridge of the coaster, never mind on the sub. Weir killed two more men before the others realised they were under attack. One of them made a dash along the walkway towards the open hatch in the casing, but had only taken a few paces before Weir shot him. Another tried to hide behind the fin, but Weir put a bullet through his arm, changed the magazine in the rifle as the man staggered into view and put a second bullet through his stomach and spine. The body tumbled into the sea. The sixth and final man had been sitting in the inflatable boat. He let go of the securing rope and was turning the boat away, trying to get the submarine's hull between him and the *Union of Sark*. Weir couldn't see the man who was now lying in the bottom of the inflatable. Four well-placed shots ripped the boat apart and killed its occupant.

By now, the coaster was only thirty metres from the

submarine and still closing. Weir kept the conning tower covered while McCready, standing next to him, covered the open hatchway down aft. He was using an American semi-automatic Barrett M82A2.

Grappling hooks were thrown and the coaster was pulled alongside the submarine. There was a gentle bump as the two vessels touched. Hunter led the way over the side, jumping the narrow strip of sea onto the sub's walkway.

An officer appeared in the conning tower. McCready's shot went through the officer's left temple and erupted out the other side. Hunter climbed up the outside ladder to the top of the conning tower. Behind him was Badonovitch. Clements and Napier headed aft for the open hatch, while Macready and Henri went forward. To make more room on the conning tower, Hunter unceremoniously dragged the two bodies over the side. One wore the three stripes of a Pakistani naval Commander, the other had the insignia of a Chief Petty Officer. The crew still in the submarine had no idea they were under attack. How could they? The noise inside the hull helped to deaden what was happening outside. Furthermore, removing some sort of obstacle from the diving planes wasn't likely to be done silently. The hatchways were small, obstructing the crew's vision of the outside world.

'Ready?' Hunter spoke just above a whisper into his microphone. 'Now.'

At each hatch, the men pulled the pins on the grenades they carried, counted to three and dropped them into the submarine. Then the hatches were slammed shut before the explosions occurred.

The yells and panic that erupted inside the hull lasted only a matter of seconds as the high-shrapnel grenades went off. The crew were cut to pieces where they stood or sat. Hunter threw open the conning tower hatch and began climbing down with his weapon of choice for close work, the Enfield L85A1. The magazine held 30 rounds and had a rate of fire of 700 rounds per minute. At only 785mm long, it was ideal in the present cramped conditions.

Two factors were working for them. First, surprise was entirely on their side and second, any weapons on the submarine would be locked in the armoury, accessible only through the Captain – who was dead.

If the sight of the four men blown to pieces affected him, Hunter didn't show it. The operations room was behind him. He turned and walked over and around the bits of bodies, pools of blood and shattered glass to get to it. The blackout curtain was in tatters, one man was moaning, his head on the surface plot table. Hunter killed him with one bullet to the head.

More gunfire could be heard as members of the crew were systematically hunted down and killed. Soon it was all over. While sea-cocks were opened, Hunter blew open the safe in the captain's cabin. He cleared it of all the paperwork he found there.

'All set? Then let's go.' As well as opening the sea-cocks they had set some heavy charges to expedite matters. It wouldn't suit them to have some ship with an inquisitive captain appearing on the scene.

They made a rapid but organised exit from the submarine and returned to the *Union of Sark*. There they repeated the process of opening sea-cocks and planting explosives. *The Flower of Allah* had come alongside the coaster and they stepped onto her deck. They recovered the chariot and, as the yacht moved away, the first of the plastic explosive charges went off, followed in quick succession by the remainder. Both vessels were sinking fast.

'Nothing on the radar?', Hunter asked.

'All clear,' said Clements, his eyes glued to the screen.

'Okay, let's get the hell out of here.' They were headed back to Oman. They urgently needed to get the device back to Britain.

Now that the action was over, a pall of gloom hung over them. It was inevitable, really. It had been carnage. Not something to be proud of. However, the thought of what would have happened if the nuke had reached Britain had sustained them. Their anger had protected them from their feelings during the action. Now reaction set in. The submarine had been a necessity. If the men on board had known what they were carrying and started talking, the information would inevitably leak. Hunter knew what the repercussions would have been. No matter what Europe's governments said, no matter how much they called for restraint, the backlash against Pakistanis living in Europe in general and in Britain in particular would be horrendous. Innocent people would be killed and seriously hurt. It didn't take much imagination to think what would happen to young Pakistani children in schools all across the Western world. And that was merely at the prospect of the bomb exploding. If it did go off? It truly was the stuff of nightmares.

Hunter reported what had happened to Macnair.

'So, all according to plan?', asked the General.

'Yes, sir. Just one thing. I counted six officers, not five, as we were expecting.'

'A visiting staff officer? It makes no difference, so well done. Right now, the USS *Port Royal* is steaming at maximum speed towards you. She'll contact you shortly.

As soon as she's in range, they'll send a Sikorsky for the device.'

'Good. We'll be glad to see the back of it. It makes me feel uncomfortable having the thing here. What will the Americans do with it?'

'X-ray the thing and let us know how to disarm it. As soon as we get the specifications they'll be passed to you. In that way, if we do get our hands on the second bomb we may be able to deal with it ourselves.'

'I thought the Pakistanis were co-operating in giving us the material we need to deal with the sodding thing.'

'They are. We also need separate confirmation that what we are being told is indeed accurate.'

'But their government . . .'

'Nick, it isn't their government. They merely tell us what they've been told. What if the man reporting to the Pakistani government is one of the conspirators? What then?'

'Ah, sorry, sir. I wasn't thinking straight.'

'That's not surprising after what you and your team have been through. Give them my heartiest and tell them the malt is on me when they get back.'

'Roger that, sir.'

The American ship was a Ticonderoga class, guided missile destroyer capable of 32.5 knots. Contact was soon made, positions agreed, and less than thirty minutes later the huge helicopter hovered into sight. The winch was lowered and the nuke was securely strapped to it. It was with heartfelt sighs of relief that the men watched as the Sikorsky headed back the way it had come.

* * * * *

'Anything in the papers they lifted from the submarine?', MacNair asked Isobel.

'Still working on it, sir,' Isobel explained.

'All right. Anything though. Anything at all, give me a call.' He sat back in his chair and looked out of his window, down to the harbour. The Americans had reported that the bomb had enough plastic explosives to kill a few hundred people in a crowded street, shatter windows and possibly bring down a nearby wall or two. The plutonium was another matter. TIFAT's guess was as good as theirs. Running the information through different computers produced a variety of results. Short-term deaths from plutonium poisoning would be in the thousands. Long term? No one could tell, except to say it would be in the tens of thousands. All services would be overwhelmed. The fire brigade, supported by the military, would have the task of cleaning it all up. At that moment the only solution they had was to wash the radiation down drains and into the sea. The ecological damage? Devastating. Add to that huge civil unrest and the whole thing was any country's worst nightmare. Whether the device exploded or not, its existence was enough to send the general population over the edge of sanity and civilised behaviour. Only one good thing had come out of it all. The information from the Pakistani government for disarming the device had been proven to be correct. Macnair sighed heavily. And there was a second device out there. Somewhere. It was late when Macnair acknowledged to himself that there was nothing more he could do. He left his office and crossed to the wardroom. He was in the bar with a whisky and soda next to him, untouched, when his second-in-command appeared.

'Care for another?' Walsh indicated the glass on the bar.

'No, thanks. I'm fine.'

Walsh turned to the barman, 'A horse's neck, please.'

They said nothing more until the barman placed a brandy and ginger ale in front of Walsh. He helped himself to ice and they took their drinks to a corner table. Isobel came in and joined them.

'Anything?', Macnair asked.

'Nothing from the submarine. However, we've found a few references to the Karakoram Highway. We first saw it mentioned when we lifted the computer from that house in Luton. Initially, I thought it might have been some sort of tourist thing. You know, see parts of the world few others have seen before you. But we found other references to it so I did a search. Even if you're mad as a hatter, it's not the sort of place anyone would want to visit.'

'Where the hell is it?', Walsh asked, sipping his drink.

'The highway runs between Central Asia and the plains of Pakistan.'

'What's the significance?', Macnair asked.

Isobel shrugged. 'I'm sorry, Malcolm, but all we've got are a few references to the place. It's not much, but right now we don't have anything else.'

'What you're saying,' said Macnair, 'is that the second bomb, if it is coming overland, could be travelling along this highway?'

'I guess I am. Nothing else makes sense,' Isobel shook her head tiredly. 'I don't know, I could be clutching at straws. I think I'll get some sleep.'

'Can I get you a drink?', Macnair asked.

She shook her head. 'Better not. I told Leo to call me if anything interesting came in and if I have a drink I doubt I'll wake up for days.' She left the two senior officers.

'You know she could be right,' Walsh said gloomily.

'She usually is. Somehow we need to confirm it.'

'Anything on the political side?'

'Not as such. Thank God, your lot are involved. I'd hate to think what would have happened if we'd handed the device over to Aldermaston,' Macnair said referring to the UK's Atomic Weapons Establishment in Berkshire.

Walsh frowned. 'Why, aren't they up to it?'

'Oh, they are. It's what our politicians would have made of it. This way, we're keeping a lid on things a bit longer. I explained to President Tahir about the possible leak from our government. He's assured me he'll keep things under wraps for as long as possible. He's backing us. Hell, he was the prime mover in getting us set up in the first place. If anyone causes any trouble, he'll just wave our mandate at them.'

'What sort of trouble?'

'Press enquiries asking us to confirm or deny any rumours. The press are beginning to suspect something is up. And as much as we may deride them, they're a canny, bloody-minded and tenacious bunch, even those who are inept.' He swallowed a mouthful of his whisky. 'Where's Nick? Are they in Karachi yet?'

'Almost.'

'Good. Then there's only one thing for it,' General Macnair said.

'What's that?'

'We're going to Pakistan. There's a President I need to speak to.'

19

Mohammed Akbar was born of a Pakistani mother and a Saudi Arabian father in a south London hospital in 1970. The combination meant he was bullied at school, treated with condescending contempt by his teachers and generally left in virtual isolation most of his life. Instead of being ground down by his experiences, Akbar grew up with an iron will to succeed and a massive hatred in his heart for all things Western and all things non-Islamic. He was also completely amoral. He began making money at the age of eighteen by dealing in a relatively new drug called ecstasy. From there to cocaine was a very small step. Unlike others in the same business, Akbar did not flaunt his wealth. Instead, he invested it in rundown properties in the Docklands area of London. While he did so, he also attended the University of Durham, where he read history and politics. He barely scraped his degree. Years later, when he was asked why he had studied that combination of subjects he said it was, 'To know my enemy. Where they've come from and where they might be going.'

By choice, in his early twenties, he spent a year in Afghanistan with the Taliban. There he came to the notice of al-Qaeda. Neither his personal bravery nor his commitment to the greater Islamic cause was ever questioned. He was seen as potentially a great asset. He was ordered to return to Britain.

By the age of thirty he was a multi-millionaire and had dummy companies, as well as real ones, set up all over the world, each one used to hide significant assets from the authorities. In Britain he pleaded poverty, claimed benefits and paid no taxes. Few people were more adept at playing the race card than he was. The slightest problem and he yelled racial prejudice. It was a ploy that worked only too well. In spite of his wealth, made from legitimate enterprises including a chain of restaurants and bars, he still imported, manufactured and distributed drugs. It wasn't for the money. It was because of the destruction and devastation that drugs caused amongst the British people. Naturally, he no longer dealt in the drugs personally. He had an army of minions to do that. All of them Muslim, all of them as fanatical as he was in their hatred of the West.

Now he sat in his rented London office, near St Katherine's Dock, and for the first time in his life he knew fear. Real fear. It had him gripped by his fat throat and was threatening to drag him down into a cesspool from which there would be no escape. He drummed podgy fingers on his desk, sweat beading his brow. From being a fit and active soldier in the army of Islam, for his height of 5ft 9ins, he had become at least 50lbs overweight. In the last few years he had tried one quack method after another to lose weight. The ones that would have helped – exercise and a sensible diet – he never managed. He always looked for the easy way when it came to his personal habits. Unfortunately, he was addicted to junk food. But right then, eating anything was the last thing on his mind. The reports coming in from all over the country were unbelievable. Not just the country! But the world!

For twenty years he had operated behind the scenes, staying out of the limelight. He had been a powerful force behind Islamic fundamentalism. Correction, he had become *the* force. Slowly but surely, he had helped to build the secret army that existed across Britain and Europe. His wealth had been his shield. But now . . .? Now, it was all gone. Every penny, rupee and dollar had vanished. He couldn't understand it. What had happened? He had tried to trace the money but kept hitting a brick wall. His accountants in Pakistan couldn't or wouldn't help him. He hadn't decided which it was, yet. But he would. And there would be hell to pay, by Allah there would.

It had been going on for a week. At first he had thought it was just a mistake, an administrative error of some sort. Like his credit card being swallowed by the machine at the bank on the High Street. Then another credit card was refused when he tried to pay for petrol. One thing after another. He still remembered the embarrassment of it, as well as the smirk on the woman cashier's face. From there, it had all been downhill. The bank where he did all his legitimate business resolutely refused to see him. That was, unless he was going in with enough cash to regularise his position. He had argued vehemently until he had finally received an appointment. It proved to be a complete waste of time however. He thought he would be seeing the branch manager; but he was met instead by a junior financial advisor. Anger swamped him as he thought of the humiliation he had felt being spoken to like that, by someone who was hardly more than a child.

He had taken his frustration out on his wife. He had hit her, hard, across the face. He had smacked her in the past, to teach her who was the boss in their house, to teach her obedience and humility. This time he had bruised the side of her face with his fist and the top of her thigh with his foot. He had stalked out of the house after heaping a load of abuse on her. He hadn't seen her or his son since.

*   *   *   *   *

Nick Hunter spoke in some detail with General Macnair. Intelligence gathering was not only sheer hard work, it was time consuming. Interpretation of the information acquired was an art form. A snippet here, a comment there, could add up to a significant amount of knowledge, provided it was coupled with a large pinch of luck. Based on the information they had gleaned from the material found on the submarine, they were as sure as they could be that the second dirty bomb was still in Pakistan, or somewhere near its borders. Hence, Hunter's orders to go to Pakistan. Which was why *The Flower of Allah* was sedately heading for the bustling port of Karachi. Even at midnight there was non-stop activity. Cranes filled the holds of ships twenty-four hours a day. Pakistan was thriving. It made more goods *per capita* than Europe. It was opening factories of various sorts on a daily basis. The nation was determined to become more prosperous than their arch-rival, India. So far, their economies were running neck and neck, but that was about to change. Pakistan was edging into the ascendancy.

Approaching the harbour, they contacted Customs and Excise and were ordered to a berth. Much to their chagrin, they were told to stay with the yacht until the morning when a Customs Officer and an Immigration Officer would visit. They needed to be in the country legally so they did as they were told. Once securely berthed, they sat in the saloon, drinking whisky and swapping stories. Like military personnel the world over, their tales were self-deprecating and often funny. When they'd relaxed and unwound, they drifted off to their cabins. Hunter took the first two-hour watch on the gangway.

In the morning, just after 08.00, the officials arrived. Papers and passports were quickly stamped, and it took mere minutes until they left again.

*　*　*　*　*

For Mohammed Akbar's wife it had been the last straw. She had collected their son from school and left. Akbar had no way of knowing that it was a move she had been planning for a considerable length of time. Systematically, she had been taking money from various accounts; accounts he thought she knew nothing about. Ever since their marriage ten years earlier, he had treated her like a chattel. A woman was owned by the man, for him to do with as he wished. At least as far as his brand of Islam was concerned. Akbar had never come to terms with the fact that she was an intelligent and educated woman. He ignored the fact that she had graduated with a better degree than he had from the university where they had met. Her degree was in pure and applied mathematics. Her ambition was to be a teacher. Shortly after her marriage, she realised she would never achieve this ambition as long as she stayed with Akbar. She had tried to make it work. How she had tried. Everything he wanted, she did. Her subservience had made her sick to the stomach. Now she had had enough and began making her plans. For five years she had stolen from him. A few pounds here, a few rupees there. The more subserviently she behaved, the more contempt her husband held her in. As a result she had a very good idea of what he was really up to. Although she did not know about the plutonium device, she did know something big was going to happen and happen soon.

A week before her husband's difficulties had begun, she had sent an anonymous letter to MI5. She had intended leaving him before sending the letter, but the temptation to watch him squirm had been too much. The beating he had given her had brought forward her timetable by a mere two days. She and their six-year-old son crossed from Dover to Calais on their way to Spain. Six months earlier she had completed the purchase of a two-bedroom villa on the outskirts of Algeciras. The money she had stolen would keep them for at least ten years – even longer, provided she didn't go mad, which she had no intention of doing. There were tears in her eyes, yet joy in her heart, as she looked out of the train window. Now there was no going back. Her husband would kill her without question. When she arrived at her destination, she would throw her burkha into a rubbish bin. It was a symbol of the subservience Muslim women were forced to display to their men. She would never be subservient again. For the first time in a decade she felt her spirits soaring. She'd done it! She tapped her handbag with a smile of satisfaction. Akbar thought himself intelligent. He was, in fact, stupid.

* * * * *

The day after his wife left him, Mohammed Akbar went into his garage and pulled the heavy cupboard away from

203

the wall. Underneath were three bricks that were not cemented in. He prised them up and took out the tin box he kept there. It was for emergencies only. Opening it, he was horrified to find it was empty. There had been at least £40,000 in notes in the box. What had happened to the money? Where . . .? That bitch! That stinking bitch! He'd kill her! He would find her and have her killed. He knew just the people he could trust.

Shaking with rage, he began making the necessary calls. As he made call after call his disbelief turned to anger, and then fear. This was impossible. No answer anywhere. Not a single person replied, either on their landlines or on their mobiles. What was happening?

Eventually, he did manage to speak to a few people. All had one thing in common – they were terrified. Then the rumours started. Where they originated, he had no idea. People were vanishing all over the country. Special forces were involved. MI5, MI6, and the biggest horror of them all, TIFAT. Fear was clouding his brain. The only people he managed to contact were minions, the small fry. They were all that was left.

Then Akbar remembered a dormant building society account he had set up nearly four years earlier. He rummaged through his papers until he found the passbook, tucked away in the back of a bureau drawer. The office where he had made the deposit had been in Plaistow High Street.

He was about to leave the house when he paused. Maybe. Yes, it made a certain amount of sense. He looked out of the window. Nothing. Nobody. A ladder with no one on it. A manhole cover with safety railings around it. But nobody watching. Still. What if his house was bugged? His jaw dropped in horror at the thought. He looked around but could see nothing. He was being ridiculous. Better safe than sorry however. He switched on his radio, which was tuned to a Muslim station. The music of his culture filled the air.

Satisfied, he hurried out of the front door and along the street. He took the District Line. He was also careful to take his driving licence, his passport and a new utility bill. The tube was hot and he fretted all the way but he needn't have bothered. Ten minutes after arriving at the building society he was back out with just over a thousand pounds in cash. Akbar took the underground back to his house and was walking towards it when he noticed the men. There was a white van next to an open manhole cover with a man not actually doing anything. A second was across the road, up a ladder, ostensibly working on a street light. Only he wasn't. Their focus was not on what they were supposed to be doing. Their focus was on his house! The realisation brought a gasp to his lips. Abruptly, he turned and walked away. His heart was pounding, sweat was trickling down his face and the back of his neck. It couldn't be. And yet, he realised, there was an inevitability to it all. The past eight days had been leading up to this very scenario and, if the truth were told, he was relieved. He now knew where he stood. No more making excuses to himself. In his heart he had been blaming his wife – in his head he had known better – and now there was nothing for him to do other than take the appropriate action. The first thing was to get the hell out of Britain. He thanked Allah he'd had the foresight to get a second passport. It had been part of his al-Qaeda training. It had been drummed into him: always be ready. There was no knowing when he might need to get away before the infidels laid their filthy hands on him. To hide his tracks.

He switched off his mobile. Thank you, he repeated, thank you Allah. It was a chant that would sustain him over the coming hours and days.

* * * * *

Macnair took the call.

'Hullo, Clive. Did you get him?'

'Sorry, Malcolm,' Owens replied, 'Akbar appears to have blown town. He hasn't taken his car so we assume he's using public transport. We have an all-points out for him, but we'll have to see.'

'When was he last seen or heard from?'

'First thing this morning. He used his phone but couldn't reach anybody.' The chuckle was dry, without humour. 'All his calls were made to men we've lifted over the past ten days.'

'Any idea what went wrong?' Macnair knew with operations like the one that had just taken place things could easily fall apart.

'A complete quirk of fate. I had two men covering the house. They were all we could spare.' He didn't need to explain. The security services and police were stretched to breaking point. 'We'd bugged his landline and mobile. We knew he was in the house. We'd established physical cover because we were about to lift him. We had a directional microphone aimed at the house but all we got was their excuse for music and thought he was still there. I can't blame my men in truth. They'd been covering Mohammed Akbar for over five hours, first from a surveillance vehicle and then nearer the house. One up a lamp post, one around a manhole cover. You know the sort of thing.'

Macnair did, only too well. He grunted acknowledgement.

'Anyway, one went to make coffee while the other went back to the van to use the toilet, which was parked a few streets away so as not to be seen by Akbar. You can guess the rest. In those few minutes Akbar walked out of the house. We thought he was still there when we raided the place. His radio was on after all. It was just sheer bad luck.'

Macnair sighed. It happened. 'It can't be helped.'

'Akbar could be anywhere. He may be lying low but he may try to get out of the country. We're assuming the latter, hence the all-points.'

'How long has he been gone?', Macnair asked.

'Coming up to five hours.'

'Enough time to get to the Continent then,' Macnair said thoughtfully.

'Easily. There are plenty of trains he could have taken. And once he's in France he can go anywhere. Thanks to the European Union we have no way of checking.'

Macnair said nothing. It was a continual thorn in the sides of all the agencies tasked with protecting the public – no border controls worth a damn.

'All right, we need to move on. If he turns up, all well and good. If he doesn't, then that's too bad. I'm flying to Pakistan tonight,' Macnair informed Owens.

'All right. If Akbar shows we'll let you know immediately.'

As Macnair replaced the receiver, there was a knock at the door and Walsh looked in. 'The helicopter's here.'

'Thanks. I'll be right with you.'

* * * * *

Mohammed Akbar caught the 12.30 Eurostar to the Gare du Nord in Paris. From there, he travelled across the city to the Gare de Lyon and, little more than an hour after arriving in Paris, was bound for Marseilles. He would arrive in the busy port as near as dammit to 19.00. Once there, his contacts would look after him. The city had a very high proportion of Muslims living in the area and many were sympathetic to the cause espoused by al-Qaeda. Akbar spent most of the journey with his head back against the seat-rest, in isolated introspection. What was happening? How had things gone so badly wrong and so quickly? And where was his wife? Was she responsible? He didn't believe it. It was impossible. She was merely a woman. His mind played with the usual tired old clichés until he fell into a fitful doze. The offer of a drink and a snack by the steward pushing his trusty trolley along the carriage brought him fully awake. He settled for a cup of tea.

20

Nick Hunter arrived at the airport with a ticket for an Aero Asia flight to Islamabad. Delays were often experienced in that part of the world, and it was well after six o'clock that evening by the time he arrived in the capital city. It was dusk, it was hot and humid, and he was not in the best of moods when he stepped outside the airport terminal.

'Nick! Over here!'

Looking across the street Nick saw Samantha Freemantle leaning out of the window of the driver's seat of a Suzuki 4x4. His mood changed in a flash and he smiled.

'What on earth are you doing here?' laughed Nick as he threw his grip onto the back seat.

'I came over with General Macnair. I've been working as liaison since I saw you on Cyprus. He's staying at the High Commission but there's no room for you there, so it's been suggested you stay at The Simara Hotel.'

Hunter snorted derisively. 'Not likely. I stayed there when I was back-packing more years ago than I care to remember. Forget it. Take me to the Marriott on Aga Khan Road. It's more convenient for the High Commission and a damn sight more comfortable. Where are you staying?'

'At the Commission,' Samantha explained. Pausing she asked 'Which way do I go?'

'Head back to the High Commission and turn up Constitution Avenue, past the Supreme Court and the National Assembly buildings. You'll see the big blue sign on the roof. You can't miss it.'

The traffic was a nightmare but Samantha gave no quarter. Close shaves didn't bother her in the least, as she weaved in and out of cars that stopped arbitrarily in the middle of the street to disgorge or take on passengers.

'Were you waiting long?', Hunter asked, merely by way of something to say.

'I'd just pulled up when I saw you. I was late but then you were too. Which is something I've learned is the norm in this country.'

'Even after such a short time?' Nick grinned.

Samantha flashed a smile at him. 'Yes! Even after such a short time,' she said, laughing. 'General Macnair is expecting you for a reception at twenty one hundred. Here's your invitation.' She handed over the embossed card.

'Black tie?' He couldn't keep the amusement out of his voice.

'Yes. Oh, I see. That could prove a bit awkward.'

'Trust the General. Turn left here and pull over wherever you can.'

She did as he said. 'Where are we?'

'It's one of the most famous bazaars in the world, second only to one in Singapore. Wait here. I won't be long.'

The street was bustling with tourists of all nationalities, pickpockets of Pakistani extraction and touts offering anything and everything at bargain prices. The fourth shop along on the right was his destination. Hunter opened the glass-fronted door and pushed through the plastic hanging ribbons into the air-conditioned premises.

An old man greeted him. 'Yes, sir? What can I do for you?'

'My name is Lieutenant Commander Hunter. If you check your systems you will find . . .'

'There is no need, sir,' the man bowed his head and clapped his hands together. 'I remember who you are.' He paused, thinking a moment. 'Scotland. Rosyth. The last item I sent to you was a white dinner jacket. Oh, and a number of cummerbunds with a special badge. You sent the design and my nephew created the badge.'

Hunter smiled. 'Achmed, your memory is famous throughout the British armed forces.' Achmed and his family had been supplying Britain's navy and army for the best part of four decades. The only time Hunter had ever been in Achmed's shop had been eight years earlier. Since then, back in Britain, he had been served by two of Achmed's sons, who toured the various British bases throughout the year. The Pakistanis had taken over from where the Chinese had left off.

'I have need of a dinner jacket, white, black trousers and all the trimmings. I'll take a cummerbund as well. Do you have one?'

Achmed cocked his head on one side, pursed his lips and said, 'Yes, Commander Hunter, we do. Delivery tomorrow?'

'Delivery in one hour at the Marriott.'

'Commander . . .'

'Achmed, please. Just do it.'

The old man smiled. 'Very well. We will get to work right away. Are your measurements still the same?'

'Yes. Also, could you throw in a pair of shoes please. Size ten. You know where to send the bill.'

Achmed nodded and Hunter left the shop smiling.

'Where did you get to?', Samantha greeted him.

'Meeting with my tailor.'

Samantha gave him an exasperated look and decided not to pursue the matter. A short while later she pulled up outside the imposing entrance of the Marriott hotel.

'Thanks, Samantha.'

'Do you want me to come and collect you?'

'No, it's okay. I can walk it faster than you can drive and I can build up an appetite. And a thirst. See you later.'

Climbing out of the car he grabbed his bag and went into the foyer. He hadn't told Samantha that he had booked a room while at the airport in Karachi. He'd been in Pakistan on previous occasions and knew the ropes only too well when it came to the military and its attitude to spending money on the comfort of its personnel.

The check-in desk took an imprint of his credit card, handed over an old-fashioned key and wished him a pleasant stay. He was told he need only telephone the desk to be given anything he required – anything at all. The meaning was obvious. He smiled in response and then explained about the delivery he expected.

Just before nine o'clock that night, dressed in his new dinner jacket, Nick left the hotel and walked on to Constitution Avenue and past the imposing National Assembly building. The evening was balmy, warm with a light breeze blowing from the south. Nick strolled along, enjoying the night. Moments like this, he knew, were few and far between. He thought about his – what to call it? – job? A ludicrous word to describe what he did. It wasn't even a calling, like becoming a doctor or a priest. It was the knowledge that without people like him and the rest of TIFAT, the world would be a far more dangerous place. In order to protect as many people as possible, they had to crawl into the sewers to clean them. Down there were people – monsters – who were prepared to kill innocent men, women and children for their perverted and pathological ideas, inevitably based on religion. How many deaths would satisfy these people? He knew the answer. There was no limit.

Nick turned left on First Road and entered the area known as the Diplomatic Enclave, and walked past the Indian High Commission on his left. The traffic was building up and it all pointed in the same direction. He noticed that there were more armed police patrols than he would have expected. A few hundred metres from the Commission he saw the barricades and the teams of men using sniffer-dogs, searching the stationary vehicles. For there to be this much activity, Nick knew, something had to be up. Now he could see the bright lights of the modern, yet imposing, British High Commission. He stopped at the first barricade and showed both his passport and his invitation. His name was ticked off a list by a fit-looking man wearing civilian clothes. He had military written all over him. A black labrador sniffed Nick while he stood still, his arms by his side. From some of the comments he was hearing, it was evident that some people were objecting to this treatment. Those that did were politely asked if they would prefer not to join the party. Their protests ceased. Temporary shelters for the armed guards had been placed along the road. Each one was occupied. Hunter knew that what he was witnessing was the result of an alert. The standard global procedures had been laid down nearly eight years ago. In fact, he had been involved with one such event a few years earlier. It meant all leave was cancelled, the drafting in of additional personnel, both British and local, maximum discomfort and distress to embassy staff and visitors, and a pain in the neck for all the other diplomatic establishments in the area. There was no doubt something was going down and Nick wondered briefly if it had anything to do with TIFAT's presence in Pakistan.

In the background, he could hear a band playing an old rock-and-roll tune from the late sixties. People were making their way into the foyer, smiling and chatting. There were surprisingly few uniforms in evidence. The men wore mainly white dinner jackets, although the occasional black one could be seen, while the ladies wore long gowns. They appeared to be a happy throng, composed mainly of the great and the good of Pakistan and the British expatriate community, with a smattering of other nationalities included, mainly diplomats. After all, if you were going to inconvenience your neighbours to such an extent, the least you could do was give them a free drink or two. Hunter skipped the welcoming line and and threaded his way past the other guests. A waiter offered him a tray laden with drinks.

'Gin and tonic, sir, or a horse's neck?', he asked.

'Ah, neither, thanks. I'll go to the bar for a whisky.'

'As you please, sir. The bar is through that door.'

Hunter nodded his thanks and worked his way into the other room. The three barmen were busy but efficient and it wasn't long before he had the equivalent of a triple whisky, soda and ice in his hand. He sipped it and coughed.

The pat on his back made him look round, into the unsmiling face of Hiram B. Walsh. 'It's worse than bourbon,' he greeted Hunter. 'It's actually Pakistani whisky. Can you believe it?'

Hunter nodded. 'Having tasted it, yes I can. How are you doing?'

'Somewhere between lousy and awful. General Macnair is upstairs in the Committee Room. I was told to find you.'

Nick looked at his drink.

'Bring it with you.'

'I'm going to leave it.' He grimaced and placed the glass on a table by the door and followed Hiram through the crowds and up the stairs.

Walsh opened the door and led the way in. The room was dominated by a large oblong table capable of seating at least thirty people. At the far end stood General Macnair, Matt Dunston, Samantha and two men Hunter didn't know. They wore uniforms, formal evening attire, complete with miniature medals, appropriate for the occasion. One was a Major in the British army, the other a Colonel in the Pakistani army.

Seeing his friend, Hunter smiled and nodded. 'Hullo, Matt. I didn't expect to see you here.'

'You really were visiting your tailor.' There was awe in Samantha's voice.

'I told you,' Hunter said giving Samantha a look of admiration. She had her hair up and was wearing a high-necked turquoise gown that suited her.

'Welcome Commander. Glad you could make it,' said Macnair, as though Nick had been invited and not ordered to attend. But then, that was just the General's way.

'Commander Hunter,' said Macnair, 'may I introduce Major Derek Phillips of the Royal Scots and the military attaché, and Lieutenant Colonel Mustapha Zardari, the embassy's liaison officer.'

Handshakes were brief. Hunter wondered if the Lieutenant Colonel was a member of the Bhutto family. Somehow, he suspected that would be the case.

'What's going on, sir?' Nick asked.

'Earlier today, we had word that there's going to be some sort of incident here at the Commission.'

'A demonstration? A shooting? A bomb?' Hunter asked.

'I am sorry, Commander Hunter, we do not know.' Colonel Zardari's English was precise, with just a trace of an accent. 'All I can tell you is that we received a warning at police headquarters. We cannot be sure and so we are taking no chances.'

Hunter knew that, unlike the days when the IRA made threats and code words were used to authenticate the danger, no such luxury existed in the world of Islamic terrorism. He also knew that far more innocent Pakistanis had been killed by the terrorists than any other nationality. The unanswered question amongst the security forces of Pakistan was what were the terrorists after? If it was political control of Pakistan they were going the wrong way about it. Hunter wondered if the threat had anything to do with TIFAT's current operation, but knew better than to broach such a subject in front of Zardari. 'I know this is a stupid question, but why has the reception been allowed to continue?' he asked.

'I'd already suggested to the Ambassador and the High Commissioner that the event be called off,' Macnair replied, waving his hand in dismissal. 'I can't say I blame them, but they wouldn't hear of it. According to them, if we abandoned or stopped a reception every time such a message was received, we would never hold one.'

'It's a hoax then?'

Major Phillips answered. 'Not to put too fine a point on

it, Commander Hunter, the best we can say is, yes, probably. I've been here nearly a year and we have yet to hold a single event without some sort of threat being received.'

'Have there been any actual incidents?' Samantha asked.

The Major nodded. 'One. About ten months ago. A small bomb exploded. There were no casualties and very little damage. However, over the last few years the Pakistani government has been highly effective in combating the fundamentalists who are trying to destabilise the country and impose their own idea of Islam.'

'It is true,' said Colonel Zardari, 'but it is a never-ending struggle.' Zardari stroked his moustache with the index finger of his right hand and cleared his throat. 'We have had confirmation that a second dirty bomb has gone missing from one of our armouries. But then, I understand, you are aware of this.'

Nobody said a word. TIFAT's operations were kept secret, at least by the men and women of TIFAT. If there were any leaks they usually came from someone in the government.

Zardari's smile was sardonic. 'It is all right, gentlemen and lady, I and my colleagues understand. If the information becomes common knowledge, we will deny it has anything to do with Pakistan. You know differently and so do we. There can be no secrets between us if we are to prevent the second detonation.' He paused and then added, 'Were it to happen, the results, needless to say, would be catastrophic. Not just for Britain but the rest of the world. If the fanatics have their way, then Allah alone knows what will happen.'

The faces of his companions were bleak, their eyes hard.

'How did one of your submarines get involved?',

Macnair asked, voicing the question on everyone's lips.

'I expected you to ask that,' Zardari said. 'We have been investigating. For the past six months, the crew changes have been slow and subtle. We have trickle drafting just as you do. We did not, could not, notice the fact that the whole crew were fundamentalists. The appointer responsible is missing. Where he has gone we have no idea. Possibly on the submarine.'

Neither Hunter nor Macnair enlightened the Colonel to the fact that they had discovered an extra officer on the submarine. Instead, they all nodded.

'When I was at Sandhurst I took part in Exercise Overkill.'

'What's that?' Samantha asked.

General Macnair answered. 'It's where a nuclear bomb explodes in Europe.'

Samantha's surprised look was reflected in her voice. 'That's an exercise? What happens?'

'In all the scenarios we've played out,' Hunter answered, 'the results are usually the same. First of all, most of the present governments of Europe will fall, not just ours, to be replaced by right-wing, ultra-conservative administrations. Riots and unrest will sweep the continent until one thing happens.'

Zardari interrupted. 'It is so. There will be one objective, one promise made to the people of Europe and only one. Revenge. The total destruction of the country considered responsible.'

'Which in this case,' said Macnair, 'will be Pakistan, because, irrespective of who has actually carried out the attack, the bombs came from here.'

'Which is why we have to stop these madmen,' Zardari said nodding in agreement.

Samantha looked at Macnair. 'But I thought you said that wouldn't happen. Because of the deaths of innocent people.'

The General nodded. 'Up to a point that's true. But everything would be different if Europe's governments change.'

'There's a follow-up to the scenario painted,' Matt said, looking at Samantha. 'The aftermath. If the revenge attacks result in millions being killed, which is highly likely, the people in Europe will be aghast at what they did. What they demanded.'

'I can see that. So what happens then?' Samantha asked.

Macnair shrugged. 'We don't know. Opinion is too divided. All we can say for sure is that the world will never be the same again.'

21

Mohammed Akbar had been at sea for three days. His transport was a dilapidated tramp steamer which had wheezed into the northern end of the Suez Canal. The welcome he received from his brothers in al-Qaeda at Marseilles had not been as fulsome as he might have wished. They were aware of the problems facing the brethren back in Britain. The British had ensured the message was disseminated to those they thought ought to know. Certain facts had been made absolutely clear to al-Qaeda. There were to be no trials. No mitigation. No pleading of not guilty. The West had finally declared war on the Muslims who had declared war on it. Indeed, in view of what was at stake, the West, in the guise of TIFAT, had gone even further. It was very simple. Not merely the friend of my enemy is also my enemy, but *you* are my enemy if you do not actively help us in our fight.

* * * * *

The COBRA meeting was attended by all the Cabinet members. The Prime Minister chaired it, sitting at the head of the table and called them all to order.

'The by-election was a disaster,' the Home Secretary began.

'We're not here to discuss the by-election,' growled the Prime Minister.

The statement was met with incredulous protests. Many of the parliamentary seats of those present were at risk. If the swing to the Conservatives stayed at the level shown, Labour would be devastated at the next election. Order was eventually restored.

'What I have to say is of far greater significance.' He saw the excitement in their eyes, their avarice for the top job - his. If he hadn't been so utterly exhausted he would have enjoyed dashing their hopes. Taking a deep breath he said, 'The President of the United States contacted me a little while ago. He made it clear that the information he was about to impart to me was top secret. No one, absolutely no one, was to be told.'

Now he had their attention. The Prime Minister was not about to resign after all. What could the President have to say that needed to be kept top secret? A few of the more astute minds in the room guessed what was coming.

'The existence of the plutonium devices has been confirmed?' asked the Foreign Secretary.

The Prime Minister nodded. Again, pandemonium broke out.

The Home Secretary sat up straighter as excitement coursed through her. Her seat was the most vulnerable of them all. Now she had what they had all been praying for, an international incident that took attention away from the government's ineptitude. She had in mind the squandering of vast sums of taxpayers' money, the destruction of Britain's armed forces and the loss of border controls, resulting in unlimited immigration, not just from the European Union but from the rest of the world as well. The list went on and on. A list that was never admitted to outside those four walls – and even then it was rarely acknowledged. The parts they had each played in events were too mind-numbing to admit to, even to oneself, unless it was over a large drink in a quiet moment, late at night. But now? Now it had all changed. If they weathered the storm – if the bombs were stopped – then anything was possible. Even another five years in power. One of those present in the room did his best not to smile as the Prime Minister described the events of the previous few days. He could expect the information to leak to the press within two or three hours of the meeting ending. It was inevitable.

'Prime Minister,' the Home Secretary said, 'if we have discovered the whereabouts of one bomb and dealt with it, why not the second?'

The Prime Minister shrugged. 'I have no idea. I'm trying to contact General Macnair in Scotland but so far have been unable to do so.'

'That monster,' retorted the Home Secretary. 'TIFAT should be disbanded immediately and its operatives arrested and tried for murder.'

There were growls of assent around the table until the Prime Minister raised his hand for silence. 'I have been told by the Americans that it is thanks to TIFAT that the first, um, device was found. Secondly I have been told in no uncertain terms to leave the organisation to get on with their job within the remit of their mandate.'

There were further protests and this time the Prime Minister regained control of the meeting by calling for order whilst at the same time slapping the palm of his hand on the table. 'Make no mistake about it, without Macnair and his lot we'll get nowhere so for the moment –

regardless of what we decide in the future – we give them every encouragement and support.'

The Foreign Secretary coughed to get attention and then said in a diffident voice, 'If the President told you not to say anything, why are you telling us?'

'Because I believe that as my Cabinet colleagues you have a right to know. I believe in collective government. Furthermore, any input you make will be gratefully received.'

They all understood the underlying message. They were in it together. The Prime Minister was not going to carry the can alone if anything went wrong. It had been his way since entering politics – which, in fact, was all he had done since leaving university. Not for him a job in the outside world, the need to make a living, the ownership of a business. Between his huge pension and the inevitable elevation to the House of Lords with its generous allowances and daily attendance money, he would see out his days not only in comfort but in relative luxury.

The meeting dragged on. Nothing of use or importance was discussed. The same comments and questions went round and round. The government was incapable of coming to the right decision. Or come to that, any decision. Politically, Britain was in paralysis.

* * * * *

He was right. He sat in his office and watched the news unfolding. It was the beginning. And once the explosion occurred . . . A wave of excitement tinged with euphoria swept through him. Those idiots at the COBRA meeting this morning had no idea. Not a clue about what was almost inevitable. Then he tempered his thinking. Even if

223

the bomb didn't explode, all hell was due to break loose. It was a shame he didn't drink alcohol. A celebratory drink would have been just right at that juncture. Instead, he would celebrate with tea, a rather fine tea from Ceylon.

*   *   *   *   *

Many Islamic groups across Europe were as appalled as everyone else at what was happening. As the news broke, the international press in particular started pointing the finger of blame firmly at Muslims, all Muslims. Even when it was pointed out that Muslims in Europe were equally at risk and that the vast majority were decent, law-abiding citizens, it was to no avail. Newspapers, magazines, TV and radio broadcasts had a common message - should a nuclear device explode in Europe, whoever was responsible would pay a heavy price. Already the media had upgraded the plutonium-based device to a fully fledged nuclear bomb. The written press and the airwaves were full of pontificating 'experts'. Bomb yields led to blast damage and expected deaths and injuries. It was all pure conjecture, as wide of the mark as it was varied, and yet on one point there was consensus. An explosion of this kind would be completely devastating and casualties would exceed those suffered in both world wars.

Panic was rife in most of the capital cities of Europe. People were fleeing London, Rome, Paris, Berlin, Lisbon and even Athens. It was mindless migration with no thought for the consequences. Looting was rife and deaths common. Police were forced to open fire during one nasty riot in Rome, and again when a group attacked a Muslim enclave on the outskirts of Madrid. The reaction of the West, the upheaval that was already occurring, was exactly what al-Qaeda had anticipated.

*   *   *   *   *

As he wallowed in the filthy steamer, Akbar could not understand the veiled animosity shown towards him. However, one thing he had learned in his years as a supporter of the one true faith was patience.

'*In sha' Allah*,' he said aloud. If God wills it. The standard excuse for anything and everything that went wrong. It was nobody's fault. It was the will of God.

Another two days passed before the ship arrived at Jeddah in Saudi Arabia. Not only was it a bustling sea port for oil exports and a vast amount of imported Western goods, it was also a disembarkation point for visitors travelling to the holy city of Mecca. It was with a feeling of relief that Akbar picked up his canvas holdall and walked down the gangway. The crew stood on the deck and watched him leave. At the gates to the port, after a two-kilometre walk, he found a bus to King Khaled International Airport. There, the first thing he did was change his money into American dollars; the currency most favoured throughout the Middle East. Once at the enquiry desk he discovered he had two options. A direct flight to Islamabad that evening for $790, or a stop-over in Dubai using Etihad Airways, the UAE national carrier, for $303. He chose the latter. He had time in hand but his cash was dwindling rapidly.

In Dubai, he crammed into a jitney that took him to the outskirts of the city. There, he found a place to sleep for just a few dollars. To save money he decided to go to bed hungry. The following morning he woke with a rumbling stomach so bought a meal known as halva puri choley. The halva was made from semolina and served sweet or salted. His was sweet. Choley was a spicy chickpea and potato curry eaten with a round, flat, deep-fried bread known as puri. He skipped the normal third course of yoghurt and cream and finished his meal with chai – black tea with no milk and plenty of sugar. After the meal, he sat back with a satisfied sigh and a guilty conscience. Nowhere else in the world was it possible to get such a breakfast.

The jitney back to the airport was cramped. The aeroplane was late as always and it was early evening before he arrived in Islamabad. This time, a dilapidated bus took him into the city and dropped him off near Sitara Market. Once there, he made enquiries about cheap hotels. They were all in the 800-rupee range but, with only $400 to his name, he decided to look elsewhere for a bed. Luckily he stumbled on the Youth Hostel Islamabad, at the Aabpara Market, where he shared a room with three other men. There were communal toilets and cold showers but no cooking facilities. The restaurant was adequate, provided you liked curries of various strengths, flavours and meats. The cost was 300 rupees.

At precisely eight o'clock that evening, Akbar sent a text message. It was simple and to the point. All it said was – *Arrived Islamabad*. Now all he had to do was wait to be contacted. He didn't have long to wait.

* * * * *

Whilst the guests at the reception enjoyed dainty canapés

and alcoholic drinks, the contingent from TIFAT made do with teas and coffees.

'Incidentally,' Macnair said to Zardari, 'thank you for the information on Rehman Khan.'

Zardari shrugged. 'It is the best we could do. We have been looking for him for many months. As we explained, our information places him somewhere near the Afghanistan border, close to the Khyber Pass.'

'We're also working on it,' said Macnair, but he didn't elaborate on what TIFAT was doing.

It was just after 23.00 when Macnair announced, 'Time to stop, gentlemen,' he smiled at Zardari and Phillips, 'if there's nothing else?'

Major Phillips understood immediately what Macnair wanted and stood up. 'Thank you, sir. Come on, Mustapha, let's leave these good people in peace.'

The Colonel nodded his understanding, said goodnight and followed the Major out.

'Samantha, there's a bottle of malt in my room. I picked it up at the duty-free. Can you fetch it, please, while I organise glasses and ice? Is there anything you'd like to drink or will whisky do?'

'Whisky will be fine, thank you.' She was back a few minutes later with a bottle of Ledaig, a single malt from Tobermory, Mull.

A waiter appeared with glasses, soda, water and ice, and the General did the honours. While he and Walsh had theirs neat, Samantha and Hunter took soda and ice, while Dunston added a drop of water to bring out the flavour.

'Thank you, sir,' said Samantha, taking the glass.

'Samantha, in the army we have the habit of calling people by their first names when in the mess, no matter what their rank. Please call me Malcolm. Isn't that right, Nick?'

'Yes, sir. Except I'm Royal Navy,' Hunter smiled.

The quip made the others laugh, easing the tension.

'Sir, I gather you didn't call us here just to listen to Zardari,' Hunter continued.

Macnair sipped his drink thoughtfully before replying. 'Isobel phoned earlier. Thanks to Colonel Zardari and the information about Rehman Khan we were able to concentrate our resources in the general area of the Khyber Pass. The satellites intercepted a call between someone in Saudi Arabia and someone at the Pass. It appears that arrangements are being made for a vehicle to be allowed into a valley called Landi Kotal. There's some sort of camp there. It's well guarded and inaccessible, with just one barely passable road in and out of the area. It's a logical staging post for someone heading out of Pakistan and trying to get to the West through Afghanistan.'

'Also,' said Walsh, 'for most of the journey, there will be other Muslims to help them along.'

'That's what Isobel suggested. It's an area we know al-Qaeda operates in. So it makes sense. And it's all we have to go on at the moment, so here's what I propose.' Macnair briefed the team and over the next hour the plan was refined further and finally agreed.

As their glasses were refreshed, Hunter asked, 'What happened when you met with President Tahir, sir?'

'He's given us *carte blanche* to do whatever is required. With one proviso – don't get caught. Tahir's military through and through, still head of his armed forces, and has no illusions as to what would happen to Pakistan if the madmen are not stopped. He's fully aware of Operation Overkill and what it means. However, he is now having to control three hundred and forty-two members of his national assembly, some of whom, incredibly, support what's happening. They want to see London devastated. And if not London, then some other Western city. If Tahir is too heavy-handed, he could face huge problems here. It's a fine balancing act, which is why he's more than happy for us to take the weight. You have to bear in mind that Pakistan has been the *only* Muslim country to keep Islam out of politics. But that was as a military dictatorship, and of course that's changing, as the assembly flexes its muscles and wields more and more power. No other Muslim country has achieved the separation of state and religion. There are forty-seven countries where the majority of the people are Islamic and only five of them are considered fully operating democracies as we understand the term, namely Turkey, Indonesia, Bangladesh, Mali and Senegal. Muslim fundamentalism is rife here in Pakistan. The reality is, democracy is on a knife-edge. The fear is, if a bomb explodes anywhere in Europe, the fundamentalists led by JIMAS will claim that it is proof of how superior Islam is to the West, or some other such rubbish. There will be war between the West and most of the Islamic countries for generations to come. And with the nuclear weapons now in existence . . . ' His voice trailed off.

Down below, the strains of 'God Save the Queen' were followed by the Pakistan national anthem. Luckily, the threat of something happening had proved to be a hoax after all. The guests departed, relaxed and happy, a mood that would shortly be shattered as news from Europe trickled in.

229

22

Following the meeting, orders were passed to the rest of the team on *The Flower of Allah*. They each had jobs to do. Flights were organised and travel arrangements confirmed. There was information to check, double-check and, if necessary, act upon. Badonovitch and Napier were called to Islamabad.

Hunter returned to his hotel, where he was soon asleep. What woke him was a huge explosion just after 06.30. He snapped fully awake before the echoes of the detonation had died down. Rushing to the window he pulled back the curtain. He looked over to his left and could make out the rising pall of dense smoke in the grey dawn. It appeared to be coming from the diplomatic compound – more precisely, he thought, the British High Commission – and in the background he could hear the sounds of sirens and bells. He went into the bathroom where he quickly shaved and showered. He hoped to God nobody had been hurt. He was getting dressed when his mobile rang. Picking it up, he saw it was Walsh.

'You and the others alright?'

'Yes. General Macnair says to stay where you are. We'll only get in the way of the emergency services. If our help is requested it'll be different. Hang on, someone's at the door.'

Hunter heard Walsh say, 'Malcolm, come in.' There was a pause. 'Nick? We need you here.'

'I'm on my way.'

Hurrying past the crowd that was already gathering, he arrived at a cordon of policemen who wouldn't allow him through.

'I guessed you might have a problem,' said Walsh, hurrying over. 'It's okay, officer,' he said to a police inspector, 'this man is needed inside.'

The policeman scowled but nodded. Hunter ducked under the police tape and followed Walsh over to a badly burned car chassis. There were a number of people looking at it, including Napier and Badonovitch.

'Hullo, Boss,' Jan Badonovitch greeted him.

'Jan, Douglas.' Handshakes were brief. 'When did you guys get in?'

'A few minutes ago,' replied Napier.

'Do we know what happened?', Hunter asked Walsh.

'Suicide bomber. The car was stopped at the first checkpoint and then up it went. It looks like one dead body inside although they can't be sure until they've counted the pieces. Three Commission lads killed. They'd been on guard duty.'

Three devastated families, thought Hunter. Each attending the funeral of a loved one. The Last Post sounding over the graveside. The ceremonial folding of the Union Jack before it was handed to a wife, a mother, a father. Bastards!!

'We have to be thankful that less than ten percent of the explosives actually detonated.' Napier said.

'How do we know?' Nick asked.

'Take a look,' said Napier.

Hunter stood surveying the scene. He could see bits of plastic explosive scattered over a fairly wide area. 'Misfire?'

'Had to be, boss,' said Badonovitch.

'Do we know how come?' Hunter asked.

'Not yet,' replied Walsh. 'Douglas and Jan are going to take a look. Some of the Commission lads will be here shortly. They've been told to scrape this lot up.'

Hunter looked around the perimeter. As far as he could tell only the outer wall had been flattened. 'If the whole lot had gone off this area would have been flattened. The loss of life would have been horrendous.' He nodded across to the nearby buildings. 'Both the Iranian Embassy and the Indian High Commission would probably have been demolished.' He paused and then added, 'I'll give them a hand. We might find something useful, but I doubt it.'

'General Macnair wants you Nick. Jan and Douglas can manage here,' Walsh said.

'Where is he?'

'Inside, talking to the Ambassador and the High Commissioner. He's suggested breakfast.'

Walsh led the way towards the imposing double doors and they went upstairs. A buffet breakfast was laid out on a sideboard. Hunter realised he was hungry and helped himself to scrambled eggs and bacon. Walsh was doing the same when Samantha and Malcolm Macnair arrived.

'What a mess,' the General greeted them.

The other two nodded.

'Look at this,' Macnair said as he switched on the television and flicked it to BBC News, whose reports showed the panic that was sweeping Europe. Already mosques were being attacked and burnt and Muslims across Europe were under a state of siege. Deaths were being reported, albeit mercifully few so far. Hunter had taken only a couple of mouthfuls of food when he lost his appetite. He sat back, sipped his coffee and watched events unfold. He noticed that the others were doing the same. After some minutes, Napier and Badonovitch came in.

'That didn't take long,' said Macnair.

'Basic stuff, sir,' Napier replied. 'We've sacked the plastic. Our lads have taken it. They'll burn it later.'

'Why didn't the whole lot go off?' Walsh asked.

'The detonation cord had been cut through and it was only hanging together by the outer plastic. They obviously hadn't noticed. Sheer luck. Stupidity on their part,' replied Napier. 'The plastic was sweating a bit, as well.'

'How old?' Hunter asked.

'I'd say six or seven years. What do you think, Jan?'

'Yes, I agree, and I would say Chinese.'

Although the explosive was a Czechoslovakian invention, it was now manufactured under licence in various countries around the world.

'Why Chinese?' Macnair frowned at him.

'The oil, sir. You can tell,' Napier replied.

Hunter said, 'That's true. If it has a dark veneer of oil then it's either Chinese or Brazilian. And Brazilian doesn't make any sense.'

Macnair nodded. There was a great deal of interference in the area by the Chinese, one of many bones of contention between East and West. So the conclusion made sense. 'Be that as it may, we were incredibly lucky.'

It was Samantha who posed the question that had just occurred to Hunter. 'Are we, personally, the target? Or is it just part of the on-going campaign against the West in general?'

Macnair scratched the side of his nose, screwed up his face and reached for his coffee cup before replying. 'Was it a coincidence? I don't know. What I do know is that I don't believe in coincidences.' He sipped his coffee before adding, 'Which is why we're moving out in two hours. I won't risk any more lives here. Besides which, I don't want the Ambassador or High Commissioner making a fuss. Our presence here is a personal favour extended by the Ambassador – the government would never condone it – so we'd better get a move on.' He looked at Hiram. 'Everything fixed?'

'Yes, sir. There'll be a cleaners' van coming for us. It will pull in at the back canopy. With luck we won't be noticed. Not with all that's going on around here.'

'Right. I need to talk to Isobel. I'll leave you to sort out everything. One other thing, the large-scale map of Pakistan, please Hiram.'

Walsh spread the map on the table.

'Take a look at this,' said Macnair. 'This is where we're going. You see this valley? It's about five miles long and ends in a very steep cliff. You can see how narrow it is.'

'Are those houses?' Hunter asked, pointing a finger.

'Yes. Water comes from this stream. No electricity. So far, satellites indicate a minimum of a dozen or so men guarding the mouth of the valley. It varies. They are well dug-in and know the terrain. In short, a death trap for an entrance. Agreed?'

The others nodded.

'This end of the valley is empty. The cliff face is actually sheer in some places and very loose scree in others. A dangerous death trap but without the requirement for armed guards.' He looked around the table at the sombre faces staring at the map.

'Hence the para-foils,' said Hunter.

'Correct,' replied Walsh. 'We go in behind, not from the end of the valley, but from over here.' He placed a stubby forefinger almost ten miles from the target. 'Thanks to the new foils, it should be a walk in the park.'

'More like a float in the dark,' replied Hunter. 'With your eyes shut.'

'We've run the scenario past Cuthbert and it has predicted a better than eighty percent chance of success,' Macnair said.

'How come it's so high?', Dunston asked.

'It's thanks to the new foils. The old ones would have had us trailing in the low sixties,' replied Walsh.

'How are we getting there?', Hunter asked. 'It looks to be a hard climb.'

The General answered. 'Hi, Hi. From twenty miles out.' This meant a parachute drop, high altitude, high opening, resulting in maximum drift. A dangerous and often unpleasant experience. 'There's a Hercules waiting for us at the airfield. Normal departure, no flight alteration, hence the Hi, Hi. Hopefully, we'll be undetected. Okay, that's it. Get ready to move out. I'm just going to have a word with Isobel.'

Macnair went through to the communications room where he was patched through to Rosyth. In spite of the fact that Britain was five hours behind Pakistan, Isobel was there waiting for his call. Her caffeine intake was helping to keep her awake.

'Anything new?'

'No, sir. The best information we have by far is what you passed to us. There are plenty of rumours, each one sending us in different directions. We are checking everything we can, but it's tediously slow work.'

'It was ever thus,' said Macnair heavily. His call had been a last-ditch effort to ensure that what they were doing and where they were going was the best use of their time and resources. It appeared to be the case.

'Malcolm, did you see what happened with the London Stock Exchange yesterday?', Isobel asked.

'Yes. It was inevitable. Presumably it'll be closed again today.'

'It also looks as though all European markets will be shut as well. They are saying that they may not re-open for many days. Or at least until the crisis is over. Literally hundreds of billions have been wiped off the worldwide value of shares.'

'We've been watching BBC News,' said the General. 'There's nothing we can do until we find and stop the second device. I also heard some of the statements made in the House of Commons last night. Bloody idiots. They're adding to the fear, not reducing it.'

'So all the political analysts say,' Isobel explained. 'But did you realise there were only a couple of dozen members in the House? The rest of them have done a bunk. That's causing its own furore as you can imagine. Gutless bunch of cowards. And,' Isobel added, unable to keep the sarcasm out of her voice, 'that's me being polite.'

The press around the world were having a field day. The big question they were asking – was there another nuclear bomb on its way to Europe? The consensus of opinion – more than likely. The US President had been forced to acknowledge the existence of the first device. When he did so he emphasised that it had been a plutonium dirty bomb, not a nuclear one but it was to no avail as far as the media was concerned. As a result the distinction was wasted on the general public. Whilst a profound fear was sweeping Europe, euphoria was being engendered in some parts of the Islamic world. Rioting across Europe was gaining momentum. Mosques were being burnt and Muslim institutions attacked. So far, more by luck than judgement, relatively few Muslims had actually been killed, although hundreds had been attacked and hurt. Many were quitting Europe to return to their homeland. Even Iraqis who had fled the war and Iranians who had fled the regime were going back. Macnair sighed in genuine sorrow. Many of the people leaving were law-abiding, upstanding citizens who contributed greatly to the well-being of their adopted countries. Be they doctors, engineers, accountants, mothers, fathers or just ordinary workers, they contributed. Their loss was something Europe would find very hard to recover from. It was imperative for TIFAT to move fast and decisively.

Isobel confirmed that, from the analysis made by Cuthbert, based on the additional information given to Macnair the previous night, the dirty bomb was to be found in the valley near the Afghanistan border. Cuthbert gave a seventy percent chance of the device being there.

'We know what we have to do,' said Macnair. 'Let's get organised. Samantha, you'll have to return to Rosyth. We need to work together more than at any time in our history. Bring MI5 and MI6 fully up to date.'

23

The train journey had been worse than Mohammed Akbar could ever have imagined. The third class compartment had been cramped, full of people and various animals – mainly goats – and the seats had been wooden slats, as hard as Hades. The train never once exceeded 30mph, and seemed to stop anywhere and everywhere. People and animals got on and off, it seemed to Akbar, at will. The whole experience sorely tested his patience but the train eventually arrived in Peshawar.

In the teeming city he went to the offices of the Khyber Political Agent to collect documents which would allow him to travel along the Khyber Pass. At a cost of 5,000 rupees, or just over £41, he was able to travel to Landi Kotal, forty-two kilometres away. The journey took nearly four hours, two steam engines pushing and pulling the little train up 600 metres in thirty kilometres, passing through thirty-four tunnels and crossing ninety-two bridges. There were two stops after leaving Peshawar station, the first at Peshawar airport to cross the runway and the second at Shahgai Fort for tea. The refreshment was included in the price of the ticket, as was the return journey. Akbar did not intend to return however.

At Landi Kotal he was met by two men driving a battered old Land Rover. Their greetings were brief as well as surly. Akbar didn't care as excitement grew within him. At last he was to meet the exalted one. The leader who would one day be revered as a true man of the one God. Of Allah! A prophet for the twenty-first century! A man to be talked about in the same breath as the Prophet Mohammed, blessed be his name! Akbar had studied the history of the great and devout man. He knew there was nobody alive who understood, or who could recite, the Qur'an like him. His devoutness was legendary amongst Islamic fundamentalists the world over.

The journey by road was just as uncomfortable as it had been so far but at last they were approaching the secret valley. The Land Rover didn't stop but bounced on over the rough ground, swaying violently, only inches away from striking the steep walls either side. Above them, at various intervals, ledges had been cut into the rock to shelter the armed guards on duty. Akbar counted eight of them. After about one hundred metres the walls suddenly opened out and the valley lay before them, stretching into the hazy distance, surrounded by high mountains. It was a breathtaking view, somewhat spoilt by the cluster of stone houses in the near distance and the swirling smoke from their chimneys. The car stopped outside the largest building. Akbar climbed down and stretched his aching limbs. What a journey! However, his mood quickly changed to one of almost uncontainable excitement when he was led inside. Sitting on a mat, cross-legged, his balding grey hair under a dirty white scarf, sat the great man himself. The long beard was matted and filthy, the hands encrusted in grime, the nails black. The stench of body odour made Akbar want to

239

vomit. Standing behind the seated figure were two heavily armed guards, each watching him closely. Akbar counted another eight sitting on stools around the room. Looking at their glorious leader he tried hard not to show his huge disappointment. He knelt down and bowed his head. Greetings were brief. The man on the mat looked Akbar in the eyes and began speaking. His voice was monotonous with no hint of censure either in the tone or the language used. Akbar found it difficult to concentrate on what was being said, to understand what he had to do. Finally, the briefing ended. It had lasted nearly forty-five minutes. Throughout that time, no notes were referred to and none of the other men had spoken. From time to time, when certain information was given, a man sitting alongside handed Akbar an envelope. Each one was of importance, containing such things as a train timetable, train tickets and reservations. Then came the last item. One of the men stepped into an adjoining room and returned with an aluminium case not much bigger than a briefcase. The man was helped to his feet, where he stood, a little taller than Akbar, in spite of the fact that he had a pronounced stoop. His emaciated, gaunt features looked at the other man without a hint of kindness in his eyes.

'Do not fail. If you do, your death will be a very bad one.'

With his two guards helping him, each with a hand under an elbow, the old man shuffled towards the door. Akbar stood, his knees aching, fear mixed with joy in his heart. He watched the other man go out into the fading sunlight and climb into the Land Rover that had brought Akbar to the valley. The engine burst into loud, smoke belching life and with a crunch of gears set off back the way it had come. Mohammed Akbar stood there at a loss as to what he should do next. One of the men who stood next to him spoke.

'Come. We will eat before we leave.'

* * * * *

The Hercules C130 took off as planned on a heading agreed with Air Traffic Control. It took the team to within sixty-five miles of their landing position. The jump was at 20,000ft. What they were going to attempt would have been impossible a few years earlier. However, the technology had come a long way and now, it was not only feasible but the whole operation verged on being safe. Naturally, there were downsides. Not least was the weather. Luckily, it was about as good as they could have wished for. Most importantly, the gentle breeze was from the south-east at 5,000ft and below. The high winds associated with being four miles high weren't as bad as they usually were, and the 50mph winds were going to be an asset on this jump. All gear had been checked and double-checked. The only equipment they had with them was what they carried on their backs. It wasn't a great deal but it should be sufficient. Isobel reported that, according to the infra-red detectors on the satellite, there were twenty-two people in the valley.

'Ten minutes,' the pilot announced over their earphones.

* * * * *

For General Malcolm Macnair, it was the most significant time in his life and career. His excuse for being there was that they were stretched to breaking point. Not a single front line person available. In the circumstances, an extra gun could make all the difference and frequently did. But, he admitted to himself, that wasn't the real reason. For a number of months now he had been wondering about his right to give the orders he was obliged to issue. To send his men into such dangerous situations that their chances of survival were often ludicrously slim. In the past two years they had lost a number of very good operatives, a fact that he took to his bed every night.

Closing his eyes, he leaned back against the inadequate soundproofing, analysing the real reason he was on the plane. He knew the answer. He had proved himself often enough in the past, as a more junior officer, but did he still have what it took now? He hoped that he did and this was his chance to prove it. He couldn't help a small smile at the melodrama of his thoughts, because it wasn't the gun-battle they would soon be facing that he was most concerned about. TIFAT was facing its two most deadly and implacable foes ever. The first was Islamic fundamentalism and their hatred of everything Western. The second was the British government because of their political correctness and desire to shut TIFAT down.

He acknowledged it wasn't merely political correctness that was the trouble with Britain's government. It was their lack of control over TIFAT. They had spent a decade and more micro-managing the country to such an extent that the people were on their knees begging to be left alone. Targets for this, paperwork for that. All neatly filed. All ignored. All the boxes ticked, just in case someone wanted to check. Britain now had more interference from its government at every level than a communist country. The irony was, the populace weren't fully aware of it, though they were finally beginning to wake up to the facts. Macnair wasn't without his supporters – important players in both the political arena and the military – but what was happening was his battle and his alone.

From the very beginning TIFAT had been underfunded. The teams received lousy pay for what they did and, most significantly of all, had been given inadequate equipment. Which was why, when they raided the bank accounts of their enemies, TIFAT kept the money. What else could they do? They couldn't leave it in the accounts of terrorists and criminals in case others got hold of it. Also if it was left long enough the banks could declare the accounts dormant and take control of the money themselves. But having acquired the money, what were TIFAT to do with it? Compared to national budgets it was peanuts. And which government should get it? The Americans? The British? The Russians? Or, God forbid, the European Union? The list comprised most of the free world. Therefore, the solution was an obvious one which benefited many people without creating any arguments and which succeeded in giving aid and succour where it was needed. A committee comprising the General, Isobel, Walsh, Hunter, Dunston and Tanner decided where the spoils went. Some went to charities all around the world, some was put to operational use, particularly in the purchase of the latest and best equipment, and a small part was paid in bonuses to the men and, when an operative was killed, to their families. Was what they were doing illegal? Probably, but who was to say? To Macnair's mind it was a neat solution. Punish the enemy by taking their assets.

Macnair dragged his thoughts back to the fight to save TIFAT. He began making a mental list of allies. It took his mind off the coming jump.

*   *   *   *   *

Hiram B. Walsh was in a quandary. Two weeks earlier he had been told that he had been selected for promotion to Brigadier General. It was a big step up at his age – he had hit forty a few months earlier – but would be the fulfilment of his dreams. It would mean command and a big job almost immediately, probably in Iraq. It would be a very good move career-wise and one that he would have given his eye-teeth for a couple of years ago. But now? Now it was all so very different.

He glanced around at the five other men in the Hercules. He knew that the likelihood of his ever meeting such people again was remote. Oh, he'd have good people under his command. No doubt about that. But these guys were something different. Their specialist knowledge was awesome, whilst their dedication had to be seen to be believed.

Brigadier General, it had a nice ring to it. One that he could get used to. More than that if he played his cards right he could end up being *the* officer commanding the Marines. It was one of the reasons he wanted in on this operation. A possible last front line action. Hopefully, it would enable him to make up his mind, one way or the other. To go or to stay? He had given up a hell of a lot for the sake of his career – although he liked to think it wasn't all his fault. He and his first wife had split up early, each acknowledging it had all been a mistake. He no longer knew where she was or what she did. His second wife had subsequently married a successful corporate type. He rarely saw his daughter of fifteen and son of seventeen. The fact was, he didn't actually like them much. Their mother had not only spoilt them rotten but had spent years poisoning their minds against him. She blamed him for it all, naturally. He felt sorry for the poor bastard who had taken her on.

He dragged his thoughts back to the operation. He found he was rather looking forward to parachuting from an aircraft at 20,000ft. I must be mad, Walsh told himself.

*   *   *   *   *

Jan Badonovitch was looking forward to jumping from the plane, although an old saying he'd heard before, that you had to be either crazy or a member of Spetsnaz, to jump from a perfectly sound aircraft came to mind. If he survived this operation he had made up his mind that he would put in a request to extend his time with TIFAT for another year. Thanks to the special payments that had been made to him over the previous two years, his mother now owned her own apartment in Moscow. He had also met a girl he thought he would like to marry. But he didn't want to return to Russia. He loved being in the West. He loved the freedom and he loved the variety of life to be encountered around the world. If he returned to his unit, he would lose all that he had come to enjoy and hold dear. He had never made friends in Russia like those he had made at TIFAT. There was still far too much suspicion in the former Soviet Union about everybody and everything. Badonovitch was something of a rarity. He was completely honest with himself. He also admitted that the money they lifted from the bad guys and gave to various charities all over the world, like the orphanage in the village just outside Moscow, was highly satisfying. That had been his doing but Doug Tanner had helped as well. He smiled to himself. The big black man was his closest friend which, for a Russian, would normally be thought impossible. In Russia, prejudice against a man because of the colour of his skin came naturally. Closing his eyes, he made up his mind. Come hell or high water, he intended to stay at Rosyth.

*   *   *   *   *

Lieutenant Douglas Napier hated jumping out of aeroplanes. He did it because it was a part of his job. Give him the sea anytime. Whether on it, in a small boat – powered or paddled didn't matter – or under it, using pure oxygen or nitrox gas mixtures, it was all one to him. He just had a natural affinity with the water.

His father had gone from Sandhurst, the Army officers' college, to a Cavalry Regiment. He had retired as a Lieutenant General and was now on the board of a successful arms-manufacturing company. When Douglas had announced he was joining the Royal Marines his father almost had an apoplexy. Instead of congratulations Douglas received a lecture about the great family tradition of serving in a Cavalry Regiment, like the previous generations, going all the way back to the beginning of the nineteenth century. The more his father preached at him, the more determined he became to defy him. From the Royal Marines to TIFAT had been an easy decision for him to make. Ironically, as a result, his father had done a complete about-face. He now whole-heartedly supported what his son was doing. Douglas suspected the change had come about as a result of Macnair talking to his father. Douglas knew that the two men went back a long way.

His captaincy was due in three months. With the promotion would come the offer of a job, within the Royal Marines, that he knew he would be obliged to take. It was part of his career, fundamental to any future promotion. He didn't want it, but the fact was, he had defied his father once and hadn't enjoyed upsetting the old man. This time, he decided, he would ask his advice.

*　*　*　*　*

Matt Dunston knew he was an oddity. He had gone through Sandhurst, been selected for the Special Air Service where he had been promoted to Captain. He went into 22 SAS, the Counter-Revolutionary Warfare/Counter-Terrorism regiment based at Credenhill, Hereford, in the heart of England. Dunston was used to jumping out of perfectly sound aircraft which, according to regular army units, was a pretty idiotic thing to do. His next move was astonishing, even to him. He still didn't fully comprehend why he had done it. He had always been religious but he had kept his faith pretty much to himself. The SAS wasn't the place to preach tolerance and forgiveness. Even so, he took Holy Orders at the age of 29. His was the most bizarre of careers, and anyone who looked at his record would have agreed. Once ordained, he spent much of his time in Bosnia and Iraq, in the thick of it, giving succour and comfort wherever and whenever he could. He still remembered the day he killed his first man as an ordained priest. Not his last, by any means but definitely his first. It was at the orphanage outside Baghdad. He had gone there with a bag of goodies for the kids: toys, sweets, clothes. Then those four men from the Iraqi secret police had arrived. Sitting in the plane, listening to the drone of the engines, the memories came flooding back.

He had been with the Principal and his deputy, sitting in his cluttered office, partaking of a cup of mint tea, when four armed men entered. They were dressed in the uniforms of the Iraqi police. Dunston had immediately

247

stood up. Warning bells were ringing loudly in his head. They demanded money. Politely, they were informed that there was none. One of the men, the one who had done all the talking, took out a handgun and pointed it at the head of the Principal, a kindly man. Looking after one hundred and twenty plus children was not easy but, thanks to his and his deputy's dedication, he was doing a very good job. Dunston, ignored by the intruders thanks to his dog collar, remembered standing next to the man and watching as the policeman began to pull the trigger. Instinct took over.

The gun had been, ironically, an Israeli Jericho 941 pistol. The magazine carried sixteen nine millimetre rounds and there was a manual safety catch at the left rear of the slide. Dunston had used such a gun on many occasions. As the policeman pulled the trigger the priest had acted.

He rammed the little finger of his right hand between the trigger and the butt and at the same time smashed the extended knuckles of his left hand into the gunman's throat. It was a killing blow. As the man gurgled and began to collapse, Dunston twisted the pistol out of his hand. The other three men stood with mouths agape, slow to react until it was too late – but only just. Although, he acknowledged to himself, without the intervention of the Principal and his deputy he would have been killed. They had flung themselves onto two of the intruders who were already lifting their weapons to fire, while he had shot the fourth man twice in the heart.

The deputy had leapt onto the back of one of the men, while the Principal smashed into the solar plexus of the second, knocking him to the floor. Dunston put the gun into the side of the man carrying the assistant on his back and fired three shots in rapid succession. The Principal had fallen clear of the third man and even as the man was lifting his pistol Dunston shot him in the head.

He remembered the aftermath. The two Iraqis proved to be very brave men. In spite of being terrified for their own safety they had acted swiftly. The Principal and his deputy had seen a great deal of death and knew how close they had all been to their own. They didn't hesitate to cover up what had happened. After all, what were four more missing people in a land as lawless as Iraq had become?

It was days of meditation and thought that finally convinced Dunston that turning the other cheek was not an option. At least, not for him. As a result he had joined TIFAT and had embarked on the most interesting period of his life.

Subsequently, he had been forced to kill on other occasions. But, he liked to tell himself, no one died who didn't deserve it. It also meant that he was in a unique position when it came to counselling the men. Nobody could accuse him of not being there, not having done it. The respect he received he had earned the hard way. Now here he was, about to undertake the most important and dangerous mission of his long and illustrious career. The maniacs they faced had to be stopped, no matter what.

*   *   *   *   *

Hunter sat with his arms folded and his head back, thinking about his future. Not the immediate future. That was taken care of. He had played through the coming events in his head and was as content about what might happen as it was reasonable to be. He had risked his life for Queen and country on numerous occasions and didn't regret a single time he had done so. But now it was different. He knew about the General's battle to save

TIFAT. His father had told him, having heard it from a senior Member of Parliament, a Griffiths. Stopping the men with the plutonium device was proof of how vital TIFAT was to the security of the Western world. The problem was the British government's hostility to the organisation. There was an option that Hunter knew was being contemplated about the future of TIFAT – moving the operation to another country, probably to America. But that wasn't the solution and he and the General both knew it. There was far too much anti-American feeling in the world. TIFAT's strength came from the fact it was truly international in scope and personnel, and operated without fear or favour.

The last time he was home visiting his parents, he had sat in the study, discussing his future. There had been no definitive conclusion but it had been an opportunity to throw ideas back and forth. If he returned to general service within the navy proper, what were his chances of promotion to at least four-ring captain or even flag rank, rear or vice admiral? One important consideration was the rate of reduction of the fleet. The two aircraft carriers promised to the Royal Navy were on hold and for the first time since Nelson's day, Britain now had a smaller navy than the French. Right now he had two-and-a-half stripes and was in line for promotion. He could be offered his third stripe and the rank of Commander at any time. The next step and the one after that basically saw him through middle age and into retirement. That was a depressing thought. Sitting there with the aircraft's engines droning through his entire body, he made up his mind. It was TIFAT or nothing. Returning to general service was not an option. He made another decision. There had been far too much pondering over the last few days. It was time to just get on with the job. The thought gave a lift to his spirits and brought a cynical smile to his lips.

'Two minutes. Stand-by,' the co-pilot announced over the broadcast.

24

Walking down the lowered ramp was text book stuff. Odd numbers threw themselves to the left, even numbers to the right. All the men assumed the frog position and felt the air around them change direction. It was no longer pushing up at them but felt as though it was coming from 45 degrees below and in front, their posture sending them forwards as well as down. A quick communications check confirmed everyone was okay. From now on everything that happened was programmed.

The parachutes deployed at 500ft. Aerofoils snapped into action, legs dropped, shoulders jerked and they were skimming through the air. A glance at the readout on his wrist showed Hunter that they had 55 miles to go and 19,350ft to fall. This meant a glide path of one mile for the loss of 351ft. Exactly as calculated by the computer for the prevailing wind and weather conditions. A press of a button and another glance at his wrist told Hunter that the prevailing wind was dropping off quickly. At 15,000ft there were 42.6 miles to go. So far, so good. He checked his oxygen flow and bottle contents. Perfect. Suit temperature: 22°C. Just about ideal. The team checked in. Their landing place had been programmed into their computers: each man would be touching down at three-second intervals, 30ft apart.

Macnair called a check and all five radioed in. At their height they could still see the sun, though it was moving rapidly towards the horizon as they dropped lower. Touchdown, ideally, should be as near to sunset as possible. That would give them time for the second flight, before darkness finally fell. At 8,325ft they entered a storm cloud. That was when all hell broke loose and the winds and rain battered them and their parachutes. Under normal conditions, with the old rigs, it would have meant death or injury. As it was, the computers began giving detailed instructions: pockets in the wings filled with, and emptied of, helium as and when required. This helped to reduce the sudden plummeting as a downdraft caught one of them, or the sudden surge skywards when an updraft hit. Even so, it was an uncomfortable ride. However, course, speed and height continued in the bracket for an accurate landing. The only problem was how safe the landing would be. The thought of a broken leg, or worse, chilled each man to the bone.

'Report in,' Macnair ordered at 5,000ft and with just over fourteen miles to go.

They did so. Seconds later the cloud passed and they were in clear air once again, following behind the storm, travelling in the right direction. Hunter was the last down. His parachute flared, turned into the wind and he landed gently on the slope, one foot on firm ground, the other on a small rock. Immediately, he struck the release button on his chest and the harness lifted away, floating across the scree even as the wing collapsed.

Every man had touched down safely. There was no talking. They rolled up their wings and shoved them into a narrow crevasse out of sight. They adjusted their backpacks and all six of them moved out. They had less than half a kilometre to yomp up the shallow incline to the summit overlooking the valley where they hoped to find the terrorists and the bomb. The going underfoot wasn't bad. The scree had been left there tens of thousands of years ago after the last ice age, when the rock and mountains had been scraped to their present shape. Dusk was now falling fast and they hurried. They wanted to reach the summit before it was pitch black. Although they carried backpacks and had different pieces of gear attached to their belts, not a sound was made by any of them. All equipment was wrapped in a thin layer of black foam which was designed not to interfere with its use. Near the top, the only noise was that of the General sucking in air.

'Sir,' said Hunter, 'we'll rest for ten minutes. We're safe here and I want to spend some time looking at what's ahead of us.' As he spoke, he removed a pair of binoculars from his belt. He and Walsh, the only other person with binoculars, moved up to the lip of the summit. They lay side by side, quartering the landscape.

'Clear,' Hunter said after a few minutes.

'Agreed.' Walsh kept below the skyline and inched backwards before standing up. Hunter stayed where he was, still looking.

'What have we got?', Macnair asked Walsh.

'Just as we thought, sir. You can see the houses easily enough. There is a truck parked this side of them. The only problem that I can see is that the valley floor is strewn with boulders, some of them pretty big, so landing could be a problem.'

Macnair nodded. 'Let's get started. But nice and slow. There's no hurry. We know from Isobel that there are ten people in the houses – probably sleeping – and there are two guards outside. The rest are scattered along the valley, guarding the entrance. Seems like overkill.'

Walsh said, 'Probably because of the bomb being there, sir. It makes sense to have extra guards.'

'You could be right,' Macnair agreed.

Badonovich and Napier had rigged their para-glider wings across their shoulders. Unlike the wings they had used for the hi-jump, hi-opening, these were manually controlled. They had double wings, connected with tubes of the same material, giving them the look of an old-fashioned bi-plane. They were inflated with helium. The resultant up-lift was considerable, in spite of the fact that they were barely eight feet long and four feet wide in the middle. Napier went over the edge first, launching himself down the vertical wall like a diver off a high board. The wing immediately bit into the air and he began to float down the valley. He knew that Badonovitch was ten seconds behind and about forty metres higher. The jump would have been suicidal, or at least highly dangerous, if it hadn't been for the night-vision goggles both men wore. Unlike the old-fashioned ones that gave the night a green edge, these gave it a very slight blue tinge. However, distances weren't distorted, nor lines of sight given small kinks like they were with the older goggles. It also meant that if you had to shoot someone, you had a better chance of hitting the target. They had no intention of flying down the valley. Napier turned and doubled back as he drifted lower. Then he turned one last time. He was twenty metres above the ground and looking for a safe landing place. The valley floor was strewn with large rocks. If he landed there, he would be in serious trouble. He reported the fact over his radio and flew further along the valley. By injecting more helium using the control button on the right side of the rig he gave himself some lift. To the left, 100 metres further on, the big boulders had been reduced to smaller rocks. A small stream tumbled down the steep side of the valley, and over the millennia, during floods, the water had eroded the boulders to the size of tennis balls and footballs. Napier swung around, came to hover a couple of feet above the ground and then gently let out some helium. He touched down as gently as gossamer and he reported in. A moment later Badonovitch arrived alongside him and the two men moved out to secure the perimeter. Once in position, the others followed the same flight pattern. Hunter was next, followed by Walsh, then Dunston and finally Macnair.

As soon as Hunter landed, he removed his rig and followed the other two to cover the landing site. Walsh landed safely. Dunston, a minute behind, was caught in a slight squall which lifted him rapidly skywards. However, as an experienced para-sailor, he corrected the movement and landed safely.

The General had done the required jumps to earn his para-glider wings. He had also kept up to date. Normally, there would have been no problem. As it was, the squall heralded a passing storm cloud and thunder and lightning suddenly engulfed them. Instead of an uplift, the General was hit by a fast downdraft and was too slow to react. He hit the ground heavily, his right foot landing on a football-sized rock and twisting under him, throwing him to the ground, stunned and gasping for breath. He lay there for several seconds until he felt somebody's hand on his arm, pulling him around, hitting the quick-release button to remove the wing. He got his breath back. 'I'm okay. Thanks,' he said through clenched teeth. His damned foot!

Sitting up, he looked into the worried features of Dunston. 'It's my ankle. It's either broken or a bad sprain. Take a look, will you?'

Dunston had completed numerous medical courses. His basic first aid knowledge was excellent. He even knew how to remove a bullet, provided it wasn't lodged too near a vital organ. Tenderly he felt around Macnair's ankle. The General couldn't prevent himself from wincing.

'I can't be sure,' said the Chaplain, 'but I think it's merely a sprain. Albeit a pretty bad one. You won't be walking far on it, that's for sure.'

'Strap it up nice and tight and shove some painkillers in me,' Macnair ordered.

Knowing better than to argue, Dunston did as he was told. Walsh stood and watched before he said, 'Malcolm, I think you should stay here. We'll come back for you.'

'No, I'm coming. I can cover using the sniper rifle. Finished? Good.' He clambered to his feet, took a step forward and would have fallen flat on his face if Walsh hadn't caught him.

'Malcolm . . .'

'Get Jan. He can piggy-back me. You can share his gear between the rest of you. Do it!'

Walsh didn't argue further. He knew his boss only too well. Not only was Macnair a brilliant tactician, he was also bloody-minded and about as tough as they came in spite of his age, Walsh thought to himself, hiding a wry smile.

When told what was required of him, Badonovitch acquiesced immediately.

They set out. It was just after 22.00. The squall had passed as quickly as it had appeared, and a half-moon crept over the right side of the valley. They walked slowly, carefully checking the ground for booby-traps, although they weren't very likely at that end of the valley. Still, they knew there was no such thing as being too careful. It was why they were still alive. Hunter had point, leading the others. He stopped a couple of hundred metres from where the houses began and knelt beside a large boulder. Using his binoculars, he quickly located the two guards sitting – less than ten metres apart – either side of the dirt track that ran between the stone houses. The others joined him and took a look.

'Thanks, Jan,' Macnair whispered as Badonovitch placed him gently beside Hunter. 'We'll go in at midnight as planned. Once we take out those two. Jan, if you take me over there,' Macnair indicated a boulder a hundred metres from where they were, 'I'll be able to cover the houses and the track.'

'General' A voice spoke in his ear. They all received the same transmission.

'Yes, Isobel.'

'Two people are missing. We only count twenty now.'

'Are you sure?'

'Positive. We've double-checked. It'll be an hour before another satellite passes overhead again, but we are as sure as we can be.'

'All right. I guess that makes our lives easier.'

In spite of the fact that all six of them had been in many situations where waiting was a prerequisite before action, time still dragged. Finally, midnight arrived and they were just preparing to move out when lights came on in the houses and voices could be heard. The team stayed where they were, wondering what the hell was happening. It didn't take long. The guard changed and the place settled down in under ten minutes.

'Give them half an hour,' said the General. 'They'll be in their deepest sleep then.'

At last it was time to move out. Badonovitch hoisted the General onto his back and quietly stepped around the boulder and along the right side of the track. Hunter and Napier were slightly ahead, each with a rifle and night-sights, watching the two guards in their seats. One suddenly stretched, yawned and lit a cigarette. The other said something in a low voice and did the same. Both men's night vision had been affected. Idiots, thought Hunter. At a hundred metres Hunter knelt beside one boulder, Napier another. They each took aim.

'Ready,' whispered Hunter into his throat mike.

'Ready,' copied Napier.

'Shoot,' ordered the General.

The noise was like sheep coughing in the distance. They were head shots and both guards died instantly. One slumped in his seat without a sound while the other, Hunter's target, flew backwards and hit a wooden veranda with a noisy clunk. Nothing happened. No one came to see what the noise was about. No one called out. Hunter handed his rifle to Macnair. The team moved in. Each of them now had the same weapon, a silenced Glock 18. The pistol was based on the world-renowned Glock 17, manufactured by the Austrians and sold to numerous countries for use by their police and military. About forty percent of the weapon was made from plastic materials and had the 33-round magazine in the butt. The weapon was light, accurate and – thanks to specially adapted 9mm Parabellum rounds – had that most important characteristic known as stopping power.

There were six houses, three either side of the track, and according to Isobel four were unoccupied. This had appeared to be the case when the guard changed, but, not relishing the idea of a surprise from the rear, they first checked them out. As expected, the houses were empty.

The house Hunter and Dunston entered had two downstairs rooms and a stone stairway running along the furthest wall. The first room was about five metres square, the floor was rough concrete, the walls unadorned stone. A fireplace in the wall opposite had last been used in the spring. A small stack of firewood stood next to it. Hunter wondered briefly where it had come from: there were no trees for miles around. Two trestle tables with benches either side were the only furniture. The second room was the kitchen. A cooking range with a dampened-down fire threw out some heat. Here, firewood was stacked high along one wall. The men lived in virtual squalor and discomfort that would have been unacceptable in the Western world. Hunter and Dunston moved slowly and carefully up the stairs, Hunter in the lead. There was a door to their left, another to the right. They took the left-hand door first. It opened with the faintest of squeaks as the two men slipped inside. There were two cots occupied by snoring men. Hunter and Dunston took up positions a metre from them, bent over to cot height, arms extended. Both fired simultaneously into the men's temples. The bodies jerked and lay still and silent.

'Two down,' Hunter whispered into his throat mike.

'Two down,' Walsh immediately announced. Unlike the set-up in the house Hunter and Dunston had gone into, Walsh and Badonovitch had found both downstairs rooms held sleeping men. 'Another two down,' whispered Walsh.

Hunter and Dunston went into the second bedroom and quickly despatched another two men.

Walsh and Badonovitch went upstairs. The first bedroom they entered was empty. The second was occupied by the final two men. That accounted for twelve of the enemy.

A painstaking search of the buildings and the dilapidated lorry failed to establish the whereabouts of the dirty bomb. They found plenty of guns, ammunition and explosives, all with Chinese markings, but no case that looked like the one they had found on the *Union of Sark*.

'I have a bad feeling about this,' said Macnair. 'We were positive the device was here. Damnation!' He hit his right fist into the palm of his left hand in frustrated anger.

'The two men who left, sir,' said Hunter, 'could they have taken it with them?'

'It's the only explanation. We need to find out where they've gone and get after them,' Macnair stated the obvious.

'We need to finish off what we came to do first,' said Hunter.

261

25

Mohammed Akbar was satisfied. He had met the great man and had received his blessing. He would, when the time came, die with gladness in his heart. But why had there been such hostility? He did not understand.

Kaman Al-Zawahiri, a distant cousin of Osama bin Laden's deputy, who was accompanying him back to London, said: 'It is simple, my friend. We do not trust anyone who lives in the West.'

'But I am one of you! I have proven myself time and time again! I am not hesitating to complete this glorious task we have been set.'

Al-Zawahiri shrugged. 'All that you say may be true, but,' he searched for the words, 'it is in our nature not to trust others. We are taught it from the cradle, just as we now teach others. Trust your family, then the village, then the tribe, then the people if they are of the same religion. And, under no circumstances whatsoever, trust anyone who lives in the West,' he repeated.

Akbar digested this information and found it sat heavily on his stomach. Then he rationalised, it was natural. They had been treated so badly it was not surprising they should think as they did. After all, he hated the West and he had spent most of his life there. Suddenly the car they were in hit a pothole bursting one of the tyres. They had been travelling slowly so no additional damage was done. The two men reluctantly climbed out of the vehicle and started rummaging in the boot for the car-jack. The spare tyre was so badly worn that canvas showed through in places. It took them over an hour to change the wheel because the nuts were rusted into place.

'I will drive,' announced Mohammed Akbar once they had finished. 'We need to take it very slowly or we will never reach our destination.'

Al-Zawahiri, a poor driver at the best of times, merely nodded. They had covered about 30 miles so far, of the 90 miles they had to drive to reach Kabul. There was plenty of time. The train wasn't due to leave until midday.

Back in the valley the first two of their comrades had just been killed.

*   *   *   *   *

'So far, so good,' said Douglas Napier.

The team had moved slowly along the track. Macnair was now travelling under his own steam, using a sweeping brush tucked under his arm as a crutch.

'You okay, sir?' Badonovitch asked quietly.

'Fine, Jan. You just concentrate on what's ahead. Don't worry about me.' Macnair wiped the sweat off his face with the sleeve of his left arm.

Badonovitch said nothing, knowing the General was being economical with the truth.

According to the information supplied by Isobel, the four guards were stationed along either side of the steepening ravine, sitting on ledges above the dirt track. Hunter was in the lead and spotted the first one just as he

263

approached a bend in the track. Signalling to the others to wait he crept forward slowly and silently, his Glock in his hand. Napier stayed at the bend with a rifle to his shoulder and the man in his cross-hairs. If Napier had to fire, the body would most likely tumble down the side of the cliff, possibly making enough noise to warn the others that something was amiss. If, on the other hand, Hunter could get close enough and shoot the man from the side, throwing him against the cliff face, then the likelihood of that happening was significantly reduced.

The ledge the guard occupied was about four metres above the valley bottom, two metres long and a metre wide. The guard was looking outwards, not expecting any trouble from behind. but then two things happened. First, the man stood up and stepped to the edge of the ledge. He started to undo his trousers to urinate. Secondly, Hunter saw that he was wearing night-vision goggles. They were the old-fashioned ones but still more than adequate. The guard saw Hunter and uttered a loud oath. Just as he was reaching for his rifle Hunter opened fire. It was a snap shot and an excellent one in the circumstances. However, it only hit the guard in the right shoulder. Napier's shot blew his head open like an over-ripe melon hit with a heavy hammer. As they had feared, the guard made a hell of a racket clattering down the side of the steep valley.

A voice called out. It called out again louder, this time with more urgency. None of the team understood what was being said. They moved forward quickly. The second guard was about fifty metres away on the other side of the ravine. He was standing and looking towards the valley. He too had night-vision goggles. He saw Hunter at the same time as Hunter saw him. This time Nick's snap shot killed the guard a fraction of a second too late as the man's reflexes pulled the trigger on his rifle and the noise of the shot echoed up and down the ravine. The bullet went high into the air.

The team advanced in a disciplined movement. Hunter and Dunston took the lead, either side of the narrow ravine. Napier and Badonovitch were right behind with Walsh and Macnair in the rear. There were six guards left and each one had to be taken care of if they were to get out of there alive. Hunter heard a foot crunching on stone around the next bend, which was about five metres away. He held up his hand and the team paused. He pointed ahead and at his left ear. They understood. He'd heard something. Dunston, bent double, moved quickly forward at the same time as Hunter. Their rubber soled canvas boots were silent underfoot. It was Dunston who saw the man first. He fired two shots, both into the guard's torso. The man was thrown back with a loud crash and a gurgle. A volley of shots sounded and the rock face around the team erupted in splinters of stone.

One bullet ricocheted off the floor and smashed into Napier's leg, bringing the young officer heavily to the ground. Hunter had his gun on automatic and was firing at a rate of 1,300 rounds per minute. The magazine emptied in seconds. One terrorist died. Dunston did the same and had the satisfaction of seeing another man fall dead. That left four. There was a pause in the shooting as both sides took stock. Badonovitch inched forward, taking out a fragmentation grenade from a side pocket as he did so. Pulling the pin, he threw it overhand, high above the barrier of boulders that were hiding the gunmen. They heard the grenade land and voices raised in consternation before it went off. As the echoes of the loud explosion died away, the team took up defensive positions and waited. It was too easy to assume that all the terrorists were dead and walk into a trap. They'd seen it before, culminating in the last desperate action of a dying man.

After ten minutes they went forward slowly and carefully. This time Walsh was in the lead, with Hunter at his shoulder. Walsh stepped around the boulder and knew it was a mistake. Only his lightning fast reflexes saved his life as he flung himself backwards. The bullet hit him in the shoulder and passed through, missing Hunter by fractions of an inch. It was Hunter who attacked the other man with a shot through the forehead that blew away half his skull. There were no more al-Qaeda people left alive.

However, the worst part of it all was the fact that they didn't have the bomb, nor did they have a clue as to where it was.

Back near the houses, Dunston patched up the wounded while they discussed their options. Walsh had a shoulder wound and Napier had a pretty nasty thigh wound. General Macnair was struggling with his damaged ankle. Hunter, meanwhile, checked out the cab of the battered five tonne lorry. The keys were in the ignition, but the grinding cough of the engine wasn't encouraging. He tried again and eventually it burst into life.

'Now we have transport out of here,' he said to the others.

Macnair said, 'You know we don't need it. A helicopter will be here in a few hours.'

'I was thinking more along the lines of driving into Afghanistan to follow the two men who escaped,' Hunter explained.

'Which way do we go? They could be anywhere,' said an ashen-faced Walsh.

'Not we. Matt and I,' was Hunter's reply. As he spoke, Badonovitch, who was on guard duty at the entrance to the valley, transmitted.

'We have company. One car. I can't see how many people are in it.'

'How far away?', Hunter asked.

'One, maybe one and a half kilometres.'

'I'll be right there,' said Hunter. 'Matt, stay with the wounded. I'll take care of this.'

Nick hurried along the ravine. When he got to the entrance, the car was only a few hundred metres away and making very slow progress. There were no signs of the dead bodies as Badonovitch had dragged them out of sight as soon as he'd spotted the car. Now he stood behind a boulder, watching the approaching lights. He had placed a pile of stones across the track and there was no way the car could get past unless it stopped and someone removed them.

'Good work, Jan,' Hunter greeted him.

Due to its worn springs the car was bucking and swaying, its lights down on the ground one moment, illuminating the cliff behind the TIFAT men the next. It stopped just before the stones.

A voice called out but they ignored it. They waited. Voices could be heard inside the vehicle.

'Two?' whispered Hunter.

'Three, I think, boss.'

'Yes, you're right. We want at least one of them alive Jan. We need to know where the hell that bomb's been taken. Look, the passenger door is opening.'

'And the driver's.'

A man emerged and stood by the car. The man from the passenger side called out. His voice echoed down the

267

ravine. He turned and said something to someone in the back of the car. Then the two men walked forward and began shifting the rocks. As they bent down they were shot through the crowns of their heads. They collapsed without a sound. The car's lights illuminated the scene but there was no reaction from the person still in the car. Hunter and Badonovitch rushed towards the car, and pulled open the doors. The man inside was working intently on a laptop computer which was evidently connected to the Internet. He looked up in total shock as Hunter thrust a pistol into his face.

'Do you speak English?' enquired Hunter pleasantly.

The man's eyes were open wide in a mixture of horror and fear. Hunter repeated the question. There was no response.

'No? Shoot him, Jan,' he ordered.

'No! Wait . . . I . . .'

'Good, you do. Get out. We have a short walk ahead of us. You okay here, Jan?'

'Yes, boss. No problem. I'll move the car.'

Hunter took the laptop from the man and prodded him along the roadway. Maybe they were going to learn something useful after all.

Once back at the houses, Hunter made the man sit on a rock. It didn't take a lot to get him talking especially when he realised that all the other men were dead. It never ceased to amaze the TIFAT operatives how the possibility of life made men talk. His name, they discovered, was Sheikh Mohammed Al-Sari. He had been sent because he had information for their great leader. He had not expected to meet the great man because he was continuously on the move, staying ahead of the infidels. He would be redirected to a new destination. This would happen three times until he came face to face with their glorious leader, Allah's blessing be on his head.

While Hunter and Macnair questioned him, Dunston and Walsh searched the computer. They uploaded file after file to Rosyth. An hour later the team was preparing to pull out. Their prisoner died with a bullet in his head. There was far too much at stake to leave the man alive. Instead of waiting for the helicopter to arrive, Macnair, Walsh, Napier and Badonovitch, started back towards Peshawar in the lorry. They would be met somewhere along the road by the Pakistani army helicopter, arranged by Lieutenant Colonel Mustapha Zardari. Hunter and Dunston headed into Afghanistan in the car. They were aware there wasn't a moment to lose. There were only four hours before the noon train left Kabul.

26

Crossing into Afghanistan was easier than Nick and Matt had anticipated. At the border town of Torkham they had been told that there was a forty-eight hour wait for the necessary visas. One hundred American dollars, and the problem was soon dealt with. Next came the queue at the border itself. On the Pakistani side lorries were being carefully examined for contraband and illegal stowaways. The customs officers were slow and slapdash. Usually, a fistful of rupees helped to speed up events.

'At this rate, we'll be here all day. I'll go and have a word,' Dunston said as he set off walking in the dusty, dry, hot air past the stationary vehicles and up to the border post. He went inside. Minutes later he was back on the street and waved to Hunter to pull out and come forward. They went through the barrier. To Hunter's querying look, Dunston replied, 'A mere ten dollars. Also, as we pass the booth, take a look over to the right. There are a couple of squaddies.'

'I see them.'

'You can't see it from here, but a bit further on is a heavily armed contingent of our troops which includes a couple of tanks.'

'I did wonder. It makes sense for the Afghans to be manning the border crossing with back up from our lot.'

This was one of the busiest crossing points between Afghanistan and Pakistan. After years of border disputes and acrimony, the two countries now had a semblance of co-operation. Illegal drugs one way, manufactured goods the other. Or so the cynics said. After all, Afghanistan was the world's leading producer of heroin and it needed a market, not only in the east but especially in the west.

No-man's land stretched for fifty metres. Nick didn't wait in the queue but drove up to the Afghan customs post. An officer approached and spoke angrily and tried to wave them back but Nick held up a $10 note. It was swiftly palmed and they were waved through.

'It's good to see that bribery and corruption are so whole-heartedly embraced,' Nick grinned at Matt.

The town was bustling. People were hawking goods, offering all sorts of items for sale, from matches and shoe laces, to a toffee-like substance that looked disgusting. Although, if the flies were anything to go by, it was a very sweet concoction.

'Good grief, look Nick! There's an Avis. Let's see about a car. A one-way hire to Kabul. We can't trust this piece of junk.'

Hunter agreed and turned into a side street. The office was air conditioned and a welcome respite from the relentless heat and dust outside. The agent behind the desk was delighted to receive them, offering coffee and biscuits. Both men declined, explaining that they were in a hurry. There was one car available. A French Peugeot. Only two years old. Air conditioning and a full tank of petrol. They said they'd take it.

'How long you want?'

'One day,' said Hunter. 'We also need a one-way hire to Kabul.'

That was when the problems started. The car had to be returned to that office. They could use it locally but not to travel to Kabul because it was not safe. Too many bandits. Even the convoys were attacked. And so it went on for about five minutes until Hunter handed the man $200 as a gift, plus the cost of the hire. He also gave him the keys to the car they'd been using, telling the man to keep it.

It was a relief to climb into the Peugeot, switch on the engine and let the air conditioning kick in. They placed their weapons in the side pockets of the doors and under the front seats for immediate access. It was a long 140 kilometres to Kabul and Hunter had no illusions about the dangers of two Westerners making the journey through such hazardous terrain. They found a supermarket that sold cans of cold drinks, pre-packed processed meats and fresh bread. They would eat and drink on the move. Hunter took the wheel and they headed out of town. They had two and a half hours to get to the train station in Kabul. In theory, it was possible. In practice, they both knew it would be touch and go.

The highway was made of badly applied tarmac, pitted with holes that tested the springs and tyres of the vehicles that used it. It was also single lane in either direction and overtaking took nerves of steel and the reflexes of a Formula 1 driver. The road meandered along valley bottoms, over hills and was composed of bends that had the road doubling back on itself for up to half a kilometre or more. Scattered along the way were broken-down vehicles of all descriptions. They regularly came across abandoned lorries, some of which had turned over on their sides. Mainly they were tankers, either oil or petrol carriers. All of them bore the scars of attack in the form of bullet-holes in the doors of the cabs and shot-out windows. They were entering highly dangerous territory. It was also one of breathtaking scenery.

The gods had been smiling when Sheikh Mohammed Al-Sari had arrived in the valley. He had proved to be a goldmine of information. The TIFAT personnel at Rosyth had quickly and relatively easily opened the various folders transmitted to them from the valley. In return, Hunter and Dunston had received names, photographs, an itinerary and a timetable. They now knew that Mohammed Akbar was accompanied by Kaman Al-Zawahiri and that they were meeting Rehman Khan in Kabul. The former Pakistani Inter Service Intelligence agent was now high on the most wanted lists of both his home country and that of TIFAT. It appeared that he would be riding shotgun with the two men for the journey to the West. It had also been established that they could rely upon a good deal of help en route. Their route would take them from Kabul to Iran, then into Turkey and to the Mediterranean Sea. There they were to board a modern super-yacht which would take them to Italy where they would catch a train for London. The preferred target may have been the British capital but a nuclear device exploding in any major city in Europe would have the desired effect.

*   *   *   *   *

The helicopter picked up General Macnair, Walsh, Badonovitch and Napier twenty miles to the west of Peshawar. The flight to Islamabad airport took a mere half an hour. At the airport, Macnair's ankle was examined by a Pakistani army doctor. The doctor confirmed it was a bad sprain and bound the ankle tightly. Walsh's shoulder and Napier's thigh were treated and dressed. They were told that time would heal them both.

Finally, Zardari showed up. Macnair brought him up to date with events.

'We have to stop them! Somehow, we have to find these men and stop them!' Zardari said as he frantically paced the room.

'Hunter and Dunston are two of my best. If anyone can catch up with them, it's those two. One thing is clear. We're running out of time.'

Walsh said, 'Even without the bomb exploding, they're winning.'

Macnair nodded. It was true. There was hysteria across the whole of Europe and it was escalating. Cities were being abandoned. Motorway pile-ups were occurring with alarming frequency. Mosques were being trashed and set alight. Attack was followed by retaliation. So it went on. Round and round. Europe was sinking into a form of anarchy undreamed of in its history.

'I need Internet access and a webcam,' Macnair said.

'No problem,' Zardari answered. 'Back at my office.'

'Good.' Taking out his phone, he speed-dialled Isobel.

'You okay, Malcolm?' Isobel asked.

'Yes, thank you. It's just a sprain.'

'And Douglas and Hiram?'

'They'll be fine. I need you to do something for me. Contact the Prime Minister. Tell him it's vital we have a web meeting with Europe's Heads of State and their military advisers. Or at least the ones he can contact.'

'What if he wants to know why?'

'Tell him truthfully that you don't know. That I requested it. Stress the urgency.'

'I'll do my best,' Isobel said.

'I'll host the meeting while you move people around the screen.'

'What time?', Isobel asked.

Macnair looked at his watch. 'An hour from now. That should give the Prime Minister's staff time to set it up.'

'Malcolm, you know what he's like. He probably won't agree.'

Macnair sighed. 'You're right. Tell him we're chasing the second device along the road to Kabul. That ought to be enough to whet his appetite and ensure some co-operation.'

Macnair had no way of knowing that he had just made a huge error.

* * * * *

They were high up in the hills, about halfway to Kabul. They had passed numerous stationary vehicles by the side of the road, their drivers sitting and watching as they drove past.

'Have you got a feeling something's wrong?'

'An itch in the back of my neck,' said Hunter. 'Nothing's come towards us for the last fifteen minutes or more.'

'That's what I noticed. And nothing is moving in our direction. What do you make of it?'

'I don't know but I'm damned sure I don't like it.'

As they swept around a bend they saw a barrier across the road about one hundred metres ahead. Hunter's reflexes were superb. He slammed on the brakes, changed down from fifth to second gear, lifted his foot off the brakes, dragged hard on the handbrake and turned the wheel. The car spun around as though it were on a turntable and they then accelerated back towards the bend before the men on the barricade realised what was happening.

'Where on earth did you learn to do that?' Dunston yelled.

'*Top Gear*,' was the laconic reply.

Around the bend Hunter slammed the car to a halt. Grabbing weapons, they dived into the drainage ditch on the side of the road.

'Anything?'

'Not that I can see,' Hunter replied. He hefted a Glock 18 while Dunston held an Enfield L85A1. 'We can't stay here. Cover me. I'll go up that hill first. You follow.'

Climbing out of the ditch, Hunter made his way quickly up the slope, keeping to one side, Dunston covering him. At the summit, he dropped to his hands and knees and crawled the last few feet on his belly. Moments later he was joined by Dunston. They counted six heavily-armed men standing behind the barrier about one hundred metres or so ahead.

'Who are they after, I wonder? A convoy? You and me?'

'Hard to tell,' Hunter replied. 'It could be us, but I don't think so somehow. Maybe it's one of the convoys?'

'That makes no sense. We're the only ones moving,' he added. 'And I don't believe in coincidences.'

'Me neither. One thing's certain, we can't hang around here for much longer. They could already have reinforcements on the way. You stay here. See that hillock over to the right Matt? I'll get behind it. I'll let you know when I'm ready. You take the front guys. I'll start on the back.'

Hunter squirmed backwards below the skyline, got to his feet and hurried down the other side of the hill. He darted around two more hills before he was in position, hidden behind a large boulder. The men were talking and gesticulating animatedly. Hunter was sixty metres behind them. He took aim at the head of the man standing to the rear of the group and then said into his radio, 'Now.'

Hunter's first shot blew the man's head apart. Dunston's target was the man standing in front of the barrier. He died the same way. The four survivors stood still, their reactions numbed by shock. The TIFAT men each downed a second target before the ambushers had the good sense to throw themselves flat on the road. They were now hidden from Dunston but not from Hunter, although the field of fire wasn't as clear as he would have liked. They were still looking forward, unaware that two shots had come from behind. One of them called out something which neither TIFAT man understood.

Dunston yelled back, 'Speak English!'

The two men spoke excitedly together before one of them called out, in a heavy accent, 'Please. Do not shoot. Come down. I wish to talk.'

'Why are you blocking the road?'

'Please, it is all a big mistake. All my friends are dead. I am alone. I hold up my hands. I stand up. Please do not shoot.'

'There are two still alive,' Hunter radioed. 'Keep them busy.'

'Roger that.' Matt raised his voice and shouted. 'There are two of you. Both stand up and drop your weapons and I will let you live.'

There was more excited chatter between the two men. While their attention was focused on Matt, Nick inched his way slowly forward, trying for a clearer shot.

'I swear, there is only me. Please, let me live. I have a wife and children. I am only trying to make a living.'

'Matt,' Hunter whispered into his microphone, 'show yourself and call on them to do the same.'

The two guards were prone on the ground now at about forty metres, their feet pointed towards Hunter. He could probably have hit them from where he stood but he doubted they would be killing shots. All he could be sure of was that they wouldn't be able to sit comfortably again for a long time. Hunter was now out in the open. Dunston moved into a kneeling position, cradling his rifle across his body. 'Show yourself!'

One of the robbers slowly rose to his feet and raised his empty hands, his gun in easy reach on the top of the barricade.

'Matt, stand up nice and slow,' Hunter whispered. 'The second man will make his move first. Yes, he's moving his legs ready to stand.'

Dunston stood up, every nerve tingling, ready to fling himself back behind the hill. Hunter aimed his gun at the back of the man getting ready to move. The angle wasn't quite right. It was still a difficult shot. He had been stepping closer each second and was now less than twenty metres away when the man suddenly stood up and at the same time raised his gun. Hunter's shot smashed into the middle of his spine and broke it in two and at the same time threw the body across the barricade. As the other man grabbed his gun he was hit front and back, one shot from each of the TIFAT officers. Hunter approached and was surprised to see the man was still alive.

'Why did you attack us?'

'Told to stop . . .' His head slumped to one side and he was dead.

'Matt, get the car. I'll drag this lot out of the way.'

Nick dragged the bodies off the road and into a nearby ditch. Dunston brought the car around. Together they threw rocks and handfuls of dust over the dead guards. It didn't take long before they decided enough was enough. The bodies were hidden from view and any cursory search. Anything more however and they would soon be found. Hunter climbed into the passenger seat.

After a few minutes of thoughtful silence, Matt said, 'They were waiting for us.'

'Yep,' Nick said.

Neither man said anything further. Nick broke out the bread, cold meats and a can of coke each. 'How did they know we'd be on this road?' Nick asked.

He gave Matt a sandwich and put the coke in the holder by the handbrake.

Matt glanced at Nick. 'There's a traitor somewhere, which means they know we're chasing them.'

'We could use some help. Let me check and see what General Macnair can offer in the way of back-up.' He looked at his mobile. 'Typical. No signal!' He paused, leaned back and closed his eyes. 'I'm knackered.'

27

They crested a rise and there was Kabul, spread out in the far distance. Hunter woke up with a start. He looked at Matt.

'Sorry, I must have dozed off,' he said.

Matt chuckled. 'You were snoring like a contented pig. I hadn't the heart to wake you. It's been a tough thirty-six hours.' He rubbed his face. 'If you're anything to go by, we must look a right pair.'

Hunter rubbed his chin and then pulled down the sun-visor to take a look at his reflection. 'Actually, it's not that bad. We'll blend in that much better.'

'You realise we're running out of time?' Matt offered.

Hunter glanced at his watch and cursed. 'Damnation. There's another roadblock ahead.' He sat up straight, automatically reaching for his Glock.

'It looks like Police and Army.'

Hunter put the binoculars to his eyes and focused. 'Ours, thank Christ.'

Dunston pulled out of the queue and drove past an endless line of trucks and cars. He stopped at the barrier. A Sergeant approached with an Afghan policeman in tow. The policeman said something unintelligible.

'Sergeant, let us through,' Hunter said showing his TIFAT ID. 'We're in a hurry.'

The Sergeant casually looked at the plastic card, squinted at the photograph and then at Hunter before he said, 'I'll have to check this out.'

Hunter replied harshly, 'Sergeant, you recognise the ID? The soldier nodded.

'Good. If you don't open that sodding barrier and let us through I'll have your guts for garters. Now shift it.'

The Sergeant stiffened, hesitated and then shrugged. What the hell? It was no skin off his nose. And the man was a bleeding officer. Only the real thing spoke like that, due to them being born bastards. He waved the car through.

If Nick and Matt hadn't been so tired, the penny would have dropped sooner. Roadblocks weren't uncommon in the region but three in such quick succession was over the top. At the third one, Hunter said suddenly 'They're looking for Mohammed Akbar and the other two. General Macnair must have arranged it. Pull over there. We'd better check and find out what time they moved into place.'

Dunston pulled the car off the road. They were now on the outskirts of the city. The houses and apartment buildings needed a lick of paint at best, a load of maintenance at worst.

Hunter approached the barrier and flashed his identity card at a Royal Marines Lieutenant, who snapped to attention and was about to salute when Hunter said swiftly, 'No! Don't! Please!'

'Sorry, sir. How can I help?'

Hunter showed him a photograph on his mobile phone display. 'Are you looking for him? And him?' He showed a second photograph which had been copied from Rehman Khan's identity card.

'Yes, sir. How do you know about this?'

Hunter replied, 'We're chasing them. Have been since oh crack sparrow fart. What time did you set up the roadblocks?'

'Just under two hours ago, sir,' The marine said looking at his watch.

'I take it there's no sign?' Nick asked.

'No, sir. I don't think they're coming this way.'

'Why do you say that?' asked Dunston as he joined them.

'We'd have got them. I kid you not, when we close this city it's as tight as a duck's . . .'

'Do you know what they are supposed to be carrying?' interrupted Hunter.

'No, sir. Only that we are to look out for a silver-coloured suitcase. Oh, and we're to stop these guys in any way we can. Um,' he coughed and added, 'we're to use extreme force if necessary.'

The other two nodded. Hunter took a deep breath and exhaled heavily. 'Lieutenant, can you direct us to your HQ?'

'No problem sir. Go straight down the road for about a klick. You'll see another roadblock on your right. Through there and we're on the left. That's the road to the barracks.'

They nodded their thanks and followed his directions. A kilometre down the road they came to the roadblock. Hunter's ID card got them through. Fifteen minutes later they presented themselves to the Officer Commanding, Lieutenant Colonel Patrick McLaren, Royal Marines. His office held a battered desk on which sat three telephones.

There were four hard-backed chairs facing the desk. The only piece of kit that could be deemed to make the occupancy of the room bearable was a coffee-maker on a side table. It was obviously a non-military item.

Handshakes were brief. 'I've been expecting you,' McLaren greeted them. 'Help yourselves to some coffee.' He added, 'You know there's no sign of the bastards?'

Hunter nodded as he topped up a mug of coffee with milk. 'Any chance they could have got past?' He took a sip and added, 'I needed that.'

McLaren shrugged, 'I'd say no. Not likely. How certain? Ninety percent.'

'Not a hundred?' Dunston too drank some coffee, a sigh escaping his lips.

'No. There are far too many al-Qaeda sympathisers in the country.' He leaned back in his chair and scratched a greying sideburn. 'But, I don't see it. They are supposedly heading for the train station. The service is unreliable and slow. There isn't a dog's chance of them being on a train and getting more than a dozen klicks out of town before we'd catch them. The noonday train, which is expected to leave around 14.00 hours, will be inundated with police as well as our boys. So no, I don't see it.'

'Any word from General Macnair?'

'He's still in Pakistan and he ordered the roadblocks. I don't suppose you know about the video conference?'

'What conference?', Dunston asked.

'He's speaking to the heads of European governments and their military advisers right now. I was informed about it when I was told to search for the two men and the device. The General says someone will phone for a sitrep when the conference is over. How long that will take, is anyone's guess. One thing you can be certain of, it'll drag on for a hell of a long time. They'll all want to say something. Have you heard anything on the news?'

'No,' answered Hunter. He waved his mug in the air. 'May I?'

'Help yourself,' McLaren said. He leaned back in his chair and put his hands behind his head. 'The Foreign Secretary has announced that it is better to jaw-jaw than to war-war.'

'He said what? You have to be kidding,' said Hunter in a hoarse voice. 'Who do we jaw-jaw *with*?'

The other two shrugged. The comment was incredibly stupid even for a government minister in the current Parliament.

'Europe has never faced such danger, ever,' Hunter added.

McLaren poured himself a coffee. 'We know. We also know that al-Qaeda can call on the help of hundreds, if not thousands, of men and women. For them, this is the big one. They will be mobilising help from here to London. Do you have any idea about what's happening in Western Europe right now?'

Dunston said, 'The last we heard it was pretty chaotic and getting worse.'

'The situation is deteriorating rapidly. "Riots" doesn't come anywhere near describing the anarchy that's sweeping across the Continent. Muslim groups are holing up in mosques from Scotland to Bosnia. Hundreds have been killed. So have many of the attackers. The trouble is, although the police and the military have been called in to give protection, some are on the side of the non-Muslims. Britain isn't as bad as the rest of Europe but it's still terrible. The death toll in London alone was around eighty at the last count. Two of the dead are young teenage girls who were in a shopping centre dressed in full black costume including their veils. A security guard watched as a group of youths attacked them. He made no attempt to stop them.' McLaren shook his head in genuine sorrow. 'I don't like the way they dress, I don't like their religion,' he spoke honestly, 'but I do believe they have the right to it. The last I heard, which was on CNN about half an hour ago, things are getting worse by the hour. If you have five minutes, take a look at what's on the television in the mess.'

'It's only to be expected,' said Hunter. 'If we don't stop the bomb, then tens of thousands of people will die and God alone knows how many will be injured. We know it. The people know it. They're not stupid. I also suspect the media is milking it for all it's worth, which makes matters even worse.'

Dunston said, 'Be fair, Nick. That's hardly surprising. They can't pretend everything is going to be all right. Just reporting the facts without any embellishments is bad enough. We know. We've run the simulations. Presumably flights out of Europe are jam-packed, roads to the country are solid with cars and trains aren't able to cope?'

The Colonel nodded.

Dunston added for good measure, 'And the powers-that-be are running around like headless chickens.'

'That about sums it up.'

Hunter said, pensively, 'It makes you wonder just how it leaked so quickly. It was inevitable it would come out at some point, but so soon?'

Dunston said, 'It plays right into the hands of the terrorists. With Europe in such an uproar, finding and stopping them is virtually impossible. They also have time on their side. And,' he emphasised the word, 'in the meantime, there's chaos in Europe. We need a lead. Something to go on.' He was aware that he was stating the obvious. Lack of sleep was catching up with him.

'I don't know if it's true or merely scuttlebutt,' said McLaren, 'but rumour has it that the leak originated in Downing Street. If not from there, then certainly from somebody in our government.' The phone on his desk rang. He grabbed the receiver. 'McLaren.' He listened, thanked the caller and hung up. 'Nothing. No sign of any of the men or the device.'

'Any chance we can talk to General Macnair?' Hunter asked, stifling a yawn.

'Not until after the conference.' McLaren paused and then said in a kindly tone, 'The pair of you look about all-in. Go and get some sleep. I'll call you if we hear anything. In the meantime I'll let the General know you're here.' The Colonel telephoned the officers' mess, gave instructions and sent the two of them away. Hunter and Dunston were shown to a couple of rooms. They were basic, cramped, yet clean. Both fell asleep as soon as their heads hit their pillows.

* * * * *

'Gentlemen, thank you all for joining me. The position is this. I am currently in Pakistan. As soon as I finish this call I shall be heading back to Rosyth. According to the information we received, the second dirty bomb was due to be leaving Kabul on the noon train. The train has not left and won't be departing anytime soon. It has been thoroughly searched but nothing has been found. There is also no sign of the men we're looking for.' Macnair stared at the camera, fatigue etched on his face. On his computer screen were the Chancellor of Germany, the Presidents of France and Italy, and the Prime Ministers of Britain, Denmark and Spain. All the attendees were listed on the right hand side of the screen but they could not be seen unless their names were in the top six. The list was not as long as expected. It had been impossible to contact many senior politicians and their aides. Together with their families they had fled to safe destinations. Many had already quit Europe. Senior officers from most of the military services that existed in the West were in attendance. They recognised where their duty lay. Isobel had control of who appeared within the top six. Aides typed messages into the text chat box and insisted that their masters be moved up the list to allow them to have their say. It was utter chaos. The opinions and suggestions were almost as varied and numerous as the attendees. Translation was a problem. Mistakes were inevitable. Keeping order was tough. Macnair, aware of who he was addressing, said, 'With all due respect,' a statement used when no respect was intended. Luckily, the non-English speakers didn't realise the fact. 'I suggest we seal the borders.'

'Impossible!' was the politest of the comments he received at the suggestion. For the next hour the arguments raged back and forth. With so many people on the move, how on earth were they going to control the borders? People were desperately trying to get out of Europe. They wanted to go anywhere they thought might be safe. Besides which, the police were stretched to breaking point and the military was no better. Ambulance services and fire brigades were working ceaselessly across the whole of Europe.

'I appreciate all that,' said Macnair. 'We have already

declared a state of emergency but it's nowhere near enough. We cannot cope. It's impossible. So I suggest we create a militia. Call up every man and woman who is ex-military and ex-police. We needn't arm them but they can help us to control the borders. Have armed back-up to deal with any situation that gets out of hand.'

This resulted in further heated argument. What about accidental deaths? What about a mob attacking a contingent of guards? Who would have the courage to stop them? How could they be stopped? By shooting them? It was unthinkable.

'What's unthinkable,' said Macnair, 'is a dirty bomb exploding in Europe.' His statement brought a semblance of order. 'I'm not suggesting we try and stop people leaving. I am suggesting we prevent people entering Europe.'

'It will take days to do as you suggest,' said Germany's Chancellor.

'I agree. Therefore, the sooner we start, the better. We could get lucky,' Macnair explained.

'Is that all we have to rely on?' Britain's Prime Minister asked. 'Luck?'

'Every agency involved in security is working on the problem. So far, we've got nothing. Co-operation is at an all-time high and TIFAT is co-ordinating anything we get in. We can't do any more. Believe me.'

'What are your men doing?'

Macnair looked at the picture of his country's leader and managed to keep his face deadpan. 'We're working on a number of scenarios but we have nothing concrete so far.' In view of the probable leaks coming from the office of the Prime Minister, he had no intention of sharing anything more with any of them.

After almost four hours of debate it was agreed. The periphery of Europe would be sealed. Nobody would be permitted to enter. Announcements would be made to the press. Macnair nodded, satisfied. It was all he wanted. All he had hoped for. He knew that at best it was a gesture. But there was nothing else. He hoped it would calm things down. Reduce the rioting and deaths. Ease the tension. Even just a little bit might help to save lives. The meeting ended and Isobel closed the conference room down. What Macnair had not said, and had no intention of sharing with any of the people who had been in the meeting, was what he was about to say next. Macnair telephoned Kabul. Hunter was dragged from the depths of the soundest sleep he had ever had.

'Sir?' Nick sounded more alert than he felt.

'We now know what the terrorists' back-up plan is.'

28

Mohammed Akbar had a smile on his face. They had been warned in plenty of time about the situation in Kabul. Rehman Khan had telephoned. They had adjusted their plans and simply skirted the city and were now sixty kilometres north-west of it. They had met Khan on the outskirts and he was driving a car that was less than three years old. The man with Akbar turned the old car around and headed back the way they had come. He had no papers to allow him to cross more borders so it was not worth going any further. Besides, he had other work to do.

The biggest problem Khan and Akbar faced was that the farther they travelled the worse the roads became, but they were far from impassable, and unlikely to hinder their journey too much. The comfort of the car and the air conditioning helped to make the journey more bearable. An hour later they stopped to get some food and drink and were joined by Kaman Al-Zawahiri.

Their next stop was at sunset. The three men got out, got down on their knees facing the direction they believed was Mecca and said the *Maghrib*, the fourth of the daily *salat* prayers. Each man recited: 'We enter upon the evening, and so doth the creation of Allah, lord of the worlds.'

Moments later they were back in the car and speeding towards the Iranian border, Rehman Khan at the wheel. The bomb was on the back seat, alongside Mohammed Akbar, who refused to let it out of his sight. They opened bottles of water, and shared dried meats, bread, and fresh olives. Khan rubbed his temples. A headache was coming on but he was determined to ignore it. To suffer the pain until it was so bad he had to take a pill. It was all part of his martyrdom in the service of the one true God.

'God is with us,' said Akbar, munching discontentedly on an olive. He wished for a burger with all the trimmings.

'We have a long way to go,' replied Al-Zawahiri. He was in his early thirties, thin and wiry, with a thick beard already streaked with grey. He wore traditional dress over grubby brown trousers.

'It is true,' said Rehman Khan, 'but what Mohammed says is correct. God is with us. Has he not smiled on our efforts so far? We know that the Western powers are in panic. They have no knowledge of where we are. Everything is going according to plan. Leaking the fact that a second bomb is on its way to London was a stroke of genius that only Osama could have understood.'

'At the time you didn't think so,' said Al-Zawahiri, smiling.

'I know. I admit it. But look what it has achieved. The West in an uproar, people being killed, hatred is being stoked up, stock markets are in collapse! It could not be better. And when the bomb explodes,' his eyes were shining, the smile on his face turning to a look of awe, 'we will become the most famous, the most revered people in history. They will speak our name in the same way as they speak of Muhammad, peace be upon him.'

They had taken the northern road through the Shibar Pass. It was dark when they entered the town of Bamiyan. The area, one of the poorest in Afghanistan, was also one of the most isolated yet most beautiful. The river and surrounding landscape was a magnet for the intrepid tourist. It had been a major centre for Buddhist pilgrimage until the Taliban destroyed the two huge statues to Buddha that once dominated the valley. Although isolated now, the town had once been an important stop on the Silk Road. Pilgrims and traders would flock to the area to visit its temples and, as a result, Bamiyan exported its art, a mixture of Indian, Persian and Greek. War brought it all to an end and now the town barely existed.

Driving through the empty streets they eventually found the Bamiyan Hotel, hidden behind high walls and surrounded by a pleasant garden. After checking in, they met in the restaurant for a meal of soup, lamb chops with potatoes and fruit with *krut*. The meal cost a mere two hundred afghanis, or two pounds sterling. With the meal they drank bottled water and followed it with thick, very sweet coffee. Khan slipped a pill into his mouth. His head was splitting but he was determined not to reveal his distress.

'I have spoken with our contact in Iran,' said Khan, as the pain eased. 'Everything has been arranged. The date has also been agreed. Two weeks from today. The first Friday in June. It will give the West plenty of time to, what shall we say, fall apart?'

They chuckled.

'I have had a message from our contact in Pakistan. He tells me that they have no idea where we are or what we are planning. We must keep it that way.' It was just as well that none of them knew about the telephone call taking place that very minute. Otherwise they would not have been so blasé about their situation.

* * * * *

Matt Dunston was lying on his bed, his hands behind his head, deep in thought.

The twisting of the laws as formulated in the seventh-century Qur'an was an obscenity. The Qur'an gave women explicit rights to divorce, inheritance and property for the first time in history. It was specific when it came to preventing violence against female children and women, as well as abuse in family households. For centuries women had the right to pursue a divorce and seek compensation if their husband could not satisfy them sexually. Sharia law had ended all that. Such enlightened thought and laws had become warped and twisted, and women now found themselves with fewer rights than some animals. Sharia-minded funda-mentalists treated women with utter contempt. One example, and contrary to what the Qur'an taught, was that a woman's testimony in court was worth only half that of a man. Furthermore, Sharia law did not distinguish between consensual sex, adultery and rape. The result was that victims of rape and sexual abuse were often charged with a crime and stoned to death. What made this punishment even more abhorrent was that the Qur'an did not sanction or allow stoning to death for any crime whatsoever. Where Sharia was the law of the land, such as Saudi Arabia, women weren't allowed out unless accompanied by a man. They were forbidden to drive, and had to wear black from head to foot as well as a heavy veil. This was in spite of the fact that black absorbs heat and is wrong for a desert climate. Naturally, the men all wear white.

Shaking his head, he got up. A cup of coffee followed by a shower was the order of the day. He went in search of one but instead found Hunter on the phone. He gestured to Dunston to pick up the extension.

'Matt's on the line as well, sir,' Nick explained.

'Good. Listen up, both of you. There is no doubt that we have at least one leak and possibly more. We don't know who and we don't know where. Therefore, there will be no co-operation with any other agency – with the exception of MI5 and MI6 – under any circumstances from now on. Is that clear? Samantha Freemantle will help to keep them in the picture. I'll deal with all other agencies. Do not believe anything you are told unless we've cleared it first. Two things have been working in our favour to date. As you both know, we've been able to access the computers of the people we've lifted. As a result, we've accumulated a vast amount of material, some of which we will be sharing with other agencies. Some of it we won't. At least not until we identify who's responsible for informing the terrorists about what we know and what we're doing. This, in turn, has led us to look more closely at some Internet addresses. Luckily, whoever is using them thinks they are safe. It's one of the reasons I intend to keep everything under wraps. I don't want anyone thinking about *how* we've discovered the information. We've been intercepting messages back and forth for the last few hours. Thanks to Isobel we've also discovered their back-up route. They are currently driving cross-country to Iran. They will travel through Herat and then on to the border crossing at Islam Qala, which is Taybad on the Iranian side. We now have their timetable as well.'

'When?' Hunter found he was grasping the receiver hard.

'They plan to set the bomb off in fourteen days' time,' Macnair explained.

'But why so late?' Dunston asked.

'To create the maximum disruption in Europe. Think about it. From now on there's going to be a bigger and bigger feeding frenzy about the prospect of a nuclear device exploding somewhere. Even changing the description of the bomb to a euphemism such as a plutonium-enhanced plastic explosive device won't help. Knowing the great European public it would probably make matters worse. Anyway, each day that passes ratchets up the tension. Already we're practically in meltdown. Today we agreed to close the borders to anyone trying to enter Europe, but . . .'

'That's not much use,' interrupted Hunter. 'The border's far too long.'

'We know that. I'm hoping it will help to alleviate some of the chaos. It won't be by much, but it may save a few lives and reduce any rioting.'

Neither Nick nor Matt said anything.

Uncharacteristically, the General added, 'I know it's a long shot, but what else can we do?'

'Nothing,' replied Dunston.

'Things are getting worse. Aeroplanes are flying out of Europe full and returning empty. However, the supply of aircraft is dwindling.'

'How come?', Dunston asked.

'The crews are refusing to return. Most of them are smuggling their families onto the planes and so have no incentive to return.' Macnair sighed. 'It's not surprising if you consider that most planes fly from capital cities and that's where most of the crews live. People are also being ingenious. Yesterday, there was a phone-in on BBC Five Live. It lasted all morning and it was about places to go. Tens of thousands of caravans are being towed north right this moment, to loads of different places but mostly to the Scottish Highlands and Islands.'

'I caught something on the news about jammed motorways,' said Hunter.

'All part of it. Between caravans flipping over because of excessive speeds and literally dozens of accidents, it's lucky no one has been killed yet but I've no doubt that will change pretty soon. That's not our problem. What is, is finding these bastards and disarming the bomb. I've sent instructions that a helicopter is to take you to Herat first thing in the morning. I've also arranged for you to get any help you ask for in regard to weapons. I'll leave that in your capable hands.' Macnair paused and then said, 'Nick, Matt, let me make something clear. I cannot risk asking for help now. If it were to be leaked that we are in Herat because we're expecting the men and the bomb to pass through the city then I fear the terrorists will find out somehow.' Macnair repeated, 'I just can't risk it. Right now, we have a step-by-step guide as to where they are going. It will enable us to look for a suitable killing ground of our choosing. Hence, in Herat there will only be the two of you. I am, however, sending Tanner and Henri to join you, but it will be forty-eight hours before they get to you. Any questions?'

'You said the bomb is due to be detonated in fourteen days time. Do we have their short-term timetable? Where they are going to be and when over the next two weeks?', Hunter asked.

'Just some hints and suggestions. We've underestimated them. We've become used to them making a plan and sticking to it religiously.'

'That's always been their way, no flexibility,' said Dunston. 'It's one of their shortcomings. One of many, thank goodness.'

'Well, not any longer. The order of the day is definitely flexibility. They'll change routes, transport, deadlines. You name it. They'll do whatever it takes to get the device into the West. To do so they have ample cash and paperwork. Anything else?'

'Yes, sir. Let's be optimistic for a moment. Please send me instructions on how to defuse the bomb. We can live in hope.'

'I've asked the Americans. You'll get detailed info within the next twenty-four hours. Anything else?'

'When do you want us to leave for Herat?' Hunter asked.

'In the morning. Get some rest. You both know that hunting a moving target is damned difficult.' The General didn't need to expand. 'Anything further?'

Hunter and Dunston exchanged glances. 'No, sir. Matt and I understand what we need to do.'

'Good. I'm heading back to Rosyth, but you can reach me in the usual way. Keep me in the loop.'

They hung up. Coffee and a quiet corner in the officers' mess gave them time to digest what they had been told. It didn't enhance their position by as much as a degree. After that they were left with time on their hands. Nothing happened for the rest of the day. They sat around watching the news on television. The situation in Europe was going from bad to worse and for the men and women serving their country in such an inhospitable country as Afghanistan it was particularly hard to watch. They all wished they were back home protecting their loved ones. Hunter and Dunston had an early night. There was a limit to how much bad news one could watch.

Breakfast was early and by 09.00 they were at the airport and climbing on board a helicopter for Herat. On landing they were met by a Sergeant driving an unmarked Land Rover. After handing over the keys to Hunter, the Sergeant took a taxi back to his base. Using his mobile, Hunter requested an update from Rosyth by text. In reply, he was informed that they could expect the three men plus the bomb to arrive in Herat in about twenty-four hours, not before. Further information about the route was provided soon afterwards.

Nick and Matt drove into town to the Marco Polo Hotel, on the street known as Jad-e Badmurghan. It was clean, boasted twenty-four-hour hot water, a free, non-alcoholic mini-bar in each room, and a breakfast of bread, cheese, fruit, different yoghurts and eggs to order. Neither man expected to be there for breakfast however and, after quickly ditching their bags, they climbed back into the Land Rover and headed east, past the airport. They were driving over a poor road through countryside that was flat and wide open. The wind blowing from the south east was called *Bad-e Sad o Bist*, the wind of one hundred and twenty days that lasted from spring to autumn and carried a desiccating dust at a temperature in the high twenties or low thirties centigrade. Halfway to a town called Marveh, about thirty miles from Herat, they found what they were looking for. The road, a single lane in either direction, narrowed and ran alongside a fast-flowing river. It made a good spot to stage an ambush. Now all they had to do was to identify the target. They walked along the side of the road. On the left ran a deep ditch. It was designed to drain away the winter flood waters. On the right was the river, as well as a tributary that came down from the distant hills. Just past the confluence of the two they had some luck. Sometime in the distant past a bank of stone and earth had been built to a height of about three metres, obviously to try and prevent flooding. From their point of view it was ideal. It gave a good view of the traffic heading towards Herat for at least two kilometres, with the road from the city being hidden by a bend. Most importantly, the tarmac was worn and cracked. Placing explosives would not be a problem.

29

Satisfied with the location, Nick and Matt returned to Herat. They received word from Rosyth that their target was expected in the Herat area the following morning. It was evident that the terrorists had plenty of time in hand. They were in no hurry. Before dawn, Nick and Matt left the hotel and returned to the ambush site. There was no traffic and the run out of the city and into the country was fast and smooth. Hunter hid the Land Rover out of sight in a copse of stunted trees, close to the river. Taking a canvas satchel and a pick and shovel, the two men made their way to the road. Dunston swung the pick and Hunter scraped at the mud and stones until they had made a narrow channel, under the tarmac, about one metre long and twenty centimetres wide.

Reaching into his knapsack Nick took out a small bowl and a can of 3-in-1 oil and poured the contents into the bowl. He added a kilogram of plastic explosives and then kneaded the putty-like substance, making it more compliant. When he was satisfied, Nick created a shape that resembled a Toblerone bar and placed it at the end of the narrow channel. He primed the plastic explosive with two detonators from which ran electric cable. He ran the cable up to the vantage point while Dunston covered it with earth. Hunter attached the end of the cable to a small electric dynamo. When they were ready, all he had to do was pull up the handle, twist it 90° and plunge it home. Half an hour after arrival the trap was set. All they had to do now was wait for the right moment to spring it. The explosive charge would kill the occupants of the car instantly. Any collateral damage would be minimal – probably no more than a hole in the road – but if another vehicle happened to be passing at the exact moment of the explosion then that too would be destroyed. However, in view of the deaths and damage that would be the result should the bomb explode, that was an acceptable risk.

Both men settled down for what was left of the night. Wrapped in sleeping bags they sat in companionable silence. There was no traffic at that early hour of the morning and time dragged slowly. Hunter thought about his parents back in the sleepy village of Balfron and wondered what they would be doing. One thing he was certain of. He knew neither would be in a panic. They were the sort of people who never panicked, no matter what the situation. He smiled to himself. One thing he was also positive about. The house, by now, would be packed solid with relatives from down south. The Griffiths family, his mother's side, were extensive and close-knit. His mind wandered. Of all the operations he had been on, this was the most critical. Western security services knew that one day there would be a catastrophic failure. It was inevitable. The killings and destruction that had occurred in America on 9/11 were an indication of what a small yet determined group of terrorists could accomplish. There was also no doubt whatsoever that there were many like-minded people wishing to harm the West. Also, the proliferation of nuclear weapons was equally inevitable. Put it all together and the future looked terrifyingly bleak. Nick sighed. He and Matt were trying to stop a catastrophe of unimaginable proportions. Just the two of them. Here and now.

'It's unthinkable,' the words broke into his thoughts.

'What was that?' Matt asked.

'Sorry. I thought you were dozing,' Hunter said, glancing at the dark outline of his best friend.

'I can't. I'm thinking of what it is we're trying to do. What the price of failure means. It's like nothing that we've done before. Nick, whatever happens, I've made up my mind to leave the ministry. One way or the other.'

Hunter asked, 'Why?'

'Faith is one thing. But this beggars belief. If there is a God how can He allow this to happen? I know the arguments. I've had them more times than I've had hot dinners. The usual excuse has always been man's free will. Man's inhumanity to man has always been explained away. But this? Where will it lead? What happens when the fundamentalists get hold of a fully-fledged megaton nuclear bomb with the capability to deliver it? This alone has the potential of being worse than during the first and second world wars combined! If we don't stop the bomb . . .', he shook his head.

'But why leave the ministry? Do you no longer believe in God? Is that what you're saying?'

Dunston sighed. 'I've no idea. I'm probably too knackered to think coherently. Perhaps I'll speak to my Bishop when we get back. *If* we get back. And why leave? I'm a hypocrite. I'm a so-called man of the cloth, yet I kill people. I shouldn't carry a gun let alone use one. So it's time to change. Alternatively, I could leave TIFAT and go

302

back into general service. But with the world in the mess it's in, I think that would be running away.'

'Matt, we've had similar discussions in the past. Your conscience had always played hell with you. I've said it before and I'll say it again. To the best of my knowledge, you've never killed anyone who didn't deserve it. Hopefully, neither have I. Jesus Christ wasn't meek and mild. That's a fallacy and a ludicrous myth. He used a whip on the money lenders in the temple. He was tough-minded and aggressive when he needed to be. Otherwise Christianity would never have taken root.'

'I acknowledge all you say, Nick, but as we sit here I realise that I've made my decision. And you've no idea what a relief it is to admit this. If the General will have me, I can maybe get my old rank back. Hell's teeth, I was the youngest sodding Major in the army at one time.'

Hunter grinned. 'And destined for much higher things. And before you say it, yes, you achieved them by serving God.'

Dunston chuckled. 'Well, I won't make General now. But on the other hand TIFAT is more important than the army. The real war is the one we're fighting. That's not to say our lads aren't doing a vitally important job in Iraq, here and elsewhere. They are. It's just that clandestine operations are where it's at.'

'I know. Which is why I joined as well. I read the paper the General wrote a few years ago and agreed with everything he said. You do know about the problems he's having with our government, don't you?'

'Yes, the idiots, especially this Prime Minister. Most of the free world thinks that TIFAT is a good idea. That its mandate should be extended.'

'The problem is, politicians like having control. It's why the world is in such a mess.'

Their debate carried on until there was a perceptible lightening of the sky. With the dawn came the realisation that they had not managed to solve any of the problems they had been debating.

A text message hit both their mobiles simultaneously. *Intercepted message. Device less than 1 hour from Herat. Possible additional support with them. Cannot confirm.*

'I wonder what "additional support" means?' Dunston asked.

'We may never know. But just in case, we had better be ready. Always expect the unexpected. That way you may live longer.'

'Only may?'

Hunter grinned. 'Better than no chance.'

'Amen to that. Okay, I'll have the rifle and scope to hand. You watch the road while I bring a few rocks up here and make something of a barricade.'

Fajr, or morning prayers, had finished and traffic was beginning to move along the road again. Not a lot, but enough to require them to watch each approaching car through binoculars and to check on the people inside. Due to the poor road surface, the cars and lorries moved slowly, bouncing over the potholes, lousy suspension making for an uncomfortable ride. The sun was over the horizon but hidden behind a bank of cloud. Hunter locked his binoculars on a car that was approaching. After a few moments he tensed, looking from the driver to the front-seat passenger.

'This is it,' Hunter said.

'Sure?' asked Dunston.

'Positive.' The car was about half a kilometre away.

Hunter swung the glasses up and said, 'There's another car behind. At least two people inside and there could be others farther back. I think they're covering our target.'

'What gives you that idea?'

'They're too close. There's only about thirty metres between them. Look at the other traffic. It's not normal.'

The other vehicles were distanced further apart, which was what they were used to seeing.

'I think you're right. Another minute. Once the dust settles I'll open up,' Matt said.

'Roger that,' Nick said. Now that they were about to go into action he was as cool as ice. His thinking was crystal clear, his focus on the target was absolute.

'Standby,' said Dunston.

Hunter pulled out the handle on the palm-sized dynamo and twisted it at right angles, locking it in position. The car had almost reached the explosives. Now! Hunter began the move that would send a surge of electric power through the wires and blow the car to kingdom come.

Matt Dunston's reactions were extraordinary. His left hand shot out and clamped around the plunger, preventing Hunter from creating the electric surge required. A noise had caused him to look over his shoulder in time to see a bus full of animated schoolchildren coming around the bend. They arrived at the booby-trap at the same time as the car.

Nick hadn't been aware of the other vehicle. 'What the . . .'

'It's a bus full of kids, Nick. We can't!'

30

Malcolm Macnair welcomed Hiram Walsh, into his office. 'How's the shoulder?'

'Fine, thanks. Your ankle?'

'It'll do.' Macnair was leaning back in his chair. His right leg was elevated, his ankle resting on a cushion. 'I've been summoned.'

Walsh frowned. 'Where to?'

'Downing Street.'

'I trust you told the Prime Minister to shove his summons where the sun doesn't shine?'

Macnair smiled ruefully. 'I was highly tempted. The nerve of the man beggars belief. Although I do have to say one thing for him. Much to my surprise, he hasn't abandoned his post. Yet. I do wonder how much longer that'll be the case. The original demand for my presence came from the Secretary of State for Defence. I pointed out in no uncertain terms that TIFAT is not answerable to the British government but to *all* those who back and endorse what we do. I even e-mailed another copy of our mandate and the standing orders which set out our rules of engagement.'

'What did he say?' Walsh sat opposite his boss and stretched out his weary legs. He'd been at it non-stop for the best part of thirty-six hours and he was in dire need of his pit and a few hours sleep. His shoulder ached like hell in spite of the competence of the doctor in Pakistan. Their own medical staff had taken a look on his return and pronounced there was nothing more to be done. The same had been said about Napier's leg, although it would take longer to heal. He was currently laid up in the sick-bay.

'Nothing. He acknowledged receipt and that was that. Then I got this further communication.'

'Are you going?'

'To be frank, I wasn't intending to. I was going to send the Prime Minister the same stuff I sent the Defence Secretary and politely decline his invitation.'

'Was it an invite or a command?'

'The latter dressed up as the former. However,' Macnair emphasised the word, 'I took a call from Summers. He's put me in the picture and also asked me to be there.'

'What did William have to say?'

'Just that he and Clive Owens would appreciate my attendance. He gave me some background information which I won't bore you with, but suffice to say he's right. I need to be present.'

'When?'

Macnair looked at his watch. 'Thirty minutes. Helicopter to Edinburgh airport and a BA flight to Heathrow. There's not a dog's chance of getting to the airport by car. The traffic is at a standstill. Clive has arranged for a car to pick me up. I should be back tonight.'

'Are cars moving down south?'

Macnair nodded. 'I've just checked the traffic conditions. There's nothing heading towards London.'

'That figures. In the meantime, I'll give Nick the details. They should get everything they want and need,' Walsh said, adding pensively, 'I'd sure like to know what went wrong with the ambush.'

'I believe it was something to do with the dynamo.'

The two men exchanged cynical looks.

'We'll find out one day,' said the General.

'Malcolm, it's still very much touch and go. If the terrorists stop talking to one another we'll be in deep crap up to our necks. Did you get the information from Isobel about the Saudis?'

Macnair nodded. 'It was part of the argument MI6 used to get me to go to the meeting.'

Walsh nodded. 'They are unbelievable. Did you see how much they stand to earn? It's trillions! Actually, earn is the wrong word. Defraud is more like it on the back of a huge number of deaths and massive destruction.'

'I've never understood it myself,' said the General, 'being a simple soldier. But I gather the forward selling of their huge stocks and shares portfolios somehow makes them a fortune.'

'I'm like you when it comes to finance,' said Walsh, rubbing his itching chin. He was in need of a shave. 'In a nutshell, that's what it amounts to. It also means that the Saudis are almost certainly financing this whole thing; including the purchase of the bombs in the first place.'

'According to Isobel we don't have sufficient proof. At least, nothing that would stand up in a Court of Law.'

'Since when have we bothered about evidence good enough for a court?'

Macnair waved his hand, as though dismissing the whole notion of some sort of legal process. He lifted his leg down and reached for a black lace-up shoe. It was identical to the one he was already wearing on his left foot but it was two sizes bigger. It slipped over his bandaged foot without any difficulty. He tied the laces tightly. Climbing awkwardly to his feet, he reached for a cane. His foot ached now that the painkillers had worn off. He wasn't due to take any more for another two hours which would be about the right time to give the pills a chance to work for his audience with the Prime Minister. One thing he was sure about, the Prime Minister wouldn't be alone. Macnair was expecting the full Cabinet.

'I'll speak to you later. Things have quietened down now. Go and get some rest,' Macnair said.

Walsh nodded. He knew that over-tiredness could lead to bad decisions.

Macnair limped awkwardly out of the room and climbed into his car. Minutes later he was strapped into a helicopter and, with plenty of time to spare, had soon arrived at Edinburgh airport. From then on he was just an ordinary member of the public. The queues were non-existent. The flights north were full, those going south virtually empty. He showed his passport as a means of identification and had his briefcase x-rayed as he went through to departures. It was only a short wait until the flight was called. There were six passengers. He sat with his head back, thinking. He had seen it all before, although not at this level of decision-making. A combination of fear and the sheer overwhelming horror of what they faced paralysed people. Both the Home Secretary and the Foreign Secretary displayed all the symptoms of such a reaction. They were in some sort of denial. Well, today they would damn well listen to what he, Owens and Summers had to say before it was too late. There was hardly a bump as the British Airways flight touched down and the plane taxied to the gate. In a short while the General had limped through the airport and out of the building. A chauffeur approached and asked if he was General Macnair. On learning that he was, he made a casual salute and opened the back door of the limousine. They were in a deserted area of the airport and Macnair commented on it.

'Everyone's leaving, General. No one's arriving. You should see departures. That's another story. There's been riots and all sorts. Hell, I wouldn't have got here if I hadn't had a police escort.'

'Where's the escort now?'

'Not needed for the trip back. Like I said, sir, everyone's leaving London. The roads are empty.'

'Where are you from?'

'Originally? Kenya. Came over because of the troubles. That was fifteen years ago.'

'How come you haven't gone like the rest of them?'

'Where to? Anyway, I figure I'd be of most use here. We need to stop them bastards, not run away.' He paused and then added, 'I know what's real about the plutonium-based device. See, I even know its correct name. I listen but keep my mouth shut. It's the nature of what I do.'

Macnair nodded, impressed by the man. 'What about family?'

'Wife, son of twelve, daughter of nine. Them's different. Them I've sent to my wife's sister in Devon. I ain't risking their lives just because I won't run.'

'What's your name?'

'Fred. Fred Mungo.'

'Well, Fred, this country would be a damn sight better off with more people like you in it.'

'That's nice of you to say so, sir. Hey, you must be someone important to get a limo and all to pick you up and take you to Downing Street.'

Macnair's smile held no mirth. 'Some people may say so. Others wouldn't. I have to say, you're right about the roads. I've never seen anything like it.'

The car was speeding along the M4 towards the city while the motorway on the other side was jammed solid with stationary traffic. Of one thing he was certain: even with a police escort, the likelihood of getting a return flight was negligible. A brief phone call to TIFAT and he made other arrangements.

* * * * *

Nick didn't have it in him to kill a bunch of kids, no matter what the greater reason. He would be eternally grateful to Matt for stopping him. The car was already passing around the bend when Dunston grabbed the rifle to shoot. Before he could, two things happened. First of all the car passed out of sight and then the second car halted in front of them and somebody opened fire. The bullets ricocheted off the rocks that Dunston had placed as a barrier, missing the clergyman by inches. He dropped to his knees as Hunter drew his Glock and took aim. Before he could open fire, a machine gun emerged through the back window of the car and bullets erupted all around them. The barrier of rocks was becoming flimsier by the second. Hunter grabbed the dynamo and pushed the handle down hard. A split second later there was an almighty explosion and the shooting stopped. Both men waited a few moments before Dunston craned his neck around the right side of the barrier. The car had stopped with its front wheels over the plastic explosive. The resultant explosion had thrown the car into the air and onto its back and set the petrol alight. Two dead bodies were sprawled out of the windscreen, on their backs. At that moment the petrol tank exploded and the car was completely engulfed in flames. Other cars and lorries came to a halt. This being Afghanistan, explosions, shootings and dead bodies were commonplace. Men were climbing out of their vehicles to take a look, searching around them for the perpetrators. Every one of them carried a rifle of some description.

*   *   *   *   *

Limping along Downing Street, Macnair heard his name being called and looked over his shoulder.

'Hang on, Malcolm, I'll walk with you.'

'Hullo, William, I thought you'd be there by now.' The two men shook hands. Summers looked harassed.

'I had to chase up some information. What have you done to your ankle?'

'Just a sprain. Nothing much. It only hurts when I laugh. Which, luckily, isn't too often nowadays.'

Summers managed to smile at that but it quickly turned to a scowl. 'The information I was after. You know about the Saudis?'

Macnair nodded. 'They're financing the whole thing. The Iranians are backing it, though keeping a low profile, and let's not forget about the involvement of the Pakistanis.'

'After you.' Summers let the General walk through the world's most photographed door first. They were shown into Cabinet Office Briefing Room A where they took their seats alongside each other, opposite the politicians. Macnair was surprised that there were so few people attending the meeting. There was only the Defence Secretary, the Home Secretary and the Foreign Secretary, drinking coffee, sitting silently. They acknowledged the arrival of the two men with brief nods; there were no smiles and no handshakes. Clive Owens, hot-footing it from MI5, arrived a minute later. All three men accepted the coffee offered to them by a white-jacketed steward. Another man appeared and announced, 'The Prime Minister will be with you in about two minutes.'

It was closer to ten minutes, but finally the door opened and the Prime Minister entered. Out of deference to the office, not the man, they stood and said hullo. The Prime Minister went around the table shaking hands with Macnair, Summers and Owens. If he noticed Macnair's walking stick he didn't mention it.

'Thank you for coming, gentlemen. I know how busy you all are.' It was such a nonsensical platitude that Macnair, for once in his life, was struck dumb. 'Please, be seated. We have a great deal to get through.' Addressing the Foreign Secretary the Prime Minister asked, 'Is there any sign of the bomb?'

'You had better ask these three gentlemen,' the Foreign Secretary replied

'Well?' the Prime Minister barked looking across at the bosses of MI5, MI6 and TIFAT. It was clear to everyone around the table that the man wasn't handling the crisis at all well. He appeared on the edge of collapse.

'I think the best person to answer that, Prime Minister, is General Macnair,' Summers replied. The three security chiefs nodded. It meant that neither Owens nor Summers would have to lie to their government. For Macnair, it was different.

The Prime Minister continued to watch Summers. 'Is MI6 not involved?'

'Of course. We are helping in every way possible. But we, along with everyone else, are stretched to breaking

313

point.' He knew it wasn't the time or the place to talk about cutbacks and under-funding. Particularly by this government.

The Prime Minister looked at Macnair. 'Well, General, what have you to say for yourself?'

Macnair looked at the Scotsman with a blank face, masking the anger that was bubbling just below the surface. He knew he had to hold his temper and watch his words. He was not going to tell the politicians about the operation currently going down. 'I have to agree with William. We are doing everything in our power.'

'And?' The Prime Minister sat up straight and then leaned forward, the nail-bitten fingers of his right hand tapping rapidly and irregularly on the table before him.

Macnair leaned forward. 'And nothing. We have no clues. No idea where the men with the bomb are. Nothing. It's like searching for a needle in sewage. It's there somewhere, but there's pile of shit to scramble through to find it.'

'That's not good enough,' the Prime Minister thundered.

Macnair shrugged. 'It's all I can tell you.'

The Prime Minister changed his tone. From hectoring and bullying he was now pleading. 'There must be something. There must be.'

The General opened his briefcase and took out a file. 'Have you been told about the best and worst-case scenarios?'

The four politicians nodded. The Home Secretary said, 'We'll become a Third World country overnight.'

Macnair looked at her without revealing his dislike. 'That's correct. But it'll go further than that. If such a thing is possible.'

*   *   *   *   *

314

Nick and Matt had slipped over the skyline and back to their Land Rover. Hunter had started the engine, rammed it into gear and they were now in hot pursuit of the other car. They slammed into potholes, bounced over cracked tarmac and risked getting bruised from being thrown about. They knew that any car they saw ahead of them would be the one they were after. At least until they reached the airport and other vehicles joined the road.

Matt Dunston was busy sending a sitrep to TIFAT by text. As soon as he finished, he received a reply.

'What did they say?'

'There's a lot of traffic from the terrorists. They've repeated a code word that our lot don't get the meaning of. Translated, it means "fly the bird". There's no reference to it in any of the stuff we've found to date.'

'What about setting up blockades?'

'No chance. There's no British army this way and we've been told not to trust the police. Aeroplanes ahead.' A passenger plane was in the distance, lining up to land while another was just taking off.

The road improved marginally and Hunter put his foot down, sending the vehicle up to 110kph.

'There's a car ahead,' said Dunston.

'I don't think it's the one we want. No, it's just a taxi.'

Hunter swung around the taxi and cut back in, narrowly missing a lorry approaching them from the other direction. He got a blast from both horns as he accelerated away. Five minutes passed and there was nothing ahead of them. Another two minutes and the outskirts of the city appeared. They went as fast as they dared through the streets, which were becoming more congested by the minute. Finally, they were moving at barely walking pace.

'Text Isobel and tell her what's happened,' said Hunter, as

he slammed on the brakes, just missing a cyclist who shot out of a side street. There was no need. Information was already being sent to them. None of the news was good.

* * * * *

They crossed the border into Iran without any problems. The tension in the car visibly eased.

'Thanks be to Allah,' said Kaman Al-Zawahiri, 'we can relax for a few days as we cross the country.'

'We will not be interfered with?' Mohammed Akbar asked.

'No. It is all arranged.' Rehman Khan lit a cigarette and blew the smoke out of the open window. 'We have their blessing. Not only will they not try and stop us, they will do all in their power to help should we need it. However,' he stressed the word, 'there is to be no contact unless absolutely necessary. They wish to be able to deny all knowledge of our existence.'

'That is understandable,' Akbar smiled. 'Are all the other arrangements in hand?'

'Yes,' replied Khan. 'I have had confirmation by text.'

'Good. Then we should easily make it in four days,' said Akbar.

The road they were travelling along was wide, flat, well-maintained and relatively busy, in sharp contrast to what they had left behind in Afghanistan. After a few miles they saw a service station, and they stopped to fill up with petrol and to take advantage of a decent cup of coffee and something to eat. They also took the time, along with dozens of other men, to take out their prayer mats, kneel on them, bow to Mecca and say the second salat prayer of the day – the noon prayer known as *Dhuhr*.

31

Macnair drank some of his coffee before continuing. 'The Home Secretary sums up the situation beautifully. We'll become a Third World nation. But it won't be just us. The whole of the Western world will be affected. To date, we have looked at the immediate aftermath of an event such as the one we're facing. I have a Pentagon report about the long-term situation. Apart from the financial meltdown, there will be looting, rioting and murder on a grand scale with little chance of restoring order for years.'

He had their undivided attention, their gazes unwavering. They were rabbits caught in the headlights of a truck thundering down upon them.

'Our neighbours will not be able to help. Just the threat of another device exploding in, say, Paris or Rome will cause even more panic. Then we come to survival. All the things we take for granted – light, heat, food, drink, transport and employment – will be affected. It goes on and on.' He prodded the file before him. 'I'll leave you to read about it later but it goes even further. Not a single mosque, not a single Muslim will survive in Europe. Millions of innocent, law-abiding, upstanding citizens will be forced out of Europe or killed. The vast majority of them are citizens who contribute hugely to our well-being and could do so after the explosion. However, they won't be given a chance. And bear in mind, many of them are as European as you and I.'

The Foreign Secretary asked, 'What about America?'

'America will pull up the drawbridge. Anti-Muslim feeling will run high and they'll experience the same problems. The world will become completely polarised. Each tragedy piling on tragedy. Britain might become a Third World country, but relations with the Islamic world will be equivalent to those of the middle ages.'

So it went on. Macnair didn't pull any punches. Some of the facts were known to the others, some weren't. The worst case they'd been presented with by their own people was nowhere near as bad as what Macnair was now telling them. But then, political advisers always put a spin on facts, irrespective of reality. Finally, the General paused and looked at Owens. 'Clive, have you reported on the names, addresses and numbers of those people we believe are involved with Muslim fundamentalism in Britain?'

Owens nodded. 'Yes. The original report is nearly three years old. But we have it regularly updated. The latest reassessment, in view of what we are facing, was when this whole episode kicked off.'

'Thank you. Have you read it?' Macnair looked into the faces of the four politicians.

The Home Secretary said, 'I skimmed through it.'

'You?' Macnair looked at the Foreign Secretary.

He fiddled with a pen on the desk in front of him. 'To be honest, I haven't had time. I've had other things to deal with and think about.'

Macnair left the comment hanging in the air. It spoke for itself.

The Defence Secretary said, 'I read it. Cover to cover.' He

paused and looked at the three security bosses. 'It's the most frightening document I have ever read.'

'That's because the situation is overwhelmingly catastrophic.' Macnair turned his attention to the Prime Minister. 'Well?'

The dark jowls wobbled slightly as he nodded. 'Yes. I skimmed through it. I am not sure I agree with all the findings.'

'These are the conclusions of some of the finest brains we have in this country working on the problem.'

'But to round up over two thousand people. To arrest them! Where do we put them?'

'Any number of places. Pack them into prison cells six at a time for all I care. Take over the old army barracks down on the edge of Dartmoor and shove them in there. And have the army guard them. Anything, just stop them being able to help the men bringing the device into Britain.'

'We can't do that!' the Home Secretary said in a shocked voice. 'These people have human rights. You can't just go locking them up, willy-nilly. It's unthinkable.' Her next statement, as far as the security bosses were concerned, was incredible. 'The lawyers would have a field day. We'd be castigated by the Courts!'

If Macnair hadn't been so disciplined, his jaw would have dropped open at the sheer stupidity of what he was hearing. If it was true that a country got the politicians it deserved, then what on earth had Britain done that was so terrible?

'Do not talk about human rights,' said Macnair. 'After the July 2005 bombings you know damned well that a survey was carried out here in Britain. Twenty percent plus of Muslims either understood or supported what had happened. You saw the report. Or you should have. If they get anywhere near Britain with that damned device we're in more trouble than it's possible to imagine.'

'Yes, but two thousand people arrested!' The Home Secretary sat in a daze, unable to keep the overwhelming apprehension she was feeling out of her voice. 'We are meeting with the Muslim Council of Britain. It is as concerned as we are and has pledged its support.'

The three security men exchanged looks. It was too much for Macnair who smashed his fist down on the table. He yelled, 'What's the matter with you people? The Muslim Council of Britain is concerned is it? It has pledged its support? What the hell planet are you living on?'

'General . . .' The Prime Minister tried to interrupt.

'Listen to yourselves! What difference will the Muslim Council make? What?'

The politicians looked at each other. None of them looked at the three security chiefs.

Macnair leaned forward. 'A dirty bomb is heading this way which, unless we stop it, will kill many thousands of people. So tell me this,' his voice was now dripping with contempt. 'What will the Muslim Council do?'

The question was met with silence. They hadn't been spoken to like that for many years, if ever. A shocked silence descended like a blanket over the room.

'Look, we don't like it any more than you do.' Owens admitted. 'We keep saying, over and over, that the vast majority of Muslims are decent, law-abiding people and even if many do have sympathy for al-Qaeda it doesn't mean they're going to do anything actively to support the organisation. But there is that rump. Whether they feel disaffected, have a loyalty only to their religion or think we shouldn't be supporting Israel, whatever the reason, they are here. We know that they are helping to foment trouble.'

The arguments went round and round until it became evident that nothing would be achieved.

Owens gave it one more try. 'The people involved cover all ages, both sexes and the spectrum of employment and the professions. One man has started a small group of fundamentalist supporters for the legal profession. So far he has recruited nine solicitors and a barrister. They are demanding Sharia law.'

'Good God!' The Prime Minister exclaimed.

'Now maybe you can begin to get some perspective on what we're facing. We can deal with the political and legal fallout afterwards,' said Summers.

As he listened, Macnair finally acknowledged to himself that they might as well give up. British government was never going to take the action required.

'Why isn't the Chancellor of the Exchequer here?' Macnair suddenly asked.

At the beginning of the meeting he had noticed that he was conspicuous by his absence. He couldn't help asking. The four across the table exchanged uncomfortable glances before the Prime Minister replied, 'He's gone to Scotland to be with his family.'

'I take it you are all going to do the same?' The General's contempt was plain to see. 'I have had word that Her Majesty and Prince Philip are staying. That when Prince Charles was told to leave by his mother, he also refused.'

The looks on the faces of those opposite said it all.

'I trust that Princes William and Harry are not in London,' said Macnair. 'For the sake of the future of the monarchy they must be sent somewhere safer.'

It was Owens who answered. 'Harry is back in Iraq. He insisted on going. As he pointed out, the press have far more important issues to worry about than writing

321

nonsense about him. William is on duty with his regiment here in Britain, Essex, I think. Neither has ever shirked their obligations, just as their father never has. Unlike so many of our parliamentarians.' Owens paused and then said, 'We have to move on.' He was about to address the Prime Minister as 'sir' but stopped himself. Instead, he merely looked at the man. 'Have you read the report dealing with the Saudis?'

'I have,' the Prime Minister said heavily, 'and I find it incredible.'

'I take it,' said Macnair, 'that you don't believe it? Or you're not prepared to act on it?'

'Quite right, gentlemen, on both premises. Now, if that is all.' The Prime Minister looked at his watch.

'No, it isn't all. We must deal with the Saudi issue,' said a frustrated Macnair.

'I have a plane waiting for me. We have your written report on the Saudis and will give your proposals some consideration.' The Prime Minister stood up, followed by Summers, Owens and Macnair. The politicians remained seated. The Prime Minister was about to proffer his hand when the other three about-faced and walked out.

In the street, Macnair turned to the other two.

'We're on our own,' he said to Owens and Summers as the three men left Downing Street and walked into Whitehall. 'Any suggestions?'

'It's what we expected Malcolm,' Summers said. 'We need to continue tracking down the ringleaders.'

Owens nodded. 'It's all we can do. I have every available resource looking for the swine. Together, we're making inroads. I just hope it's going to be enough.'

Macnair's phone rang. 'It's Rosyth. I told them to call only in an emergency. Excuse me a moment.' He listened intently before saying, 'Any idea why? No? Right. I'm on my way back.' He terminated the call and turned to the other two. 'I'm afraid Hunter and Dunston have experienced a setback.'

'Do we know what?' Owens asked.

Macnair shook his head. 'I'll find out soon enough. As soon as I know, you'll know.'

Summers asked, 'Have you contacted my man in Iran?'

Macnair nodded. They said their goodbyes.

As General Macnair walked down towards Parliament Square one of his favourite poems came to mind, which he couldn't help paraphrasing. Enemies to the right of us, enemies to the left of us and parliament behind us were volleying and thundering. *The Charge of the Light Brigade* about summed it up.

32

Nick and Matt landed in Tehran after an uneventful flight from Kabul and were met by Doug Tanner and Simon Henri. They'd been forced to return to Kabul to get the correct visas and paperwork for their journey. The examination of their documents in Tehran however was cursory. They showed the letter from the Minister of Culture inviting them to visit Iran to look at her wonderful historic treasures and architecture. If the timing of their visit seemed odd to the Immigration Officers, in view of what was happening in Europe, they didn't comment on it.

Walking out of Tehran Airport terminal, Dunston said, 'You know something, I actually like Iranians. At least, the ones I've met in my time.'

'I remember an Iranian girl,' said Hunter. 'About ten years ago. She was beautiful, witty and intelligent.'

'So you had nothing in common,' Matt teased him.

'Amen to that,' said Doug Tanner, smiling broadly.

'Absolutely not a thing,' Hunter smiled.

Laughing, Matt asked 'Where to now?'

'We're going to be met,' Hunter said looking around. 'That guy waving to us from that people carrier. Looks like he's our MI6 contact.'

The men hoisted their bags and crossed the pavement.

'Are you waiting for someone?' Hunter asked.

'Yes, Allah and Father Christmas. Please get in.' The man had short black hair with dark eyes to match and was clean-shaven. He was in his early thirties, of medium height and build and spoke impeccable English. Introductions were brief. He gave his name as Omar Zand. They knew he was MI6 and had been working in Iran for some time. He would be leaving soon, though not until the crisis was over. Too long in one country and there was a danger that a front line agent could go native. It wasn't unheard of. What Zand didn't tell them was that his real name was Oliver Smith. Zand was his maternal grandfather's name and Smith that of his father. He had been raised in a tolerant household, where religion was rarely discussed. That changed, as it did for so many people, on 11th September 2001. The rejoicing in the Islamic world when 2,646 Americans were killed, plus 327 foreign nationals from 54 countries, was short-lived. When the sheer horror of what had been done had finally sunk in, people around the world were appalled although Muslim hard-liners and fundamentalists continued to celebrate. Of the 67 Britons who lost their lives, one was Oliver Smith's older brother. Oliver had just graduated from Oxford, where he had been reading European History. It was there he had been approached by the security services. It was known that he spoke almost fluent Farsi, thanks to his maternal grandparents, and had a working knowledge of Arabic. If MI5, or better still, MI6, could recruit him, he might become a significant asset. Oliver Smith jumped at the chance to fight for his country in a worthwhile and meaningful way. Now here he was, at the end of his third year in Iran, and a veteran of numerous operations. Back in Britain he was highly thought of as a man who would, with luck and God's blessing, go all the way to the top.

They threw their bags into the rear and climbed into the vehicle; a Ford Galaxy people carrier.

'Do you have anything new?' Hunter asked.

Zand shook his head. 'The latest is that they are still on their way here.'

Zand drove them to Khordad Avenue, on the south side of the city, near the Tehran Bazaar. The journey was long, tedious and fraught. As Tanner put it, how the hell were the drivers managing to miss each other instead of having a smash-up four times an hour? But, as Zand explained, any accident wasn't the driver's fault: it happened because it was God's will! Eventually they reached Zand's house and drove quickly into the small, enclosed courtyard. The stone villa was very well appointed, with four bedrooms, all en-suite, a large lounge and a mammoth kitchen with a table that could cater for ten people.

'Some house,' said Tanner.

'It belonged to an American diplomat back in the early eighties. It has been vacant for about ten years. MI6 own it through an investment company based in Kuwait.'

'I didn't think that sort of thing went on in Iran,' said Hunter.

'You'd be surprised. Follow me.' Zand stepped across to a wooden door, unlocked it, switched on a light and led the way down a flight of steps. In the basement was another door, this time with a combination lock. He tapped in the number. When he pulled open the heavy door he revealed a cupboard jammed with communications equipment.

'Pretty impressive,' said Tanner.

'I have recruited people from all over Iran,' Zand

explained. 'Messages are sent here, I encrypt them and forward them to MI6. There are some new messages. Let me see.' He fiddled with a switch and then said, 'I'll just play them back and listen to what they say.'

The first message was in Farsi. Whatever was said, Zand nodded as he listened. The following messages were the same. 'Good. You will be pleased to know that the messages confirm that the dirty bomb was brought over by three people. Does the name Rehman Khan mean anything to you?'

Hunter nodded and explained what he knew about the man.

'And Kaman Al-Zawahiri?'

'I don't think so, but his name does sound familiar.'

'His cousin is Ayman Al-Zawahiri, bin Laden's deputy.'

Hunter nodded. 'Now I know who he is. He's been on and off our radar for quite a while now. Who else?'

'Mohammed Akbar.'

'I know of him,' said Hunter. 'A nasty piece of work.'

'We have a file inches thick on the little bastard,' said Zand. 'I've also received confirmation that a group of men have joined them. Could be as many as a dozen, and they're definitely heading this way. However,' he glanced at his watch, 'we lost them about two hours ago. We're intensifying the search. It's all we can do at present.'

'How long will it take them to get here?' Dunston asked.

'They won't arrive here until morning. They're in a convoy of four cars, so we ought to pick them up sometime. Right,' Omar rubbed his hands together, 'would anyone like tea or coffee?

*

327

Supper was eaten in a local restaurant where the food was excellent, and cheap. The five men sat at a corner table. Nothing was said about the operation. Zand had warned them: you could never be sure who was listening. Iran had one of the most comprehensive spy networks – principally for internal work – in the world.

When they returned to the house, Hunter and Zand sat in the kitchen while the other three went to their beds.

'I've never understood the desire to create such destruction,' Omar said reflectively. He looked at Nick with a penetrating gaze. 'Have you?'

'No. I've said it before and I'll keep saying it. Violence, death, destruction and war should only be found in books and on film. Life is too short and the world far too small for us to continue what we're doing. Look at the global issues we have to contend with. Overcrowding for one. Every day the world's population increases by two hundred thousand. And what is there for the kids? Pollution's out of control and there's a huge lack of natural resources such as gas and oil. That's one of the main issues here.'

'What is?' Matt asked entering the room.

'Can't sleep?' Nick asked sympathetically.

'No. I heard your voices and thought I'd come and join you. Pity we haven't got a bottle of something to lubricate the larynx.'

Zand smiled. 'Will a single malt do?'

'Ssh! Keep your voice down,' Dunston whispered, 'Tanner and Henri can hear the words "single malt" whispered at one hundred paces.'

Zand got the bottle, ice, cold water and glasses. Within minutes they were clinking glasses. 'What were you saying about oil?' He looked at Hunter.

'We know that the oil reserves are being rapidly depleted in Saudi. They have maybe two or three decades or so left. Now, for many people in the country that isn't too important. They have assets and investments, and they're helping to lead the world in some innovative industries like electricity production using wave and wind power. However, there is a very powerful clique, near to the throne, for whom, as far as they are concerned, enough is never enough.' He shrugged. 'That's what General Macnair was telling me. They have sold forward, I was about to say a small fortune, but that's a euphemism for a very, very large fortune, in worldwide stocks and shares. Vast amounts of precious metals and other minerals are being bought which, if the bomb does go off, will cause the expected meltdown. The Saudis will benefit from trillions of dollars in profit.'

'Trillions?' Zand looked at Hunter, his mouth agape.

'So I believe,' Nick shrugged. 'It's a sum I can't come to terms with, like most people. What happens to it? Where does it go? All we're sure about is that the Saudis are supplying the funding for what's happening. They also have some personnel involved as well but we have yet to identify who. We will, make no mistake about it. Some gear has also been supplied to the terrorists. You know, if you think it through, then at one horrendous level it makes sense. The Saudis become even wealthier, which will give them enormous power around the world.'

'There's a huge downside for them,' said Dunston. 'What will the world do about it when they find out?'

Zand nodded. 'Yes! What will we do?'

Hunter replied. 'Some people will believe it. Others won't, no matter how much proof we have. Can you

329

imagine the arguments in courts around the world? And what will Muslims do?'

'Rejoice?' Zand suggested.

'The vast majority of Muslims wish to live in peace, raise a family, grow old. It's what we all aspire to. But a large and strong minority see Islam as the world's dominant religion. And don't forget something of vital importance. The Saudis have one of the best armed military set-ups in the world. With the very latest weapon systems, they are a force to be reckoned with.'

'As was Saladin all the way back in the twelfth century,' said Dunston, 'and Egyptian to boot. Although he did conquer Syria as well as giving the crusaders a bloody nose.'

'It's only some Saudis, hence only some Muslims. It's like saying that from the seventies until only a few years ago, all Roman Catholics were supporters of the IRA. We know nothing was further from the truth. It's a fact we have to keep reminding ourselves of when dealing with the billion or so innocent Muslims in the world.'

'I know what you mean,' said Zand. 'I really do. Despite the fact that my brother was killed in the 9/11 attacks. I came to understand a long time ago that we are dealing with the fanatics. The fundamentalists. Such people are equally bad whatever the religion.'

'That's a fact,' said Dunston. 'I've known a few Christian zealots in my time and they scared the Bejesus out of me.'

'That's my point exactly,' said Hunter. 'It's imperative we keep everything in perspective.'

'What will happen to the Saudis?' Zand asked reasonably.

'That's not our problem at the moment. Stopping these sons-of-bitches with the sodding bomb is. Thanks for the drink, Omar,' Hunter placed his glass on the table, stood and stretched, 'but I'd better get some sack-time.'

'Me too,' said Dunston, standing up.

'I'll stay here. If there are any messages, I'll call you.'

No messages arrived and the team had an undisturbed night. Breakfast was boiled eggs, sangak bread – long, thick and baked on a bed of stones – and strong coffee. The morning wasn't really wasted, even if they did sit around drinking coffee, fretting. Rosyth had sent a detailed sheet of instructions to Hunter. It demonstrated how to defuse the bomb. It was the middle of the afternoon before they finally received any further word from TIFAT. Mohammed Akbar and Rehman Khan had been positively located. They were in a convoy of four vehicles and had just passed through the town of Semnan. That put them on the main A83, about 200 kilometres or so from Tehran.

'There is another feature of the house I would like to show you.' Oliver led them down into the basement, moved some empty boxes from the furthest wall and pushed at the corner of a stone. There was a click and a section of wall swung open.

Tanner stepped forward and gave a low whistle. 'This is some armoury.'

'It's been put together over the years,' said Zand, 'bit by bit. There are quite a few collections like this around the country. It was always felt that, come the uprising would come the need.' He shrugged. 'Somehow, I don't think it's going to happen. At least not for a long while. Iran, in spite of its problems, is pretty solid. The ruling party holds the country in a powerful grip and the Mullahs have massive sway. So please, help yourselves. Take whatever you want.'

33

They were ready to move out. They had Glocks and plastic explosive with all the trimmings. Now all they needed was a target. Their quarry had disappeared from sight again. This time, it was Zand who had located them. Through his contacts, he finally received word that fourteen men in four cars were passing through Tehran. Zand thanked his informant and arranged a meeting. Suitable payment for all those involved in collecting and passing on the information still had to be made. Commerce never stopped, no matter how great the death and destruction.

'Can we be sure it's them?' Hunter asked.

Zand shrugged. '100 per cent, no. 60 per cent plus, yes.' Zand then asked an astute question. 'We all agree they must be stopped. What if the price is the thing exploding in the middle of Tehran? It will kill thousands of innocent people.'

Dunston replied for them all. 'It won't detonate unless they set it off. However, none of us is absolutely positive that's really the case. Could a stray bullet cause it to detonate? Not according to what we've been told. But, and it's a big but, what if they're wrong? What if there's the tiniest possibility of a bullet hitting the wrong part of the mechanism and setting it off? It's unacceptable even with those odds. Which is why we'll track and ambush them somewhere quietly away from the city.'

Zand nodded, satisfied with the answer.

Tanner summed it up for all four of them when he said, 'My Momma didn't raise no mass murderer and that's for sure. We stop them at all costs, that is at all costs to us. But we do it right.'

'Good. I think it's time we rolled,' Oliver said.

Hunter looked surprised. 'Are you coming with us?'

'Is that a problem? You need me to show you the way. Besides, fourteen against five is slightly better odds than fourteen to four.'

'No argument there,' said Dunston, nodding.

'Oui, he is correct,' said Henri.

'Okay, that's fine with me. Only you do what I say, Omar. Is that clear?'

'Of course. Now,' smoothing out a map of Tehran, he pointed, 'this is where they were. This is where they are headed. This is us.' His phone rang. The conversation was brief. 'We need to hurry. It looks as though we'll be playing catch-up.'

They loaded up the Ford Galaxy. It had been modified by Zand and was a smuggler's dream, with hiding places for any amount of contraband and certainly more than they needed for the weaponry they were taking. They set out. The streets were just as busy as when they'd arrived but Zand deftly steered them through the traffic.

Zand received another message. 'They have now reached the outskirts of the city and are heading north-west towards Qazvin. That's 180 kilometres away.'

'We'd better step on it,' said Hunter.

A major accident was blocking the road ahead. Thanks

to Zand's knowledge of the city they managed to get round it but they had lost a lot of time. The sun was setting as they arrived at the city limits and turned on to the road to Qazvin. The road was wide and well maintained. Zand floored it.

'Where's all the traffic?' Dunston asked in a baffled tone.

Zand gave a wry chuckle. 'It takes some getting used to. But it's like this all of the time. The city is jammed and here it's empty. There's some traffic during the day, but not a lot. It's mainly trucks. They don't run at night.'

The latest piece of intelligence they had received from TIFAT was that the men and the device were close to or at Qazvin. Where they had gone to ground – if they had gone to ground – was unknown. Zand used his phone to made a brief call. He used it again when they were about halfway there. It was a lengthy conversation. When he'd finished, Zand said, 'I didn't want to say anything earlier, since it was a long shot. I do have one contact – the mayor – in the city.'

'The mayor?' Hunter looked surprised.

Zand smiled. 'Let's just say I helped him with his election campaign. He's spoken to the police. A number of men have checked into the Hotel Iran on Peyghambarieh Street. I know the place. It has a new block of rooms at the back with en-suite toilets and showers.'

'Are we sure it's them?' Hunter asked.

'As sure as we can be,' said Zand.

'Do you trust this mayor?' asked Henri.

'Good grief, of course not! That's why we'll move extremely cautiously. Slow and easy, nice and gentle.'

'Now there,' said Hunter, 'we're on the same wavelength.'

* * * * *

'We cannot thank you enough, my friend,' Mohammed Akbar said as he shook hands with the man who had been in charge of their escort from the Afghanistan border.

'*Mashallah*,' said the man. 'It is God's will. You have important work to do. We have merely helped you. You still have a long journey ahead.'

'All aboard!' came the distant call, followed by short blasts on a whistle.

'You had better get on the train with your friends. You should be in Tabriz at first light. Sleep well, my friend. And go with God.'

Akbar climbed onto the train. It pulled away with a slight jerk as he leaned out of the window and waved goodbye. He would never see the man again. At least not in this world, but certainly in the next. It was 21.30 and the journey ahead of them would take eleven hours.

34

It was just after 22.00 when they entered the foyer of the Hotel Iran. The public rooms were still relatively busy – mostly men drinking Zam-Zam – a form of cola – or some orange or black fruit drink – and over in two separate corners were sat men with their wives, who drank using straws fed up under their heavy veils.

Zand did the talking. He paid cash for the rooms which had been booked by the mayor. They were not en-suite; the showers and toilets were at either end of the corridor. One shower and toilet served ten to twenty people depending on whether the rooms were single or double occupancy. Once in his room, Hunter wondered how on earth two people managed to share. There was just enough room around the double bed to squeeze along the wall. The single cupboard enough space to hold two coat hangers and a narrow shelf.

Zand tapped on Hunter's door and went in. Hunter was sitting in the dark, his curtains open, looking out of the window. The hotel's new build was three sides of a square. According to the brochure they'd found at the check-in desk, the hotel extension boasted rooms big enough to hold a double bed, a writing desk and a chair along with the separate shower and toilet. It was single-storey, although a sign said that a second level was due to be built the following year. Six of the rooms opposite held the men they were after.

Zand opened a holdall and took out a small directional microphone with earphones. 'Let's see if we can learn something useful.' He switched it on and aimed it across the quadrangle at a room opposite.

'Anything?' Hunter asked.

Zand shook his head. 'No.' Suddenly he paused. 'Wait! One man has just wondered what the others are doing. Where they are going.' He paused and frowned. 'Another has said it is in the service of Allah and against the infidels.' He paused. 'There's more about the blessings of Mohammed. Wait! One man has just said he wishes them a safe journey.'

Hunter snapped alert. 'Do you think the device has gone?'

'I can't tell. Not yet.' He placed the microphone on the windowsill, still pointing at the room opposite, and placed his hands on his earphones, pressing them closer to his head. His eyes were now closed in concentration. 'Two of them are going out to get food.'

'Omar, if they've got the device we'll take them out, grab the bomb and move like the wind for the hills. Classic evasion and escape tactics,' Nick said.

Zand nodded. 'And if they don't have it?'

'If we take out those men and they don't have the device then we're running and hiding for nothing. I have a healthy respect for the Iranian police. They're not stupid and they have the power to shut down the country. We'll never be able to keep up the chase. We'll be too busy trying to avoid being arrested. Whichever way you look at it, it's a can of worms, so we have to be 100 per cent certain

337

the bomb is here. We . . .' Zand raised a hand and Hunter stopped talking.

'Damnation. It's gone,' Zand said. 'The device is on the night sleeper. It'll be in Tabriz tomorrow morning. Arrangements are being made to meet the men who have it and take them across the border. I can hear one of them on a mobile phone.' Zand could not disguise his concern as he looked at Hunter.

'Are you sure?' Hunter asked.

'As sure as I can be,' he shrugged, thought about it, and nodded again. 'I'm sure.'

'Where's Tabriz?' Hunter asked rhetorically as he opened their map of Iran. He pointed. 'Just over 300 miles. Any contacts there?'

Zand nodded. 'A senior, but disillusioned, policeman. Probably my best contact in Iran. What do you propose?'

'Hit the road. Try and get to Tabriz before the train. Tell the others to get ready to move.' While Zand went into the corridor and knocked on the doors of the others, Hunter sent a text to Rosyth detailing the developments.

Having paid for their rooms in advance, their departure was swift and unannounced. The others took the change in their plans as a matter of course. Zand drove them out of the city. They soon reached the turning for Karaj, the next city on their way to Tabriz.

Hunter announced, 'Dog watches, two hours at a time starting with Omar, then Simon, Doug, Matt and then me. So settle down lads and make yourselves as comfortable as possible.'

There was no question of a comfortable ride. The road stayed quiet. Occasionally they passed a car heading into the city, but nothing was travelling in their direction. Zand handed over to Henri when they were just outside Karaj.

Henri stayed at the wheel until they arrived at Zanjan. It had been an uneventful, boring ride, ideal as far as the team was concerned. Unknown to them however, the train they were chasing had only just departed Zanjan. In the centre of the city they came across a huge bus station, eerily silent at that time of the morning, but packed with vehicles. Zand directed Henri through the city. Once they reached the outskirts, Doug Tanner took over the driving. The roads were quiet and they arrived at the outskirts of Tabriz just as Dunston was coming to the end of his stint. It was a few minutes short of 06.00 and the train was due at 08.30, so they had plenty of time. They parked up in a lay-by, where they managed an hour's sleep. Hunter kept watch. A lorry thundered past and woke the others up.

'We'll hit town,' said Hunter. 'Recce and deployment are the order of the day. We know the train terminates here so they'll have to change. From here there are three lines, one to Turkey, one to Iraq and one to Azerbaijan. Or they might decide to hire a car which is what I'd be more inclined to do. It's more flexible.'

'Did you know,' said Dunston, 'that the Ajichay River used to flow out of the Garden of Eden, placing the city at the gates of Paradise?'

Tanner, ever the cynic asked, 'What, this dump?'

'According to the Bible,' said Dunston, 'this dump. It's had a truly amazing chequered past. In 1727, as many as 77,000 people died in what was reputed to be the world's worst earthquake. It's awesome when you consider the level of art and culture that existed in this area when we were barely out of caves.'

It left them all thinking about the irony of what they were now seeing. The people carrier reached the western end of Bahman Street, near the train station. They parked in an empty bay. Zand moved to the driver's seat.

'Okay, let's go. If we see them, we follow. We make no moves until they're out of the city,' Hunter instructed. 'If they get suspicious we take them, grab the case and get the hell out.'

The others nodded.

'We have plenty of time, so nice and slow. Hopefully, there's the Iranian equivalent of Starbuck's somewhere.'

The station was already busy, with local trains taking commuters across the city. Just like any other station, anywhere in the world, Hunter thought. The arrivals board rotated its list of trains and when they were due with the usual clatter. There were few delays showing. The team spread out across the concourse, and kept in contact using their personal radios. Each member was sitting or standing at a booth drinking coffee. The sixth train on the board was the one they were waiting for. According to the arrival information it was delayed by forty-five minutes. The time dragged very slowly. Because they were tanned, wearing Westernised clothes obviously made somewhere in the Middle East, and all in need of a shave, they tended to blend in. Nobody took any notice of them as the minutes ticked down. As the train approached the station however everything turned to rats.

35

Across Europe, parliaments reacted in almost identical fashion. First of all, they were in total and utter panic. Many parliamentarians had used their positions to get themselves and their families out of the capital cities. Roads were clogged, accidents were frequent – many fatal, many more where the injured required hospital treatment – and often led to violent recriminations, as each party blamed the other. Such attacks were particularly violent if Muslims were involved. Hospitals were staffed with skeleton crews, as many doctors and nurses had also joined the mass exodus. The largest percentage of staff who stayed to help were Muslim. A fact ignored by the media. Panic instilled more panic. Political leaders across Europe made broadcast after broadcast telling the people *not* to panic, not to leave the cities. To sit tight. To wait for more information.

The British Prime Minister made his regular broadcasts from his constituency. But then, all of Europe's leaders were somewhere they considered safe. For the previous forty-eight hours Europe had been at Bikini state Black Special. This meant an increased likelihood of attack, no defined target and a potential terrorist threat. Within the past few minutes the British government had been given no choice but to change their threat level to Bikini Amber. As far as Britain was concerned there was a specific and substantial threat, although the actual target was still unidentified. It also meant High Alert which could be a transition to war. The armed forces were ready to mobilise. The Chief of the Defence Staff, had already briefed the Cabinet on the meaning of the next alert level. He explained about the ultimate warning state – Bikini Red – which meant information had been received about a *specific* target, that Britain was at war, but most significantly, that there was likelihood of a nuclear strike. Whatever the Bikini state, the same problem persisted. Who was the country at war with? The Bikini states had not been designed to handle the situation the country now faced.

Later that morning the Chief of the Defence Staff telephoned General Macnair.

'Malcolm? Sorry it has taken me so long to get back to you. Have you seen the news?'

'Yes.'

'I've been briefing the Cabinet on Bikini Red.'

Macnair interrupted. 'I thought they'd all left London?'

Taff's laugh was mirthless. 'They have. It was a conference telephone call. The Prime Minister is in Scotland and the rest have all scattered.'

'What about you?' Malcolm asked.

'I'm staying put,' Taff replied. 'Come hell or high water, this is where I belong. I've made it clear to my staff that I expect nothing less of them. And to be fair, not one has complained, asked to be excused, or done a runner. Not unreasonably, those with families have made arrangements for them to leave London. And we've helped with the ferrying. After all, if you're giving your life for your country, the least your country can do is protect your family. Now, how can I help you?'

'The reason I called you earlier was because I need to get some personnel into Turkey.' Macnair explained the situation and finished by saying, 'We need a NATO asset, a helicopter.'

'I'll get your team air-lifted into Timbuktu if it's required. Leave that to me. Is there anything else you need?'

'Not for now. How are you coping?'

'We're stretched to breaking point. You've read all the reports Malcolm. For a decade we've warned the idiots what would happen if you stretched the armed forces too thinly. This government has done so and they're having to face the consequences. I take very little satisfaction in saying I told you so – even to a pompous oaf like this Prime Minister – but maybe once it's all over we can get some sense back into the situation. We'll have to see.'

'You don't, for one minute, think that's likely, do you?' Macnair couldn't keep the incredulity out of his voice.

'Of course not. But I live in hope. Always in hope.'

* * * * *

A large number of Iranian army personnel had suddenly appeared at the end of the concourse.

'Christ! What's going on?' Hunter asked Dunston who was standing next to him.

'No idea. But I don't like it one bit. What shall we do?'

'Nothing. If they've come for us there's sod all we can do about it.' He transmitted to the other three. 'Keep calm. Simon and Doug walk away slowly. Go back to the car. Let's see what happens.'

Along the concourse they watched as Henri sauntered

one way and Tanner another. Nobody tried to stop them.

'There are at least a hundred of them.' Hunter turned his back. 'If they've come to meet the train there isn't much we can do about it.' He turned again to look. The platform on which the train was due was now lined with soldiers. 'Damn! Here comes the train.'

The train was pulling slowly into the station. It came to a halt right up against the buffers and, after a few seconds of calm, doors burst open and voices called out. Hunter and Dunston walked across to a coffee bar, where they had a better view of the disembarking passengers. They spotted and recognised the three men they were after. Rehman Khan was carrying the case. An officer approached them and saluted. He said something and the man holding the case nodded. Dunston surreptitiously used his phone to photograph them as they walked along the platform. The officer gave an order and the soldiers surrounded the men and led them out of the station. Within seconds the three men were being driven away in a Mercedes Benz which quickly disappeared from sight. Hunter and Dunston returned to the car.

'Nick,' said Zand, as the others climbed in, 'I've just had a call from my contact. They are being given an escort to Bazargan. That's about 240 klicks from here.'

'Damn! I hadn't expected the Iranians would want to be so involved,' said Hunter. 'We'd better follow. I've never heard of the place. Is that Iraq or Turkey?' he asked.

'Turkey. I know it. I've used it a couple of times. The customs/immigration post sits on a hilltop about two and a half kilometres from Bazargan village. The border is hellishly busy and seriously chaotic. The worst bit is westbound, on the Turkish side. You need a Turkish visa to enter and the office you get them from is shut half the time, even though the border is supposed to work all night,' Zand snorted. 'Not forgetting the go-slows at meal times, of course. Clearing customs is a nightmare. It can take anything from three to twenty hours.' He paused and then added thoughtfully, 'If the Iranian authorities have fixed things then I expect they'll be across in no time at all. We, on the other hand, could have a hell of a job.'

'What are the roads like? How long will it take them to get to the border?' Hunter asked.

'Pretty good. They should be there in about three hours, I'd say.'

As they followed in the wake of their prey, Hunter updated TIFAT and Dunston transmitted the photographs he'd taken. They were approaching the outskirts of the city when they were forced to stop in a stationary queue of traffic. In the distance, they could see the army lorries escorting the Mercedes as it pulled effortlessly away.

* * * * *

Rehman Khan was satisfied. His contacts in JIMAS had been true to their word. An escort to the border and a further escort once they had crossed into Turkey. It was holy jihad and the West was going to pay. Praise be to Allah, how they would pay. Islam would rise to be the dominant religion and greatest force in the world. At last. The future would be glorious. His name, along with that of Akbar and Al-Zawahiri, would go down in history, to be revered for all time alongside that of the Prophet himself. *Their* names to be spoken in the same breath, with the same honour and exultation! He smiled to himself. It was a glorious prospect. They may still have a long way to go, but nothing could stop them now. His smile widened. He had upped the dosage of his pills to two and they were proving highly effective. The tolerance he was building up against the drugs was irrelevant. He wouldn't live long enough for it to matter.

'You are amused, my friend?' Akbar asked, looking at Khan.

'I was merely thinking of what the future could hold,' replied Khan.

'Not could, will.'

Khan's smile broadened. 'Thank you, my friend. I stand corrected.'

'I, too, have thought of little else.' The overweight Akbar smiled in return. 'It is an amazing responsibility we have. And look how the Islamic world has come together to help us achieve our objective. Our brothers in Saudi Arabia have arranged all this. An escort to the border. A second special escort across the border and then the journey to the sea. We cannot fail.' There was awe in his voice.

'Those are precisely my thoughts. Praise be to Allah. As well as all thanks to the Saudis,' said Khan.

Al-Zawahiri said, 'Our time has simply come, my brothers.'

They continued their banter, pleased with their progress so far and excited by what lay ahead of them. Their escort was forcing other cars out of the way and they moved rapidly towards Turkey. In just over two and a half hours they reached the border. Normally, they would have had to wait in line before they could cross into a country that, though Muslim, was an important member of NATO. However, the Saudis had been at work. A lot of money had changed hands. The officials currently manning both sides of the border were not only JIMAS supporters but had been well compensated for their compliance. As they

346

approached the border, they could see the low hill in the distance, with the border post sitting in splendid isolation. At the foot of the hill were various buildings including an hotel and a number of bars. To the left of the road was a white customs and immigration shack, a pole stretched across the road and a very long queue of traffic leading up to it. They drove past the stationary vehicles. Their escort, with flags fluttering on the wings of the bonnet, ensured nobody blew their horn or gestured angrily at such flagrant abuse of power. The Iranians were used to it.

The car stopped outside the hotel. A customs official approached, saluted and handed over the necessary documents. The three men walked up the hill with him. He escorted them across no-man's land where they met another man and who took them down the other side where another Mercedes was waiting. They climbed inside and it roared away. Their destination was a town called Dogubayazit, 40 kilometres from the border and the nearest place with a decent hotel or restaurant. Everything had gone exactly as planned. Their passing went virtually unobserved. The very long and powerful reach of the Saudis was at work across the region. It seemed there was nothing to stop the three men with their lethal cargo. However, Omar Zand also had a long reach.

36

The helicopter had dropped the team at the regional airport in Erzurum, Turkey. From there, they had taken a taxi to the Marriott Hotel. Omar Zand had stayed in Iran. Their farewells had been brief. While Nick rang General Macnair, the team took the opportunity for a work out in the hotel's fitness and sauna club.

'Thanks to Zand, we've learned that a car with three occupants was escorted through the Iranian/Turkish border in double quick time. It passed through a town called Dogubayazit on the main E80. Since then, it's vanished,' Hunter explained.

'We're talking to the Turkish police right now,' General Macnair said 'but I don't hold out much hope.'

'Do we know where the Turks stand in all this, sir? How much can we trust them?'

'I've spoken to Varol Sandal, the Director General of their Security Forces. I believe you've met him?'

'Yes, sir, at the European security conference last year. He came across with all the right words, but apart from that, I can't say,' Nick replied.

'He's doing so again. Turkey is desperate to join the European Union so their co-operation appears to be all that we can hope for. He says he has every available man working on the case, looking for Khan and his companions.'

'Does he know that they have the bomb?' Hunter asked.

'He's not stupid. You'll be pleased to know that Zim Albatha is on his way to you.'

'Excellent! Some good news at last. We could certainly do with him.'

Zim Albatha had helped TIFAT on a number of other occasions, including tracking down a terrorist in Scotland and fighting a Russian crime cartel in Europe.

'Hold on a moment Nick. Isobel's here.' A few seconds passed. 'I'll have to call you back.' The General abruptly ended the call.

While he was waiting for General Macnair to call back, he telephoned the desk and arranged for two Skoda Superb cars to be delivered. He was assured they would be with him in less than twenty minutes. The General rang back soon after.

'Isobel has intercepted a message that suggests our three targets have holed up somewhere.'

'Any idea where?' Nick asked.

'None whatsoever. Just sit tight. If we've not heard any more by tomorrow I want you to move west. We know that's where they're going so you may as well stay ahead of them. We may get an opportunity to set a trap.' The General could not prevent a sigh escaping from his lips. 'Nick, you have no idea about the sort of resources we're throwing at this. Even if we stop them, it's going to take a hell of a long time before Europe recovers. Financially, politically and in every other way. Race relations have been flushed down the toilet. It'll take decades to recover. Have you seen the news?'

'Yes. I've been watching CNN. The riots and burnt mosques tell their own story.'

'The death toll is in the many hundreds, possibly thousands and mainly Muslims. It's unjust, unfair and downright wrong.'

'You won't get any argument from me. The only hope we've got is to stop these three maniacs.'

'Correct. And once we've done that, we'll go after their leaders,' Macnair promised.

'And who are they, sir?'

'That's what Isobel came to see me about but we need to confirm some details first. In the meantime, as soon as we have any news, I'll be in touch.'

After the fraught and hectic time they'd had, the team spent what was, for them, a quiet afternoon and evening. They had just sat down for dinner in the hotel's restaurant when they were joined by Zim Albatha. He entered the room like a whirlwind, his height and size making it impossible for him to go anywhere quietly.

'Will you join us?' Hunter invited after they'd exchanged handshakes and delighted smiles.

Albatha nodded. He waved to the waiter and ordered a large steak with all the trimmings. Next, he downed a glass of red wine, belched his appreciation, and filled his glass again.

'I guess,' he said, quietly looking Hunter in the eye, 'that the men you're chasing have the bomb?'

'How do you figure that?' Dunston asked, a faint smile playing around his mouth.

'A number of reasons. Knowing you and knowing General Macnair, it can be the only reason that brings you to Turkey. A Pakistani device across country is how I see it.' His eyes narrowed as he looked around the table. 'Also, I heard the Turkish Minister of State for Immigration speaking about it.'

'Who to?' Hunter asked, leaning forward with interest.

'I do not know. Maybe we will find the answer if I get the chance to ask him one day soon.' He then proceeded to give the details of the bugging operation he'd carried out.

Hunter nodded. 'Well, it makes a lot of sense. Anywhere west of Turkey could be a target. We do know their preferred destination is London. From Athens to Edinburgh to Lisbon there are at least seventy or eighty cities they can destroy.'

'And you believe they are here, in my country?' Zim asked.

'As sure as we can be. We're using all available resources. Tomorrow we move westwards to Erzincan or perhaps Refahiye because the E88 splits off from there.'

Albatha nodded. 'That is the way to go if they head for the Mediterranean. If they go by land then it will be the E80 all the way to Greece.'

'We believe we're ahead of them at the moment,' said Hunter. 'If we can identify them we'll take them out. I take it you've no problem with that?'

Albatha shook his head. 'Your mandate allows for it. And we signed up to your mandate. So, no problems with us. I am here to give you every help that is possible. I have a squad of men near here, in another hotel. It is a dump but good enough for – what do you call them – squaddies?'

There were nods of assent.

'They are to be used as we together agree. What about roadblocks? Let the eastbound cars through but stop the westbound?'

Hunter nodded. 'We can try it. But you know as well as I do how many back streets there are. If they get so much as a hint of what we're up to, they can easily vanish without trace.' He paused. 'I suppose a road block on the main road is better than nothing, until we get better intelligence.'

'*If* we get better intelligence,' Dunston interrupted.

Hunter nodded gloomily. 'Okay, we set up on the main road. If we keep the traffic moving at a reasonable speed they probably won't realise what we're up to. We only need to check cars, not lorries and buses, so with luck they'll just think it's normal traffic.'

'What if they've changed vehicles and are now on a bus? Or in a lorry?' Henri asked.

'I've no answer to that,' said Hunter. 'All we can do is hope they're not. We'll do four hours on, four off. Doug and I will take the first watch. Matt, you and Simon next. If we see the Mercedes and the men, we take them out, there and then, no hesitation.'

The order was greeted with enthusiastic nods.

Albatha looked at his watch. 'It is just after 21.00 hours. My men are eating right now. What if we aim for 22.00 hours to begin?'

'Fine with us,' said Hunter.

Just then their food arrived. The best that could be said for it was that it was adequate. Or, as Tanner put it, the steaks filled a hole. They looked longingly at the wine and switched to bottled water. Albatha followed suit.

*　*　*　*　*

He had been a soldier in the Turkish army for three years and seven months. He liked to say that he had been a

352

Muslim all his life. He would help to man the roadblock just before the road entered Erzurum. He used a mobile to send a text message to the number he had been given. For use in an emergency, the Saudis had said. Well, from what he could gather, this was an emergency. He didn't know precisely what was going on but he could guess. The thought of it filled his heart with joy and left a warm feeling in his stomach.

* * * * *

The result of the soldier's action was twofold. First of all, there was no sign of the three terrorists. Secondly, the warning had been sent by text and it wasn't picked up until nearly eight hours later. That was when Macnair received the report about the traitor amongst the Turkish soldiers. Hunter was woken just before 06.00 from a sound sleep, to be told of events. Cursing like hell, he quickly showered and shaved and then went in search of Albatha who was two doors away. Hunter's second knock brought the big man to the door.

'Nick, what is it?'

'Bad news, Zim. The General called a few minutes ago. ECHELON intercepted a text message last night. It was sent to somebody in Saudi Arabia. We're pretty sure it was then forwarded to the terrorists. From subsequent intercepts it appears they've gone into the mountains and are probably past us by now.'

Albatha's eyes narrowed in suspicion. 'Where was the first text sent from?'

'You're not going to like it, Zim, but from here. This area.'

'Do you think it is one of my men?' Zim asked.

Hunter shrugged. 'We can't be certain but it looks likely. I think we should proceed on that assumption. If we are wrong then we will have to look elsewhere.'

Zim then broke into a torrent of Turkish while he was getting dressed. 'You know it is one of my men, don't you?'

By way of a reply, Hunter shrugged again. 'The message was sent only minutes after your briefing and before the roadblock was set up.'

'I think it is one of my men,' he said savagely, roughly shoving his arms into his jacket.

'Zim, do you know any of your men well enough to trust?'

'Not really. The Sergeant has a good reputation. But that means nothing.'

'No one else?' Nick asked.

'No.'

'It can't be helped.' Hunter pondered the problem for a few seconds.

'There is one thing,' Zim said almost as if he was thinking out loud. 'I would be surprised if any of them had mobile phones.'

'How come?'

Albatha shrugged. 'Not on their wages. I have one because of the nature of my work but I doubt even the Sergeant has one.'

'That makes life easier.'

'I'll kill the bastard if we find him,' Zim fumed.

'I think a nice friendly chat won't go amiss,' said Hunter.

'You're right. Let's go.' Albatha looked at his watch. It showed 06.35. 'The Sergeant will be having breakfast.'

Only minutes later they were sitting with the Sergeant at his table in his hotel. Albatha spoke rapidly to him. There was no mistaking the anger in the professional soldier's response. He replied swiftly to each of the questions and Zim relayed the information to Hunter.

'He says there is only one man that he knows has a mobile telephone. He comes from the province of Hakkari.' Seeing Hunter's perplexed look, he went on to explain. 'That's down in the south-eastern corner of Turkey on the Iran/Iraq border. It's a hotbed of Islamic dissidents. He's been posted at the roadblock and is due back here in fifteen minutes.'

Hunter nodded. 'Zim, bearing in mind what you said earlier, does your Sergeant have any explanation for how he acquired the phone?'

'It's so unusual to have one that the Sergeant did ask him about it. He said it was given to him by his uncle who is a rich merchant.' Albatha shrugged. 'That's all the Sergeant knows. It has caused trouble. The other men do not like the fact that he has one.'

The Sergeant spoke again and Albatha nodded. 'They are naturally jealous. The Sergeant has had to warn the man not to flash it around.'

'Is the Sergeant sure there is no other phone?' Nick asked.

'He says he cannot be absolutely sure. However, he does not know of any other.' Zim paused. 'Of course, it may be the wrong man, but right now he's our best bet.' Albatha frowned.

At 07.10 four off-duty soldiers walked through the front door and into the dining room. The Sergeant pointed out the second man to Albatha. He was of medium height, slim to the point of skinny, with hair over his ears and a bushy moustache. He looked shambolic. His khaki uniform was unkempt and ill-fitting. He held a cigarette in his hand and was taking quick, short puffs. He seemed nervous.

'Tell the Sergeant to call the man over.'

The Sergeant proved to be a canny operator. He called two of the soldiers over and asked for a sitrep on the night's activities. The two soldiers exchanged exasperated glances but they dragged their feet across the wooden floor to stand at the table. The Sergeant said something and held out his hand. The soldier who owned the phone looked startled, his eyes darting everywhere. At that point, he panicked. He turned to run. Albatha, quick as a flash, stuck his foot out and the man tripped, knocking his head on a nearby table. Albatha and Hunter exchanged looks.

'Guilty as hell,' said the Turk.

They found the phone in the man's leg pocket. Hunter took it, with the intention of sending it to Rosyth. There could be something useful to be found in the 'sim card'. The other soldiers had been watching in complete surprise, wondering what was going on. They were even more surprised when the Sergeant and two of the soldiers handcuffed him, took the man away and placed him in his room on the third floor of the hotel with an armed guard.

Albatha said, 'What now?'

'I've no idea. I need to speak to General Macnair to see what he can suggest. In the meantime we may as well recall the men from the roadblock. It's damn-all use.'

Hunter telephoned TIFAT and got the General out of bed.

'Sorry to disturb you, sir,' he began.

'That's all right. What have you got for me?'

Hunter brought the General up to speed.

'Zim, we're on the move,' Nick said. 'General Macnair is arranging for an EH One Zero One to pick us up, courtesy

356

of NATO. We can be in Refahiye in two hours.' The AgustaWestland helicopter could carry thirty passengers with all their kit.

'In that case,' said Zim, 'we'll take the prisoner with us. When do we leave?'

'We've got time for a quick breakfast. I'll let my lot know,' Hunter said as he hurried away.

Half an hour later, they were en route to the airport. The helicopter was waiting for them and they were soon airborne and heading west to Refahiye.

* * * * *

Unknown to TIFAT, Rehman Khan, Mohammed Akbar and Kaman Al-Zawahiri had already reached Erzincan, having driven like maniacs through the night. There, they had turned left, and followed the Euphrates River towards Divingi in the south-west. Thanks to the warning they had received from the soldier in Erzurum, they had changed their plans yet again. Now they were heading for Osmaniye and the coast. There, the Saudis had arranged for a yacht to meet them and take them across the Mediterranean. They had slipped through TIFAT's fingers and there was nothing Hunter or his team could do about it.

* * * * *

The soldier who had warned the terrorists had no additional information of any value. Zim Albatha arranged for him to be held in a military jail. It would take some months, but eventually he would be court-martialled and given hard labour for thirty years. He would die in prison. But before he did, he would be in for a very uncomfortable time. The remainder of the soldiers returned to their barracks.

37

The next forty-eight hours were the most frustrating that Nick Hunter had experienced. Refahiye itself was very pleasant. Situated along a river that fed into a large lake. The north side was high hills, white with snow in the winter and a deep, lush green in the summer. There was only one road in and one road out. If the terrorists were headed west they had no choice but to pass through the town. So where the hell were they?

'Sir,' Hunter reported to Macnair, 'either they're headed somewhere else or they've holed up for some reason.'

'That's what we originally thought. However, we've been running the figures again. It's just possible, if they received the warning early enough and they drove as fast as they could, that they'd beat you to it.' The General sighed.

'Is it likely?' Nick asked.

Macnair couldn't keep the frustration out of his voice. 'Likely, no, possible, yes. We can't tell with any accuracy. However, if we're right and they have already passed by, we think the most likely scenario is they're headed for the Mediterranean. Again, there's no way we can be sure. Give it another twelve hours. I'll arrange for the helicopter to pick you up. You may as well stay where you are and continue what you're doing. After that, I'm thinking of deploying you to Tarsus. It's a gamble, I know, but we don't see any other choice at this moment in time.'

'Did you get anything from the mobile we confiscated?' Hunter asked.

'Yes. That was very useful. We've tracked down his contact. Have you heard of a Saudi prince by the name of Khaled Aziz bin Abdullah?'

'Wasn't he in the news recently? Something to do with the half million dollars a year that's paid to all the members of the House of Saud? Or the princes, I should say. Aren't there about three thousand of them?'

'Nearer four. Thirty to forty new males are born to the House of Saud every month. Khaled Aziz's tenth son is a recipient. That's what the fuss was about. Especially as the average Saudi citizen's annual income dropped from US $14,600 in 1982, to less than US $ 7,000 in 1998. That was when the last income survey was done. Taking inflation into account, it's still dropping as the Saudi national debt rises. God alone knows what it is today.'

'And Khaled Aziz sent the message?'

'Possibly. All we can say for certain is that it was sent from a phone registered to him.'

'Does that mean he's involved? Or does it just mean that somebody in his household has access to his mobiles?'

'That's what we're trying to figure out. We do know that he has over fifty mobiles in his name.'

'Fifty!' Hunter couldn't keep the surprise out of his voice. 'What does he do with fifty mobiles?'

'They're used by various members of his household as you suspected. Your guess is as good as ours. However, one thing we have discovered, although we've yet to prove it; it looks like he's involved with JIMAS. They're

360

causing a lot of trouble all across the Middle East, calling for a holy jihad against the West.'

'I saw it on a CNN bulletin,' Nick explained.

'Right now we're focusing our attention on Khaled Aziz bin Abdullah mainly because we've nowhere else to go. With his wealth, power and influence there's a certain logic to him being involved, especially with the financial situation the Saudis have manoeuvred for themselves. Come what may, if he does prove to be involved, I'll make sure that he doesn't enjoy his victory for very long.'

'Is there anything else I need to know, sir?' Hunter asked.

'Not at the moment. We'll contact you again should we learn anything. Anything at all.'

The helicopter returned just after 20.00, picked up the team and Albatha and headed for Tarsus. There had been no sign of the terrorists, no reports that were of any use whatsoever, and nothing to help to calm the situation in Europe. The result of which was that the air of panic across the Continent was at epidemic proportions. Most businesses were closed, all European stock markets were shut and hospitals and emergency services were now completely overwhelmed. Food and drink were selling for astronomical prices as none of the supermarkets or corner shops were being replenished. The black-market was thriving, some people were getting rich, many people were dying. Armed gangs roamed the streets, resulting in a great deal of robbery and murder. People were in constant motion and accidents of all sorts were occurring from the Black Sea to the Atlantic. Most roads across the Continent were jammed. The traffic trying to get out of the cities was backed up in every direction. Although politicians in many parliaments were calling for emergency sessions, most couldn't muster enough representatives for a quorum. The European Parliament had been closed. They had all, using one excuse or another, fled their capital cities. Across the Islamic world the press was deafening in its silence. Any condemnation at the threat of the bomb was quickly extinguished. As a result, many people in the West were calling for a nuclear strike against Islamic countries. When saner heads pointed out that the vast majority of Muslims were innocent of any involvement, the cry naturally went up that if that was the case, why wasn't there a far greater outcry from the governments and press of the Islamic countries? The silence persisted. One thought was uppermost in the minds of many people who tried impartially to contemplate the situation Europe faced. If this was the result of the threat posed by a plutonium dirty bomb, what would the situation be like if a nuclear bomb was to explode? Then, finally, the Islamic dam broke. Politicians from across the Islamic world started to demand an end to the idiocy. They pointed out that should a nuclear bomb explode it would be just as bad for Muslims. The prospect of Western retaliation finally made the headlines. Polaris nuclear rockets were a thousand times more powerful than what was heading for Europe. But would the West dare use them?

General Macnair spent a great deal of his time on the phone or in video conferences trying to persuade the powers-that-be not to retaliate. That was when he could find any political leaders to talk to. He asked for more time for TIFAT and the rest of Europe's security services. His arguments and pleadings were falling on deafer and deafer ears.

JIMAS rejoiced. They wanted the isolation. They wanted their world to be for Muslims only. It was what they had planned for, dreamt of, for generations past. And now it was almost upon them. Their holy jihad would succeed where all others had failed.

It was then that TIFAT finally had a little luck. Not much, but enough to give them a lead.

It was Isobel who telephoned Hunter. 'Nick? We have an intercept. Unfortunately, not with the quarry. However, it may prove just as good but we're not sure. We've spent the last couple of days accessing just about every mobile phone supplier in the world. Naturally, we've concentrated on the Middle East. Leo wrote a simple programme to identify certain names. From that we lifted the phone numbers and locked on to them.' Isobel paused, collecting her thoughts.

'Sounds complicated,' said Hunter.

'Actually, it's easier than you think. Once we were in, the systems ran themselves. The only constraint was time. The computers had hundreds of millions of names to trawl through. However, once we'd set things in motion we could forget about it. One major flaw in the whole plan was . . .'

Hunter interrupted her. 'What if the phone was in the name of a company? Which we know the Saudis tend to do because the princes pay very little tax.'

'Exactly. That thought occurred to Leo after the programme had been operating for a couple of hours. Well, he amended what he had already written, only this time to break into the Saudi equivalent of Companies House and find out if there are any companies where Khaled Aziz was a director and/or owner.'

'What did you find?'

'He holds directorships in nine companies. Apart from the fifty mobiles registered to him personally he also has a further twelve mobiles registered through these companies . . .'

'Twelve! What in hell's bells does he do with another twelve phones?'

'They're given to his wives and children.'

'Why fifty in his name and twelve in the companies' names?'

'God alone knows. Anyway, we've got nothing so far from the original fifty so now we've tapped into the other twelve. From what we can gather, these are used by his two senior wives and their children. Honestly, some of the stuff the two wives talk about would make a courtesan blush.'

'Who are they talking to?' Hunter couldn't help asking, intrigued by the very idea.

'Each other.'

'Each other? Don't they meet?'

'Not very often. As far as we can tell he has four houses, each with a wife and offspring. Two are deemed senior, two junior. The first two are older than the other two. Anyway, be that as it may, we also picked up one conversation between Khaled Aziz and a man we think is the master of Aziz's luxury yacht.'

'So?'

'We've double-checked the translation but, in a nutshell, the master appears to be saying that he has taken delivery of the package and will be proceeding to sea immediately.'

'It could be just a package of some sort.'

'I told you it wasn't much. But it's all we've got,' Isobel said, sighing.

'Presumably you're thinking a package is code for the three men and the bomb.'

'Correct.'

'Where's the Saudi yacht?'

'We're still checking. We think somewhere between Turkey and Cyprus.'

'You think?'

'Sorry, Nick. We're doing everything we can. It really is the best we've got at the moment. We're also still trawling everywhere we can think of but there's not even a hint of them being anywhere else.'

'What are we going to do?'

'The General is talking to the Admiralty right now, to see if we have any assets in the area. If we want the Royal Navy to help we need political permission. There are a number of problems about securing that permission. First of all, the time element. How quickly would we get the green light? If at all! Secondly, there's the leak. But who is it? If it is coming from the political end, is it actually a Member of Parliament or is it one of their staff? If the men and the device are on the yacht and we show our hand what then? We go round and round. Hence the General's determination to keep everything under wraps. He's calling in every favour from every contact he can think of. We also have MI5 working on the problem, checking and vetting information and backgrounds. We have GCHQ eavesdropping every mobile, landline and computer they can find. This lead is known only to us. You know about it. My team know as do the senior command,' Isobel explained.

'Okay. So what are you proposing?'

Isobel chuckled. 'Actually, it's the General and his lateral thinking. He has proposed a joint exercise. The Royal Navy putting a TIFAT team into action. Making sure communications are right, chain of command working and so on. Hence not an operation, merely an exercise. Permission therefore, would not be required.'

'What a farce,' said Hunter with a heartfelt groan. 'We're faced with a nuclear device that could kill tens of thousands of people, if not more, and destroy a large chunk of a Western city yet we're playing games. It's not credible!'

'I couldn't agree with you more. But that's the way it is,' Isobel said.

'Okay, what are our orders in the meantime?'

'You're on the move again,' Isobel answered. 'Helicopter to Cyprus for equipment. I believe you know Captain Trevellyan of the Royal Scots Dragoons?'

'Yes, I met him when I went looking for Samantha Freemantle and the team from MI6. Is he still on Cyprus?'

'Yes. He's expecting you. You'll be billeted in the mess. Nick, anything you want you get. General Macnair made it clear I was to tell you that.'

'Okay. Is the helicopter arranged?'

'Yes. Also, in view of the help he's provided, we think Zim Albatha should accompany you.'

'I have no problem with that, but why?'

'He's a Muslim. In the long run, we want to be able to scream from the rooftops how much help our Muslim brothers have been. Nick, stopping these maniacs is a priority but it's only half the picture. What happens afterwards is of vital importance to the stability of the world, even the peace of the world.'

'I realise that. We've been talking about that very thing here. Taking Zim along is fine with us, assuming he wants to come. And assuming he can come.'

'He can, he's been seconded to TIFAT for the duration. His boss should be telling him even as we speak.'

'All right, that works for me,' Nick agreed.

'One other thing. Jan Badonovitch will meet up with

366

you on Cyprus.'

'Excellent, Isobel. We could sure use more help. Many thanks. Can you arrange for Jan to bring re-breathers, five sets. He'll know what we need. They don't have any there.'

'Will do, Nick. The General or I will be in touch.'

With the conversation at an end Hunter went to find the others and brought them up to speed. Within the hour, they were airborne and reached the base on Cyprus in time for last orders at the bar. One thing Hunter was only too aware of was that time really was running out. As the device travelled further west it was becoming a real danger.

38

Nick Hunter rose early the following morning. He had too much on his mind and couldn't sleep. He needed time to think. He changed into running gear and set out around the Cypriot base. He hadn't gone far when Matt Dunston fell in alongside him. Neither man said a word, but both slowly began to increase their pace. Forty minutes later, panting for breath, they faced each other and went through a series of fighting katas, using different disciplines. Their hands and feet were a blur, each movement stopped before contact – most of the time – but the occasional blow or kick sometimes connected but at nothing like the force if each man had followed through. Their concentration was total. It needed to be, otherwise one of them could have been seriously hurt or even killed. Finally, they stopped.

'It gets harder,' gasped Dunston as he bent over, his head down, hands on knees. 'I must be getting old.'

Hunter managed a chuckle. 'You're doing well, considering how ancient you are.' He sucked in air.

'Less of the ancient or I won't hold back next time.'

'Yeah, yeah. I've heard that one before. Come on. Time for breakfast.'

They made their way in companionable silence back to

their quarters. Breakfast was bacon and eggs with all the trimmings. The remainder of the team drifted in and helped themselves at the buffet. All of them looked more presentable than they'd done the evening before, due to the simple expedient of shaving.

'The General has arranged for us to get anything we need from the NAAFI. Looking at us, it would be a good idea to get some clothes. We can't hang around here looking like tramps.'

'Hullo, boss, hullo, you guys.' Badonovitch walked across the room.

'Hi, Jan,' they chorused.

'Grab a pew,' said Hunter. 'Good flight?'

'You know Crabfat Air. Attractive stewardesses. Good food. Plenty to drink.' Although they always spoke disparagingly of the RAF, in reality it was a good service, considering the aircraft they had for ferrying military personnel around the world.

They kitted up at the NAAFI. Its range of clothing was small but adequate for their needs. The team spent the morning with Captain Trevellyan, going through various items of equipment. Not knowing what they might need they earmarked quite a range, from plastic explosives, and other weapons, to diving gear. After lunch Nick was summoned to the communications centre for a call from General Macnair.

'I've spoken to the Royal Navy,' the General explained. 'There's a minehunter at Malta on what was originally a goodwill visit. In view of what's happened that was turned into aid. They've been helping to keep order, although Malta appears to be one of the few places where there's been little trouble so the crew are no longer needed. The ship was due to sail to Marseilles but those orders have

369

been amended. I believe you know her. HMS *Atherstone*?'

'Yes, sir. My old ship. She was my first job after qualifying as a clearance diver. She'll have all the gear we need and then some. On reflection Jan needn't have brought all that kit with him.'

'We weren't to know. Anyway, better safe than sorry. They're being given orders even as we speak. Sailing time to Cyprus is three days which is way too long. A Hercules will take you and drop you.'

'Roger that, sir. Are we sure the terrorists and the bomb are on the yacht?'

'No. But we are now certain about its owner's involvement. And truth to tell, it's still all we've got. We've mounted an operation in Turkey, stopping and searching trains, setting up roadblocks, even having known fundamentalists arrested.'

'What about their Minister of State for Immigration, Syed Azam?'

'He's been kept fully in the picture about the operation. What only a handful of people know, of course, is that the briefings are meaningless. However, with luck, it'll give those on the yacht a false sense of security.'

'Do we know where the yacht is?'

'There's a suggestion she's heading for Tunisia. That's as much as we've got. We have satellites searching the Mediterranean. She'll show up some time.'

'When we find her, how about the Crazy A blowing the sodding thing out of the water?' Hunter asked, using the *Atherstone*'s nickname.

'There's no doubt you'll have to put a shell through the yacht, otherwise she'll be out of range about two minutes after you hove into sight.'

'That's what I was thinking. And if the yacht is blown

apart or just sunk we can then go looking for the device.'

'That's what minehunters do best,' said General Macnair.

Using sophisticated sonar and tried and tested techniques to search the seabed, if the yacht didn't blow up, she would be found in no time. Divers would do the rest. On the other hand, even if she was obliterated into tiny pieces, the chances were that the case and the device would be intact. The search procedures would be the same, the task merely more difficult and taking longer to achieve.

'Why is it we haven't claimed we've got it? Tell the press. It might help to calm matters.'

'We've thought of that, but it's impossible. Far too many people know what's happening. We'll never be believed. No, our only option is to recover it or watch it detonate. Even then, it's going to be hell's own job to be believed around the world. In fact, worldwide acceptance will never happen until enough time passes to show there's no danger. And throughout that time the fanatics will be denying it all. They'll still be claiming the bomb is heading our way. Which means the riots and disruption will continue for quite a while. It'll make the world recession look like a tiny blip of inconvenience.' Changing the subject, Macnair added, 'We've asked the manufacturers to supply photographs of the yacht. I'll forward them to you. Also her specifications. Size, speed and so on.'

'What about the crew, sir?'

'Eight-strong and she has cabins for eight guests. Her top speed is thirty-two knots. She's quite some beast, I can tell you.'

'If they're headed for Tunisia, do we follow them into whichever port they use? Or if they're there already, do we go in?' Nick asked.

371

'I don't know yet. It all depends on what happens. In view of the lack of information we have about the blasted thing, it looks like there's a good chance they are already there.'

'So why don't we know? Surely the port authorities . . .'

'We have to be careful. This is clandestine with a capital C. We've called in favours from people we can trust but they are few and far between.'

'I suppose that's hardly surprising considering the help and support they're getting from fundamentalists around the world, not just the Middle East.'

'Not only that. If they've gone into port with a different name painted on the side who's to know? It's not as though they're entering an alert European port where the paperwork is checked. A handful of any currency of the Western world would see them alright.'

'True enough.'

'The satellites are concentrating on the Tunisian coastline but let's not forget it's the best part of 800 miles long with dozens of ports of all sizes and usage. It's one hell of a job, despite using Cuthbert's identification program to assess the photographs sent to us by GCHQ. If they know or guess we have such a program it wouldn't take much to alter the shape of the upper deck. A few pieces of planking placed in strategic spots would be enough to confuse the computer.'

'This is getting worse by the second.'

'You never said a truer word. Right, enough doom and gloom. The Hercules is being prepared for take-off so you'd better get along.'

'Okay, sir. We're on our way.'

Their gear was packed into three specially reinforced plastic flotation units and thrown into the back of an army lorry, which headed for the airfield. They took off into a beautiful, clear blue sky, the Hercules thundering and shaking. Once airborne, they helped themselves to coffee supplied in flasks, courtesy of the RAF then settled back into their seats. As with all jumps, there was an anticipatory mood of excitement tinged with trepidation.

'Thirty minutes!' came over the tannoy.

They each changed into wetsuits and packed their clothes into the waterproof containers that held the rest of the gear. The aircraft began to slow down to jump speed.

'Five minutes! Stand by!' was the penultimate announcement.

Now under the control and watchful eye of the jump-master, a Sergeant in the Royal Air Force, the team lined up facing aft. They hooked up their release cords to the overhead wire and stood in expectant anticipation. The rear door opened hydraulically, which brought the wind whistling around the exit. The red light turned to green.

'Jump! Jump! Jump!'

The canisters of gear went first and the team followed. Hunter jumped first and was followed by Dunston. Badonovitch, Tanner, Henri and Albatha jumped in quick succession. They jumped from 4,000ft. Their parachutes fully deployed a mere 200ft below the Hercules, leaving them to enjoy what was a very pleasant experience in the warm sunlight. There was only one ship to be seen, the grey-hulled HMS *Atherstone*, which was sailing at slow speed as she launched both of her inflatable Gemini craft to pick up the team and the canisters. Hunter could read the ship's pennant number – M38 – emblazoned on her sides.

The first Gemini, manned by two sailors, approached one of the white canisters and hauled it inboard along with its parachute. The second Gemini did the same with another canister. By this time, Hunter had hit the sea. As the water reached his waist, he thumped the quick-release and his parachute drifted a few yards before settling on the surface. Hunter plunged down into the warm water to a depth of a couple of metres before his lifejacket automatically inflated and he rose back to the surface. He swam over to his parachute and attempted to roll it up.

Moments later the first Gemini was alongside and helped him into the boat. The parachute was dragged on board. The second Gemini collected the third canister and was now helping Albatha. Hauling divers and their equipment out of the water was a common activity for the ship's crew. Within minutes the Geminis were back alongside the minehunter, one to port, the other to starboard, hooked on to a bow rope which towed them though the water. This kept the Gemini alongside the ship's hull, facilitating handing up the canisters. The team quickly followed by climbing a rope jumping-ladder.

'Welcome on board, sir,' the Petty Officer said as he saluted Hunter. He grinned broadly.

'Tam! What a pleasant surprise,' said Hunter. Having saluted the quarter-deck where the ensign flew, he then shook hands enthusiastically with Petty Officer Tam Chapman. They had served together when Hunter had been the First Lieutenant of the *Atherstone* and Chapman had been a leading seaman. A man with two stripes on his shoulder stepped forward, hand outstretched.

'Nick, good to see you again,' First Lieutenant Paul Cooper greeted him.

'Coop! I thought you'd moved on.'

'Another month. Then I'm going to the Northern Diving Group at Faslane.'

Hunter made the necessary introductions and then followed Cooper to the bridge. There, waiting to greet him, was the ship's captain, Lieutenant Commander Mike Thompson, on his last job before leaving the Royal Navy.

'Welcome on board Commander Hunter,' said the captain. 'My instructions are to do as you tell me but not to endanger the ship.' His greeting was neither friendly nor unfriendly. If Hunter had to describe it he would say the man was indifferent. This was, Hunter knew, a very common reaction in officers who had been passed over for promotion and were just biding their time before leaving the service.

'Thank you for that. I'd like to get out of this wetsuit. Then perhaps we can go to your cabin and I'll put you in the picture? It would be an idea if Cooper came as well.'

Hunter went below, showered and changed, then returned to the bridge. He, Thompson and Cooper went below to the captain's cabin. A fresh pot of coffee was sitting on a hot plate. The Captain poured coffees for the three of them, courteous but with a resentful air about him. Coffee in hand, Hunter began to brief the other two. As he did so, there was a distinct but subtle change in the Commanding Officer's attitude.

'I had no idea about what you are involved in Nick. Those bastards! Being here, we are, to all intents and purposes, out of the loop. The crew are worried sick. What if Portsmouth is the target?' He held up his hand. 'I know, I know, it's not likely but you can't help wondering. Also, we've seen the news reports. The shortages, the riots! Forget the bit about endangering my command. I'll do whatever it takes. Have you the slightest idea where this yacht is right now?'

'Only that we believe she's headed towards Tunisia. That was the last update we received. ECHELON is still looking. It's the best chance we've got of finding her.' He reached into his pocket and took out his phone. 'These are the photographs I was sent, along with the yacht's specifications. We can enlarge them and print them off and hand them to the lookouts. You never know, we might get lucky and spot the damned thing.'

'Can I see?' Cooper asked.

Hunter handed over his mobile.

'Bloody hell. She can outrun us without even trying.'

Thompson said, 'We can put a shell through her. That would stop her. Even sink her.'

Hunter said, 'You've got it. There is virtually no chance whatsoever of the device exploding unless the shell makes a direct hit. Even then we're looking at a burst container as opposed to an explosion, and our radiation dosimeters will tell us if there's a leakage.'

The CO said, 'Then it's hands to minehunting stations. More coffee?'

Hunter nodded. 'Thanks.'

'I'll get them,' said Cooper, reaching for the coffee pot. Cups were refilled and for a few minutes silence reigned. Hunter absorbed the feel of the ship, her gentle movements, her smell as the memories came flooding back. Those were the days when life was a damned sight simpler and a lot less dangerous. He suddenly felt a sense of loss, but with it came the realisation he could never go back.

'Range to fire say seven miles,' said the Captain. 'We need to get that close for a positive identification. They won't be expecting us so it shouldn't be a problem.'

Hunter nodded. 'That's pretty much what we thought.'

The Captain turned to his First Lieutenant. 'Number

One, we'll go to Condition Yankee and close down to Condition Alfa. Get sprinklers and hoses rigged as soon as we finish here.'

'Aye, aye, sir,' Cooper acknowledged.

Hunter had prepared the ship in the same way many times. Then it had always been for exercise purposes; this time it was for real. Condition Yankee meant that certain watertight doors were kept closed due to a potentially hazardous situation like entering or leaving harbour. However, it was also needed when a ship closed down to gas tight Condition Alfa. This meant all openings to the outside world were tightly closed. If the device exploded then there was a likelihood of a plutonium dust-cloud being created, through which the ship could pass. If it did, the sprinklers were there to wash away any dust into the sea.

'And if it doesn't go off we hunt for it. Finding the yacht will be child's play,' said Cooper.

'You're right,' said Hunter. 'However, I glanced at the chart on the bridge. What depth are you worked down to?'

The question was aimed at Cooper, as the diving specialist on the ship. 'We've just done our eighty.'

'Excellent. That's a bit of luck. It gives us some flexibility. I reckon as far as twenty miles or so from shore.'

Hunter knew that no diver, no matter how well trained, could dive straight to 80m without being adversely affected. If he tried it, he would have one of two sensations. Either he would have a feeling of the world spinning out of control, or that he was tumbling at high speed. The resultant feeling of nausea, or actual vomiting, was not only very unpleasant, it was extremely dangerous. So the team dived deeper and deeper over a few days until they were finally at 80m. It took incredible skill and technique to achieve it.

'Any further?' asked Cooper.

'Any deeper, we keep station and send for a saturation team,' Nick explained. A saturation diving team could easily get to the seabed anywhere in the Mediterranean and if necessary, spend days at depth.

'What if we don't find anything?' Thompson asked.

'It's a dense piece of kit,' said Hunter, 'with a thin coating of lead and an aluminium case so we ought to be able to locate it.'

'I think,' said Thompson, 'we should go to defence watches. That way we'll have the personnel closed up for a rapid response. Agreed gentlemen?'

'Right away, sir,' Cooper said.

'I'll talk to General Macnair and check if he has anything further for us, and then I can brief him on what we're doing,' Hunter said.

*　*　*　*　*

The yacht was steaming steadily towards Tunisia. Sicily was a blip on the north-eastern corner of the radar screen, nearly fifteen miles away. They were keeping to the starboard side of the channel as they passed through the narrow waters, in accordance with the Rules of the Road. Everybody on board was in fine fettle. Everything was going according to plan. The latest information they had received confirmed that the idiots in the West had no idea where they were. Allah be praised! Nothing could stop them now!

'When do we next make our report?' Rehman Khan enquired.

The three men were sitting in the yacht's opulent saloon, enjoying their cups of strong Turkish coffee. Khan swallowed his pills with his coffee. The pain was gradually intensifying and he had doubled the dose yet again.

'Not until we are safely alongside in Bizerte,' replied Mohammed Akbar, licking his lips appreciatively.

'We are indeed fortunate to have such a mentor as the glorious Prince Khaled Aziz bin Abdullah,' said Kaman Al-Zawahiri. 'Allah bless his name.'

The other two nodded agreement.

'I have been speaking with the captain,' said Khan. 'He says we will stay in port for twenty-four hours in order to refuel, take on water and stock up with food supplies. Once we leave Tunisia, we shall cross the Mediterranean to the European side. Then we will follow the coast. Should anyone try to stop us, we will make a run for the shore. The captain knows what we are doing and is prepared to sacrifice his life for the greater good. Once we reach Europe, even if we have to detonate the bomb before we reach a major city, the loss of life will still be great.'

'When will we get to Tunisia?' Akbar enquired.

'During the night we will arrive at Cap Bon. That is the north-eastern corner of Tunisia. We will cross the Gulf of Tunis and arrive at Bizerte at first light. It has been well planned, my friends, and well implemented. We cannot fail!'

A servant appeared at the door and enquired if they were ready to eat. They walked through to the luxurious dining room, where they sat at a table of polished mahogany, in comfortable chairs. Two servants waited on them. They started with vegetable soup. The second course of exquisite lamb kebabs, cooked in a mouth-watering sauce, was followed with a sorbet made from real strawberries. Throughout the meal they drank only bottled water. Afterwards, they had more coffee, before going up to the bridge for a breath of fresh air and to watch as the sun set on the distant horizon. It was a beautiful night. One that made all three men glad to be alive. However, they knew, having been told many times by the Imams, that Paradise would be even more beautiful.

39

Nick Hunter and the team enjoyed their fish and chips followed by cheese and biscuits. Afterwards, following a contemplative turn around the deck, Hunter went to his pit. He was sharing the First Lieutenant's cabin, where there was a second bunk, while a couple of camp beds had been set up for Matt Dunston and Simon Henri in the wardroom. Doug Tanner and Jan Badonovitch had been berthed in the Chief Petty Officer's mess. All that night and the following day, the *Atherstone* steamed along the north Tunisian coast a couple of miles outside the ten-mile limit. A new contact appeared on radar every few minutes, which had the ship steaming in its direction to investigate. Thanks to the photographs of the yacht, the contacts were quickly dismissed. Many of them proved to be small fishing boats, although a few coasters were also spotted. As the day wore on, the officers and men on board the *Atherstone* became more despondent. They had all known that finding the yacht would be more by luck than judgement, but even so they couldn't help feeling low.

'So that's the sitrep, sir,' Hunter said as he reported the lack of progress to Macnair.

'The fact is, we didn't expect anything else' General Macnair admitted. 'In light of this we've been pursuing permission for a goodwill visit by the *Atherstone* to Tunisia, to refuel and take on supplies. We're asking if either Tunis or Bizerte would be possible.'

'Why those two ports, sir?' Hunter asked.

'They are the most likely ports where the yacht could refuel, and we calculate they will have to do so soon. We are concentrating all our satellite assets on the area, so we have high hopes something will break soon,' Macnair explained. 'I'll call you back. Something has just come in!'

Hunter went up top to the bridge.

'Signal, sir,' said the Chief Yeoman, appearing from the signals office and handing over a clipboard to Thompson. It was a message from Admiralty, informing the Captain that approval had been received for the ship's visit to either Tunis or Bizerte anytime in the next forty-eight hours. Liaison for the visit was to be through the British Embassy in Tunis. A phone number was included.

'Bridge, ops,' came over the loudspeaker.

The Officer of the Watch replied. 'Bridge.'

'Contact bearing green five zero, far.'

The ship was in defence watches. Half the men were on watch, and half of them were relaxing. The operations room was manned, with a watch being kept on the radar and the plotting table. During normal peacetime steaming this wasn't the case, with only a quarter of the ship's company being on duty. Then it was part of the Officer of the Watch's job to keep an eye on the radar. By plotting the contact on the table it was easily calculated in which direction and at what speed it was travelling. Usually, such information was used to *avoid* a contact. Now it was different.

'Did you get that, Able Seaman Jones?' The OOW called to the starboard lookout.

'Yes, sir,' came the reply. 'I can just make out the masthead sailing light.' Then he added, 'I think.'

'Thanks, Jones. I have it.' The OOW focused his binoculars on the contact. After about twenty seconds he said to the Captain, 'Sir, you might like to take a look. It's moving pretty fast. I think it has a white superstructure.' He looked at the photograph on the bulkhead behind the chart table and added, 'It looks something like that.'

The Captain picked up a microphone. 'Ops, captain. Get me a course and speed on the contact bearing,' he leant over the compass and lined up the sights, 'two nine five.'

'Roger that, sir,' came the reply from the Leading Seaman on watch in the operations room. Two minutes later, as the ship's engines picked up revolutions to maximum speed, he was able to make his report.

The OOW was also tracking the contact on the bridge radar. 'I concur with ops, sir. The yacht is heading for Bizerte.'

'At twenty knots,' said Thompson, 'we'll never catch her.'

Hunter's phone rang. It was General Macnair.

'Nick?' said the General. 'We've some good news at last. GCHQ has intercepted a message from a vessel about six miles offshore from Bizerte and heading that way. It was sent to Khaled Aziz. The message says "Going in to refuel. Will depart in twenty-four hours".'

'We have the yacht on visual now, sir, though she's too far away for us to do anything except follow her in.'

'We'll contact the embassy and arrange for them to sort out the port authorities.'

'Right, sir. I'll speak to you as soon as I have anything to report.' He turned to the Captain. 'Mike, TIFAT confirms that's the yacht.'

'Okay,' replied the Commanding Officer. 'Officer of the Watch, hands to harbour stations.'

The Navigating Officer appeared on the bridge.

'Pilot, we're going into Bizerte,' said the Captain.

'Aye, aye sir. I've got the chart ready for entering harbour, just in case. I can brief you when you're ready.'

Thompson nodded. Taking the microphone, he explained to the ship's company what was happening. In spite of the gravity of the situation, there was a muted cheer from below. No sailor, in any navy, anywhere in the world, could resist a run ashore in a foreign country. Hunter and Thompson had discussed the possibility of leave. They had agreed that if it wasn't allowed then it would seem odd to anyone taking an interest in them so leave would be granted to some of the crew.

'The harbour master has given permission to enter harbour, sir,' reported the Navigating Officer, replacing the VHF handset.

The Navigating Officer bent over the chart he had now placed on the table. 'We're to go alongside here,' he said, pointing with the tips of a set of dividers. 'I recommend eight knots from now, sir.'

At that moment the First Lieutenant appeared on the bridge, saluted the Captain and reported that the ship was ready to go alongside.

'Very good, Number One. Have the hands fall in for entering harbour.'

'Aye, aye, sir.'

The ship's company fell in, six hands for'ard and six hands aft, standing at ease, in a line, legs apart, hands behind their backs. There was an edge of anticipation amongst the crew as they watched the lights of Bizerte coming closer. The HMS *Atherstone* steamed through the harbour entrance and turned to port. They had been directed into the canal and ordered to go alongside, just down from the water-sports centre which was shown clearly on the chart. Thompson stopped the ship in the middle of the canal, put his port engine half ahead, his starboard engine half astern and finally his wheel hard over to starboard. The ship spun round as though she was sitting on a turntable. He took her port side to the wall, which meant she was facing the right way in the event of having to make a rapid departure. The First Lieutenant ordered the bow rope and stern rope out and dockyard workers dropped the eyes of the ropes over bollards and the ropes were taken to capstans, fore and aft.

'I have the ship, sir,' the First Lieutenant reported, as he ordered the slack to be taken down on the ropes and then, as they tightened, pulled the ship safely alongside to lie snug against her rattan fenders.

'Finished with main engines,' said the Captain. 'Ring off and tell the Chief Engineer I want the ship at immediate notice for sea. Number One, sort out water and fuel. Leave for port watch only. Leave to expire at 23.59. Emphasise that all those ashore should stay within hearing distance of the ship's siren and if we start blasting, to come running.'

'Aye, aye, sir.' The First Lieutenant saluted and left the bridge to speak to the coxswain and issue instructions.

Hunter appeared on the bridge and said, 'The yacht has gone into the Old Port.' Looking at the chart, he pointed, 'She's about there. I'm going to take a walk with Matt and have a look-see. In the meantime, my lot are getting the diving gear ready.'

As the gangway went out, Thompson became distracted by the arrival of a man from the harbour master's office, along with a customs and excise officer who only stayed on board for a few minutes. The former required papers to be signed. Berthing fees would be collected from the embassy. Both Matt and Nick wore jackets to cover their shoulder holsters, each containing a silenced Glock 18. They walked along the canal front before turning left onto Boulevard Habib Bou Guetfa. In the distance they could see the bright lights of the casino with a constant stream of cars pulling up outside. The town was a busy place. They passed women sitting on the pavement wearing white from head to toe, but with black facemasks that even covered their eyes. They held out their hands begging for alms. The two men ignored them. They knew if they did give them something, they would be pestered for more.

At the roundabout outside the casino, with its garish lights and flashing sign, they turned left and then right. They were at the Old Port and there, one hundred and fifty metres away, was the yacht. There was absolutely no doubt it was the vessel they were looking for. With a great deal of anticipation, they followed the path around the wall. The port was principally filled with fishing boats, all gaily coloured, some alongside, others at anchor. In the background, to the right, was the minaret of the Great Mosque, and to the left of it was the minaret of the Rebaa Mosque. It was an attractive enclave, very much like the fishing villages found in Greece or Spain. The bars were busy. Although the country was mainly Islamic, it grew its own grapes which were turned into wines of good repute.

'I didn't expect such a cosmopolitan place,' Hunter said.

'It's an example of what Muslim countries could be like if they came into the twenty-first century,' replied Matt. 'If we get the chance, you should try a drink they call boukha, a fig brandy served very cold as an aperitif.'

'Somehow I don't think we're going to have the opportunity Matt.' They approached the yacht. 'I can't see any crew, can you?'

'Yes. On the other side of the bridge. Sitting on a chair.'

'Ah, yes, I see him.'

They were now only a few metres from the stern of the yacht. She was a fair-sized vessel, 30m long, 8m at the widest part of her beam. They only saw the one guard.

'There's nothing more to see,' said Hunter. 'Let's get back. I suspect there will only be the one guard all night.'

The two men turned away and quickly left the area. Within minutes they were back on the *Atherstone*.

The team and the ship's officers congregated in the wardroom.

'What's the plan, boss?' Jan asked.

'The yacht is in shadow, but the approaches are brightly lit. One thing we can be certain of is that they'll be well-armed. We don't know how many of them are actually on guard but we only saw one.'

'So it's wet and quiet,' said Tanner.

'You got it, Doug. The quieter the better. Gear ready?' Nick asked.

'Just about,' said Tanner.

'Okay, in that case we go at 02.00. Try and get some rest until then. We'll split into watches and keep an eye on the yacht. Doug and myself, then you two,' he said to Badonovitch and Dunston.

'That won't be necessary,' said Thompson. 'I'll set a couple of lads to keep an eye on the yacht.'

'Are you sure?' Hunter asked.

'Positive.'

'We do appreciate it. It's going to be a long night.'

Hunter sat alone in the wardroom looking at the information he had received from General Macnair about how to defuse the bomb. The Americans had sent a series of diagrams showing each step of the process. On one level it was simple enough, on another it wasn't. The hardest part was being in the field with the device ticking down to zero. Nick left the wardroom and went out onto the quarter-deck and along to the diving store. It only took a few minutes to find the tools he needed. Collecting a small, thin-bladed screwdriver and a slim pair of wire cutters he then found a piece of neoprene, wrapped the tools in it and used a short length of sail makers thread to tie it up. As satisfied as he could be, he went along to the communications centre. His last task, before getting his head down for a few hours, was to report to Macnair and bring him up to speed.

'Let's just hope that the device is on the yacht. Have you had a chance to look at the material the Americans sent about dismantling it yet Nick?'

'Yes, sir.'

'You OK with it?' Macnair asked.

'I won't know until I try. There are two booby-traps. They are pretty basic but the Americans managed to dismantle the first one successfully and I'll be using the same information.'

'Then all it leaves me to say is good luck. Call me as soon as you return to *Atherstone*. As we've discussed, we'll broadcast the distress signals along with a position while you make sure there's as little evidence left as possible.'

*   *   *   *   *

Mohammed Akbar said, 'I tell you, I do not like it. It is too much of a coincidence that a Royal Naval ship arrives immediately after us.'

Kaman Al-Zawahiri said, 'Then why send their crew ashore if they are here for us? It makes no sense. Besides, when the time comes to leave, we get out of port and go at full speed. We can travel at least twice as fast as they can. They will never catch us.'

The yacht's master said, 'They may not be able to catch us but they could blow us out of the water with their gun.'

'They can do nothing,' said Akbar, his voice dripping with contempt. 'We can be away within minutes and out of range of their pop-gun soon after we pass the breakwater. They would never dare shoot at us while we are in the territorial waters of another country. The stupid British always play by the rules.'

The others nodded and Rehman Khan said, 'What you say is true. I have sent a message to our glorious Prince Khaled Aziz informing him of the situation and asking for advice. We must wait and see what he says. What is the position with the water and diesel?' he asked the master.

'We have almost finished filling the tanks.'

'Good.'

It was just after midnight and they were sitting in the guests' saloon, drinking alcohol-free sherbets and eating local figs one of the crewmen had purchased. Khan's phone rang.

Once Khan had finished speaking he looked at the other two. 'That was his Highness, Prince Khaled Aziz. He is saying we must leave for Tabarka. There is an airport there and his private jet will be arriving in five hours. The pilot knows where to take us.'

'Is there anything else?' Akbar asked.

'That is all,' said Khan. 'He has obviously learned something about the Royal Navy ship.' He paused and added, 'I think we should wait here and leave in time to get to the airport as the plane lands so that we are not waiting too long at the airfield. Here we are protected.'

'That makes sense,' said Akbar. 'We need to enquire about a taxi.'

A crewman was sent ashore to find one. He was away for only a few minutes before he returned and reported to the master, 'There is a man watching us.'

'Are you sure?'

'Yes. He is behind the wall, in that direction.'

'How many?'

'I saw only one.'

'There may be more. We must proceed very carefully.' The master's instructions were explicit.

Three of the crew went ashore, heading for the casino. They entered the building through the main entrance and exited through a side door.

A fourth man went in search of a taxi. He saw one approaching the casino and flagged it down. At first the driver refused to go to the airport which was 100km away but the tip offered changed his mind.

When the crewman reported back, he said, 'The driver suggests that you leave between 2.00 o'clock and 2.15. At the very most, a few minutes later. He will pick you up behind the casino.'

'Good,' said Khan. 'Now we must decide how we get away without being seen.'

'That is easy,' said the master. 'We will slide the inflatable into the water, near the bows. Nobody will be able to see us doing it. You go down a jumping ladder and one of my crew will row you around the end of the wall. You will get to the back of the casino without any problems.'

'What will you do?' Akbar asked.

The master shrugged and smiled. 'Nothing! The infidels will wonder what we are doing. They will wait and worry.'

There was a knock on the door and one of the three crewmen who had been sent ashore entered the room.

'Well?' asked the master.

'There are two of them. You cannot see them very well from here but they are easily spotted from the other side of the wall.'

'There are no more?'

'No, sir. We searched carefully. What do you wish us to do?'

'Where are the two men I sent with you?'

'In hiding, watching them.'

'What are you going to do?' Al-Zawahiri asked.

The master drew a forefinger dramatically across his throat.

'Why do such a thing?' enquired Akbar.

'It is simple, my friend. We must add confusion to confusion. All that is important is that you get away. We will dispose of the bodies. What will they think? What will they do?'

They nodded. It was a good plan.

* * * * *

At 01.30 the team mustered on the starboard side of the ship. It took them twenty minutes to get kitted up and ready for the water. They would be swimming in groups of two, at two minute intervals. Hunter was buddied to Badonovitch, attached by a three metre nylon line from the top of each of their right arms, while Dunston was

391

buddied with Henri. Albatha and Tanner had entirely different jobs to do. Tanner left to go along the road, past the casino and up to Fort Sidi Henni situated at the edge of the breakwater. He took with him an Accuracy International L96A1, a standard sniping rifle used by the British Army. At the fort he broke a lock on one of the gates and climbed the ramparts. From there, he had a clear view of the yacht. Tanner's job was to cover the team's back. Albatha, meanwhile, headed for the Old Port. He took up position where he was hidden by a low wall but had a perfect view of the yacht. Albatha looked at his watch. He knew the team should be arriving in about twenty minutes. He settled down to wait. With luck, it would all be over in an hour.

'Nick,' Thompson appeared down aft, 'I can't raise the two lads I sent to keep watch.'

'Has anyone gone to look for them?' Nick asked.

'The Coxswain and the Buffer. I don't like it. I told them to be very careful.'

'Zim,' Hunter transmitted, 'can you see either of our lookouts?'

'No,' Albatha replied quietly. 'Wait!' There was a pause. 'I've got a pool of blood here.'

'Thanks, Zim.' He broke the connection and looked at Thompson. 'Zim has found blood.'

Thompson closed his eyes and shook his head. 'Damnation!'

'We can only carry on,' said Hunter. 'They may still be alive and on the yacht.'

Thompson said heavily, 'Yeah, and I believe in Santa Claus.'

'We'd better get moving.'

*

Hunter and Badonovitch slipped like ghosts over the side of the *Atherstone* and into the water. A quick check for potential leaks and they left surface, feet first, causing not so much as a ripple. At a couple of metres under the water, they flipped over and swam under the keel of the ship and up to the harbour wall. From there they swam at a depth of three metres, Hunter feeling the wall on his left, Badonovitch following his boss. It was, by Royal Navy standards, an easy dive. Breathing pure oxygen, there were no tell-tale bubbles escaping to the surface. Hunter had a Glock 18 with silencer in a specially made waterproof bag attached to his left side and a diver's knife strapped to his right calf. The special tools he'd acquired were in the pouch on his right shoulder. The other three had employed the same arrangement with their weapons.

They arrived at the corner of the entrance to the Old Port and went straight across, swimming the eight metres or so to the harbour wall on the other side. There they turned left, and this time Hunter kept the wall to his right as they swam the short distance towards the yacht. As they approached the hull, it loomed before them, white and ghostly in the darkness. They felt along the bottom to the stern. They were surfacing when Hunter bumped into an object that was floating beneath the surface but anchored to the seabed. It took him only seconds to realise that he had found the two missing seamen. They surfaced, their heads barely breaking clear of the water, to appear next to the fixed ladder that led to the deck. 'I found the two sailors,' he whispered in Badonovitch's ear.

Badonovitch nodded. 'I know,' he replied softly.

Still keeping his voice low, Hunter radioed Tanner. 'Fort this is Seal One, over.'

Immediately Tanner replied, 'This is Fort. All clear. Out.'

Hunter and Badonovitch shucked their diving gear and attached it to the bottom rung of the ladder. Carefully and quietly, Hunter climbed onto the deck. He slipped over the guard-rail and waited for Badonovitch. Bent low, they could not be seen by anyone ashore. They moved forward a few metres and waited. Minutes later they were joined by Dunston and Henri.

'Let's move out,' Hunter whispered.

Guns in hand, the two teams split up. Hunter and Badonovitch went up the port side, Dunston and Henri moved along the starboard side. Climbing a short set of steps, Hunter stepped onto the bridge wing and straight into a startled lookout.

40

There was no hesitation. Nick Hunter put a bullet in the man's forehead, silencing him forever. Stepping onto the bridge, he looked around for other crew members. Dunston appeared on the other side. The four men went below. While Henri and Badonovitch went to the crew's quarters, Dunston and Hunter checked the guest cabins. They were empty.

'Jan. Henri,' Hunter whispered into his transmitter, 'I want the master. He has a few questions to answer.'

'Roger that, boss,' Badonovitch replied.

Suddenly one of the doors at the end of the corridor opened and a crew member stepped out. Seeing Badonovitch he yelled at the top of his voice. Badonovitch reacted like lightning and fired one round into the man's stomach and a second round through the crown of his head. He fell back with a clatter. Other voices joined in the chorus of yells. Another door opened and a head appeared. Henri fired a snap shot but missed. The door slammed shut and the man began yelling to the other crew members. Badonovitch, standing to one side, took hold of the handle and pressed it down. It was lucky he was standing where he was, because the man inside opened up with an automatic pistol. The bullets smashed through the door and would no doubt have killed Badonovitch. As it was, he was able to kneel, throw open the door and shoot the man straight through the heart. It was a very lucky shot. Hunter and Dunston had joined Henri and Badonovitch in the crews' quarters. Hunter knelt down by another door, Dunston stood next to him and turned the handle. Immediately, the cabin's occupant opened fire, with his weapon on automatic. After a few seconds the shooting stopped and Dunston shoved the door open. Bullets skimmed past their heads. Hunter shot twice. The first bullet smashed the man's elbow and the second hit his sternum. He was dead five seconds later.

'Boss,' Tanner said, from his vantage point on top of the fort, 'one of the men is climbing through the window. He's reaching up for the deck.'

'Shoot him,' was the stark reply.

There was pause of a couple of seconds and then Tanner said, 'Got him. He's just fallen into the water.'

'Is everything still quiet up there?' Hunter asked. 'The gunfire down here is enough to wake the dead.'

'I can hear you up here,' said Tanner, 'but nobody else seems to have done so. Or if they have, they're ignoring you. I can't see anyone at the moment. What about you, Number Two?'

'Nothing,' said Albatha. 'No sign of anyone, though the shooting is pretty loud.'

'We'll need to hurry,' said Hunter to the others. Just then one of the crew opened fire. One bullet hit a door hinge and was deflected into the corridor. It hit the steel fire-extinguisher that was hanging on the bulkhead and ricocheted into Henri's side. He went down with a grunt of pain as blood began to seep through his wetsuit. Badonovitch stepped to the door, knelt, looked through the cracks, saw the crew member and shot him between the eyes.

'Two more cabins,' said Hunter. He tried the nearest door. It was locked. He placed his Glock against the lock, flipped it to automatic and opened fire. Six shots blew it apart and the door flew open. Dunston fired the shots that killed the single occupant who was cowering on the other side of the cabin.

'According to the information the General sent, there should be eight of them. That leaves two to go and one cabin. That one there,' he nodded at the door at the end of the corridor. 'Right, change of plan. Simon, you okay?'

'I think so. It hurts like hell but not a lot of blood.'

'Okay. Stay where you are. Jan, up top. Use a flash/bang. When you get into position let me know. I'll shoot the lock. Doug, put a couple of rounds through the window. Jan, you throw the flash/bang. Okay everyone, let's move.'

A minute later they were ready.

'Right, Doug, shoot,' ordered Hunter as he began firing at the lock. There were more shots, followed by the clatter of shattering glass, a yell and an explosion that ripped through the yacht. The two men in the cabin were blown off their feet, their ears ringing in pain, nausea sweeping through them in waves. Then Hunter and Dunston rushed in, and standing astride the writhing figures lying on the deck, jerked their arms behind their backs and wrapped plastic ties around their wrists. They dragged them to their feet and hustled them along the corridor to the stern of the yacht. Dunston had already called the *Atherstone* and given a brief sitrep. It was then that Thompson learned about his two crew members. The Gemini, which was in the water and ready, came roaring around the end of the quay and into the Old Port. Petty Officer Tam

397

Chapman was driving, while Paul Cooper knelt in the bows. The boat came alongside and the two prisoners were dropped unceremoniously into it.

'Nick,' said Cooper, 'we've received the distress signals, right on time. The position is as agreed. We're flashed up and ready to go.'

'Good. Are you ready Matt? Then let's go.'

They started in the engine room, placing charges on the ready-use fuel tank. Next they did the same to the main tank and then the petrol stowage. Each body had plastic explosive strapped to it. The amount of explosives they used was excessive. It wasn't wanton destruction for the sake of it. With the *Atherstone* gone, leaving dead bodies behind wasn't a good idea. Questions could be asked. Even with the excuse of responding to distress signals at sea it could be awkward. With the yacht and bodies blown to smithereens what questions could be asked? Where were the crew? Had they blown the yacht to pieces and, if so, why? Nobody would believe the *Atherstone* didn't have something to do with it, but that was irrelevant. What was important was the authorities' inability to prove anything. It gave the Tunisian government a way out. They could shrug and say there was nothing to be done. The timers on the charges were set for 07.15. Time enough for the *Atherstone* to depart territorial waters. Badonovitch recovered the bodies of the dead sailors and passed them up to the two men in the inflatable. He hauled himself out of the water and into the boat.

Overloaded as it was, the Gemini trundled slowly back to the *Atherstone* while Albatha and Tanner were already hurrying along the quay. Dunston and Hunter were right behind them. Even with the noise of the flash/bang nobody had come to investigate. The Tunisians were not a nosy people. The *Atherstone* had her engines running and her berthing hawsers singled up. The Gemini arrived back alongside the minehunter. The boat was emptied of gear, the bodies of the crew were passed up carefully and the two terrorists manhandled as roughly as possible. They hit the deck with a great deal more lumps and bruises. Even as the Gemini was being hoisted up, the head and stern ropes were let go. Two engine orders and a wheel order had the ship moving majestically away from the wall and towards the open sea canal. Technically, the port was closed, so no ship was allowed in or out. However, there was nothing across the harbour entrance to prevent them leaving, and so they departed as quickly and quietly as they could. The time was just after 03.15.

Once at sea, Thompson turned to Hunter and asked, 'How did they die?'

'Their throats were cut.' The words were stark and blunt. There was no other way to put it.

'Bastards!'

'I'm really sorry, Mike.'

'Don't be an idiot, Nick. I could have sent more men, had them in different places and better hidden.'

Hunter knew that Thompson was right. It still didn't help much. The two prisoners were placed in the locker room in the fo'c's'le. Tanner was left on guard while Dunston prepared the SSM. It wasn't long before he was injecting the drugs into them. Henri was in the wardroom, having his injuries seen to. The wound wasn't deep, but it was painful. He would be laid up for a few days.

*　*　*　*　*

Macnair, Walsh and Isobel were in the General's office,

sitting in silence, when Hunter called in. His sitrep was brief and to the point. The reaction of the three of them was unprintable.

'How in hell,' asked Walsh, 'did they know you were coming?'

'We can't be certain that was the case,' replied Hunter, 'it just seems that way.'

'I agree with Hiram,' said Isobel. 'They knew alright.'

'They may have seen the lookouts and put two and two together,' Hunter said. 'Or it may have been a coincidence. Or it could be a part of their plan all along.' He couldn't keep the frustration out of his voice. 'We won't know until we question them.'

Isobel said, 'It seems we take two steps forward and one back. I'll get Gareth and Leo working on some more intercepts and we'll see what we can find out.' As Isobel finished speaking Gareth entered the room.

'Sir, I thought you might like to see this. The intercept is timed just after midnight. I've only just got the translation off the computer. The voice is confirmed as that of Prince Khaled Aziz. He spoke to one of the men on the yacht by phone and said "You must leave for Tabarka. There is an airport there and my private jet will be arriving in five hours. The pilot knows where to take you."'

'Is that all?' Macnair asked.

'Yes, sir. Leo is currently hacking into the computer at the airport to see if a flight plan has been filed.'

'Good work,' said Macnair.

'Sorry it took so long. Everything is coming in time order. There's so much data to process it takes a while.'

'Did you get that, Nick?' Macnair asked.

'Yes, sir,' Nick confirmed.

Another extension rang and Macnair pressed a button

that also put it on speaker. It was Leo.

'General? The Sheikh's plane will be landing shortly. It has a flight plan for Venice. I've looked up the details about Tabarka airfield. It is about 100 kilometres from Hunter's position. No plane is allowed to take off before 06.00. So they could still be there.'

'Is that likely?' Hunter asked.

'It's all we've got, Nick,' said Leo.

'Think you can make it?' Macnair enquired.

'No idea, sir. We can try. Bizerte is about five miles astern of us. We'll go ashore and see about transport. With a bit of luck we could get there in time. But we'll have to move fast. We have just under two hours.'

'All right,' replied the General. 'Get going. We'll speak later.'

Within minutes the *Atherstone* had turned and was steaming towards the shore, aiming for Cap Blanc, the northernmost tip of Africa. Hunter, Badonovitch, Tanner and Albatha changed into dark civilian clothes, armed themselves with Glocks, hand grenades and some plastic explosive. The *Atherstone* was a couple of hundred yards offshore when a Gemini was launched and the First Lieutenant ferried them in. The beach at Cap Blanc was sandy and smooth. The team disembarked without so much as getting their feet wet and ran towards the cliff and the pathway they could now see in the early dawn. The outskirts of Bizerte were a couple of kilometres away and they fell into a fast run. For the TIFAT team it was no problem, but for the unfit Albatha it was purgatory. He was quickly gasping for breath and falling behind.

Hunter called over his shoulder, 'Zim, stay here. We'll come and pick you up.' With that he picked up speed , the other two right behind him.

Luck, at last, was on their side. They had only just reached the suburbs of the town when an outside light came on above the door of a substantial villa. A short, fat man was seen waddling towards his car – a top of the range Citroen – parked in the drive. The engine started and the car approached the shut gates. It stopped and the man got out. The team stood in the shadows and watched as the furthest gate was pulled inwards. The man's back was to the team as he pushed open the second one. Hunter stepped silently from behind the wall and up to the Tunisian. A blow with his open palm across the back of the man's neck rendered him unconscious. The team tied and gagged the man and hid him behind bushes on the other side of the road. Hopefully, he wouldn't be found for hours.

They piled into the car and returned to where they had left Albatha. Hunter drove as fast as he dared. They were on a secondary road. It was empty, reasonably straight and in good order. They were passing through the region known as the Mogods. The area had an annual rainfall of 600 inches and specialised in cattle-rearing and dairy-farming. As a result they drove through lush green pasture where stands of cork and evergreen oak trees abounded. Hunter had no time to enjoy what little scenery he could see in his headlights. It took twenty minutes before they joined the main highway running from Bizerte to Tabarka. Finally, Hunter was able to put his foot to the floor and the big Citroen surged forward.

Albatha announced, 'Sign ahead says airport 40 kilometres.'

'Less than 15 minutes with luck,' Hunter replied. 'What's the time now?' He didn't dare take his eyes off the road.

'Twenty to six,' replied the big Turk. 'There's still a chance we'll make it.'

41

The men paced impatiently up and down the runway. After the jet had landed, the pilot had wanted to leave as soon as his passengers had arrived. The flight controller, who was on night duty in case of emergencies, point-blank refused. He had allowed the plane to land precisely because the pilot had claimed he had an emergency. Now the pilot was insisting that the problem appeared to have resolved itself. The flight controller wasn't stupid. He knew he had been duped. That had made him angry. He had insisted that no plane was allowed to take off before 06.00. Not even theirs. It was more than his job was worth. When the pilot insisted that he would leave regardless, the flight controller prevented him from doing so by ordering an oil tanker to block the runway.

It was now 05.50 and at last the tanker was being moved. The pilot assumed that meant they had permission to take off and told the others to climb aboard. The plane, a Yakovlev Yak-40, was a small, three-engined jet airliner. As the three men climbed into the plane, the engines began to whine and whistle. It taxied to the end of the runway, turned and waited a few more moments for the engines to warm through. Nobody on the plane noticed the Citroen smash through the single pole barrier at the far end of the airfield and speed towards their tail. The plane began to roll and rapidly picked up speed. The car was gaining but the jet was out of gunshot range. The plane began to ascend, the wheels retracted and its speed accelerated rapidly. The Citroen was left behind, already a tiny dot far below, as the Yak-40 turned north and headed for Europe.

Only a few minutes into the flight a steward handed Akbar a message. He looked at the other two and chuckled. 'It seems our presence on this plane is known by the authorities. We are to be met at Rome and arrested.'

Rehman Khan laughed. 'The imbeciles.'

*   *   *   *   *

Hunter slammed on the brakes and the car skidded to a halt. Climbing out of the car he watched as the plane vanished. He slammed his fist onto the roof of the car in sheer frustration.

'Boss!' Badonovitch called. 'We'd better get the hell out of here, before security comes.'

Hunter climbed into the car and accelerated back the way they had come. The barrier they had smashed through was unmanned and somehow their presence still hadn't been noticed. As they hit the road and headed east the sun rose over the horizon, bathing them in warmth and bright light.

Hunter handed his phone to Tanner. 'Call General Macnair. Tell him what's happened and ask him to tell *Atherstone* we're heading for the coast road. If they keep close inshore we'll see them and I'll give a series of five flashes.'

While Tanner contacted Rosyth, Hunter concentrated on the road, overtaking vehicles with reckless precision. An hour later, they spotted the *Atherstone*, hugging the coastline. Hunter flashed his headlights and immediately the ten-inch signal lamp flashed back. The team jumped out of the car and made their way down a gentle slope to the beach to meet the Gemini which was heading inshore. Within minutes they were alongside the ship and climbing the jumping ladder. Even as they did so, the *Atherstone* was turning to starboard and the open sea, revolutions rung on for fifteen knots. The team were gutted with frustration. However, there was nothing else for it but to have breakfast and turn in. A few hours sleep wouldn't go amiss. Before he did though, Hunter went for'ard to speak to Dunston.

'Get anything?'

'Sorry, Nick. The master had a heart attack about ten minutes after I injected him.'

'And the other one?'

'He died only a few minutes ago. He knew what was happening, but only in the broadest sense. He was ignorant of the details. For instance, he knew about the three men flying to Europe but didn't know where they were headed.' Pausing, Matt added, 'He killed one of the lads.'

Hunter looked over his friend's shoulder at the inert bodies. 'It's a pity you didn't slit his throat. However, the extra SSM you gave him achieves the same end.'

'I didn't give it to him.'

'Oh? Then what happened?' Nick asked.

'Cooper did it.'

Hunter looked surprised. 'Good for him. I'll speak to Mike. We can get the bodies weighted and thrown overboard.'

* * * * *

It seemed to Hunter that he had barely climbed into his pit before he was interrupted from a deep sleep. The General wanted to speak to him in the communications office.

'Nick? We have some information. Thanks to Isobel's lot we now know who's been leaking information to Prince Khaled Aziz.'

'Who?' asked an intrigued Hunter.

'Have you ever heard of an MP by the name of Saddiq Ali? He represents a constituency around Hounslow. Big Muslim enclave. Friend of the Prime Minister.'

'Never heard of him.'

'That's not surprising. However, not only is he an MP but he's also a member of the security oversight committee and has had access to just about everything that's been going on around here. Or most of it, anyway.'

'What can you do about him?' was the blunt question.

'For now, we're using him. Later, we'll see. We've been feeding information into the system under the guise of co-operation with the government and a desire to make amends. We've already sent a report stating that we believe a plane with the terrorists and the dirty bomb on board is headed for Rome and that an all-out effort was to be made to arrest the men when it landed. We have also made it abundantly clear that ECHELON has gone down and that we are trying to re-establish contact with the satellites. Furthermore, we are unable to carry out any form of phone intercepts and we expect the problem to last a minimum of twenty-four hours.'

'With what in mind, sir?' Hunter asked.

'We are going to do our best to lull them into a false sense of security. We know their preferred target is London. That they will do their damnedest to get to Britain. However, if they fail, detonation of the bomb anywhere in Europe will be just as bad. What we have learned from the intercepts is that they're headed for a trans-continental train. If they catch one and they feel in any way threatened they can set off the bomb.'

'What do you want us to do, sir?' Nick asked.

'For now, just sit tight. A helicopter is on its way. You and the team will be flown to Sicily. There you'll liaise with four training Harriers belonging to the Italians. They'll fly you to Verona.'

'There are five of us.'

'Dunston will be staying behind.'

'But, sir . . .' Nick began to protest.

'But me no buts, Lieutenant Commander.'

'Yes, sir. Why Verona, sir?'

'You're catching a train.'

'To where?'

'It's not so much as where, as which train. The terrorists are joining the Venice Simplon Orient-Express in Venice.'

'How can you be sure?'

'We're as sure as we can be. Now they think they're safe from us listening to them, they're talking back and forth almost non-stop. Their excitement is growing by the hour. A lot of Islamic mumbo jumbo is being spouted. A personal message from Osama bin Laden has been forwarded to them which seemed to send them into a paroxysm of happiness. We've also discovered there's a network of agents helping them along the route. We're identifying each one for future action.'

'I thought they had a fourteen day timetable?'

'They did but clearly it's changed. Why, we've no idea. Not that it matters now.'

'Is there anything else, sir?'

'There are no train reservations in the names of Rehman

Khan, Mohammed Akbar or Al-Zawahiri.'

'That's not surprising. They know we're after them. They'll be using false identities. It's an obvious precaution.'

'You'll join the train at Verona. It leaves at 13.10. You should make it in plenty of time. We need you to identify them but you must not make a move until you arrive at the Arlberg Pass.'

'Yes, sir, that makes sense.' If the bomb exploded there it would cause the minimum of damage and the least number of deaths. The plutonium fallout would also be trapped in the pass. It was the best option they had.

'Train tickets will be available for you to collect at the station. Have you still got the updated photographs of the three men?'

'Yes, sir.'

'Incidentally, you did a good job with the yacht. There's been hell to pay but we're denying all knowledge of it.'

'What about us leaving early?'

'I'm not saying the Mayday ruse actually worked, but everyone is going along with it. So, in the best tradition of the Royal Navy, the *Atherstone* cancelled all leave and set sail to give aid and succour to those in peril on the sea, as it says in the hymn. As a result, we're claiming the moral high ground and taking an indignant stand at the suggestion we had anything to do with the yacht being wiped off the face of the earth.'

At the end of the call Nick thoughtfully replaced the handset. Minutes later he woke Matt and briefed him on what was happening, while at the same time explaining to his friend the news that he wouldn't be joining them.

'I'm sorry Matt, there just aren't enough places and the General's given his orders.'

'I should go instead of Zim.'

Hunter shook his head. 'We *need* a Muslim in at the kill. You know that.'

'Nick, be careful.' Matt said.

'Don't worry, old friend, I will,' Nick said. 'Right, I'd better brief the others.'

Shortly afterwards a Sea King HAR3 appeared. Hunter, Badonovitch, Tanner and Albatha were lifted off the *Atherstone* and flown directly to Catania on the eastern coast of Sicily. There, four training Harriers were waiting for them. Each member of the team climbed into a designated cockpit and rammed bags of equipment at their feet. It was damned uncomfortable. Minutes later the vertical take-off jets lifted into the air. In seconds the planes had accelerated to their top speed of 600 knots and were passing through 30,000ft. The distance to go to Verona was five hundred and sixty miles; flying time, just over forty-five minutes.

* * * * *

Akbar was handed yet another message which caused him to break out in a smile. 'I do not know how it is done, my friends, where the information comes from, but here is very good news.'

The other two sat up straight in their luxury seats and leaned forward.

'Tell us,' said Khan, urgency in his voice.

'All efforts to find us have been switched to Rome. We are to divert to a small airfield outside Venice, and not land at the main airport, just in case there are people looking for us there. The pilot will approach the field and radio that he has an electrical problem. Not serious, but will need to land as a precaution. No airfield can refuse such a request. We will be met and taken to the railway station from there.'

'What then?' Khan asked.

'Again there is a change of plan. We will not be going to Dieppe to meet *The Flower of Allah*. We will be going all the way to London.'

'Why is that?' Kaman Al-Zawahiri asked.

'There is no ship.'

'What has happened?' Khan had difficulty keeping the fear out of his voice.

'Do not worry, my friend. It was always a possibility. The ship was coming from Cyprus to meet us and take us across the Channel. She has been missing for many days.'

'How?' Al-Zawahiri asked.

Akbar shrugged. 'We are not sure. Perhaps the crew have run away. If they have, may Allah curse them for eternity. Or perhaps they are dead. There is no way of knowing.' He suddenly smiled. 'Come, my friends, let us enjoy our good fortune, and may the blessings of Allah continue to shine down on us.'

The other two nodded.

* * * * *

There was no chatter between the pilots and their passengers. The pilots had too much to occupy them. Normally, the skies would have been crowded, but now there was barely a plane heading in the same direction. Those that were, were privately owned. Why they were heading for Rome was anybody's guess. For the pilots, it was an interesting operation. For the team, it was sheer boredom. When they landed in Verona they were met by a police escort. The General really had pulled out all the stops.

The police inspector shook hands with each of them and they climbed in. They had barely left the airport when they were forced to slow down. Both sides of the road were clogged with cars and people all headed out of the city.

'This is hellish,' said Hunter.

'It's been like this for days.'

'Where are they going?' Albatha asked.

The Inspector shrugged. 'Who knows? They certainly don't. They just want to get out of the city. To safety. Away from the killings. But there is nowhere to go. It is not just here. It is happening all across Europe. And in Britain, as well. You see that smoke, there, there and over there?' He pointed at the rooftops in the distance where billowing black clouds of smoke rose into the heavens.

'What's happened?' Albatha asked.

'Two mosques and a church have been set alight. Many Muslims have been killed here and throughout Europe. They are now organising themselves, to defend their mosques and properties and to protect their lives and the lives of their children. Atrocity follows atrocity and it is now, how do you say, out of hand. It is a tragic time, not just for Europe but for the whole world.'

Eventually, after a frustrating journey, they were deposited at the station. The goodbyes were necessarily brief because the inspector was called away to a shooting incident. They collected their tickets from the booking office, where the clerk told them that the train was full and that they were lucky to get tickets. The long arm of Macnair had reached out again.

Hunter asked the clerk, 'But where are they all going? To London?'

The clerk shook his head. 'No. Most are only going as far as Zurich. Some are for Paris and London but not many.'

411

Hunter shook his head. 'Why Zurich?' But he knew the answer even as he asked the question.

'It's where the money is kept.' Out of habit he smiled and said, 'Have a good day.' He pulled the blind down on his window.

Looking along at the other windows, Hunter could see that they were already closed. He hurried across the concourse and handed out the tickets. 'We have one more important thing to do before we get on the train. Let's go. We'd better hurry. The train leaves in forty-five minutes.' They followed him outside the concourse, where he pointed at a men's clothing shop. 'We're going in there.'

'What for, boss?' Badonovitch asked.

'We'll stick out like sore thumbs dressed like this,' he explained. 'I've been on the Orient-Express before. In the evening men wear dinner jackets and the women wear evening dresses. I doubt that'll be the case in the circumstances so we needn't go that far. But we need to look a lot smarter and tidier if we're to blend in.'

The others nodded. It didn't take a lot of haggling to get a very good price for suits, shirts and the accessories they required. Being Italy, there was no problem getting what they needed to fit, Albatha included. The shopkeeper was very grateful for the business. As he said, nobody was currently in the market for such items. Money was being spent on basic items, such as food and drink.

'How is it you're still here?' Hunter asked the man.

He shrugged. 'You see how it is. Where are they running to? Where is safe? Until the bomb is found the answer is nowhere.'

'That's true.'

'The television, the papers, all say stay calm. That things aren't really that bad.'

412

'Is that helping?'

Again he shrugged. 'Who can say, signor? I only know that I think it is more dangerous out there than in here. My family is safe in the apartment above me. We have enough food for now. So I think it is better that we stay.'

'That makes sense. I wish you luck,' said Hunter.

'And you, signor. Where do you go?'

'Us? Why do you think we're going anywhere?'

'The clothes. They tell me you are catching the train. The special one. Is that not so?'

Hunter nodded. 'That is so.' He held out his hand. 'I hope all goes well.'

'Thank you, signor.'

They shook hands. If TIFAT was right, the little man and his family would be safe where they were.

They needed one more item each. In a nearby luxury leather goods shop they bought four shoulder bags of the sort used by men. It was the only place to put their weapons. The bags on offer were of varying colours and design. They chose black with a single pocket and a flap held by two studs. They walked back across the concourse towards the platform. Hunter wore a light-grey suit, a white shirt and red tie. Badonovitch was dressed in a brown suit and open-necked, light green shirt, Tanner wore a cream-coloured suit and an open-necked black shirt, while Albatha wore grey trousers, a double-breasted black blazer and a light-blue tie. The change in their appearance was startling.

Hunter looked at the other three, 'It's true after all.'

'What is?' Tanner asked, a puzzled look on his face.

'It's clothes that maketh the man, not manners.' The comment raised only a slight chuckle.

They were entering the station when Hunter's phone rang. He was surprised to see whose name was on the screen. 'Samantha?'

'Hi Nick. I'm at the coffee kiosk by the toilets.'

'What did you say?'

She repeated herself. 'I'll explain when you get here.'

Hunter looked at the others. 'Samantha's over there.' They pushed their way through the crowds.

'What the hell are you doing here?' Hunter greeted her.

Tucking her arm through his, she smiled sweetly and replied, 'Nice to see you too.'

'The General sent me. Four tough looking reprobates like you lot could easily cause suspicion. I'm background colouring.'

'Just so long as you stay in the background,' said Hunter, not sure whether to scowl or smile. 'As we're here, we may as well get some coffee while we wait for the train.'

They bought coffees and snacks, both of which were extortionately expensive. However, they didn't bother protesting. There was no point. It was a seller's market for food and drink. The crowds were pushing and shoving, moving in all directions. Different languages could be heard as people called to one another, waving, hugging, weeping. Exquisitely tailored men and women were giving orders to flunkies and servants carrying their bags as they tried to cross the concourse.

Finally, the train rolled majestically into the station. As it did, hoards of people began shoving their way towards the platform. There were yells, screams and a great deal of profanity. Some people tripped over, others were pushed, some stumbled and fell.

Hunter said, 'Split up and let's go. We must not miss this train. Samantha, you follow me.'

The team moved out. They muttered platitudes, apologies, even asked to be excused but didn't pause as they made their way towards the platform. Taking one look at them was enough for most of the crowd to let them through. There was only one incident when a Frenchman tried to prevent Badonovitch from passing. Without pausing, Badonovitch merely used his right arm to sweep him out of the way, knocking him to the concrete. Their carriage was halfway along the train. An attendant stood at the door, holding a clipboard. Nick and Samantha arrived first. They showed their tickets, he ticked off their berth numbers and pointed along the corridor. A few minutes later the others arrived. They had three adjacent cabins. The compartments were on the right side of the train, the windowed corridor on the left. Each compartment was set out with a comfortable, upholstered sofa, facing the direction of travel, together with a coffee table and two upright chairs. The sofa would be turned into bunks by the staff later in the evening. The compartment was vintage 1929, one of the Orient-Express's famous LX series of Pullman coaches. There was no doubting the luxury of their surroundings.

Hunter and Samantha settled into their cabin, looking through the information pack detailing the services available. The train lurched slightly and slowly pulled away. Hunter looked at his watch and said, '13.10. Exactly on time.'

There was a knock on the door and the other three entered. There wasn't a lot of room, but Tanner and Badonovitch sat on the sofa while Albatha leaned against the door.

'What's the plan, boss?' Doug Tanner asked.

'There are three restaurant cars at the front of the train,

so we'd better split up. Samantha and I will take the one nearest the front. Doug, you go to the middle one and you two take the third one but sit at separate tables. I don't need to tell you to take your time. Get something to eat and drink. We'll stay in the restaurants until Innsbruck. If we don't see any of them, then Zim, you stay where you are, facing down the train. We'll start a routine of wandering the corridors. We can use the toilets, look out of the corridor windows. You know the routine. We'll spell each other in the restaurant car about every hour. OK? Right, let's go.'

Albatha opened the door and checked that the corridor was empty then gestured to the others to follow him. Passing other travellers they wandered slowly along the corridors of the carriages, gradually getting further apart from one another.

Albatha entered the first restaurant car. To the right of the carpeted aisle were the dining tables. Draped in stiff white cloths, with bowls of flowers in the centre each could accommodate four passengers comfortably. Albatha and Badonovitch sat separately from each other while Tanner walked past them into the next carriage, which was about two-thirds full, and sat down facing the way he'd come. Hunter and Samantha strolled past him and entered the last restaurant car. Hunter sat down at the last empty table with his back to the engine.

'Have you spotted any of them?' Samantha asked as she sat down opposite him.

'No not yet but there's plenty of time. They can't stay holed up for the whole trip.' Nick smiled at her. He had to admit to himself she was looking extremely attractive. 'Your presence is an unexpected pleasure.'

She smiled impishly, dimples on either cheek giving a

416

soft edge to her looks. 'A pleasure?'

Hunter smiled in return. 'Actually, yes. Provided you do as I tell you.'

Her smile vanished. 'Now, hang on a minute . . .'

'Samantha, that's not a request. That's an order. Don't let the way the team and I speak fool you. When I say jump, they know they'd better be moving. There's only room for one boss, and on this caper that's me. We've all run our own ops at one time or another and we discuss and dispute but once we're in action there's a chain of command.'

Samantha looked as though she was going to argue when the steward arrived to take their orders. They both asked for smoked salmon sandwiches, coffee and an Orient-Express Special Torte.

Samantha nodded her head at the door behind Hunter. 'That's obviously where the kitchen is, along with the attendants' quarters.'

The waiter returned, placed the food and coffee on the table and with a harried, 'Enjoy your meal,' went to assist some customers at a nearby table who were clamouring for more drinks.

'Nice coffee,' said Hunter, 'and excellent sandwiches. How the hell did they manage to cater for everyone with what's going on?'

'I've no idea. This torte is delicious.'

They exchanged smiles. Hunter took out his phone. A quick text to each of the others established that the men they were looking for weren't in any of the restaurant cars.

Kaman Al-Zawahiri chortled. 'My friends, I cannot believe we have had such luck.'

'It is not luck, my friend,' Mohammed Akbar said. 'It is thanks to the far-sighted brilliance of Prince Khaled Aziz.'

'You are right,' Rehman Khan nodded. 'We are now properly armed and have three bodyguards. Nothing can stop us. It is only a matter of time. We arrive at Innsbruck shortly and depart at fifteen minutes before six o'clock. Tomorrow we reach Paris at nine o'clock in the morning, and then London at a quarter past five. Surely, Allah is smiling upon us.'

'What shall we do about food?' asked Akbar. 'I am becoming hungry and I don't want to stay locked up in here for the next twenty-four hours.'

Khan said, 'We shall take it in turns, one at a time, to eat. Two will stay in the compartment at all times. If it becomes necessary, one can protect the other to give him time to detonate the bomb.'

'You must show us how that is done, my friend,' said Al-Zawahiri.

'It is easy,' said Khan. 'You set the time by pressing this button, holding it down and moving the digital time shown there.' He demonstrated the simple procedure and watched each man repeat the same steps. There were nods of satisfaction as a contented feeling descended on the three men.

42

When the train pulled into Innsbruck the team, along with a few other passengers, alighted, and walked up and down the platform, ostensibly to stretch their legs. They each carried the bags holding their weapons. If their targets decided to quit the train and make a run for it, then the team needed to move fast.

Hunter and Samantha strolled along the platform arm-in-arm.

She smiled at him. 'Isn't this romantic?'

Hunter looked down at her and returned the smile. 'Another place, another time, sweetheart and yeah.'

She tapped his shoulder. 'If that was an American accent it was terrible. And who was it meant to be?'

'Cagney?' he suggested, raising an eyebrow.

'Idiot.'

'See anything? Anyone?'

'No. With so many blinds drawn it's impossible to see anybody.'

'All aboard,' was called in German, French and English and was followed by a warning whistle. The Venice Simplon Orient-Express left Innsbruck station on schedule at 17.46.

While Zim Albatha returned to the first restaurant car,

the others went along the train into different carriages. Doug Tanner stood at a window at one end of a carriage and watched the scenery unfolding. Occasionally a passenger walked past him, smiling tentatively. He smiled and nodded in return. Badonovitch was two carriages further on, doing the same thing. Hunter strolled to the rear of the train and back. Samantha did the same thing, except in each carriage she paused, entered the toilet cubicle, waited a few minutes and re-emerged. Tanner took Albatha's place and the others swapped around. The evening passed slowly. The scenery they travelled through was breathtaking. They were surrounded by snow-capped mountains and green and beautiful valleys but the views were wasted on them.

Darkness fell. There was no longer an excuse to stand in the corridors and so they returned to their compartments. Hunter acknowledged that there was a limit to the number of times someone could walk up and down a train and not be noticed. Hunter and Samantha were joined by Albatha and Badonovitch while Tanner took his turn in the restaurant car.

'Any ideas?' Hunter asked.

'What about getting our hands on a couple of attendant's uniforms?' suggested Badonovitch. 'We could work our way along the train, knock on all the doors and tell the people we've come to make up their beds.'

'That might not be a bad idea,' Hunter said. 'Samantha, take a wander towards the front and see if there are any attendants not in the restaurant cars.'

Samantha nodded, got to her feet and went out.

'Let's consider the worst-case scenario,' said Hunter. 'If we don't find Khan, Akbar and Al-Zawahiri we'll have no choice but to stop the train in the tunnel at the Arlberg

Pass. If the terrorists panic and set off the bomb the explosion will do very little damage and the fallout will be kept to a minimum. However, we may be able to convince everyone on board that the train has broken down and that passengers need to walk through the tunnel to join a replacement service. Khan would understand the limitations of detonating the bomb in the tunnel and, having come this far without being intercepted he may not suspect anything. After all, as far as they know, it could be true. And if it was true, then they'd still stand a chance of getting to London or some other city.'

Albatha nodded. 'Yes, you are right, Nick. They have come this far, so why wouldn't they expect to complete their journey.'

'So we take them out then?' Badonovitch asked.

'I'm not sure this is going to work,' Samantha said as she returned to the compartment. 'I've just been watching an attendant working his way along the next carriage knocking on doors. He was telling people that it was time for the first sitting for dinner. Most people didn't open the door to him and many didn't even bother replying.'

'So the terrorists wouldn't respond either,' said Hunter thoughtfully. He looked at his watch. 'OK. Plan B. Soon after midnight, we must make our move. Jan and Zim will go forward to the engine cabin and stop the train in the tunnel. I don't know how you'll do it but make sure the train is immobilized. I'm going to need you down on the tracks with me, so the last thing we want is for them to be able to drive the train out of there. Samantha, you get one of the attendants to announce over the tannoy that the train has to be evacuated. In the meantime, Doug you go to the rear in case they try to get out of the tunnel that way.

421

Samantha, you join him as soon as you can.'

'What then?' Samantha asked.

'Then we take them down. Hard and fast. There should be enough light from the train for us to see what we're doing. Right, that's it. Who's first for dinner?'

At 19.00 Albatha and Tanner went along to enjoy an excellent fillet steak. They sat at separate tables, each in his own way lamenting the lack of a glass or two of decent red wine. An hour later, Samantha and Hunter appeared. Samantha opted for salmon fillet while Hunter chose the steak.

'This is superb,' said Samantha.

'Do you do much cooking?' Nick asked.

'Truth to tell, I'm a lousy cook. I follow the recipes religiously but something always goes wrong,' she said laughing. 'You?'

Hunter shook his head. 'I live in the wardroom most of the time with stewards and chefs to see to things. Although I'm a dab hand at barbecuing.'

'Isn't it time you moved off the base? Found your own place?'

'I'm working on it. I wasn't going to buy a place in Scotland until I knew whether or not I was going to stay with TIFAT.'

'Are you?'

Hunter looked at her pensively before he nodded. 'Yes.'

'What about your naval career?'

'I think I'm doing more good with TIFAT.'

'Why?' Samantha was fascinated. She had never met a man quite like Hunter. He was so sure of himself, so confident. He made a decision and acted. He was also willing to put his life on the line if it was necessary. Something he had done often enough in the past. Hunter wasn't aware of it but his reputation was going before him. Both MI5 and MI6 thought very highly of him.

'Good question. I've thought long and hard about it. I've come to the conclusion it's because we're at war. It's a dirty, no-holds-barred war, at least as far as the enemy is concerned.'

'Who are?'

'You know damn well who they are. Like the scumbags who want to kill tens of thousands of innocent people using a dirty bomb. And let's not kid ourselves. If they could get their hands on a nuclear bomb, say with a 15 to 20-kiloton yield, then they'd use it. Each kiloton is equivalent to 1,000 tons of high explosives. If it was delivered and detonated in any city it would kill hundreds of thousands. Then would come the effects of the radiation. That's their intention, and we need to do everything in our power to stop them.' He kept his voice low and he leaned across the table as he spoke. Even so, there was no hiding the passion and commitment he felt.

Samantha nodded. 'So, back to where we started. Where would you live? Edinburgh?'

'Probably.'

'That's a bit of a commute, isn't it?'

'We're not like the regular military. We present ourselves to the outside world as such but we don't fall-in on parade, salute the flag and report at 08.00 every morning. It's not possible to operate like we do under such restrictions. So the commute wouldn't be a problem. What about you?'

'What about me?'

'Are you staying in Scotland or heading back south?'

'Back south, I should think. I'll have to see.'

'Is that what you want?'

Samantha looked at him thoughtfully. 'I haven't made

423

up my mind yet.'

Hunter smiled and said, 'Let's get back to the compartment. If none of them come for dinner then we're going to have to carry out Plan B.'

Badonovitch had the fish goulash. There had been no sign of the terrorists and the steward had just announced again that this was the last sitting. If they didn't show up in the next fifty minutes it would be too late. The kitchen would be closed. He sat for a little longer sipping his coffee and as he did so Rehman Khan walked into the carriage. Badonovitch recognised him immediately. Taking out his phone, he tried to text Hunter. There was no signal. He thought for a moment about wandering along the corridor to tell the others, but decided against it. There was no point. Khan could go nowhere except back the way he'd come. It didn't take four of them to follow him, quite the reverse. Most of the time the corridor was empty. Too much activity would send alarm bells ringing in Khan's head.

Khan ordered some sort of lamb dish with all the trimmings.

Badonovitch called the waiter and asked for cheese and biscuits.

Khan picked at his meal and after only a few minutes pushed it away, barely touched. He also left the double helping of ice cream he had requested but he did drink his coffee. Badonovitch watched as Khan swallowed some pills from a bottle he kept in his pocket. When Khan got up to leave Badonovitch followed. He kept his distance, giving Khan plenty of space. He walked quickly and had already entered the next carriage while Badonovitch was only halfway along the corridor. As Khan stepped out of sight, Badonovitch ran quickly to reach the door and see where he went. Khan was still hurrying and was nearly at the end of the corridor when Badonovitch stepped through the door. So far, the Pakistani had not looked back and had no idea he was being followed. If Khan did look behind him Badonovitch would step into one of the toilets to be found at either end of the corridor.

* * * * *

Khan was sure the man behind was following him. But who was he? Why was he following him? Did he know who he was or was he merely being paranoid? Did the man know about the nuclear device? He told himself to get a grip. He was imagining things. Khan had reached the last carriage on the train and hurried along to his compartment. As he opened the door and stepped in, he looked back. The man was still behind! He was . . . No! He was just going to the bathroom!

The doors opened outwards, away from the direction of travel so Khan couldn't look along the corridor. Instead, he held the door open a few millimetres and tried to listen.

'What are you doing, my friend?' Akbar enquired.

'I think I was followed from the restaurant car, but I am not sure.'

'Followed by whom?' Al-Zawahiri asked, picking up his Kalashnikov AK-74, and flipping the safety catch on the right side to give it full automatic fire.

'There was a man in the restaurant car. When I left, so did he.' Khan thought a moment. 'Though it's true to say he had finished eating.' He frowned as he tried to recollect what he had seen. The truth was, he had not noticed Badonovitch until the last carriage. Had the man been following him and he hadn't noticed? It was possible, he supposed. After all, the lights had been dimmed for the night so visibility was not good.

'There is no sign of the man. He must have gone into one of the end berths.' Khan shrugged and closed the door.

'We cannot be too careful,' said Al-Zawahiri. 'We had better stay here and not go for any food.'

Akbar vehemently protested until the other two gave in and agreed he could go and get something to eat. He left before they could change their minds.

'I shall go and speak to the others,' said Khan. 'We must have maximum alertness for the next twenty-four hours.'

*   *   *   *   *

Badonovitch was an old hand at surveillance. He went into the toilet and stayed there. He had noted the compartment Khan had entered and that was all he needed to know. Not spooking them was the most important thing he could do right then. He opened the toilet door slightly so that he could see along the corridor. In his right hand he held his Glock. If there was trouble, he was ready. Stepping out of the toilet he crossed into the next carriage and along to Hunter's compartment. He gave the diving signal of five bells – two quick raps, another two quick raps followed by a fifth – so that inside, Hunter would know it was him and that all was well.

The door was unlocked and he entered. He announced, 'I've seen Rehman Khan.'

'Are you sure?' Hunter asked.

'Positive. He's in the last carriage, two-thirds of the way along. I also saw Mohammed Akbar heading for one of the restaurant cars.'

'We'll go and take a look,' Hunter said. 'Well done, Jan.' The smiles on their faces said it all. He looked at his mobile. 'We've a signal. Phone HQ and let them know we've found them.' With that, he and Samantha went out of the door, Hunter with his satchel slung over his shoulder.

There was no sign of Mohammed Akbar in the first restaurant car but as they entered the second they saw him, halfway along, facing the way he had come. Hunter and Samantha sat two tables behind him, Hunter looking at the man's back. There was no doubt as to his identification. Akbar had already ordered, and was spooning soup into his mouth while at the same time taking bites from a bread roll. He ate as though no food had passed his lips for a month.

'We've already eaten, thanks,' said Hunter, 'but can we have some wine?'

'Yes, sir. What would you like?'

'The Chardonnay, please.'

When the wine came they raised their glasses and sipped. They chatted quietly, ignoring Akbar. Unlike his compatriot he bolted his food and ended his meal with three helpings of ice cream together with a large cappuccino.

'Is he still eating?' Samantha asked quietly.

'Like a pig.' Hunter smiled at her. 'He's just finished. He's about to leave.' He threw some euros on the table, more than sufficient to cover the cost of the barely-touched bottle of wine.

Akbar was in something of a hurry as he walked along the corridor. Hunter, trailed by Samantha, followed at a more leisurely pace although his long stride enabled him to keep the man in sight.

'Stay here. I'll see which compartment he enters,' Hunter whispered to Samantha as they passed their compartment.

Hunter stopped at the door to the last carriage and hid in the shadows, looking through the window onto the corridor. He watched silently as Akbar entered one of the compartments and counted the doors. It was the same as Khan's. He returned to his own compartment where the team was sorting out the gear.

'Did you speak to the General?'

'Yes, boss,' Badonovitch replied. 'I told him what we are planning.'

'Good.' Hunter turned to Samantha and said 'Get back to the restaurant car and find an attendant. We need to know what time the train gets to the Arlberg pass.'

She nodded and hurried away.

'Are you finished?'

'Just about, boss,' Badonovitch answered. 'Just got this detonator to prime.'

Samantha quickly returned and said, 'We'll reach the pass just after midnight and the tunnel about fifteen minutes later.'

'Okay, that gives us plenty of time. Let's go through the procedures once again. There must be no errors.'

As the briefing progressed Sam became more and more agitated until she burst out, 'What about me?'

'As soon as the carriage stops, I want you down on the tracks. Get close to their compartment. If one of them tries to climb out of their window shoot him.'

Samantha nodded.

'OK! Let's get kitted up,' Nick ordered.

The first thing they did was to put on their Kevlar vests. The new ones were an improvement on the old. The monomers of plastic, linked together to form polymers, were now connected by a stronger hydrogen bond than previously. Now when a bullet hit the vest its force was distributed over an even wider area. Even at close range a bullet would no longer penetrate, although the force would knock the victim off his feet. Next came their webbing with the plastic explosive, detonators and associated gear. Finally, they double-checked their Glocks, then it was time to move.

A glance showed them that the corridor was empty. Quickly, they went along to the end carriage. They paused while Hunter and Badonovitch got to work. Between the carriages they placed shaped explosives along the floor. The force of the blast would be downwards. They wanted to isolate the carriage in the tunnel. Once the plastic explosive detonated, it would all come down to a matter of speed. If Rehman Khan managed to detonate the device, deaths and damage would be kept to a minimum. However, the TIFAT team would know nothing about it. The detonator had a fifteen-second fuse. They were ready to go. Tanner led the way through the door. He held his silenced Glock in a two-handed grip, arms extended. He walked bent over at the waist. Albatha walked behind him, with his gun held in the same way. If they saw anything, either of them could fire. Badonovitch followed, his weapon in his hand. Everything was quiet. Tanner had reached Khan's door. He didn't dare try the handle in case the occupants saw it moving. So there was no choice. From his satchel he took three small mounds of plastic explosive, each wrapped around a knot in the ends of short lengths of detonation cord. They had already made the measurements needed for the detonation cord using their own door. The knot meant that no detonator was required at the plastic explosive end, only an ignition at

the other end so that all three lumps exploded simultaneously. This was fixed and ready for the pin to be pulled.

Hunter said, 'Countdown on one. Three, two, one.'

He pulled his pin and stepped through the door and
along the corridor. The other three did the same and
stepped away from the door. They each put on night-
vision goggles. Hunter's explosion reverberated through
the carriage. The lights went out and the carriage was
rapidly coming to a halt as automatic brakes kicked in.
This was a safety feature on most trains. Almost
immediately the second explosion blew the cabin door
off. Now it was all noise and confusion. People in other
compartments were yelling and screaming. Seconds
seemed like minutes. Albatha was already inside the
cabin, kneeling. Tanner was standing in the doorway, his
left side in the compartment, his back to the corridor, half
in and half out. One thought was uppermost in their
minds. Would the world end for them in the next few
moments? Khan had the device on his lap and was
frantically trying to set the timing mechanism. Akbar,
who had been in the top bunk, was struggling to
disentangle himself from the sheets and reach for his AK-
74. What none of the team saw was a door opening, three
compartments behind Tanner, the muzzle of an AK-74
appearing and opening fire. At the same time, the doors in
between opened and two men looked out, drunkenly
wanting to know what was happening. They were killed
instantly. However, that didn't stop the bullets which
stitched up Doug Tanner's back, throwing him forward
and into Albatha, spoiling the latter's aim. Tanner had
been hit in the neck. The bullet severed his spine and a
second hit him in the base of the skull. He dropped to the
floor, dead. Hunter's reactions were like lightning. He

threw himself forward, and was in the air, horizontal to the floor, when he opened fire. Two bullets hit the man who had shot Tanner. They were head shots. Hunter hit the floor with a breath-expelling thump. Khan was sitting in the far corner of the compartment, his head bowed, the device on his lap. His hands were shaking so badly his fingers slipped off one of the buttons he needed to hold down. The digital readout stopped. His head was throbbing, he knew death was only moments away. He tried to press the button again. Badonovitch stepped over Albatha and opened fire. His Glock was on automatic. Four shots hit Khan in the chest, knocking him back against the compartment wall, killing him instantly. The device fell onto the floor. Akbar lifted his AK-74 when Badonovitch shifted aim and both pulled their triggers at the same time. Badonovitch was hit in the top of his left arm, the bullet slicing through his muscle. However, it did nothing to affect his aim. Two rounds shattered Akbar's right shoulder. A further two blew his face apart.

'Clear,' Badonovitch yelled loudly.

Hunter lay still, facing the man he'd shot. A second man appeared, pulling the trigger of his AK-74 which was on fully automatic. He was screaming '*Allah Akbar*'. The bullets went high, while Hunter's smashed into the man's chest. The man hit the door, throwing it open, blocking the men in the third cabin who were now coming through the door. They were firing wildly at waist height. They had been sitting with their cabin lights on when it went dark. They had no night vision and could see nothing. Their shots knocked the door closed, giving Hunter a clear sight. Kaman Al-Zawahiri was in front. Hunter shot him in the chest. The Arab went flying backwards, knocking the other man off his feet. The man lay on his back, the soles of his shoes pointing along the corridor. Hunter emptied his gun into the man's crotch, the bullets travelled through the guard's body and stomach and lodged in his heart. He took a few seconds to die. Suddenly, it was all over. There were yells and screams coming from the other compartments, some calling in French, others in German and others in English. Pushing himself to his feet Hunter ignored the commotion and stepped into the cabin.

Just then, an attendant who was berthed in a small cubby-hole at the back of the carriage, switched on the emergency lighting, supplied by a bank of batteries.

As Hunter removed his night-vision goggles he recognised the device as being similar to the previous one. On the floor was an empty case. He looked at the dial on the front. His guts churned and his stomach muscles tightened. Khan had set it going. From the look of it, it would explode in ten minutes and forty-five seconds. Why he hadn't set the thing off Hunter had no idea. Panic, he guessed. It was easily done. Or maybe he hadn't had time to turn the dial all the way to zero.

Badonovitch, who had been checking his American friend, said, 'Doug's dead, boss.'

'Bugger!' Hunter spotted the blood seeping down Badonovitch's arm. 'Are you okay?

'I'm okay. Just a flesh wound.'

'Shut that lot up and get everyone off the train and get moving.' Glancing at the display he said 'We've got ten minutes to get as far away as possible before this sodding thing goes off.'

'What about you?' Albatha asked.

'Someone's got to try and defuse the bastard. Come on, move it. Get the sleeper attendant. Tell him what he needs to do.'

'He's here,' said Albatha, looking along the corridor at the man hurrying towards them, doing up his blue tunic, his hat perched on his head. He was speaking loudly and wildly in Italian. In view of what had just happened, either the man was very brave or plain stupid.

The team knew the attendant spoke English and Badonovitch said in a loud voice, 'There is a bomb. We must get everyone off and as far away as possible.'

'No! No! We must stay here and I will contact the police. You will all be arrested.'

Albatha pointed his gun at the attendant and said, 'No, we leave and we leave now. We are special forces working for the government. That is the dirty bomb we have been looking for. So it is time to go. Now hurry!' The last command was yelled.

The attendant gulped and nodded. He didn't need any more persuading. He rushed along the corridor telling the passengers to get their shoes on and to depart the train immediately. There was a bomb. He did not say it was nuclear.

'Come on, boss,' said Badonovitch.

'Get lost, Jan. I'll see you later.'

'Come on, Nick,' said Samantha. 'We can't do much more.'

'I said go. That's an order. No arguments.'

Hunter looked at Badonovitch who nodded. He knew better than to argue. He grabbed Samantha's hand and dragged her with him.

Hunter yelled after them, 'Don't let the train driver back up. Stop him, use threats if you have to, but get everyone out of the tunnel.'

From his coat pocket, Hunter withdrew the neoprene-wrapped tools and broke the sail makers string. He sat on

433

the bunk with the device in his lap. He ignored the two bodies as he sat contemplating the case for a few seconds. He turned it over. As he expected the cover was held in place with four screws. He took the screwdriver and set to work. Each screw came loose quickly and easily. Next, he forced the tip of the screwdriver into one corner and prised the cover up about a centimetre. He took a pencil torch, switched it on and peered inside. One wire was attached to the cover on the other side. It was booby-trapped.

43

'Move it, you people,' Badonovitch yelled. 'Move it! There's a bomb. Hurry.'

The message had even penetrated the brains of the intoxicated who stumbled along the tracks in fearful panic. One woman was carrying a young baby in her arms and was holding the hand of a little girl who was crying as she stumbled over the railway sleepers.

'Samantha, take the baby,' yelled Badonovitch.

Samantha snatched the baby from its mother's arms while Badonovitch scooped up the little girl. 'Don't worry,' she yelled to the mother, 'just concentrate on running.'

The woman nodded. Ahead, they could see the lights of the train moving slowly towards them. A man was walking in front, swinging a torch. Badonovitch was the first to reach him.

'Here, take the child,' he thrust the little girl into the arms of a startled attendant. 'Get these people on board fast while I tell the driver to get the hell out of here.'

'No! No! I cannot! I cannot!' The attendant wailed. 'We must go back. To the missing carriage. Take the child. Here!' He thrust his arms out, holding the screaming child under her armpits.

But Badonovitch was already running alongside the

train which had now stopped. The other passengers were arriving and scrambling to get onto the train, pushing and shoving, completely panicked. Some of that panic instilled itself into the attendant and he dropped the child and started doing the same.

Using her free arm, Samantha bent down, picked up the little girl and shouted to the mother, 'Come on. We'll try another carriage.'

The woman nodded, unable to speak, sobbing and gasping for breath at the same time. Only two doors along nobody was trying to climb into the train. Samantha stood on the bottom step and wrenched open the door. Awkwardly, she jumped up into the carriage and then turned round to help the mother.

'You okay?'

'Yes! Yes, thank you. Oh, thank you.'

'Don't thank me yet. We need to get out of here.'

The driver had his head out of the window, trying to see what was happening. He thought he could see people on the tracks. He had stopped the train because the torch was no longer waving back and forth and so had thought that perhaps they had reached the end carriage. Why didn't that idiot of a guard come and explain matters to him? And who was this running alongside the train?

Badonovitch stopped, looked up at the man and asked, 'You speak English?'

'Yes. What is happening?'

'There is a dirty bomb on the train. We must get away. Now! Go!'

The driver hesitated for only a moment, nodded and said, 'Come up here.' He pushed open the door he had been leaning out of. Badonovitch climbed into the cab as the train moved forward.

'I suggest you go as quickly as possible. We've about five minutes before the bomb explodes.'

* * * * *

Turning the device around, Hunter gently lifted the opposite corner and took a long and careful look. It was similar to the first device. If he lifted the cover off, the wire would accelerate the timing device and it would explode instantaneously. He held the torch between his teeth and aimed it inside the device. Carefully reaching inside with the pair of wire cutters, he snipped the wire. While he worked he couldn't help rationalising to himself why he had not gone with the others. It had been the result of a recent discussion he'd had with Macnair. They were both fully aware of what it would mean if the device exploded in the tunnel. Deaths and contamination would be at a minimum. The best they could possibly have hoped for. But the fact that it had happened would ratchet up the fear out of all proportion. Retaliation would be off the scale, beyond belief. But *if* it didn't explode and emphasis was given to the vast amount of help received from Muslim governments around the world, then maybe, just maybe, they would be able to weather the storm. Or at least prevent it from intensifying. So there was more at stake than just his life. Even so, he still wasn't a kamikaze. He hoped.

Lifting off the cover, he put it to one side and sat looking at the insides of the device. Like all such pieces of kit it was fundamentally a basic mechanism. A timer operated by batteries, through to an arming mechanism and the detonator. All he could see was the clock ticking down on the outside casing and the housing for the detonator on the inside.

Now there was the second booby-trap to deal with. He mentally shook himself. It's identical to the first device that the Americans had sorted, he told himself. Identical! Get on with it! The clock showed he had just over four minutes to complete the task. Enough time, thought Hunter. The Americans had taken hours to defuse the first device because they had taken x-ray after x-ray of gradually longer exposure. This gave them a picture right through to the core. As a result, he knew that the inner core of plutonium was only a centimetre in diameter and surrounded by a lead shield. After all, no scientist in his right mind would want to be tampering with the stuff if he was going to die of radiation poisoning soon after.

The second booby-trap was similar to the first but was attached to the bottom of the detonator. He placed the long-nose screwdriver into the two slots on either side of the detonator housing and turned it anti-clockwise. It moved smoothly and easily. He quickly finished unscrewing the cap and checked it could be lifted out. Now came the tricky bit. He glanced at the timer. There was still one minute and twenty-nine seconds left.

The wire allowed about three millimetres of space between the bottom of the detonator casing and the housing for the plastic explosive. If he lifted the detonator out too far the circuit would complete, the detonator would be aimed into the plastic explosive and be close enough to set it off. He could jerk it away and hope for the best meaning that if he moved fast enough the plastic explosive wouldn't go off. However, the blast from the detonator would certainly blow his hand to pieces. Apart from that, if he wasn't fast enough, the plastic explosive would detonate and that would be that.

He placed the wire cutters on the floor next to his right foot. Using his right hand he very carefully lifted the detonator housing up until he had a space of about two millimetres. He slipped the nail of his left thumb into the gap and put his index finger on the top, pressing down, holding it in place. Reaching for the cutters, he placed them on the rim of the hole, parted the handles and slid them inside. He gently closed the blades, felt a slight resistance and then they shut together. Unhesitatingly, he took hold of the detonator casing and lifted it free. He sat with the device in his left hand, the detonator housing in his right and he looked at the timer. He still had twelve seconds to go.

Nick sat like that for some time. His mind was frozen. Slowly at first, but building momentum, came the thought that he'd done it. He'd done it! He put the device down on the bunk, the detonator next to it and reached into his pocket for his mobile. There was no signal which shouldn't have come as a surprise considering how far underground he was. The General could wait.

Hunter stood, looked at the two bodies and stepped into the corridor. He knelt by Tanner's body. 'Bye, old friend. It won't be the same without you.' He threw a blanket over Tanner's body and stood up.

He moved further along the corridor, looking into the compartments until he found what he wanted. He threw away the contents of a half empty glass, poured in some brandy, added ice from a well-insulated ice-bucket and topped the glass up with soda. He took a mouthful of the drink and then sat sipping it, unwinding after the tension, not just of the last hour or so, but of the whole damned operation.

He was on his third glass when Badonovitch, Albatha

and Samantha returned to the carriage about twenty minutes later.

'You okay?' Samantha asked.

'Couldn't be better,' Nick said. 'What brings you three back?'

'There was no explosion so we figured it was safe to return,' Samantha replied.

Badonovitch said, 'I phoned the General. He said he'd already seen to things. NATO personnel are on the way together with a specialist engineer. He'll take charge of the device. Swiss army are also on their way. We have to take the bodies to the base outside Munich in one of the helicopters. He'll have a Hercules waiting for us.'

'Anything else?'

'I don't think so.'

'How's the arm?'

'I'll live,' Badonovitch stopped speaking.

'I know . . . Doug. Of all the lousy things to happen,' said Hunter. 'He was a great man and a good friend.' There was silence for a few seconds. 'Anyone want any brandy?'

All three nodded.

'I'll find some glasses,' Samantha said. She was back in a few moments and poured the drinks. Badonovitch and Albatha took theirs neat. Samantha added ice and soda. The four of them sat resting, heads back, not speaking, sipping the brandy. There was nothing left to say, not yet, anyway. The adrenaline rush was wearing off fast. They stirred when they heard voices outside the carriage. The Swiss army had arrived and with them came the men from NATO and the engineering specialist from Aldermaston dressed in a full anti-radiation suit. He held a monitor over the device, pronounced himself satisfied and took his hood off.

440

Other NATO personnel joined them, along with a Major from the Swiss army who organised body bags to take away the dead.

'Are we finished?' Hunter asked. 'Good, then let's go. Where are the helicopters?'

The journey to Rosyth was uneventful, with the four of them sleeping most of the way. When they landed at Edinburgh airport, transport was waiting for them. A base ambulance was there to transport their dead friend's body.

Hunter reported to the General. 'How's the ankle, sir?' was the inane greeting he opened with.

'Getting better. A fine job, my boy. A very fine job.'

'Thank you, sir. Losing Doug Tanner was a bitter blow.'

'Yes, it was that. He'll be a very hard man to replace. I gather his body has been taken to the chapel?'

'Yes, sir' Hunter frowned. 'Where is everyone? The base is empty.'

'Scattered across Europe. Thanks to Isobel, GCHQ and ECHELON, we discovered a lot of people plotting terrorist attacks of one form or another. Once the nuke exploded, they intended to carry out atrocity after atrocity in every major city. We've uncovered dozens of planned attacks that would have resulted in many deaths.'

'And what about the MP? If it wasn't for him, Doug and probably thousands . . .', Nick paused.

'MI5 are keeping a discreet eye on him in case he tries to make a run for it,' General Macnair explained.

'Is that likely, sir?'

'We've no idea. So far, it doesn't look as though he intends to. But you never know.' Looking at his watch,

Macnair added, 'It's 18.00. Time for the bar. I'd like to buy you a large drink.'

'That's very kind of you, sir, but I'd like to call my parents first. Also, I could do with a shower and a change of clothes. Can we meet in an hour?'

'By all means.'

Hunter left the office and crossed to the officers' accommodation block. Once he was there, he sat on the edge of his bed and rang his parents.

'Hi, Dad.'

'Hi, son. You okay?' Tim Hunter asked.

'Sure. I just wanted to let you know that I'm back in Rosyth.'

There was no disguising the relief in his father's voice.

'Thank God for that. We've been listening to the news. The bomb being found. Know anything about it?'

Nick said, 'I found it.' It was a simple understatement of staggering proportions.

'Somehow, I am not surprised. When will you be coming home?'

'As soon as possible. There's a lot of noise in the background.'

'Yes, half the family's here. Your mother's gone up to the supermarket. I'll tell her you called.'

'Thanks, Dad. I'll call again later.'

Instead of a shower, Nick relaxed in a hot bath, listening to the news on the radio. It was all about the nuclear device. When the water began to get cold he climbed out, shaved and dressed. A little while later he went down to the wardroom where the General, Albatha and Walsh were standing at the bar. Macnair put a large malt, with ice and a dash of soda, into Hunter's hand.

'I've agreed with Zim's boss that he can stay for a few

442

days,' said the General. 'He's going to help us with some of the clean-up jobs. Tomorrow, Owens and Summers arrive to discuss where we go from here and I want you to join us at 14.00 Nick.'

'Aye, aye, sir.' Nick replied. The General was never off duty, no matter what he was doing.

It was inevitable that they talked about the situation facing Europe in particular and the rest of the world in general.

Hunter made a valid point when he said, 'What about ordinary Muslims? How in hell are we going to get peace back? Listening to the news on the radio, the attacks and riots are still going on as badly as they have been for the last week or so.'

Macnair sighed. 'It will take time. I suspect a great deal of time. Though you're wrong, it's not as bad as it was a couple of days ago. But you're also right about what is, in reality, an even bigger issue. The bitterness and hatred across the whole of the continent is deep and wide. Perhaps we'll never fully recover. It's impossible to tell.'

'There have been thousands of arrests, Walsh added, 'both of Muslims and white people of all ages and both sexes. Every police cell in the country is at bursting point.'

'That can't last,' said Hunter.

The General said, 'From what I can gather, many of them will be set free in the course of the next few days and told to go home, behave and get back to normal. Of course, you will still have the idiots fomenting unrest, but that's inevitable. The fact that they are on both sides of the fence means that we have twice as much to deal with.'

At that point Isobel joined them. 'I've not come for a drink,' she said, excitedly, refusing the offer of a gin and tonic. 'We have confirmation of the whereabouts of Prince Khaled Aziz.'

'Oh?' Macnair lifted a quizzical eyebrow.

'Yes, at his palace on Qishrān Island.'

'Are we sure?'

'Positive, sir. There's a meeting taking place. From the guest-list it looks like a Who's Who of the Islamic terrorist world. There are men from here, the US, parts of Europe, Africa, the Far East and the Middle East. Everywhere.'

'How many?' asked a thoughtful Macnair.

'One hundred and forty seven,' Isobel confirmed.

'Hmm. This is too good a chance to miss. When?'

'Eight days from now.'

'Any indication of staff numbers? Other visitors?'

'Staff no, but he'll have plenty we know. Other visitors? Such as who?'

'Not to put too fine a point on it, prostitutes and little boys,' the General replied.

'Oh, I see. There doesn't appear to be anyone but we'll keep checking. I wasn't sure what you'd want to do about it, but Gareth has downloaded detailed plans of the island and the buildings. They're on your desk.'

'Thank you. Hiram, Nick, you know what's required. Work on it tomorrow.'

'Yes, sir,' they chorused.

'Now, Isobel, about that drink,' Malcolm smiled at her. She settled for a gin and tonic.

It was then that Samantha Freemantle joined them. To Hunter's way of thinking, she looked ravishing. When asked, she opted for a horse's neck with ice. The gong sounded for dinner and just as they were trooping through to the dining room Matt Dunston appeared. In spite of what the future did or didn't hold, much of the evening was spent dawdling over dinner, with a glass or two of palatable wine. The meal ended with a vintage port with cheese and biscuits. Afterwards, in the bar, Hunter flirted outrageously with Samantha. She, in return, gave him cause for hope. It was a tantalising prospect. When he finally went to his pit, Hunter was slightly the worse for wear, something he rarely experienced.

The following morning he was up bright and early, running off his hangover. He followed this with his usual series of katas and, having worked up a good sweat, returned to shower and climb into his uniform. After breakfast, he spent the morning with Hiram Walsh. The two men pored over the plans of the island where Khaled Aziz was to be found. An initial strategy was quickly agreed and they worked on the detail until lunchtime. At 14.00 precisely Hunter presented himself at Macnair's office. Clive Owens of MI5 and William Summers of MI6 had already arrived.

'Good work,' Owens said as Nick entered.

'Thank you, sir.'

'Yes, let me add my congratulations as well,' said Summers, then he added, 'I take it you know why we've asked you to join us?'

Hunter shook his head.

'We've been discussing how to deal with Saddiq Ali,' Macnair said.

'That's correct,' said Owens. 'We can clearly demonstrate the man's involvement but we are unable to prosecute him because of the way we acquired the information. Also, truth to tell, there would be little appetite for such a prosecution, especially amongst our political masters. The potential fallout would be devastating for this party in particular and for politics in general. Worse, of course, is that if we show a Muslim MP was involved then there won't be another Muslim in Parliament for a hundred years. It will also stir things up even more when we are desperately trying to calm matters down.' He shook his head, as though wishing to deny the facts, even to himself. 'At the moment, it's one hell of an uphill struggle. Imagine what it would be like if Ali's involvement was public knowledge.'

Summers said, 'That's the *legal* side of matters. Now we come to another side.' He nodded at Owens.

'I have here a detailed report on Saddiq Ali's current whereabouts and his movements this coming weekend. It makes fascinating reading. You'll also find the keycard useful. I have prepared the information myself. There are no copies.'

Hunter took the file with a puzzled frown. A quick flick through told him all he needed to know, however, and he nodded. 'I see. May I ask who, apart 'from we' four, is aware of what we plan to do?'

'Not a single soul,' Macnair replied.

'There is one thing, and it's up to you,' said Summers. 'How do you feel about having Samantha Freemantle with you? As back-up?'

Nick thought about it for a few seconds. He shook his head. 'I'll deal with it alone.'

Summers nodded. 'As you wish.'

They spent the next hour discussing the assignment further. The heads of MI5 and MI6 professed themselves satisfied and stood up to leave. The men of the security services were in revolt once again.

44

After they'd gone, Macnair asked, 'Any questions Nick?'

'No, sir. I'll see to it. If it's convenient, will you accompany me to Hiram's office? We'd like to go over our plans for Khaled Aziz.'

Macnair nodded and climbed to his feet, lifting his walking stick. 'Blasted thing.' Whether he was referring to his foot, the stick, or both, Hunter didn't know.

The plans of the island and the surrounding area had been scanned into a computer linked to a projector. Walsh opened proceedings with an overview of the island. He went through point by point until he said, 'Nick will you explain about HMS *Atherstone*.'

Hunter leaned back in his chair and said, 'The *Atherstone* is now in the Eastern Mediterranean on a goodwill visit to Cyprus. We propose she makes a second goodwill trip to Jeddah. Our ships call in there from time to time, especially as the Saudis are our biggest customers in the arms trade.'

'That's very true. It would also be useful in showing the world how we are willing to let bygones be bygones. Bridge-building is the order of the day,' Macnair said.

'*Atherstone* has all the gear our teams need. We can fly as many people as we wish into Jeddah. After all, it has one of the busiest airports in the world, with all the visitors

447

who pass through on their way to Mecca.' Hunter aimed a remote control at the projector and flicked the picture back to an Admiralty chart of the area. He stood up, walked over to the wall screen and pointed. 'As we know, the palace is on an island one hundred miles along the coast. *Atherstone* gets a three day visit to Jeddah showing the flag, holding cocktail parties, doing the usual and then, on the afternoon of the third day, departs. They are offshore the island at about zero two hundred. The team goes in quiet and careful. If there are any guards about Isobel ought to be able to identify their whereabouts. We take them out. The amount of explosives we need is significant but we ought to be able to get plenty from Cyprus. If you look at these architectural plans of the place,' Hunter flicked screens, 'you can see what we think are the main load-bearing walls and pillars. Of course, we can check that with an architect.'

'Leave that to me,' said Macnair.

Flicking back to the plan of the island, Hunter pointed. 'Again, using Isobel and the satellite pictures, we can establish if the beach here has any lookouts. We can spend the next week watching what they do. We can check if they patrol the palace, the island, or even use boats to patrol around the shores. It gives us time to build a picture of the place.'

'Except it might all change when the other men get there,' said Macnair.

'That's so,' said Walsh. 'But then flexibility, as always, is the name of the game.'

'How many in the team?'

Hunter replied, 'Hiram and I discussed that. Sixteen. The *Atherstone* goes in slowly until she's about three miles off-shore. We've had a sliver of luck. According to the

Nautical Almanac, at that time there won't be any moon. Moonrise isn't until 07.38 and then it'll be full.'

'Thank God for small mercies,' said Macnair. 'Inflatables?'

'Six,' Hunter said.

'Why so many?', asked the General.

'We go in with the team plus as much gear as they can handle. The Geminis return to the ship while the beach is checked and we ensure there's no one there. The *Atherstone*'s crew ferry the remainder of the gear. While they do so, the team heads for the palace. Slow and easy they take out any guards. While doing so, they plant what explosives they're carrying. All being well, the ship's crew bring up the rear with the rest of the equipment.'

'It sounds like a lot of explosives,' said Macnair, thoughtfully.

'It is,' replied Walsh. 'We need to raze the place to the ground. Not a brick left standing. Everyone inside killed. Send a message to them that we won't tolerate any more attacks on the West.' He shrugged and added, 'Not that it'll do any good. The fanatics will keep coming.'

On that gloomy note they continued to the end of the briefing. Attack time would be 05.00, the darkest hour before dawn.

Macnair nodded. 'I'll speak to Admiralty. We'll make a fuss about the goodwill visit with the press. How we are all working together for the good of humanity. That there is no animosity between us and Muslims in general. You know, the usual stuff. Which happens to be true. Right, leave this with me. Hiram, you and I will pick the team. You'll be going on the *Atherstone* to co-ordinate the op.' He turned to Hunter, 'You'd better get off. And good hunting.'

'Thank you, sir,' said Hunter as he stood to leave the

office. 'Incidentally, what's happening to Doug's body? And to the bodies of our two who died in Tunisia?'

'The bodies off the *Atherstone* have been flown to Glasgow where they will be handed over to their families.'

'Could we . . .?'

'Already taken care of under the guise of a special insurance policy.'

'Thank you, sir. And Doug?'

'In accordance with his wishes, he's to be cremated and his ashes scattered over the Forth. He's specified he's paying for his wake and has asked that the rest of his money goes to a service charity. I can't remember which one, but it's in his will. The funeral won't be until the teams return.'

Hunter nodded. As he reached the door, the General called out to him. 'Incidentally, I've put you up for a gong.'

Hunter, his hand on the doorknob, stopped in complete shock. 'I beg your pardon?'

'A gong. The George Cross, to be precise. You deserve it after what you did.'

'Thank you, sir,' Hunter said, faintly.

Back in his cabin, Nick called his uncle in London. After the usual greetings, his uncle, as always, asked Hunter when was he going to quit serving his country and serve the company instead. As always, Hunter gave his standard reply of one day. He then asked his uncle for a favour which was immediately granted. Next, he packed his gear. He collected various pieces of kit from the armoury, as well as a diving set from the store. He packed his MG Roadster and was on the road soon after six o'clock, heading for Glasgow, then the M74. The motorway north was still jammed with vehicles moving slowly. The road south was getting busier as people decided it was safe to return to their homes in London and the south-east. The message seemed to be sinking in.

Nick broke his journey that night at the Hilton Park Travelodge but he was up early the following morning, eager to reach his destination and avoid heavy traffic. He still had the best part of two hundred miles to go. Near Bristol, he followed the sign to an out-of-town retail park, where he found an electrical goods store. There, he bought three identical digital cameras, each with a wide-lens option and a tripod. As the day was pleasantly warm, he took down the car's roof before continuing. It was early evening by the time he reached the hill at the top of Dartmouth. He always felt a twinge of nostalgia as he approached. It was fourteen years earlier that he had joined Dartmouth Naval College on the journey to becoming a Royal Naval officer. Who would have thought he'd end up like he had?

He stopped outside a supermarket and made a phone call. He was relieved to be told the boatyard had received a fax to expect him. His family kept a 40ft cabin cruiser on the Dart, at Dittisham. It was ideal for his requirements. She had already been taken off the slips and put in the water. Named *Saint Louis*, after the American city where his mother's family had settled back in the 1890s, she was fast and comfortable. He drove into the town and booked into the Dart Marina Hotel.

In the file was the information that Saddiq Ali would be arriving later that evening and staying at the Dart Marina Hotel. Being ahead of your quarry was a huge advantage. People on the run looked over their shoulder, not ahead of them. Nick sorted out what he needed and went up a floor to the MP's room. The corridor was empty. He let himself into the room with the keycard supplied by MI5. The layout was virtually identical to his room. It took him only moments to plant two listening bugs. He stuck one behind the bed's headrest. The other was placed under the coffee table. He departed the room less than a minute and a half after entering.

In that part of Devon there appeared to have been very little trouble. It was an oasis of calm and peace, where people were trying to get on with their lives.

Although it was almost six o'clock in the evening when he finally arrived at the yard he found the owner still there. The owner was sixty-five if he was a day and still going strong. When asked why he didn't retire he always replied, 'To what? The old trout has enough hours in the day as it is to nag me. Any more would drive me crazy.'

'Hullo, sir,' he said in his soft Devonshire burr.

'Hullo Fred. And I've told you before. You must call me Nick,' Hunter said to the man in oil-stained overalls.

Fred looked over towards the *Saint Louis*. 'She's been checked over and is watered, fuelled and ready for departure.'

'Thanks, Fred.' In the background he could hear her two engines throbbing gently. Together, they carried Hunter's bags and groceries down to the landing stage. Nick climbed aboard and Fred passed over the stuff.

'Give me a shout when you're ready to leave and I'll come down and let go the ropes,' he said.

'Thanks again, Fred. I'll manage. Don't trouble yourself.'

'No trouble. If you need me, I'll be in the shed.'

Nick stowed the groceries away and switched on the coffee percolator. He checked out the Calor gas bottles, went aft to take a look at the small inflatable hidden away in its central stowage and finally, mug of coffee in hand, he went up top. In the cockpit, he unclipped the canopy and put it in its stowage. He stood for a few minutes casting his eyes over the instruments. The tachometers were in the right bracket for idling, the oil pressure gauges and engine temperatures were correct, the diesel and fresh-water gauges showed full. He flipped the bilge pumps on, heard them working and, as he expected, saw no water being pumped out. Finally, he switched on the echo sounder. He had three metres of water beneath the keel. Nick stepped onto the landing stage, removed the bow and stern ropes and threw them onboard. Taking the breast rope in hand, he stepped back onto the deck, pushing the boat away as he did so. Immediately, the gentle current of the river began to pull the boat away from the stage. Back in the cockpit, Hunter pushed the gear levers from idle into slow ahead and added a few revs. The boat swung effortlessly out from the berth and moved sedately downstream. He needed a boat for one simple reason. Saddiq Ali had the use of one.

The river was in ebb, a gentle breeze in his face. He kept her at a sedate pace, with enough way on to give him steerage. It was a peaceful and beautiful evening. Two miles and twenty minutes later he was opposite the college sitting majestically on the hilltop, dominating the town.

He turned the boat to face upstream and approached the buoy he'd arranged to use. As the buoy came down the port side, he reached over with a boat hook, hooked the eye on the top of the buoy and lifted it out of the water. He grabbed the securing rope, took it forward and connected it to the bow cleat. In the cockpit he cut the engines. Peace descended on the *Saint Louis*.

MI5 had done an excellent job. Their intelligence

confirmed that Saddiq Ali had recently taken possession of a sailing yacht, moored on the other side of the river from the town, opposite where Hunter now sat. The yacht, called *The Temperance*, was an Oyster 38, ocean-going, sleek, and a great vessel in the hands of a competent skipper and crew. Ali was not known as a yachtsman. According to MI5, the yacht had been the only boat available at short notice to get the MP out of Britain. It belonged to a wealthy businessman in Hounslow who was not only Pakistani but a supporter of Ali.

A crew of two was expected to join him. Both men were known to be Muslim fundamentalists but had only recently been introduced to Ali.

On this operation, Hunter had not shared his *modus operandi* with anyone and that included the General. This hit was going to be kept as private as he could make it.

Hunter spent some time setting up two of the cameras and making sure they were secure. They faced forward with their field of vision slightly overlapping. The result was an angle of coverage of about 260 degrees from the boat's bows out to the horizon. The third camera was set at head height and was pointed at the cockpit. He checked the pictures, made adjustments and was eventually satisfied. Next, he made a bacon sandwich, poured another coffee and lounged in the cockpit, enjoying the sunshine.

He looked up at the college, the memories flooding back. He had thoroughly enjoyed his time there; even the pomp and ceremony had been instructive. He had learned to dive in the river, using a compressed air breathing kit then, five years later, he had specialised as a Mine Warfare and Clearance Diving Officer, which had led him to TIFAT.

He put on a set of headphones to reduce background

454

noise and switched on the receiver to the frequency of the bugs in the hotel. Dead silence. Settling down on the comfortable bench in the cockpit he leaned back. The lapping of the water against the hull, along with the gentle rocking of the boat, lulled him into a deep, peaceful sleep. An hour later he came wide awake. It was a trick he had learned over the years from his time at sea. Being called to go on watch and again as the Commanding Officer of a minehunter required quick responses day and night. He sat up and looked around. Nothing had changed apart from the fact that the sun was setting. Looking across the water, he could see that the streets were packed with people, the roadside tables full, and the doorways of the pubs had their usual quota of smokers. He'd give it another hour.

Sliding the *Saint Louis*'s inflatable into the water, he climbed down, started the 10hp outboard and pottered across the river towards *The Temperance*. He placed two listening bugs on the hull beneath the rubbing strake. One was about a third of the way along from the bows, the other near the cockpit at the stern. Crossing the river, he tied up at a landing place close to the hotel.

Back in his hotel room he switched on the receiver and put it on loudspeaker. Still total silence. Taking a shower, he lay down on the bed and dozed fitfully. He came wide awake when he heard a faint noise on the speaker. A door closing. Another opening. A toilet being flushed. Then a voice, evidently on a phone, probably a mobile.

'I shall meet you tonight in the bar. Yes, nine thirty will do fine.'

The voice ceased and all Hunter could hear were the sounds associated with a single occupant in a hotel room. He looked at his watch. It was just on 20.45. He switched frequencies and heard voices speaking Urdu. There were men on the yacht.

A short while later, dressed in a smart cream-coloured suit and brown shirt, Hunter appeared in the hotel bar. He ordered a pint of alcohol-free beer and took a seat near the door. The room was half full. Hunter slipped an earpiece into his right ear and placed a small black box on the table in front of him.

Saddiq Ali MP came in just before 21.30. He was elegantly dressed in a grey suit, his well-cut jacket hiding the paunch that was beginning to develop. Ali ordered a large gin and tonic and sat at a table nearby. Hunter turned the black box until the microphone pointed at the MP.

Within minutes two other Middle Eastern-looking men appeared and joined Ali. Their handshakes were brief, their greetings cordial. They were both in their early twenties, slim to the point of emaciation, but fit-looking at the same time. Ali ordered drinks, orange juice for the two men, same again for him.

'Is everything ready?' Ali asked.

'Yes, my friend. We have been on the yacht. We sail from here tomorrow afternoon. The ship will be twenty miles south of Land's End by dawn the next day. We will arrive at about that time.'

Ali said, 'Curse the men who stopped us. May God cast them into the fires of hell to be damned for all time.'

'It is a shame, my friend,' said the first speaker, 'but we have still achieved much. Look at the hatred we have stirred up and the distrust that now exists between Muslims and the infidels. We can build on that. It may take time but we will succeed. Perhaps not in our lifetimes but Allah is patient.'

Saddiq Ali grinned without humour. 'I would have

wished for it in my lifetime. There is, I think, still time. We must start again. That is all there is to it. Someday we will detonate a nuclear bomb in London and not just a dirty bomb! I will see to that!'

45

Hunter's concentration wandered, always a problem when eavesdropping for too long, and he was forced to focus his attention again when Saddiq Ali laughed and commented, 'It will be like the *Marie Celeste*.' He just shook his head when his two colleagues wanted to know what he was talking about.

'It is time we had dinner,' announced Ali. He stood up and the other two followed.

Hunter stayed where he was. He didn't want to spook them. He had heard enough to know that they would not be running away that night. The Saudi oil tanker, currently berthed in Plymouth, would not be in position until the morning after.

Nick stayed long enough to have a second pint and was back in his room before Ali returned at midnight. He sat listening to the bugging device on the yacht. The voices were speaking in Urdu. Hunter wished he could understand what they were saying.

Returning to the *Saint Louis* he changed into his wetsuit. He slung his oxygen re-breather diving set over his shoulders and put the equipment he wanted in the diving pouches on either hip. He sat for two minutes, breathing pure oxygen to cleanse his body of carbon dioxide and nitrogen, then slipped over the side of the boat into the Dart. He checked the compass bearing of the yacht, used his hands to sink down a couple of metres and then flipped over into the horizontal position, the compass and depth gauge board held in front of him. At that time of the morning and on such a dark night, he knew he was being over-cautious using his diving gear, but with so much at stake, he wasn't prepared to take the chance. It took him just three minutes to cross the river and reach the yacht.

Nick spent a little time kneading about one pound of plastic explosives into the joint between the rudder and the hull. When he had done so, he pushed in the detonator connected to an electronic receiver. The charge could be exploded from a distance of about one mile by sending the signal through the water. He surfaced at the stern. From what he had seen of the two men, they appeared to be true to their religion and were teetotal. Cautiously, he pulled himself up hand over hand using the railings. He went very slowly, ensuring the boat stayed steady. At the hatch leading below he fed in a thin plastic tube. It was connected to a bottle of compressed Kolokol-1, a Russian opiate-derived incapacitating agent. The drug was very fast acting and would render someone unconscious for up to six hours.

Hunter waited for ten minutes before opening the doors and sliding back the hatch. A quick search revealed the men in cabins up for'ard. They were both unconscious. The radio was in the chart house next to the hatch. He unscrewed the back of it, put in some plastic explosive with the same kind of electronic detonator he had used on the rudder, and replaced the cover. Next, he searched the cupboards for any signs of weapons. He found none. Standing in the main saloon, he examined the deck for any loose planks. Using his diving knife, he prised a plank up and grinned. Two Kalashnikovs nestled between the ribs. He took each weapon in turn and using his knife, deactivated the firing pins. Nick retreated out of the yacht and closed the doors and hatch behind him. Slipping over the stern, he left the surface and returned to the *Saint Louis* on the reciprocal bearing. He climbed back on board, stripped, showered and changed and then returned to the hotel for a good night's sleep, or what was left of it.

In the morning, Hunter had an early breakfast, paid his hotel bill, bought the Saturday edition of the *Telegraph* and that week's *Time* magazine, along with a carton of milk, and went down to the inflatable. It took only minutes to climb on board the *Saint Louis* and stow the dinghy away.

It was just after 08.00 and the day had dawned bright and sunny. A slight sea mist was at the river mouth, already being burnt away by the sun. There was a steady, warm breeze from the east, which meant it was ideal for the yacht sailing westwards. Hunter made some coffee and sat in the cockpit reading. The listening device was tuned into the MP's room. Ali didn't stir until after ten o'clock. He rang room service and ordered fresh orange juice, coffee and scrambled eggs on toast.

The rest of the morning passed quietly. The two men on *The Temperance* came ashore, made some purchases in the local shop and returned to the yacht. They made no attempt to contact Ali.

At midday Hunter flashed up the engines and let them warm through. A short while later he released the buoy and headed downstream. He would stay ahead of his quarry until he made his move. He put the listening device tuned to the yacht on loudspeaker and headed south towards Start Point. About a mile and a half from Dartmouth the sounds of the men on the yacht deteriorated rapidly and were quickly lost. He turned around and headed back north, this time at less than a quarter of the speed, the boat just maintaining steerageway. Gradually, the sounds from the yacht become louder. The men were calling to each other, preparing to get underway, Hunter guessed.

There was silence for some time until Ali climbed on board from the dinghy and asked for help with his bag and a hand up for himself.

'Are we ready?' Ali enquired.

'Yes, we can go. Start the engine Siraj.'

Near the mouth of the Dart, Hunter turned the boat and started south again. He set the automatic pilot on a heading of 190° at a speed of five knots and kept watch for the yacht coming out of the river mouth. He had the radar operating and set to give a warning bleep should any vessel be on a heading that brought it within one mile of the *Saint Louis*.

The yacht appeared and turned onto a southerly heading, following a mile astern of the power boat. The two Pakistanis were busy hoisting the mainsail and jib. The yacht changed direction by a few degrees which would take her closer inshore but it was a better course with the wind coming from the east. He marked the yacht's position on his radar and did the same again exactly six minutes later. Measuring the distance travelled he calculated the yacht was doing 5.8 knots. The wind speed was showing on the anemometer as ten knots which meant the two men certainly knew how to sail.

The sea was flat calm, the sun shone, the barometric

pressure was high, the temperature was in the mid-twenties. It was an ideal day to be on the water. Hunter kept ahead of the yacht, watching her as she tacked and jibed back and forth, accurately following a base course. She was an imposing sight, and received many admiring waves from other boat users. The men on *The Temperance* ignored such friendly overtures.

Hunter kept the *Saint Louis* on automatic and merely tweaked the compass dial when he wanted to alter course. The afternoon wore on slowly. At 16.00 Hunter had Start Point four miles abeam while the *The Temperance* was still one mile astern but nearly two miles closer inshore. Rounding the Point, the yacht tacked 40° to starboard and thanks to an increase in the late afternoon breeze, her speed increased to nearly eights knots. Now they were heading 260° and running before the wind with only her mainsail and jib. Hunter was surprised that they didn't hoist their genoa which would have given their bows more lift and the yacht greater speed. However, after checking the distance to go to the rendezvous, he could see that they had plenty of time in hand.

The sea ahead was becoming less crowded. Nick looked at the radar and checked the heading of various craft and could see none were coming within a mile of his intended track. He went below to make tea and spent the next half an hour sitting in the cockpit, cleaning his weapons and checking his kit.

At sunset, the two boats were twenty miles south of Dodman Point. The wind had continued freshening and was now gusting twenty knots. The Atlantic, coming into the Channel, had developed a long, gentle roll, not uncomfortable, but unpleasant for anyone not used to the sea. After being caught unawares Ali was violently sick and had taken to his bunk. Hunter grinned sardonically. The idiot had puked over the windward side, not the leeward, leaving one of the Pakistanis to clean up the considerable mess.

Hunter switched on the navigation lights, red to port, green to starboard, and a masthead white overtaking light and white forward steaming light. Using his binoculars, Hunter watched as *The Temperance*'s lights appeared. At the top of the mast was a combined red and green lantern, whilst pointing astern, he knew, was a white overtaking light. By now there were few vessels on the water, apart from a number of large ships and coasters, some heading up the Channel and others heading out to sea. Hunter had turned the *Saint Louis* to starboard about an hour earlier and had taken her closer inshore. The yacht was five miles south on a divergent course. In order to keep track of her he was marking the radar every ten minutes, which ensured he could identify the yacht at any time. Gradually, he was falling behind, which suited his purpose. He had done nothing to arouse the suspicion of the men on *The Temperance* and they seemed to be completely unaware of his existence.

To ensure he stayed alert, Hunter made himself a strong cup of coffee and sat watching the sea. He had spent many weeks and months doing this very thing as an officer in the Royal Navy. He enjoyed it. And now he was at sea again he had to confess to himself that he'd missed it. Perhaps it really was time to return to General Service and resume his naval career. No, he'd made up his mind. TIFAT was where he belonged. At least for the foreseeable future.

At 23.59 it was obvious that *The Temperance* was on time and track for the rendezvous. Another two hours, Hunter decided, and then he would launch his attack. He had now changed direction to port and was shadowing the yacht at seven miles, keeping her on a steady bearing and distance. Even if they became suspicious, there was little they could do about it. No, his one fear had been that some other vessel, hearing a Mayday call, would become involved. Which was why he had planted the explosives in the radio.

The next two hours dragged slowly by. As the two boats went further south and west, the sea got rougher. The yacht handled it better than Hunter's craft, the sails giving her a stability that was missing from the *Saint Louis*. As a result, Hunter brought forward his timetable. There were no vessels within ten miles, and none on a convergent course. Increasing speed, he headed directly towards the white overtaking light on the stern of *The Temperance*.

At thirty knots he closed in rapidly. At just under one mile he took the transmitter and pressed the button. He wasn't sure whether the gentle thump in the night was fact or imagination.

46

After switching off his lights, Hunter turned on the cameras and cautiously approached *The Temperance*. The yacht's running lights were still burning and now the deck lights were also turned on. With the loss of her rudder, the yacht had gone into irons. This meant *The Temperance* was no longer sailing before the wind. She had turned, beam on to the wind and was drifting before it, the sails flapping ineffectively. Hunter could see the two Pakistanis hanging over the stern trying to assess what was wrong. He noticed that the stern of the yacht appeared lower in the water. Just then he blew their radio apart.

Perhaps the shock of events had proved too much for them. They stood frozen for a few seconds until Saddiq Ali appeared on deck, white-faced, distressed. As he did, he pointed at Hunter heading towards them. The two Pakistanis looked towards the *Saint Louis* which was now less than a cable away. It took them a few more seconds to understand that the approaching boat was somehow linked to what had happened. One of the men yelled something in Urdu and reached down into the cockpit. He stood up straight holding a Kalashnikov AK-74. He cocked the weapon, pointed it and – nothing. He cocked it again and pulled the trigger even as the other man did the same.

Again nothing happened. The two men were screaming words that Hunter didn't understand. Now less than ten yards away, he fired four bullets from his Glock 18 into the first man's torso. He flew backwards and straight over the side with barely a splash.

Now alongside the yacht, the other man raised the Kalashnikov above his head by the barrel and made to throw it at Hunter. Before he could make his move, the yacht lurched towards the stern of the *Saint Louis* and threw the Pakistani into the safety wire that surrounded the deck. He dropped the gun over the side and grabbed the rigging. He looked at Hunter who had stopped almost alongside the yacht.

'I bent the firing pins,' Hunter called, 'last night. While you were sleeping.'

Snarling his hatred, the Pakistani leapt at the boat's bow. Hunter stood and watched as the terrorist got his feet on to the boat amidships and heaved his torso up. One shot through the forehead sent the man flying backwards and into the water.

A flick of a switch and the deck of the *Saint Louis* was bathed in light. 'That's better, you can see what's going on now.'

Saddiq Ali stood in open-mouthed shock. As Hunter turned his attention on him, he came to life.

'Don't you know who I am?', he began. 'My name is . . .'

'Saddiq Ali, and you are a Member of Parliament.'

By now, the water was lapping at the gunwale and the yacht gave another lurch as she settled. Ali suddenly realised the position he was in and climbed hurriedly on top of the cabin.

'I demand you help me onto your boat!' he screamed, fear grabbing him by the throat. The mainsail was flapping

466

and cracking, and the yacht was now rocking slowly from side to side as she sank.

Ali was surprised when Hunter said, 'By all means. Please step on board.'

'Huh? What do you mean, step on board?'

Hunter shrugged. 'My name is Nick Hunter,' he began, 'and I am from The International Force Against Terrorism. Perhaps you've heard of us?'

'Of course I've heard of you,' Ali said. 'You're a bunch of murdering thugs who should not be allowed to exist.'

'That's one way of looking at us, I suppose. On the other hand, it could be said that we help to keep the world safe from scum like you. We know what you did. We know you are en route to rendezvous with a ship that will take you to the Middle East. We know that the Saudi Arabians are your paymasters, that JIMAS is the organisation that tried to detonate the dirty bombs in Europe and that it was Pakistani dissidents who supplied the bombs. Now, you can stay where you are and drown or climb on board.'

Ali hesitated for a second but then came to the conclusion he would die in the next few minutes unless he did something. But why rescue him if he planned to kill him? Hope surged through him. The chance to deny the charges and argue that he was merely on a cruise when he was attacked for no reason suddenly came to mind. No! Better yet, he had been kidnapped. Then he had been rescued by this man. He would heap praise on his organisation. Yes! That would be the thing to do. He would live to fight another day. With the arrogance that had taken him into politics, he jumped for the side of the *Saint Louis*. He would have fallen into the sea if Hunter hadn't grabbed him and dragged him over the side of the rails. He sprawled unceremoniously on the deck.

Ali now went into grovelling mode. 'Thank you. Thank you, for saving me. I appreciate it very much. I was kidnapped by these people. I was being taken somewhere, I don't know where. You say it was to a ship that was to take me to the Middle East. I can well believe it. As an outspoken critic of fundamentalism I am regarded by them as an enemy. I expect I was to be held for some sort of deal. Some concession they want.' The man was babbling, almost incoherent, talking nonsense.

Hunter ignored Ali and gazed at *The Temperance*. The yacht's hull was awash, the batteries short-circuited and the sailing and deck lights were extinguished. He couldn't help feeling sad at the destruction of such a beautiful craft.

Ali was suddenly silent, like a tap being turned off.

Hunter looked at him and said, 'If you make a move I'll put a bullet in you.'

Putting the engines into reverse, the boat backed away and when he had opened enough distance, Hunter turned the *Saint Louis* and headed east. The flipping of a couple of switches and the boat's steaming lights were back on. Hunter set the automatic pilot and turned his attention to Ali. They were about the same height, but the MP was not as broad-shouldered and now his expanding gut was more evident. A glance at the radar showed there were no ships headed in their direction. Also, as they were running before the sea, the boat became a far steadier platform.

'You're a real piece of work, aren't you, Ali?'

'How . . . How dare you! How dare you speak to me like that!' Because he was still alive Ali was beginning to believe he would survive the whole episode. Then he would make the thug standing over him pay. Killing innocent men. Unarmed men. Yes, he would testify to that fact. And who would the Courts believe, a murderer or an Honourable Member of Parliament?

'Oh, I dare all right. I was the person in command of the team that stopped the dirty bomb getting here.' Pausing, Hunter looked down at Ali. 'We know you were the person telling JIMAS what we were doing after you received the updates of the operation.'

'You cannot prove that,' Ali said. 'And if you try, I'll deny everything.'

Hunter chuckled. The sound sent fear up Ali's spine. All of a sudden he wasn't so sure about what was going to happen to him. Come to that, where were they going?

However, before he could say anything Hunter asked, 'Why did you do it?'

'I did nothing! Nothing!' Ali yelled.

'We know you did. We have recordings of you in contact with JIMAS and Khaled Aziz in particular.'

At the mention of the Prince, Ali jerked and stared open-mouthed at Hunter. Again, a vestige of courage surged through him and he said, 'The phone taps will be illegal. You cannot use them in a Court of Law.'

Hunter said nothing. He wasn't prepared yet to inform Ali that he wouldn't be standing trial.

'It gives me great pleasure to tell you that we know about the JIMAS meeting in the Gulf. Every person there will be wiped off the face of the earth.'

Ali sat up straight, a mixture of horror and indignation sweeping through him, his own situation forgotten for a few moments. 'You cannot do that! You cannot!'

'Yes, we can. Because of you and JIMAS, thousands of people across Europe have died. Innocent men, women and children, who just wanted to get on with their lives. That includes Muslims. Race relations have been thrown back, not decades, but probably a hundred years. Why? Explain it so I can understand.'

'You'd never understand,' said Ali, squirming backwards and onto a seat behind him, contempt dripping from his voice.

Hunter let him move. The more comfortable he was, the more likely he was to talk. And if that failed Nick could use the SSM.

'Try me. Why did you do it?'

'For Islam,' he spat out. 'To make the West understand that if they want to live in peace, then Islam must become the dominant religion.'

Hunter looked at the man in genuine amazement. 'All you've succeeded in doing is to drive a wedge between Muslims and the rest of us.'

'The bigger the wedge, the better,' Ali said with venom.

'Who else in Europe has been helping you? Who are the leaders?'

'I'll never tell you that!'

'Hunter opened a small locker and extracted a plastic box. He flipped it open and said, 'This syringe contains a powerful drug called SSM. You may know it as a truth drug. Once I inject you with it, you will tell me anything and everything I want to know. Of course,' he continued, now lying, 'you will be brain-damaged. Not to a debilitating level, but pretty seriously. You will experience memory loss and much of the time you won't remember your own name.'

Ali looked at Hunter in horror. Finally, he said in a strangled voice, 'You cannot be serious!'

'Oh, I am. My instinct is to put a bullet into your knees and throw you over the side. You'll die in agony. Or you can talk to me and we'll see about an entirely different fate.'

470

'I won't! You can't make me!' the MP said in a strangled whisper.

'Fair enough.' Hunter was standing a metre away. He kicked Ali in the side of the head, not too hard, but just enough to stun him. He grabbed the man by the scruff of his neck and dragged him onto the deck. He put his knee in the middle of his back and, taking the hypodermic, he shoved it into Ali's bicep and put his finger on the plunger. 'Do I fill you with this stuff or do you want to talk?'

'I . . . I'll talk,' Ali stuttered.

'Sensible fellow,' said Hunter. Before letting him up, he took a length of nylon cord and tied Ali's arms securely behind his back. Next he lifted him by his collar and threw him onto the seat. The MP lay gasping, tears in his eyes.

Hunter switched on a recording machine and placed it within earshot. 'Let's start at the beginning, shall we?'

Hunter had prepared questions to ask, and others occurred to him as he learned more about JIMAS and what the MP had been up to. Some of the names he was given came as a surprise. However, surprise turned to shock when Ali named two Saudi Princes. It seemed to Hunter that TIFAT was going to be extremely busy for months to come. The interrogation went on for over an hour.

One answer came as no surprise. 'All Western troops will be withdrawn from Iraq, Afghanistan and other Islamic states. That will enable us to fully implement Sharia law.'

Shaking his head, Hunter thought, Sharia. The path to a watering hole – the eternal ethical and moral code based on the Qur'an and Sunnah, also the basis for *Fiqh*. This in turn meant the jurisprudence built around the Sharia, *by custom*! Hunter had studied the subject on the basis of 'know your enemy'. He hadn't declared war on Islam,

471

Muslims had declared war on the West. Hunter had learned that the words of Mohammed had made sense. Had made for a far better society for all, particularly women, who had been so badly treated in the seventh century. But that word had been perverted over the centuries to what it was today. This had resulted in a twisted dictatorship of unimaginable proportions at the highest levels of Islam.

Finally, all his questions had been answered and Hunter could think of nothing more to ask.

Surprisingly, he made an offer. 'Would you like a cup of coffee? Or do you prefer tea?'

Saddiq Ali was taken completely by surprise. 'A . . . a . . . coffee,' he stammered.

Hunter prepared the percolator. His anger and his hatred were like nothing he had experienced before. The number of deaths in Europe alone had been horrendous, but the fact was, no westernised country had been spared. He shook his head. No, that wasn't correct. Virtually no country in the world had escaped unscathed. If non-Muslims were attacking the Muslim minorities in their countries, then in Islamic countries it was the reverse. Non-Muslims were being hounded and killed in their hundreds, if not thousands. Curiously, very little had happened in America. It was acknowledged that this was because Muslims had become far better integrated into American society than they had in Europe. Perhaps, thought a cynical Hunter, lessons would be learned from that fact. But why did he doubt it?

Whilst in the galley, Hunter had kept a close eye on the MP and was amused to watch him struggle and squirm as he tried to break free. Hunter knew there wasn't a cat's chance in hell of him succeeding.

'Milk and sugar?'

'Yes,' croaked Ali, stopping his writhing as he finally realised that it was a waste of time.

Hunter appeared in the cockpit. Taking another piece of nylon cord he tied one end to the MP's right wrist and tied the other end to the guard-rail. Next, he cut the cord holding Ali's hands together. Ali brought his hands around to his front, awkwardly massaging his wrists as he got the circulation flowing again.

Hunter handed him his coffee. As he did so, he remarked, 'Dawn is fast approaching, you can see the sky lightening in the east. It looks like being another fine day.'

Ali said nothing. Instead, he took a sip of the coffee. After a few more mouthfuls, he asked, 'What . . . what are you going to do with me?'

Hunter's smile was not pleasant. 'Did I tell you that a good friend of mine was killed on the operation? A really nice guy. An American.'

'No, you didn't tell me,' Ali said, in a strangled voice.

Hunter nodded. 'He was one of the kindest men I've ever known. All his life, at every opportunity, he did work and gave money to children in dire straits across the world. So, my first inclination still stands.'

'You cannot! You cannot! Dear God, *no*!' the last word was a scream.

'Give me a good reason why not?'

'It's barbaric!'

Hunter looked at the man in real surprise. 'How dare you tell me it's barbaric after what you did! How dare you, you bastard!' He had raised his voice for the first time, anger seething through him.

'What I did was war,' came another surprising

statement. 'And I demand to be treated as a prisoner of war.'

Hunter nodded. 'Okay. You're a prisoner of war. I find you guilty of crimes against humanity and sentence you to death. That suit you?'

'No! You cannot! I demand . . . I demand . . .', he shook his head to clear his thoughts which were beginning to turn foggy. 'What . . . what's happening to me?'

'I won't blow holes in your knees and let you drown, much as I'm tempted. However, I *will* tell you that the coffee you drank contained a very powerful drug. You will be unconscious in about two minutes and then I'll throw you over the side.' He took the mug from Ali's hand before it spilt on the deck. It would save scrubbing it down later.

Saddiq Ali began to moan and then sob. 'No . . . No . . . You cannot,' he managed to say.

As though from a distance he became aware of Hunter tying the inflatable's anchor to his feet. He was now drifting in and out of consciousness and then his head pitched forward and he was out for the count. Hunter pushed Ali's torso over the side of the *Saint Louis* and then heaved the rest of him into the water. As much as he'd been tempted to throw the Member of Parliament overboard fully aware of what was happening, he didn't have the heart to do so. Ali would die without the awareness of his impending death.

Hunter decided to examine the cameras later. Should it be necessary, he thought, he would have enough to show the two Pakistanis with their automatic weapons. He had recorded all that Saddiq Ali had said. He would edit out the last bit. After all, the MP jumped overboard and committed suicide rather than return to Britain to face the music. One thing was damned sure. He *didn't* trust this government – under any circumstances.

Ramming the throttles hard over, Hunter spun the wheel to port as the engines picked up revolutions and the screws bit deeply into the water. The *Saint Louis* came bows up and stern down as she accelerated, showing an almost boundless joy as she carved a deep wake behind her.

Epilogue

The press was trumpeting loudly the recovery of the second dirty bomb. Within only a few days, specialists from around the world were being invited to take a look at the device. Great emphasis was placed on the help given by Muslim countries in dealing with the situation. It was made clear that the chances of success in preventing both devices from exploding were considerably enhanced thanks to unprecedented co-operation between all nations. Leaders from around the world gathered together, made speeches together, praised the actions of one another. Luckily, in the euphoria of the bombs not exploding and the gradual settling of the unrest that had been sweeping across the world, nobody was asking any difficult questions. Even the media understood the need for restraint, for bridge-building, to calm the unrest that could so easily have led to nuclear Armageddon.

The only people who knew all the answers were TIFAT. And they weren't saying anything.

*   *   *   *   *

The attack on Qishrān Island was text book. Hunter led the attack team. The men had quietly joined the *Atherstone* while she was alongside at Jeddah, drifting on board over a two-hour period, ensuring they weren't noticed. The ship sailed on time, arrived off the island in the middle of the night and launched the Geminis without a hitch. Back at Rosyth, Isobel and her people kept the team informed of the location of the guards. There was nobody on the beach; the team landed quietly and quickly confirmed this fact. While they moved out, the *Atherstone*'s crew began ferrying more explosives ashore. As a back-up they also had twenty M72 LAW rockets. Strictly speaking they were anti-tank rockets but played holy hell with any building they struck. If necessary, they would help to keep down the heads of their targets.

According to Isobel, there were merely eight guards walking around the palace walls. As was often the case, being on their home territory, where they considered themselves safe, the guards were sloppy in the extreme. They were quickly and easily dealt with. It took the best part of an hour but the explosives were planted in the designated spots and primed to go up in one hour.

It was decided that no mop-up operation was required and they quietly quit the area. They were on board the ship, five miles from the island, when the huge explosion occurred. It was awesome.

The team disembarked from the minehunter a few days later in Oman. From there back to Scotland was a fourteen-hour flight.

*   *   *   *   *

Doug Tanner's funeral was a very sad occasion. He had been highly popular. His skills and knowledge would be sorely missed. One passage read out at the crematorium, written by Tanner in a farewell message in his will, was to hope that it was bucketing down with rain when it came to scattering his ashes. That brought a few chuckles to an otherwise sombre affair. The wake was loud and boisterous, full of laughter and anecdotes about their dead comrade. It was their way of coping with the realities they faced, day in, day out.

*   *   *   *   *

Lieutenant Douglas Napier, RM, returned to the Royal Marines. His tour at TIFAT was over. His promotion to Captain followed only days later. The promotion had been his incentive to return to General Service. His wounded leg healed completely.

*   *   *   *   *

Matt Dunston informed his appointer that he could no longer serve as a Chaplain. His immediate resignation was accepted. The General, using the funds TIFAT had 'liberated', hired Dunston as a consultant in the war on terrorism.

*   *   *   *   *

Although tours of duty were ending for numerous other TIFAT operatives, they all volunteered to stay. The General moved heaven and earth, called in every favour owed to ensure they did.

*   *   *   *   *

Zim Albatha had a job to do in Turkey. The first of many. There were supporters of the holy jihad who needed to be dealt with. He set the explosive in the petrol tank of the Minister's limousine. Although he had a driver, when visiting his mistress, Syed Azam insisted on driving himself, a fact his driver found highly amusing. Albatha knew where he was going and for what purpose. Following at a discreet distance, when the car was on a deserted stretch of road, Albatha sent the signal that detonated the bomb. The explosion was huge, death instantaneous. Albatha drew alongside, looked at the wreckage, turned and drove away.

*　*　*　*　*

When faced with the facts, the King of Saudi Arabia agreed. He'd had no idea whatsoever about what was being done in the name of his country. His anger was genuine, his desire to track down everyone connected to the conspiracy all too real. He had already set his security people to follow every lead. He truly wanted closer ties with the West. All stock market holdings would be at the same level as they had been before the collapse. Because of the virtual meltdown of the markets worldwide, many transactions hadn't been honoured, although the House of Saud had still acquired hundreds of billions of dollars. Luckily, in the global marketplace of the twenty-first century, cash didn't change hands. It didn't actually exist. It was all done by computers. Resetting the transactions wasn't that difficult but merely took time. Again, thanks to computers. The result was the House of Saud walked away with ten billion dollars-worth of assets. A bagatelle under the circumstances. Their donations of billions of dollars to aid agencies around the world were gratefully received.

* * * * *

Macnair's meeting in Downing Street with members of the government, and with Owens and Summers, was highly satisfying. TIFAT would continue to operate from Rosyth in its present form. None of the three security chiefs bothered telling the Prime Minister once again that he couldn't do anything to stop TIFAT operating. Nor did they bother to explain once more about TIFAT's mandate. They knew they would be wasting their breath. When they left Cabinet Office Briefing Room A they agreed one thing. They couldn't trust the politicians of this government – or any government, come to that. New operations were already in the pipeline. The mop-up work still had to be done and TIFAT would play a central part – its programme would be a busy one.

* * * * *

Samantha joined Nick on board the *Saint Louis* for a week of cruising the south coast. The weather was idyllic, the sea flat calm. Nick taught her how to dive, and how to tease lobsters and crabs out of their cubby-holes. He also showed her how to cook them – his speciality. In the evenings, they berthed alongside one of the small fishing villages dotted along the coast and enjoyed visiting local pubs and bistros.

The phone call from Hiram Walsh came as a complete surprise, as did the trickle of texts from the others at TIFAT. Twice a year, winter and summer, the Royal Navy published a list of those who had been selected for promotion. Lieutenant Commander Nicholas Hunter, GC, was now Commander Nicholas Hunter, GC. To go further up the promotional ladder he knew with certainty that he would have to leave TIFAT and return to General Service. The decision to stay wasn't a hard one to make. He had no desire for higher rank.